W9-BUC-321

A Woman of Passion

Virginia Henley

A Woman of Passion

WHEELER
PUBLISHING, INC.
ROCKLAND, MA

★ AN AMERICAN COMPANY ★

Published in Large Print by arrangement with Delacorte Press, an imprint of
Dell Publishing, a division of Random House, Inc. in the United States and
Canada.

Wheeler Large Print Book Series.

Set in 16 pt Plantin.

DU BR
LP
HENLEY
V

Library of Congress Cataloging-in-Publication Data

Henley, Virginia.
    A woman of passion / Virginia Henley.
        p. (large print) cm.(Wheeler large print book series)
    ISBN 1-56895-762-9 (hardcover)
    1. Shrewsbury, Elizabeth Hardwick Talbot, Countess of, 1520-1608—
Fiction. 2. Great Britain—Court and courtiers—History—16th century—
Fiction. 3. Great Britain—History—Elizabeth, 1558-1603—Fiction.
4. Large type books. I. Title. II. Series
[PS3558.E49634W66 1999]
813'.54—dc21

99-38382
                                                                           CIP

*This book is dedicated
to strong, vital women, everywhere.*

You know who you are.

PROLOGUE

Derbyshire, England
August 20, 1533

"**W**hat the devil are you doing?" the little red-haired girl demanded as two burly farmers lifted the oak dresser.

Ignoring her, the men hauled the dresser outside and came back upstairs for a bedstead. Bess Hardwick put her hands on her hips and commanded, "Stop!" When they did not obey her, she stamped her foot and cursed them soundly.

Clutching her rag doll closely to her chest, she ran downstairs and literally staggered with shock when she found the rooms empty. She rushed outside and saw the oxcart filled with her family's possessions. Though visibly upset, her mother stood by passively, as did her older brother and her sisters.

"No! Noooo!" Furiously, Bess ran to the wagon and began to unload their belongings. She managed to pull down a wicker linnet cage, but the rest of the furniture was tied down and far too heavy for her to budge. The little red-head threw herself on the ground, kicking her heels and screaming at the top of her lungs, in a royal tantrum.

"Do ye want me to tan her arse, missus?" one of the men asked.

"No, no. Bess has an overabundance of

passion. She feels things more deeply than others. There is nothing any of us can do— it just has to run its course before she can stop."

Bess Hardwick was in a full-blown rage, but rage was the only thing that kept her sickening fear at bay. First her father had gone and then the servants; then one by one the farm animals had disappeared. The best pieces of furniture had been sold, and now they were losing their home. Where would they go? How would they live? Where would they sleep? What would they eat? One uncertainty piled on top of another, becoming a mountain of stark, cold terror.

Bess was ready to fight, ready to take on the entire world, but the rest of her family had no fight in them.

"Come along, Bess, we cannot stay at Hardwick, it is no longer our home," her mother said, gently pulling her to her feet.

"I'm not going!" she cried stubbornly as she sat down in the dusty road, glaring daggers at her family.

After a full minute's wait, Elizabeth Hardwick nodded for the driver to start. "Bess will follow; she has no other choice."

The imp of Satan sat, unyielding as the Rock of Gibraltar, as the wagon descended the hill, getting smaller and smaller, then finally disappearing down the rutted track. When she found herself alone, with no audience but the bird and her rag doll, Bess opened the door of the wicker cage. "Well, at least you don't have to leave. You may live here forever."

2

The linnet hopped out of the cage and flew up into a large oak.

Bess got to her feet and went to stand in front of the half-timbered house where she had been born. She spoke to it, never doubting that Hardwick Manor could hear and understand every word. "You are mine! Don't be sad. I will be back to claim you. The rest of them are useless. It's going to be up to me!"

Bess's father had died and left her when she was four, but she remembered standing with him in front of the house on this very spot. She could still feel his hand on her shoulder and hear his words in her ear: "Land is wealth, my wee lass. Land and property are the most important things on earth. Hardwick! Even our family name comes from the land. Hang on to Hardwick, Bess, no matter what."

Bess swallowed the hot bile in her throat and dashed a hand across her nose and eyes, rubbing dirt into the snot and tears that ran down her face. She would be six on her next birthday, and six was far too old to cry. Bess looked at her doll. "Are you ready to go, Lady Ponsonby?" After pausing for a moment, she added reluctantly, "Then so am I." Feeling almost torn in half, she turned away from the house and walked stoically in the direction of the cart, clutching Esmeralda Ponsonby by her rag arm.

An empty feeling settled inside her and expanded until it filled her entire belly. Something warned her she had better get used to it; she doubted it would ever go away. Bess

3

hadn't gone far when the linnet deserted the oak tree and fluttered after her, twittering in distress. Bess felt it alight on her head and make a little nest for itself amongst her fiery curls. "Foolish little bird," she muttered. "I wouldn't leave Hardwick if I were you."

PART ONE

THE GIRL
LONDON 1543

❖

Gather ye rosebuds while ye may,
Old time is still a-flying;
And this same flower that smiles today,
Tomorrow will be dying.

ROBERT HERRICK

PART ONE

THE GIRL
LONDON 1543

❖

Gather ye rosebuds while ye may,
Old time is still a-flying;
And this same flower that smiles today,
Tomorrow will be dying.

ROBERT HERRICK

ONE

"**S**omething glorious will happen today....
I feel it in my heart!" The corners of Bess Hardwick's generously shaped mouth lifted in a smile
as her gaze traveled the entire length of the
gallery of the grand London mansion. She had
been with the noble Lady Zouche and her
daughters for a year now, and that incredible
year had changed her life forever.

When they had been forced out of Hardwick,
her mother, Elizabeth, had taken refuge with
her sister Marcella, who was also a widow. Bess
soon grew very close to her aunt, recognizing
that they were kindred spirits with strong,
decisive personalities. At Marcella's instiga-
tion, the two sisters had put their heads
together and concocted a plan. Listening to
them had taught Bess that the most important
goal in a woman's life was marriage and the
greatest lesson that could be learned was how
to catch a husband. Since Aunt Marcy was
rather horse-faced, with a tongue sharp enough
to clip tin, their mantrap had to be baited with
Bess's more docile mother, Elizabeth.

In what seemed a remarkably short time, Elizabeth Hardwick captured the younger son of
Sir Francis Leche of Chatsworth. Unfortunately,
Ralph Leche, Bess's new stepfather, had little
money of his own, and when the babies started

7

to arrive, he had difficulty supporting them all. Even the house in Baslow village that Ralph leased from his father, Sir Francis, became overcrowded, especially after Aunt Marcy moved in to help with the children. So once again the sisters put their heads together to concoct a plan to improve their family's lot in life.

It had been nothing short of a miracle when the noble Lady Margaret Zouche decided to pay a visit to her country home at Ashby-de-la-Zouche. Elizabeth and Marcella had known Lady Margaret when they were girls because of some distant relationship, and they decided to visit her immediately to ask if one of the Hardwick daughters could be found a suitable position in her London household. Such service with a noble family was a traditional way for children of poor kinsmen to further their education and gain experience in running a vast household. When Lady Zouche indicated she was amenable to their request, the sisters rushed back to Baslow to make the monumental decision.

Which Hardwick daughter should be pushed from the nest to make her own way in the world? "Though it's an unpaid position, it is a God-sent opportunity to make useful connections for her future. Mark my words," Marcella prophesied, "Bess will be our salvation!"

"Bess?" Elizabeth said uncertainly, for she had two daughters older than Bess, both of whom were far more suited to following orders.

"Of course Bess," Marcella said implacably. "She has your beauty and my sharp tongue, and to top it all off, her glorious flaming hair will make London sit up and take notice of her. Her sweet, biddable sisters would be dumb as doorknobs! Bess will seize the opportunity and run with it. Bess isn't sweet, she's tart, and at barely fourteen already has the breasts of a courtesan! I shall miss her with all my heart, but it is a wonderful opportunity for her."

Bess had never been separated from her family; she'd never even slept alone. She shared a bed and all her secret dreams with her sister Jane. Bess feared she would miss her gentle mother and her aunt Marcella. Her aunt dispensed such sage advice, and she wondered how she would manage without her.

The night before she departed for London, when she would be cut off at a stroke from her loving family, Bess experienced the nightmare that had been plaguing her ever since they had been thrown out of Hardwick Manor. It seemed to recur when she was feeling especially vulnerable.

Bess walked in to a room that was empty, stripped bare. She ran downstairs and found the bailiffs carrying off everything she possessed in the world. Bess begged and pleaded and cried, all to no avail. Outside, her family's meager belongings were being piled on a cart. They had been put out of their house and had nowhere to go. Fear washed over her in great waves. Panic choked her. When she turned around, the cart was gone, her

9

family was gone, and even Hardwick Manor had vanished. Bess had lost everything she'd had in the world. The suffocating terror mounted until it engulfed her.

Bess awakened, screaming...everything was gone...she was overwhelmed with helplessness, hopelessness.

The following morning, the excitement of traveling to London soon dispelled the terror of the nightmare. Once inside the magnificent treasure-filled Zouche mansion, Bess no longer harbored any doubts that she had done the right thing in leaving home. She was completely certain that she was fulfilling her destiny and had an overwhelming desire to become wealthy enough to buy back Hardwick Manor for her family.

Suddenly plunged into a world of riches and privilege, Bess became wildly ambitious. Like a sponge, she soaked up everything about her new way of life and made herself indispensable to Lady Zouche and her daughters. And now, just over a year later, on the threshold of womanhood, Bess had the feeling that something momentous was about to happen in her life.

As she descended the stairs from the third-floor gallery, Bess paused in her headlong rush as she saw young Robert Barlow coming in the other direction, gasping for breath. He was a page in the Zouche household, from the same village in Derbyshire as herself.

"Rob, sit down before you fall down," Bess said, retracing her steps to the gallery. She shoved the tall, thin youth down on a carved settle and noted his gray pallor. He was as delicate as a girl and had little vitality.

"My chest hurts terribly when I climb stairs," he gasped. Nonetheless, he managed a smile, apparently grateful for her attention.

"Go up to your bed and lie down. I think you are growing too fast and it robs you of strength." Bess enjoyed such robust health herself that the boy's languor alarmed her.

"I can't, Bess, I have to take this message to Suffolk House and await a reply."

Bess plucked the letter from his hand. "I'll take care of it, Rob. Go up now; none will even miss you." Bess knew she should delegate the delivery of the letter to a footman, but on a sudden impulse she decided not to do so. London! How she adored it, and the Strand— with its magnificent mansions that belonged to the nobility—was her favorite place to walk in the most glorious city on earth.

The letter was addressed to Lady Frances Grey, Marchioness of Dorset, who was Lady Zouche's dearest friend in the world. The first time Bess had met Frances Grey and learned she was the daughter of King Henry Tudor's sister, she had been overwhelmed. But during the past year, Bess had visited the Greys' London residence so frequently that she had come to feel at ease in the great lady's presence.

Bess had thought the Zouche residence,

which reflected the feudal lifestyle of the past, impressively grand, until she had experienced Suffolk House, where the Greys held court on a regal scale. Though they were immensely rich and powerful, Bess thought Frances and Henry Grey the kindest, friendliest people she had ever known. And even though their daughters, Lady Jane Grey and Lady Catherine Grey, were in the line of succession to the throne, they were good friends with Lady Zouche's daughters. Thanks to Bess's position as the girls' companion, she was included in that friendship.

Using a back door that led from the kitchens, Bess stepped into the warm summer sunshine and quickly walked down Bedford Street to the Strand. If the stretch of land along the river had been paved with gold, it wouldn't have seemed more fantastic to her for there stood one huge mansion after another, all no doubt crammed with riches, treasures, and servants. At first Bess thought of them as the many mansions of heaven, which Jesus had referred to, according to the scriptures. Nay, more like paradise, she decided. Her footsteps slowed as she strolled past Durham House and York House. Just imagining the vast rooms behind the tall windows, whose walls held priceless paintings, set her blood singing. Someday, Bess vowed, I will have my own town house in London. *What about Hardwick?* a tiny voice whispered. Bess tossed her red curls, dislodging the embroidered cap perched precariously on her head. "Hardwick shall be my *country* home," she answered loftily, ignoring the liveried servants who sent her admiring glances.

Ambitious men got whatever they wanted, so why shouldn't a woman be ambitious? She was only going to live once, so why not make it count? Bess was determined to be a great success and get her fair share of this world's riches. She swore it, vowed it, pledged it like an oath. Bess envisioned her future with clarity. She knew exactly what she wanted and knew there would be a price to pay. But that was only right, a mere bagatelle. She would pay the price gladly, even with abandon. She would walk through fire or barter her soul to have it all!

It had not taken Bess long to make herself indispensable to Lady Zouche. She made sure her employer saw that she was quick-witted and shrewd, and had an ability to manage people that would have been wasted in a menial position in the Zouche household. She had adapted so quickly to the lifestyle of the aristocracy, had such beautiful manners and an abundance of energy, that Lady Zouche had recognized the jewel she had acquired and appointed Bess companion to herself and her daughters.

Happier than she had ever been in her life, Bess knew that now was her opportunity to catch a husband. Though she was not of noble birth and had no dowry, she was young, beautiful, and had the benefit of influential connections in the exalted ranks of the upper aristocracy. Moreover, Tudor court circles attracted the richest, most ambitious men in England.

Bess made her way through the formal gardens behind Suffolk House, inhaling the fragrant scent of lavender and late-summer roses. She scanned the lawns leading down to the river, expecting to find Lady Frances outdoors on such a warm afternoon. Until she reached the steps, Bess did not notice the two men above her on the terrace. As she looked up, the sun dazzled her eyes so that she thought for a moment the resplendent figure before her was King Henry. Bess drew in a swift breath and sank down in a graceful curtsy upon the terrace steps. Her skirts formed a pool of pale green, and the sun burnished the tendrils of red-gold hair escaping from beneath her cap.

From their vantage point above her on the terrace, the two men were privileged to a delicious display of pert breasts. William Cavendish's mouth curved sensually. "Cock's bones, there's a dish I'd like to taste."

Henry Grey, Marquess of Dorset, jabbed his friend in the ribs and strode toward Bess. "Mistress Hardwick, surely there is no need for such formality between us?"

As he raised her from her curtsy, Bess blushed, for she could see that the man behind him was not Henry VIII. "Forgive me, Lord Dorset, I thought you were entertaining the king," she said breathlessly. She saw the man's dark brows momentarily draw together as if he were displeased at the comparison, then watched as he threw back his head and laughed. Bess was stunned. He was at least six feet tall, with thick dark hair that curled attractively about his collar. His square, determined jaw was clean-shaven, showing off the deep cleft in his chin. His eyes, brimming with amusement, were such a deep shade of brown that they looked black. All in all, he was the most compelling male she had ever seen.

"This is my good friend, William Cavendish," Henry Grey explained, as his companion elbowed him aside and lifted Bess's hand to his lips.

She knew her fingers trembled in his big hand, and her legs felt as limp as wet linen the moment he touched her.

"When did you last see the king?" Cavendish demanded.

"Never, milord." Bess withdrew her hand from his and added coolly, "but his portraits are everywhere."

"Ahh! All were painted in his prime, when he was at the peak of his vigor and virility. His vanity will not allow his subjects to see him as he really is."

Here is arrogance, Bess thought. The man thinks himself better than the king! "All men are vain, milord," Bess said pointedly.

It was Henry Grey's turn to laugh. "Touché, Cavendish, you are every bit as vain as the king, *and* as dissolute," he murmured to his friend, who took a mistress as casually as he selected a new pair of riding boots.

With difficulty, Bess tore her glance from the powerful figure of Cavendish. "I have a letter for Lady Frances—"

"You've missed her, my dear, she's gone off to Dorset House for items she plans to take to Chelsea next week. We have only just returned from Bradgate in Leicestershire. Why do ladies constantly move from one house to another?" he asked quizzically.

"For the sheer pleasure of it, milord." Bess smiled. "If you will excuse me, gentlemen, I shall seek out Lady Frances at Dorset House."

Cavendish spoke up. "Mistress Hardwick, I have my boat here. Permit me to drop you at Whitefriars' water stairs."

Bess couldn't believe her ears. Shrewdly, she covered the eagerness she felt with a show of reluctance. "I couldn't possibly take such shameful advantage of you, milord."

Her clever words were provocative, filling his head with wicked thoughts. "Nay, I consider it my duty to provide you with safe escort, mistress."

Bess wet her lips. "You offer me safe escort, milord, but who, pray, will protect me from you?"

"I refuse to take offense," Cavendish said with a grin. "You are a very wise young woman to exercise caution with the men of London. The Marquess of Dorset here will vouch for my character. I must insist on delivering you safely to Dorset House."

Bess said pertly, "If you *insist,* milord, how can I possibly refuse?"

It was her first concession to him, and Cavendish vowed it would not be her last.

"She's very young, Rogue," Henry Grey reminded his friend, deliberately using his rakish nickname.

"I'll handle her with the greatest care," Rogue Cavendish promised with a devilish glint in his eye.

As they walked down to the river, Bess assessed Cavendish openly. He was a big man with wide shoulders and a broad chest. His face was tanned from being outdoors, and he had a generous mouth that was no stranger to laughter. He had dark auburn hair and warm brown eyes that presently danced with amusement. But Bess was already aware that Rogue Cavendish was cocksure of himself, and she suspected that he was on the prowl for a pretty face. On the positive side, however, he had very influential friends and was showing a marked interest in her.

He boarded the barge first, then turned to help her. His powerful hands spanned her slim waist as he swung her into the air. Bess snatched off her embroidered cap before it fell into the river, and her glorious hair came tumbling down like molten red gold. As he lifted her to the deck, he gave the impression of sheer brute strength, and once again her knees turned weak.

The sight of her hair and the feel of her slender body beneath his hands had a marked physical effect on Cavendish. He hardened quickly.

17

Bess removed herself from his hands immediately. She was sexually innocent and knew little of male arousals, but she was far too wise to let his actions pass without a rebuke. "Sir, I must protest. I do not permit gentlemen to handle me in such a familiar manner." She moved to the stern and sat down, spreading her skirts across the padded seat to prevent him from sitting close to her.

Cavendish grinned down at her and decided to stand. He signaled his bargeman, then braced his well-muscled legs to hold his balance. Men's fashions had been set by the king, designed to show off the male physique with tight hose and wide-shouldered doublets that ended just short of covering a man's most threatening parts.

Bess didn't seem to notice. She inhaled the tangy scent of the Thames. "I love London; imagine having three houses on the river!" she said, her mind still on the Greys' holdings.

"Chelsea Palace doesn't belong to the Greys, though they have the use of it. Would you like three houses?" he asked quizzically.

"Certainly I would. Though just one on the river would satisfy me, I warrant."

"I wonder," Cavendish mused, sensing a powerful ambition that matched his own. How challenging it would be to try to satisfy her. "Do you have a first name?" His tone was still amused.

She lifted her eyes to his. "Mistress Elizabeth Hardwick, companion to Lady Zouche. Do you have a title?" she asked him directly.

Cavendish laughed. "No...not yet. I have to work for a living."

"What is it you do, sir?"

She was so direct, without subterfuge, he found it enchanting. "I am the king's representative with the Court of Augmentation."

She recoiled from him. "God's blood, is that anything like the Court of Wards?"

He considered the question philosophically. "Specifically, I deal with the dissolution of the monasteries, but both courts serve the same purpose: raising vast amounts of money for the Crown."

"You steal property!" she accused.

"Softly, Elizabeth," he warned. "You may say anything you wish to me, but accusations against the Crown are considered treason. I worked under Thomas Cromwell until he lost his head. I survived his downfall and now work directly for the king, but only because I guard my tongue."

Bess leaned forward and confided, "My family owns Hardwick Manor in Derbyshire, but because my brother, James, was a minor when my father died, the grasping Court of Wards stepped in and took it from us until he comes of age."

"I'm sorry. There are ways to avoid such losses."

"How? My mother protested, but the *bloody* Court ruled against her," Bess replied passionately.

"The property could have been held by trustees. You should have had a lawyer. They are costly but worth every penny. The side with the better lawyer *always* wins."

Bess pondered his words for a moment. "That's a valuable piece of advice you've just given me. Oh, I wish I were a man. The things they teach men are so worthwhile. Lady Zouche's daughters are taught Latin and Italian, which are nearly useless, in my opinion. I persuaded the Zouche steward to teach me to keep the household accounts, a far more practical skill."

"For when you run your own vast household," Cavendish teased.

"Don't laugh at me, sir. I *shall* have my own household!" she vowed. "I want to learn so many things...how to buy and sell property, for instance. Oh, I warrant you could teach me a lot. I am insatiable!"

His groin, finally starting to behave itself, suddenly went wild. Lord God, he thought, the things I'd like to teach you. His mouth curved. "You'd make an apt pupil."

They were at Whitefriars' stairs, and perversely William didn't want to let her go. He jumped up onto the stone steps to hand her from the barge. "You have been delightful company, Mistress Elizabeth Hardwick. Lady Zouche is an old acquaintance of mine; it seems high time I paid my respects to her."

Bess at last relented and gave him a dazzling smile, perfectly aware that she had engaged his interest.

TWO

Later that day, when Bess handed her employer a letter from Frances Grey, she suspected that she was about to be severely scolded for absenting herself all afternoon without permission.

"Robert Barlow was indisposed, Lady Margaret," she explained, "so I delivered your letter to Lady Frances myself. She was extremely pleased to see me, for she had an invitation for you."

Margaret Zouche opened the letter and eagerly scanned its contents. "Oh, how lovely. We are invited to Chelsea for all of next week. Frances and I will be able to catch up on the latest gossip! Bess, my dear, there is so much to do, I don't know where to start."

"Don't worry about the girls, Lady Margaret. I shall begin packing immediately."

"You are so organized, I don't know how I ever managed without you. Come to my dressing room; I should like your advice on what clothes I will need for Chelsea."

Bess was delighted. She took a great interest in Lady Zouche's wardrobe and had a natural flair for fashion. When she arrived in London, Bess had owned only one change of clothes, but now, thanks to her wealthy employer, she possessed four dresses. As she accompanied Lady Margaret to her dressing room,

Bess decided this was the perfect opportunity to double her wardrobe!

As the two women looked over dozens of expensive gowns, Bess said casually, "A friend of Lord Dorset bade me carry his regards to you. Now, let me think, could his name have been Cavendale?"

"Rogue Cavendish! He's Henry Grey's dearest friend and a devil with the ladies. I must include him in my next dinner party; Sir John enjoys his company, and I admit he's set my heart aflutter since I was a girl."

Bess looked unsure. "This gentleman seemed older than you, Lady Margaret." The ploy worked like a charm.

"That's most flattering, Bess, but I believe we're about the same age. He was widowed when he was quite young...he can't be much more than thirty."

"Thirty? When you wear pink you look no older than twenty."

"La! Remember the ages of my daughters! I shall take the pink to Chelsea."

"Some colors age a woman," Bess murmured.

"Really? I never thought of it before. Which colors?"

"Shades of purple, definitely, and gray is so drab." Bess stroked an emerald velvet gown covetously. "Green makes the skin look sallow, I think."

Lady Margaret gathered up the offending garments. "Here, take them; aging isn't a problem for you, dear child."

As Bess hung the precious dresses in her wardrobe, she hummed a merry tune. The sleeves were separate and interchangeable, and in her mind's eye she pictured how striking the green velvet sleeves would be paired with the elegant gray and how vividly the colors would contrast with her blazing hair. Bess had known in her bones that today would be lucky for her. She rubbed her cheek against the velvet and thought breathlessly of Rogue Cavendish. A widower in his thirties! No wonder he had seemed so worldly. And she was going to see him again. There was little doubt that Lady Zouche would invite him and no doubt whatsoever that Cavendish would accept!

Bess suddenly remembered poor Robert Barlow and ran up to the attic on the fourth floor, where the male servants were boarded. She rapped lightly on the door to his room before opening it. He was lying on his narrow bed. "Are you recovered, Rob?" she asked softly.

"I feel much better. Thank you, Bess, for what you did today. I wrote a letter home, telling them how good you are to me."

She saw the look of adoration on the boy's face and wished he would stop mooning over her. "Next week we are going to Chelsea. You will have an opportunity to rest and regain your strength while we are away."

Robert looked crestfallen. "I will miss you sorely, Bess."

"What rubbish!" she said impatiently, hurrying off to ready her charges for dinner.

In the Great Chamber at Whitehall, Henry Tudor entertained his courtiers at dinner. As William Cavendish and Henry Grey pushed their chairs away from the banquet table, the latter remarked, "As has become custom, the food and wine were far too rich and plentiful."

Cavendish drained his goblet. "Speak for yourself, Henry. He's catering to the greatest appetites in England tonight, my own included."

"I take it you are not referring to food and drink."

Cavendish's amused glance swept the hall. "The raw ambition of the people in this room tonight is exceeded only by their lechery."

"Your own included," Henry added lightly, stroking his blond mustache.

Frances Grey kissed Cavendish. "We're at Chelsea next week; do come, William; I'll arrange a hunt. You didn't come to Bradgate this summer, as you promised, so I won't take no for an answer!"

As Frances moved off toward the dancing, Cavendish thought the blood sport here tonight would be greater than anything Chelsea had to offer and was glad he had pressing business in Dover. Then he wondered what had put him in such a cynical mood. He was thankful that his occupation involved a good deal of travel and he was not expected to dance attendance at Court regularly. The king had surrounded himself with beautiful females every night since he had beheaded foolish little Catherine Howard, and most of them went willingly to his bed.

Cavendish saw his old friend, Lord William Parr, just returned from putting down trouble on the Scottish border, and sought his company. Parr was of medium height, but his military bearing and close-cropped beard gave him an air of authority. Cavendish was in time to hear Parr make an assignation with the beauteous Elizabeth Brooke, daughter of Lord Cobham. As she kissed Cavendish, she murmured in his ear, "No tales, Rogue," so William forebore to tell his friend that she had been spreading her legs for the king.

"You two seem very cozy," Parr accused.

"That is because I have just betrothed my daughter to the lady's brother." Marriage was the single most important step to advancement in Tudor society, and the espousal of children was a serious business.

"Splendid!" Parr clapped him on the back. "When I wed Elizabeth, we'll be related."

Cavendish did not ask Parr what he planned to do with his present wife.

Thomas Seymour, the handsomest man at Court, made his way across the room to greet Cavendish and Parr. Seymour's sister Jane had made him brother-in-law to the king, and though Jane was now in her grave along with three of Henry's other wives, the king was extremely fond of his late wife's brother. Thomas put his arms around both men in a friendly gesture. His golden beard curled about his laughing mouth, making him look like a young god just stepped down from Olympus. "Cavendish, you're a bloody genius. Your plunder of the monasteries has made me a wealthy man."

"God's death, that incautious tongue of yours will send us all to the block."

Seymour roared with laughter, and Cavendish couldn't help but like the good-natured young devil who hadn't a cautious bone in his body. Thomas was enjoying the intimate favors of Lord Parr's sister, Lady Catherine, in spite of the fact that she was wed to old Lord Latimer. Seymour thumped Parr on the back and said outrageously, "Do keep me informed of Latimer's health; the old swine can't hang on much longer." Wealthy widows were snapped up within a week at Court.

William Parr looked at Cavendish and quipped, "Christ, before long we'll all be related."

When Cavendish caught sight of Lady Catherine Parr Latimer, his gorge rose. Her demeanor was the epitome of respectability, yet she was cuckolding her husband with Thomas Seymour, and according to his friend Frances Grey, Catherine Parr was also the king's latest choice of bedmate. *The Court is no better than a brothel—an incestuous one at that!*

William excused himself and made his way down the chamber, for once ignoring the inviting female glances being cast his way. He noted with cynicism the men who never left the king's side. Edward Seymour, Thomas's older brother, was fawning on Henry, while the equally ambitious Lord John Dudley monopolized the conversation. Cavendish walked directly to the lord treasurer, Paulet, who immediately held up his hand to stay William's words.

"No need to tell me—your fees are late again, my friend. I am buried beneath an avalanche of paperwork and ask you to exercise patience."

"I have a solution, my Lord Treasurer. While collecting money for the Crown, I can collect my own fees at the same time. It will relieve your office of unnecessary work. I'll still submit my accounts in detail, but they will be marked *paid in full.*"

"Yes, I think we can accommodate each other in such a satisfactory manner. I'll get the king's authority for you. You did a most commendable job at St. Sepulchre's in Canterbury."

William thanked the treasurer and moved off, gratified to have accomplished the profitable business for which he had purposely come. He contemplated the cardroom and the ballroom, both overflowing with predatory, expensively gowned females willing to lift their skirts for him at the crook of his finger. But for some reason he found the company tonight unappealing.

As Cavendish left Whitehall, his mind conjured a picture of a girl with large dark eyes and red-gold hair. Elizabeth Hardwick was the antithesis of the shopworn courtesans who bartered their wares at the Tudor Court. She was so fresh and young and, yes, innocent! His chance meeting with her had shown him just how jaded his palate had become. Rogue Cavendish decided she would make a most enchanting mistress.

The following afternoon, Bess was giving the Zouche girls an embroidery lesson. She had learned needlework at her aunt Marcy's knee. Not only did Bess do exquisite work, she also drew original designs on the cloth. While the girls worked on samplers, Lady Margaret and Bess were putting the finishing touches on a pair of sleeves that were to be a gift for Frances Grey. Bess had drawn the Tudor roses, whose petals were now filled in with Spanish silk.

When the house steward announced William Cavendish, Bess was so disconcerted she pricked her finger. Her mistress, all aflutter, dismissed her daughters and flew to the mirror. When Bess arose to follow them, Lady Zouche said, "I really shouldn't be alone with him—just sit quietly and do your embroidery."

Cavendish was so gallant, he had Margaret eating out of his hand in seconds. His devilish gaze flicked over Bess in the far corner, and she knew immediately his words were meant for her.

"Forgive me for coming uninvited, but I haven't been able to get you out of my mind since yesterday."

"Cavendish, you are a flatterer and a rogue. It's been far too long since we've seen you."

"You are even lovelier than I remember."

Bess's mouth curved into a smile as she lowered her eyes and bent her head over her work.

William's glance fell on the sleeve that Lady Zouche had been embroidering. "I've interrupted your needlework. Tudor roses— I had no idea you were so talented."

" 'Tis a gift for Lady Frances; we are invited to Chelsea next week."

"I, too, am invited. I was going to decline, but you have quite changed my mind. Suddenly, I cannot wait."

His voice was deep and, to Bess, held a wealth of hidden meaning. If he did not stop, Lady Zouche would suspect something. She must find a way to warn Cavendish to guard his wicked tongue. When a footman came in with wine and wafers, Bess jumped up quickly, relieved the servant of the tray, and brought it forward.

"Thank you, dear child." Lady Zouche picked up a wineglass and, turning her back on Bess and Cavendish, carried it to a side table across the room.

With her back to Lady Zouche and a forbidding look of disapproval on her face, Bess offered him the tray and whispered, "Stop!"

His eyes glittered with amusement. He knew Margaret could neither hear him nor see what he did. "No," he murmured. He noticed the drop of blood on her finger, quickly raised it to his lips, and sucked.

Bess yelped and almost dropped the tray. She felt her cheeks begin to burn. He really was a damned rogue to toy with her right under Lady Margaret's nose. She could be dismissed on the spot.

"Is something wrong, Bess?" The question was sharp with suspicion.

"Yes, my lady, I'm afraid I've spilled the wine." Bess very deliberately tipped the glass so that it splashed over Cavendish, then bit her lip at her own daring. "Forgive me, sir. I'll get a footman." Bess glanced up into his eyes and saw that her deliberate act had not angered him; rather, it had challenged him.

Though the village of Chelsea was only a few scant miles upriver from the city of London, it was considered to be in the country. Here, too, sumptuous mansions had been built along the river, but all were surrounded by meadows, beyond which lay dense woods.

Magnificent Shrewsbury House, which was owned by the Talbots, one of the wealthiest noble families in England, was at Chelsea, and opposite Kew Gardens was the enormous, square Syon House, which belonged to the Dudleys. Just a mile away, the tall, slender brick towers of Richmond Palace rose above the Thames, and farther upriver lay the resplendent and incomparable Hampton Court Palace.

Bess was so thrilled about the Chelsea visit, she hadn't been able to sleep. The anticipation of being in the company of Rogue

Cavendish made her dizzy with excitement, yet at the same time it disturbed her. She knew that she had caught his fancy, but he was a man of the world and it might be hard to hold his interest, and more difficult still to get him to declare himself. She knew she must walk a fine line and not step over the boundaries of propriety, but skirt the edges close enough to make him want her. Bess shivered at the thought.

Chelsea Palace took her breath away. The rooms were spacious, with many windows to let in the light, and her imagination took flight. Bess decided that when she built her dream house, it would have more glass windows than walls.

Frances Grey greeted Bess just as warmly as she welcomed Margaret Zouche and her daughters, making no distinction between her noble friend and her daughters' companion. Everyone, especially Bess, loved Frances for her easygoing manner and lack of pretention, rare qualities in one of royal blood. Frances had a beautiful face and lovely golden hair, but her figure was full and could only be described as plump.

Even though Chelsea Palace had scores of servants, Frances had brought along so many ladies-in-waiting, nursemaids, and governess-companions for the Grey children, who were slightly younger than the Zouche girls, that Bess realized she would have few duties to perform apart from sitting with the two friends while they indulged in endless gossip.

Over the past year Bess had learned every scandalous detail of Henry Tudor and his royal court. She knew all about Anne Boleyn's imperious manner, sulfurous moods, and deformed little finger. She learned that Anne had kept the king panting after her for six long years without letting him bed her. When Anne did finally give in, he got her with child immediately, then moved heaven and earth to marry her. Frances had chuckled and said, "It was easy for Anne to deny Henry intercourse, for she loved Harry Percy and didn't give a fart for the king— oh, sorry, Margaret, I meant to say she didn't give a *fig for the king.*"

Bess also had heard all the disparaging remarks Henry had made about not wanting to ride that "Flanders mare"—Anne of Cleves, his fourth wife—and she had also learned every indiscretion ever committed by the wanton little Catherine Howard, his fifth. Now she sat listening as Frances divulged the very latest gossip.

"When Thomas Seymour returned from his mission to Germany, Catherine Parr fell into his bed like a peach...well, perhaps more like a persimmon, with that prim mouth and air of respectability she pretends."

Margaret interjected, "I didn't know Lord Latimer had died—"

"He hasn't, but I warrant his days are numbered!"

"Oh, Frances, how can you say such things?"

"Because I know for a fact Henry has propositioned her! She confided it to her sister, in strictest secrecy. Naturally her sister couldn't wait to tell me."

"Oh, poor Catherine."

"Don't feel too sorry for her, Margaret. She's been married to two rich, old husbands and knows to perfection how to manage men. She's learned how to suck more than persimmons. Catholic too," sniffed Frances, who was staunchly Protestant.

"But if she loves Thomas Seymour—"

"God's balls, Margaret, love pales into insignificance when pitted against ambition. Why settle for the king's brother-in-law, when the king himself waggles his weapon?"

"You think she has aspirations to be queen?"

"I do. What does she have to lose besides her head?" Frances slapped her plump thigh with mirth, and Bess bit her lips to keep from laughing at such shocking irreverence.

"But if he is having his way with her, he has no need to wed her," Margaret pointed out.

"I didn't say he was having his way with her; I said he had propositioned her. Catherine is wise enough to let him dip his dickie once, then cut him off. Cockteasing is still the surest method of trapping a husband."

Bess sat listening, absorbing the noblewomen's lessons about men. She felt disappointed when Lady Margaret's daughters came running into the salon and interrupted the conversation.

"May we please go to the stables with Lady

Jane, Mother? She has a new white palfrey."

"Bess will go with you, but you must promise to be careful."

Frances assured her friend, "There are dozens of grooms, Margaret; your young ladies will be perfectly safe." She smiled at Bess. "You must select a mount for yourself while you're down there; we are having a hunt tomorrow."

Bess's spirits soared.

"Oh, I don't think we will join you, Frances. I haven't ridden since I was in Derbyshire last year," Margaret demurred.

Bess's spirits plummeted.

"Lud, Margaret, if I can cram my bulk into a saddle, you can make the effort. No one shall be excused; everyone rides, children and all. Let the bloody grooms earn their pay."

Inside the vast stables the girls discovered a litter of kittens nesting in the hay. They swooped them up in their arms with cries of delight and carried them outside. So that the mother cat would not be distressed, Bess picked her up and began to stroke her with murmured endearments. The black and white feline, unused to such gentle attention, nestled in the crook of her arm and began to purr. "Sweet puss, do you like to be stroked?"

Bess jumped as a shadow loomed above her. The cat took such alarm, it left a long scratch on her thumb as it leapt to safety.

"Sweet puss," Cavendish murmured, pleased to see her the moment he rode in and dismounted.

Bess gasped at the pain in her thumb and at his closeness.

"Did you come to meet me?" he teased.

"You have a fine conceit of yourself, sir." She waved her thumb. "This is the second time you've wounded me."

He took her hand and saw the blood upon her creamy skin. For one erotic moment he pictured drops of blood across a creamy thigh, and the urge rose up in him to take her right there in the hay. Instead, he removed his riding glove and stroked her thumb with his, brushing the blood away. He stroked again. "Do you purr?"

She looked him directly in the eye. "I have claws."

"Sheathe them," he murmured huskily. Sheathe me! he invited silently.

Bess lowered her lashes, knowing they were long and dark and pretty. "We shouldn't be alone." With cool deliberation she pulled her hand from his.

"If I hadn't thought we could be alone together, I wouldn't have come. Besides, we're not alone; we're in a stable filled with grooms and children." Cavendish turned and spoke to his manservant, who hovered at a discreet distance. "Take my bags up, James. I'll follow shortly."

Bess stepped away and spoke to him over her shoulder. "Lady Frances bade me choose a mount for tomorrow's hunt, but I haven't yet decided if I'll join the chase."

He closed the distance between them, took her arm, and led her down a row of horse stalls, in the opposite direction from the girls. "Do you ride well?"

"I like to ride astride," she confided.

He stopped walking and stared down at her. Already aroused, he found her words acting upon him as an aphrodisiac. The serious look on her face told him she was not being deliberately provocative, she was simply stating a fact, but her facts were exciting him in a very primal way. He looked in to a few more stalls. "You'll have to ride sidesaddle tomorrow. Here's a little mare with clean lines that will serve you very well."

Bess saw that the chestnut horse was undistinguished in any way, and her glance strayed to more showy animals.

"Wear green tomorrow," he said.

Taken aback by his remark, Bess turned to look at him. He was gazing at her with an expression of intense interest.

She loved green because it provided such a flattering contrast to her fiery-red hair. But why did *he* want her to wear green? "Is green your favorite color, sir?"

"Green will blend in with the trees to make us invisible."

"Oh!" She gasped in surprise, suddenly comprehending why he had suggested the unremarkable mount for her. A small flame of hot anger kindled inside her as it occurred

36

to Bess that he was well-versed in such matters as arranging clandestine assignations with women. Was Rogue Cavendish a practiced womanizer? Was she out of her depth? Her eyes moved over his broad chest, across his wide shoulders, and came to rest on his sensual mouth. Then she wondered what it would feel like to be kissed by this powerful, attractive man. Suddenly, Bess couldn't bear the fact that other women knew, while she did not. But she felt her anger subside as she realized a man should be experienced in these matters. What good would he be otherwise?

Lifting her eyes to his, she saw that he was amused. He was so attractive, he could probably have his pick of any woman in Court circles, yet for some reason his fancy had settled on her. Clearly he had seduction in mind, and she'd be willing to bet he was a man who enjoyed the chase. The enormous challenge he represented was too much for Bess to resist. The corners of her mouth lifted. This might be a game to him, but she was deadly serious. She wanted him every bit as much as he wanted her, possibly more, though not for the same reasons. Cavendish would be an extraordinary feather in her cap.

"I've decided to join the chase after all, sir."

"Elizabeth"—he said her name like a caress—"you may call me William."

"William," she said slowly, testing the name on her lips, and liking the taste of it. Then she tossed her curls and pertly added, "You may call me Mistress Hardwick."

THREE

As Bess helped Lady Zouche dress for dinner, the older woman fretted, "I've no notion what I can wear tomorrow."

"I packed your riding habit and a pair of your favorite boots, Lady Margaret."

"You are so competent, Bess. However did you think of it?"

"Your daughters insisted I pack theirs. They said everyone rides at Chelsea."

"I finally learned the reason Frances moved upriver this week. The king has moved the Court to Hampton, and she was afraid of missing something."

"Hampton Court Palace," Bess said with reverence. "How I would love to see it."

"And so you shall, my dear. We are going there on Thursday. Little Lady Jane Grey has been invited to reside there and be tutored with the royal children. Frances wants to inspect their apartments and living quarters. She isn't sure if she will let her go this year or wait until next."

"Lady Jane is very young," Bess said, trying to contain the excitement she felt.

"She's the same age as Prince Edward, and the cousins are very fond of each other. The king thinks his son would benefit from a playmate. Surrounded by adults, he has become far too serious, like a little old man. Frances has confided that there is an understanding between her and the king to betroth the royal children if they seem suited, and of course if Lady Jane is to be Edward's future queen, it makes a good deal of sense to educate them together."

Bess thought it was a match made in heaven, for Lady Jane reminded her of a little old woman, but she had more sense than to voice such an opinion.

"I think it's acceptable for you to dine with us, Bess. Frances has such liberal ideas, she doesn't expect her ladies to go to the servants' hall."

"I'll take a tray with the girls, my lady, then see them safely to bed." Bess knew she would never be able to eat with Cavendish's bold eyes on her. Let him wait and wonder where she was; it would do him good!

Two hours later Bess changed into a dark violet gown and pinned her curls high on the crown of her head. She had no jewels, but she did have a small fan she had embroidered with silk violets. She took the long way downstairs, stopping in each regal chamber to admire the treasures and furnishings displayed so elegantly here at Chelsea.

Bess had a deep and abiding passion for beautiful things. She stood before a medieval tapestry depicting a hunt scene and marveled that it had been lovingly preserved through the centuries. Royalty never let anything out of its clutches once it had been acquired. Bess understood such behavior. If ever she was fortunate enough to possess something of value and beauty, she would treasure it forever and ensure that it would be passed down to her children and her children's children.

She saw that the dining hall was empty and the company had moved into a long gallery lit by myriad candles. Music floated down from a minstrels' gallery. As she paused on the threshold, Bess pretended this all belonged to her...*her* liveried footmen serving wine, *her* musicians, *her* guests.

While Lady Frances was ordering the servants to set up card tables—she knew full well that men much preferred gambling to dancing—William Cavendish came up behind her and fondly slipped his arms around her. She smiled up at him. "What shall it be, whist?"

He put his lips close to her ear and murmured suggestively, "I want to play with her—the little redhead who just arrived. Be a darling and arrange it for me, Frances?"

"She is a rather tempting morsel."

"She tempts me," Cavendish admitted.

Frances was willing to indulge him. She liked Bess, the girl was unusually bright and high-spirited, and it would be diverting to watch the byplay and see how well she acquitted herself. Frances watched Bess seek out Lady Margaret, and a sly idea popped into her head immediately. Knowing how much her friend detested cards, Frances pounced on her. "We need a fourth for whist, Margaret."

"No, no, I dislike the pasteboards. John should be here, somewhere." She looked beseechingly at Bess. "Has Lord John arrived yet?"

"No, my lady."

"Come, Margaret, it shall be Henry and I against you and Cavendish."

Margaret paled. "I couldn't. I would try his patience beyond bearing."

"Then perhaps Bess will help me out?"

"Yes, yes, Bess, do attend Lady Frances."

"But I have no skill, my lady."

"Nonsense, a clever girl like you will pick it up in a trice." Frances took her arm and led Bess down the salon.

The two men greeted Bess, and Henry Grey, with his impeccable manners, helped her into a chair.

"Bess may partner me since she doesn't know how to play." Frances sat down facing her and the two men took their seats. Cavendish picked up the cards, shuffled them, and informed Bess, "We'll play long whist. We use all fifty-two cards; each player gets thirteen." He dealt them out one after the other in rotation. "A game is for ten points—the holding of the honor cards is counted."

Bess nodded her head, even though she didn't fully comprehend. She focused her complete attention on Cavendish, listening to his every word, watching his every move. Gradually, it came to her that each pair of partners tried to take tricks. The ladies lost every hand against the men, and Bess was grateful that Lady Frances seemed not to mind. Bess grasped the concept quickly, learning the honor cards; then it occurred to her that if she kept track of the cards that had been played, her chances of winning would be vastly improved.

They changed partners so that Bess and Henry Grey were pitted against Lady Frances and Cavendish. "Enough pissing about, Henry, it's time to play for stakes. Rogue and I will clean you out!" Frances declared.

Bess watched the men put money on the table and place wagers. She felt terrible, for she knew that with her for his partner, Henry Grey would lose his money. Whenever she and Henry did manage to take a trick, Bess whisked it from the table with a feeling of triumph.

The three friends carried on a running conversation, rich in gossip and punctuated with jibes at each other. Bess didn't listen; she gave her whole attention to the cards and the way Cavendish played them. With every subsequent hand she picked up more nuances of the game. A footman served them wine, and after she drank a little, everything came into sharper focus. Bess now watched their faces as well as the cards, and she realized how easy it was for a player to signal his partner in subtle ways. Inside her, excitement mingled with apprehension as she anticipated that soon she would be partnered with Rogue Cavendish.

"Pay up, you damned tightwad," Frances twitted her long-suffering husband, then raked in half the silver coins that she and Cavendish had won.

As Henry and William changed seats, Bess drained her wineglass to give herself courage. Then she felt Cavendish's amused eyes on her from across the table. "Let's double the stakes." His mouth curved in a smile of pure confidence.

Bess felt as if her heart were in her mouth as she gazed back at him. He was like a master with a pupil in whom he had every faith. She experienced a moment of panic that he was putting all his trust in her. Then Cavendish winked at her boldly. Suddenly, she was filled with assurance. All her uncertainty fell away. Without him she would be vanquished; but with him she could do anything!

It was as if lady luck sat on her shoulder advising her which cards to play. Like magic, she and Cavendish could do no wrong. Bess began to enjoy herself. As well as whist, she and her partner were engaged in another game, quite overt and open, but at the same time they were linked together in something far more subtle and personal, something that excluded everyone else in the universe, something intimate and private.

They communicated in a language that had no words. Each knew the thoughts of the other; each gave and received pleasure from the other. It was not a flirtation; Bess would have lost her concentration immediately if she had engaged in dalliance. It was more basic and elemental, not only a meeting of minds, but a sharing of passionate enjoyment for what they did, like true kindred spirits.

When they had soundly trounced the Greys, Cavendish pushed half their winnings before her. "Clever girl." It was the first money Bess had ever had in her life.

"Beginner's luck!" cried Henry, rising so he could change partners.

"Sit down," Rogue murmured. "I have no intention of relinquishing her."

Bess blushed and caught the eye of Lady Frances, who gave her an admiring look. She had acquitted herself at cards and performed even better in the more exciting game played by men and women.

The hours melted away, and the pile of silver coins before Bess doubled. When Frances refused to lose one more time and their game broke up, the hour was late and most of their guests had retired. Frances handed Bess a cloth purse. "You cleaned me out; you might as well have the purse as well."

"Thank you, Lady Frances. I had a wonderful evening."

"I should thank you.... I was entertained simply watching you."

"It isn't over yet." Cavendish was at her elbow. "I know what both of us need," he murmured suggestively. Bess glanced up at him, trying to keep her alarm at bay. "Fresh air." He took her arm and led her from the salon toward doors that opened onto the balustrade.

The night air was cool as it touched their

faces and ruffled their hair. "Mistress Hardwick, you are a most apt pupil."

"You are so experienced, you make an excellent teacher, sir." She spoke to him formally, and he got the impression the intimacy they had shared during the game had somehow vanished. Her words also made him acutely aware of the age difference between them.

"God's death, you make me sound ancient."

"You mistake my words; I am most grateful to you."

How grateful? he wondered. "Well, what plans do you have for your ill-gotten gains?"

Bess had gathered forty silver shillings into her purse, which amounted to two whole pounds. "Oh, I've always wanted a little neck ruff; now I'll be able to indulge myself."

He stopped walking and looked down at her, astonished at how unspoiled she was. "A ruff? Do you not long for jewels?"

"Of course I do, and someday I shall have them," she said matter-of-factly.

His fingers reached out to touch her collarbone. "I could give you jewels, Elizabeth." His suggestive offer hung upon the night breeze. She gave no response. They were standing on the balustrade, and he watched her step back and glance upward at the unlighted windows.

"I must go up. I don't wish to disturb Lady Zouche or her daughters."

Lady Zouche can go to the devil! "If you come to my chamber, you won't disturb them," he urged persuasively.

45

"If I were gone all night, sir, I would be instantly dismissed, and rightly so."

He slipped his arm possessively about her small waist, drawing her back to him, and pledged, "I would take care of you, Elizabeth."

She gave him a level look. "I have more good sense than to allow you to seduce me, milord. I have no dowry; I must make my own way in this world. I want a respectable marriage, and without my honor that would be impossible."

Impatience rose up in him. "God's death, you are an innocent wench!"

Bess flashed him a radiant smile. "Ah, and therein lies the attraction."

Cavendish threw back his head and laughed. She was part girl, part woman, yet wise beyond her years. Her candor held him in thrall. The perfume of the night-scented stocks stole to them from the garden beyond the balustrade, beckoning them into the velvet blackness. He saw the longing in her eyes, then heard her sigh with regret.

"I must go. Now. You are far too tempting, Rogue Cavendish."

He felt his body stir with soaring desire, but crushed it down for the moment. "I'll let you go, but I give you fair warning that tomorrow I will take up exactly where I left off."

Bess picked up her skirts and hurried toward the French doors, but before she disappeared inside, she called provocatively over her shoulder, "You may try, milord, but it remains to be seen if you will succeed."

As William Cavendish sought his chamber, he was deep in thought. He dismissed his manservant, James Cromp, who had waited up for him. James knew his place and would have vanished discreetly if his master had not been alone.

As Cavendish lay abed, willing his body to relax, a full-blown picture of Elizabeth Hardwick filled his imagination. "Bess," he murmured aloud. That's what Frances had called her, and the diminutive suited her. It was softer, more intimate than *Elizabeth*.

He smiled ruefully. He had fully expected that she would share his bed tonight, but the little beauty had a mind of her own. He laughed and shook his head at her refusal. The devil of it was, he doubted that it was morals or prudery that made her hold him off. He suspected that it was her practical common sense that told her not to play the slut. She valued herself highly enough to hold out for marriage, and he grudgingly admired her for it.

Of course, he'd overcome that obstacle. Persuading her to be generous would be pure pleasure; it would simply take more effort than he had anticipated. He allowed his imagination free rein. She had proved a perfect partner tonight at cards. Following his lead, her mind in tune with his own, she had picked up every nuance and learned everything he had to teach her. Instructing her excited him. Deep in his bones he knew she would make a superb life partner...an exciting wife. The concept was a novel one; in his experience, wives were anything but exciting. Cavendish sighed inwardly and, turning over, fell instantly asleep.

In her own bed, in the suite of rooms assigned to the Zouches, Bess lay reliving every detail of her exciting evening. The luxury of her surroundings and the exalted company at Chelsea made everything seem fanciful and illusionary. Was she really here, and were these things really happening to her? She pinched herself, then stifled a giggle as she felt the pain. She reached beneath her pillow to touch the purse of silver coins and found that they, too, were real.

But the most thrilling part of the evening had been getting acquainted with William Cavendish. Just the thought of him made her feel as if she were floating on a cloud. Cavendish was an important official of the Court who worked for the king! Yet he gave her his undivided attention, and she had never been so flattered in her life.

Bess knew it would be easy to fall in love with him, but she preferred that it be the other way around. Oh, if only he would fall in love with her, just a little bit. He had offered her jewels and he had offered to take care of her if she lost her position. She had nearly screamed with excitement when he touched her. It had been almost impossible to deny him and to deny herself, but somehow she had found the strength to tell him plainly that she would not allow him to seduce her.

Bess knew a moment's panic. How foolish she had been to refuse him; he would definitely ignore her tomorrow. But hope would not be denied and rose up again to fill her heart. If he did pursue her in the hunt, after she had told him she wanted marriage, surely it would indicate that he was courting her.

In the east wing, in a great carved gilt bed, Henry Grey sank himself into the plump depths of his wife's voluptuous body. After he satisfied himself and his wife, he lay contentedly cushioned upon her generous curves.

"What do you think of Bess Hardwick, Henry?"

"Glorious breasts." His mouth sought a large, florid nipple.

"There's more to Mistress Hardwick than tits." Her hands came up to knead his buttocks.

"Mmm, breasts and brains. I wish him joy of her."

Frances milked him to the last drop. "Breasts and brains can be a lethal combination."

Despite the late hour at which the Greys got to sleep, they were up at the crack of dawn to lead the Chelsea hunt. Every neighbor who owned a mansion in the vicinity took part, including their children and their grooms.

Bess accompanied Lord John and Lady Margaret Zouche and their daughters to the vast stables. When she emerged, riding the small chestnut Cavendish had suggested, the courtyard was a deafening welter of horses, hunters, and hounds.

The head huntsman was shouting orders that were largely being ignored, the hounds were baying wildly and circling on their leashes, horns were blaring, men were arguing, children squealing, as servants carried around stirrup cups and grooms attended the young ladies who needed assistance.

Bess wore her green velvet dress; it wasn't exactly a riding habit, but it was the most suitable garment she owned. Her blazing hair was gathered neatly into a matching snood she had crocheted herself. She craned her neck looking for Cavendish, but the moment she spotted him, she pretended not to notice him. When she saw that he, too, was wearing green, her pulses quickened.

Cavendish greeted the Zouches and reined in beside Lord John to exchange a few words. Bess hoped he wouldn't single her out in front of Lady Zouche, but he did it so deftly, no one seemed to notice. His big bay gelding sidestepped away from a pair of hounds, and as he curbed its agitation, their stirrups almost touched. "Follow my lead," Cavendish instructed, then moved off to greet his friend Henry.

Three grooms joined the Zouches, one each for Lady Margaret and her two young ladies.

Bess maneuvered her mount away from the family and walked her horse slowly to the outer perimeter of the hunters. If she meekly did as Rogue Cavendish bade her and followed him it would be tantamount to throwing in her hand and conceding him victory. It would signal to him that she would obey his every command, and Bess had no intention of sending him such a signal of compliancy. Since he enjoyed the chase, she was determined to lead him on one.

When the hunt master released the hounds and sounded his long brass horn, most of the hunters thundered off after the dogs. Bess watched Cavendish. Without a backward glance he kept pace with the pack across the fields, then veered off to the left when he reached the woods.

Bess sat her horse, keeping it reined in so it could not follow the others. She wondered if her ploy would work. She had almost given up hope when she saw the lone rider emerge from the trees. Her heart soared. Cavendish had circled back to see where the devil she was. The corners of her mouth lifted triumphantly as she dug her heel into her chestnut's flank and sped off across the fields in the opposite direction of the hunt and Cavendish.

She bent low over her mount's neck and urged her on in an encouraging tone. Bess knew it was only a matter of time before he overtook her, if indeed he had taken up the chase. She resisted looking back. She would find out soon enough. His gelding was far more powerful than her horse and he was astride, while she was hampered by the sidesaddle. Once she reached the trees, she could guide her smaller mount more quickly than her pursuer would be able to guide his, but it was inevitable that the hunter would capture his quarry.

FOUR

A powerful hand took the reins and brought her horse to a halt. "Why the devil did you flee from me?" His words shot out like steel-tipped arrows.

For the sheer pleasure of it! Bess gazed at him wide-eyed, breathless. "Because I was afraid." It was not wholly a lie. Would he vent his anger on her?

"God's death, I won't rape you!"

Her breasts rose and fell as she gasped for air. "Do I have your word on it, sir?"

"Certainly." His eyes narrowed. "God's blood, you're a clever wench; you've already got me on the defensive."

"A position you detest." Her eyes danced with laughter.

"I'll show you a position," he growled, but the amusement was back in his eyes and she decided to trust him, though not too far. His hand never left her bridle, and now he led her deeper into the woods at a leisurely pace. They rode at least three miles before he found a small clearing beside a shallow brook.

"Privacy is a precious commodity." He dismounted and tethered their horses where the animals could nibble the grass. Then he moved close to her stirrup and looked up into her face. "For the next few hours you are for my eyes only."

He held up powerful arms and watched Bess linger long over her hesitation before she came down into his arms in a flurry of velvet skirt and petticoats. Audaciously, he held her captive against him after her feet touched the ground—not long enough to frighten her, but long enough to savor her lemon scent of verbena, and certainly long enough to press her breasts against his chest and brush his hard shaft against her soft belly. When she pulled away, he did not prevent her.

Cavendish wore a short, rakish cloak, which he unfastened from his shoulders and spread on the grass in a patch of sunshine. "Be at ease, sweeting."

She accepted his invitation and sat down upon the cloak. He knelt beside her. "The real reason for wearing green is so that the grass stains won't show," he murmured intimately.

"Rogue Cavendish, you are far too experienced for my liking!" she said bluntly, and made as if she would arise and leave him.

"And you are far too innocent for mine," he said, taking possession of her hand to keep her beside him.

Her dark eyes were enormous. "Liar," she whispered softly. "My innocence excites you."

He groaned. "Oh, Christ, you speak the

truth; I don't know what to do to you first."

"Oh, you rogue!" she gasped. Then she looked straight into his eyes. "Will you always be so honest with me?"

He nodded. "If my honesty excites you." He lifted her hand to his mouth and ran the tip of his tongue across her palm, then placed his lips upon her wrist to feel her rapid pulsebeat.

Bess watched him avidly as he began to toy with her fingers, tracing their delicate length, then he separated them and slipped one into his mouth. She gasped as he began to suck on it. She experienced a tiny pulsebeat between her legs, and she saw that he was so wise in the ways of women, he knew what had happened to her. She snatched away her hand and heard his deep chuckle.

When Cavendish raised his hand toward her face, Bess drew back slightly. "I promised not to ravish you, but I do intend to awaken you a little."

She considered for a moment and decided to let him take a few liberties. It was time to dispel some of her ignorance about the things that happened between men and women. Bess had heard endless gossip about sexual matters but had no firsthand experience. She had chosen him for her tutor, so why not let him commence his lesson?

When he brushed the backs of his fingers across her cheek, the corners of her mouth lifted. "You are so unearthly fair." He pulled off her snood and caught her silken hair as it tumbled into his hands. The sight of the red-gold mass took his breath away. His fingers splayed through it sensuously. "Bess, you have the most glorious hair I've ever seen."

"Why does my hair fascinate you? Is it the color?"

"Aye, it's like flames. I could warm my hands at the blaze, and it marks you as special; you make blondes and brunettes seem commonplace."

" 'Tis said it is the mark of a hot temper, and in my case it is true," she confided.

"That in itself is exciting. What man can resist the urge to tame a hellcat?"

She laughed with delight. "Tell me more."

"Do you want the truth?"

She looked into his eyes. "Always."

"It's a constant reminder that the curls between your legs must be red too."

"Oh!" Her lips parted in genuine shock. "Is that what men think about?"

"A thousand times a day," he said solemnly.

She decided he was teasing her unmercifully. "Damned rogue."

"A truthful rogue." His hands left her hair to cup her face, then slowly, with great reverence, he lifted her mouth to meet his.

Bess closed her eyes so that her other senses became heightened. His male scent enveloped her, his touch and taste intoxicated her. She opened her lips and kissed him back. "Ooh, I've wondered so long what a kiss would be like. It's such a relief to know I like it excessively!"

"Have you never been kissed before?" he asked, stunned.

Her dark eyes were luminous, her lips trembled. He reached out to trace the outline of her mouth, and her body was taken by a great shudder. Suddenly she grabbed his hand and bit down on the fleshy part of his thumb, then looked appalled.

"You shouldn't have done that, Bess."

She stared at him with enormous dark eyes.

"It reveals far too much about you, sweeting."

She managed a breath when she saw his amusement.

"It tells me your emotions run deep. It tells me you are a woman of passion. Though barely awakened, you possess an earthy sensuality that men will respond to all your life." He swept her into his arms and this time kissed her thoroughly. His mouth became insistent, and her lips parted beneath his. As he molded his mouth to hers, she clung to him, responding with fire. Heat leapt between them, threatening to melt and fuse them together permanently.

His hand was on her breast, and Cavendish knew if he did not put some distance between them he would have her naked in the grass. To his utter consternation he realized his conscience was pricking him. Abruptly, he got up from his knees and went to his horse. What the hell was the matter with him? Making love to Elizabeth Hardwick had obsessed him since the minute he'd laid eyes on her. The whole point of coming to Chelsea was to get her to lie with him!

Now they were alone in the woods; what was

there to stop him? With a little gentle persuasion he could arouse her to the point where she would willingly lie naked in the grass. She was clearly virginal, with no notion that full, intense arousal was so compelling there would be no stopping, no turning back. But afterward she would believe he had betrayed her, and the trouble was, he desired more than one tumble. He wanted her on a more permanent basis. Immediately, he realized the responsibility was his.

William opened his saddlebags and took out food and a wineskin. He closed the distance between them and unwrapped the linen cloth that held roast capon, sharp cheese, and crisp apples. Bess smiled her delight, and he knew he had himself under control. There was nowhere on earth he would rather be at this moment, and they were going to enjoy their time alone together. He would temper his wooing with soft words and gentle hands that would not take them beyond the point of no return.

William enjoyed watching her eat. She bit into a capon leg with gusto, and when the tart juice from a green apple ran down her chin, she licked it off with relish. "Let me show you how to drink from a wineskin." With his hands guiding hers, he showed her how to squeeze it with just the right pressure and how to position her mouth to catch the dark red stream of wine. The lesson involved a great deal of laughter, and William realized just how wonderful it was to be with a female who enjoyed laughing as much as he did.

When the wine was done, he lay back in the warm sunshine and pulled her down so that her breasts were cushioned on his broad chest and he could look up into her beautiful face. They spent the next hour kissing, whispering, touching, and laughing. With much difficulty William kept his rampant desire under control, but he was amply rewarded by knowing how much pleasure Bess received from his nonthreatening dalliance.

When they heard a distant hunting horn, she sat up and searched for her snood. William found it and put it on her, gathering her wildly disheveled hair into the confining net.

"Sweetheart, I have to go to Dover to do an inventory of the monastery of St. Radegund. It will take some time because I have to assess their lands and rents."

"When must you leave?"

"Tomorrow. Will you miss me?"

"Perhaps...a little," she teased.

"Tell the truth! You'll miss me fiercely!"

With mock solemnity she placed her hand upon her breast. "You take my heart with you, William."

He sat up and kissed her temple. "Sweetheart, when I return I'll have a question to ask you regarding a more permanent relationship. I want us to be together."

The horn sounded again, closer. William got to his feet and pulled Bess up beside him. "You go first so we are not seen together. Chelsea is in yonder direction. I'll join the hunt for a couple of hours." He lifted her into the saddle with possessive arms, kissing her in the process. "Remember that I adore you."

Bess rode back to Chelsea Palace in a state of wonder. Was this what it felt like to tumble head over heels in love? Rogue Cavendish adored her, he had admitted it freely. When he returned from Dover, would he ask her to marry him? It all seemed too fantastic to be real, yet Bess believed with all her heart that fate had something glorious planned for her.

The king's red-haired daughter, Elizabeth Tudor, had spent days wandering about Hampton Court Palace, exploring every nook of every chamber, antechamber, gallery, and staircase. The most spectacular of these was the King's Staircase, whose walls and ceiling had been painted by Italian masters. Remembering that this staircase led to the State Apartments was more important to the Lady Elizabeth than its artwork.

Learning the layout of a royal residence was the first order of business for Elizabeth Tudor. It gave her a measure of confidence and security, as well as providing her with an escape route from unpleasant scenes and people she detested. She remembered Hampton so vividly, recalling the happy moments with her mother and the hours of shattering sadness.

She paused as she reached the Long Gallery.

An unbearable lump of sorrow rose in her throat for her sweet stepmother, Catherine Howard. Elizabeth pictured her running down this gallery, screaming for the king when she learned she had been charged with adultery. *Lord God, was it only a year ago February that she was beheaded? It feels as if I've been mourning for years.* Then she thought again of her mother, Anne Boleyn, and knew she would always be in mourning.

Elizabeth Tudor forced the tragic memories away and let happier thoughts fill her mind. Catherine, so young and gay, had been unfailingly kind to her, mothering her as no other woman had done. Catherine Howard had been cousin to her real mother, Anne Boleyn, and she had answered all Elizabeth's questions about her mother and the fateful marriage to her father, King Henry. Elizabeth had been wildly curious for years, but whenever she had dared whisper her mother's name, she had been hushed up with slaps.

Elizabeth remembered her other stepmother, Jane Seymour, who had liked to walk in the Clock Court here at Hampton before she gave birth to the little prince Edward. Elizabeth was only four at the time, but she remembered how cruel her stepmother had been to her, coldly banishing her to Hatfield so that she would be eighteen miles away from her father, King Henry.

Elizabeth Tudor smiled a secret smile of satisfaction. *Jane Seymour schemed to replace my mother, but the sly bitch also ended up in her grave.*

Still, Jane's short reign as queen hadn't been a total loss. It had produced a brother for Elizabeth and provided her with an uncle, Thomas Seymour. Elizabeth smiled again, just thinking about him. Thomas was like a golden god and one of the very few people she loved and trusted in the entire world.

Elizabeth moved toward the latticed window, opened it, and leaned out. It was much too pleasant a day to stay indoors, and she decided to explore the gardens. She saw a barge arrive at the landing stage, and curiosity kept her at the window to see who arrived. When a gaggle of females disembarked, Elizabeth squinted her eyes to see if she knew them. She recognized Frances Grey, Marchioness of Dorset, because of her girth. She liked Frances, who never put on airs, but thought her young daughter, Lady Jane Grey, was a pious little dog turd, utterly devoid of wit or mischief.

Elizabeth was well aware the child was being considered as a consort for Prince Edward and would likely soon join the royal nursery so they could be educated together. A few nobles' sons already were being educated at Court along with Prince Edward; the schoolroom would soon bulge at the seams. Elizabeth laughed out loud as she thought of the Earl of Warwick's sons. The Dudley brothers would make Lady Jane's life hell!

Elizabeth slipped into the library and selected a book of verse to take into the gardens. Any day now the cruel winds of autumn would denude the lovely flower beds and strip the leaves from the shade trees. To avoid the visitors she made her way from the royal lodgings toward the lesser rooms of the outer courtyard.

As she cut through the Silver Stick Gallery, Elizabeth saw a female coming toward her from the opposite end of the gallery. When they got within five feet of each other, both stopped dead in their tracks and stared. Both girls, gowned in purple, had the same startling red-gold hair. Both were slim, of the same height, and each carried a book. The striking resemblance did not end there, for both had the same straight carriage and held their proud heads high. The encounter was like looking in a mirror.

"Who the devil are you?" Elizabeth demanded.

"I am Mistress Elizabeth Hardwick. Who the devil are *you*?"

"I am the Lady Elizabeth."

"*Your Grace,*" Bess gasped, sinking into a curtsy.

"Nay, I have no such title these days."

"I cannot call you *lady* when you are a *royal princess*."

"Ha! Behind my back they call me the little bastard."

"They will regret it someday, when you are queen."

Elizabeth's amber eyes turned to glittering gold. *They will indeed.* "Why have I never seen you before?"

"I am from Derbyshire, Your Grace. Lady

Zouche found me a place in her household as companion to her daughters."

Elizabeth stared at her. Mistress Elizabeth Hardwick was a farmer's daughter, while she was the daughter of a king. How was it possible they were so alike? "We even have the same name." She walked a circle around Bess, examining her closely. "Look at our hands— 'tis uncanny." They had the same graceful hands, with long, delicate fingers, though the Lady Elizabeth's were adorned with many rings. "I'm not old enough to have breasts yet, but when I am, I hope and pray to God they resemble yours, mistress."

"Please call me Bess, Your Grace."

The girl is so easy to talk with, as if we have known each other for years. "We could be sisters, Bess. In fact, I wish you were my sister; we have far more in common than the one with whom I have been saddled." Elizabeth watched closely for Bess's reaction to her slur against her Catholic half-sister, Mary. When Bess seemed amused rather than shocked, Elizabeth took a cautious liking to her. "What are you reading?"

"Oh, Your Grace, it isn't my book; it belongs to Lady Jane Grey. I was sent to retrieve it from the barge, but I have become hopelessly lost. The rooms at Hampton have no imaginable order."

Elizabeth almost choked with glee. " 'Tis my father's pride and joy. None has ever dared criticize it before. How refreshing to know someone who speaks her mind."

"I am cursed with an impulsive tongue."

Elizabeth nodded her understanding. "Retorts spring quickly to my lips also, but I have learned a measure of caution. What is Lady Jane reading?"

Bess showed her the book.

"Latin! The little dog turd carries it with her just to impress everyone. What the hell pleasure can a little girl derive from Latin?"

Bess burst into laughter, amused to hear the young princess swear.

Elizabeth joined in her laughter. "My uncle Tom Seymour taught me to swear. He's a sailor—they have very salty vocabularies. My father is going to make him admiral of the fleet." Though the princess was younger than Bess, she was wise beyond her years. "Come into the gardens with me; I want to talk."

Bess looked uncertain. "I'll be in trouble if I don't return with the book, Your Grace."

"I'll take care of that," Elizabeth said decisively. "Come." It took only a few minutes for the Lady Elizabeth to lead them into the State Apartments and ferret out the whereabouts of Lady Frances Grey.

With a murmured apology Bess handed the book to Lady Jane and saw Lady Zouche gape at the resemblance between the two red-headed young women.

"Lady Elizabeth, how lovely to see you! May I present my friend, Lady Margaret Zouche?" Frances sounded genuinely happy that Elizabeth had been brought back to Court where she belonged.

"Lady Margaret," Elizabeth acknowledged. "It is always a pleasure to see you, Frances. I would like Mistress Hardwick to attend me, if you can spare her for an hour."

When Lady Zouche appeared to have been struck dumb, Frances said, "By all means. Jane is here to visit with Prince Edward; we are presently awaiting an audience with your father."

"Good morrow, Lady Elizabeth," Lady Jane said gravely.

"*Age quod agis*—attend to what you are about," Elizabeth translated the Latin for her. *"Vivat rex!"*

"Long live the king!" Lady Jane said piously.

The last thing Elizabeth wanted was to be present when her father arrived. His mood was so uncertain. Her earliest memories of him tossing her in the air were mixed up with the times he had pointed his all-powerful finger and raged at her. Both were terrifying. She had learned to hold her own in his presence, sensing that he despised cowardice in anyone but himself. People said she was so like him—there was no denying that she was Old Harry's daughter—but Elizabeth knew that when he saw her red hair and witnessed her temper, he could be either amused or enraged.

Elizabeth took Bess by the hand and swept her from the room. The two girls walked through the Privy Garden and into the Great Fountain Garden. Bess spotted a fat bumblebee struggling in the water and immediately scooped it out and set it on the stone ledge so it could dry off its wings.

"God's death, you are impulsive. You acted without thinking."

"Nay, I thought about it. I weighed the bee's life against my being stung and decided the risk was worth it."

"Your thought processes work rapidly, as do mine, but I have learned to act with caution," Elizabeth explained.

"Perhaps because you have been stung too many times."

When they came to the maze, Elizabeth said decisively, "We'll go in here where we can be private." At the center of the maze, the pair sat on a bench. "Tell me about yourself. I want to know your philosophy, your hopes and dreams. I want to know what is in here," Elizabeth touched her forehead, "and in here," she touched her heart. "No! On second thought, let me tell you."

Bess nodded eagerly.

"You have a hot temper; you are vain; you have a thirst for knowledge and a passion for life. To top it all off, you are extremely ambitious."

"You are describing yourself as well as me, Your Grace."

Elizabeth laughed. "You are also clever, witty, and blunt."

"Do you believe in destiny?" Bess asked eagerly.

"I do. I believe in my own destiny."

"Do you believe you will be queen someday?"

Elizabeth pressed her lips together, caution coming to the fore.

Bess touched her hand. "You don't need to tell me, I know! I am so certain about what my future holds that I warrant you are too."

"Tell me."

"I shall make a great marriage and have many sons and daughters. I shall have a town house in London and a magnificent home in the country, where one day I shall entertain Queen Elizabeth the First of England!"

"It is dangerous to share secret dreams. I trust no one."

"Let's swear a pledge to trust in ourselves and trust each other," Bess said impulsively.

Elizabeth placed her hand over her heart. "No matter what." They smiled at each other. "Do you know any gossip?"

"Well..." Bess had heard gossip about King Henry but suddenly realized the impropriety of repeating it to his daughter.

"You *do* know some gossip! Tell me or I shall never forgive you!"

"Do you know a lady named Catherine Parr?"

"Certainly I do. She has become thick as thieves with my sister, Lady Mary. They go to Mass together."

"I dare not say more, Your Grace; it involves your—"

"My father? God's death, how could I have been so blind? The woman has ambitions to become queen!"

"So I have heard."

Elizabeth put her finger to her lips in warning as she heard male voices through the hedge. Two extremely dark youths came crashing through the maze. They looked inordinately pleased with themselves when they saw the females.

"Lady Elizabeth, how delightful. We were looking for a diversion." The dark boy who was Elizabeth's age made a gallant bow.

"Robin Dudley, you intrude."

The taller youth, who looked about sixteen, was even swarthier than his companion. His eyes widened as they gazed at Bess. Then he reached out a hand and touched her upthrust breast. "Are they real?" he demanded.

FIVE

Bess balled up her fist and thumped him hard in the middle of his chest. "You uncouth swine, your manners are abominable."

The Lady Elizabeth's eyes took on an avid gleam. "You shouldn't have done that, *Old Man.*"

"Why not? She's only a servant," George Talbot drawled.

Bess's anger flared hotly. "You arrogant bastard! How dare you show such disrespect in the presence of Lady Elizabeth Tudor?"

"Ha! He is a *Talbot.* They think themselves far more aristocratic than the *Tudors.* They are descended from *Plantagenets,* don't you know?"

Bess's breasts rose and fell with her anger, and George Talbot found it impossible to tear his gaze away. "Descended from baboons, more likely," she retorted.

"Is your arse blue, George?" Robin asked with a straight face.

"No, just my blood."

Elizabeth laughed, thoroughly enjoying herself. "This is my *friend*, Bess Hardwick."

"Your friend? I suppose you are going to give me a royal rebuke and jump to her defense," Talbot challenged.

"No. That is why she is my friend. She's perfectly capable of defending herself. She's worth her weight in gold—she doesn't even know that you are heir to the earldom of Shrewsbury, the wealthiest in the land, and what's more, she doesn't give a pennyworth of piss!"

Bess felt the blood drain from her face when she learned he was Shrewsbury's son. His father was the premier earl, almost considered a monarch, north of the Trent. Not only was his father lord lieutenant of Yorkshire, Nottinghamshire, and Derbyshire, he owned magnificent Sheffield Castle, not a stone's throw from Bess's home of Hardwick.

"I'm Robin Dudley." The other youth stuck out his hand to Bess. "Any friend of Lady Elizabeth's is a friend of mine. Has she given you a nickname yet?"

Bess finally realized that this young man was the Earl of Warwick's son. He was affable

good-natured, and Bess liked him imme-
.ately.

"*Vixen* would suit her temper, I think."

"Who the devil asked you?" Bess spat at
Talbot, giving a fine display of that temper.

Elizabeth smiled her approval. "*Vixen* is
good with your coloring, Bess. I call Robin *the
Gypsy* because he's so dark."

Bess found Talbot far darker than Robin
Dudley. His face was dark-complexioned;
his light blue eyes were a startling contrast to
his swarthy skin. His long hair was so black
that the sunlight gave it a blue sheen. The tall
youth was extremely lithe, with long legs and
wide shoulders. He held his head high with a
natural pride that hinted at arrogance, and he
seemed to take it as his due that everyone
would treat him with deference.

"I call Talbot *the Old Man* because he's
been married since he was twelve. Poor George
had no say in the matter. They shackled him
to the Earl of Rutland's daughter, Gertrude,
to safeguard the Talbot wealth."

"I pity the lady." Bess had taken an instant
dislike to him and could not help goading
him.

"Oh, they don't live together as man and wife
yet. Gertrude isn't old enough to be bedded,"
Elizabeth explained.

"He'll be an old man by the time he gets
some!" Dudley said coarsely, and Talbot
cuffed him across the ear.

Bess was appalled at the sexual content of
their conversation. It was extremely inap-

propriate to speak of such matters in front of the young princess, yet the Lady Elizabeth didn't seem shocked in the least.

"Lewd talk is disrespectful to ladies," Bess said primly.

"Hell's teeth, she must be up from the country, with such prudish ideas," Talbot jibed.

"She's from Derbyshire, the same place as you, *Old Man.*"

His eyes narrowed. "Hardwick, did you say?"

"Well, I think you are charming, Mistress Hardwick," Robin Dudley said frankly.

"And I think you are unique," Elizabeth added.

"Well, at least her name is apt," Talbot drawled. "She certainly makes my wick hard."

Bess gasped and raised her hand to slap his insolent face.

"Go ahead, Vixen. I'd like an excuse to give you a lesson in manners."

Dudley guffawed, "Christ, we know what you'd like to give her. We can see the sparks flying between you!"

Bess spun on her heel and began to march from the maze.

"Doesn't she know she can't leave without your permission?" Robin was choking with laughter.

"Doesn't know and doesn't give a damn— she's absolutely priceless," Elizabeth declared.

Bess prayed fervently that she was going in the right direction. If she took a wrong turn in this infernal maze and made a bloody fool of herself, she would simply die!

On the short barge ride back to Chelsea Palace, the talk was all of the king and the young Prince Edward. Bess sat apart, thinking of the Lady Elizabeth. The king's daughter had every advantage, while she was just a servant—as she had been so rudely reminded—and yet Bess realized she would not change places with her. Though the princess had palaces and jewels and servants untold, Elizabeth's future was no less uncertain than her own. If she was to realize her ambition, she would have to hold her own against great odds. But she believes in herself, just as I do, thought Bess, and if you believe something with all your mind and all your heart and soul, someday it shall come to be.

Bess thought of William Cavendish, and her heart skipped a beat. How she wished he were still at Chelsea so she could tell him all about her encounter with Elizabeth Tudor. How exceedingly fortunate she was to have met such a man and how lucky to have caught his fancy. He had warned her that his business in Dover would take some time, and she wondered how he would see her when he returned. Bess heaved a great sigh. She would leave it up to him to contrive something. Rogue Cavendish was a man of the world and would find a way to get what he wanted. How exciting that he wanted her!

Bess went over his words again for the hundredth time: *Sweetheart, when I return I'll have a question to ask you regarding a more permanent relationship.* William was going to ask her to be his wife, Bess hoped and prayed. She was certain she wanted no other husband but him. With resolution she pushed away a nagging doubt. Surely the question wouldn't involve becoming his mistress? Not when she had made it plain that she would not allow him to seduce her and that she wanted a respectable marriage? No, though he was nicknamed Rogue, he had not pressed her for more than kisses. *Mistress Elizabeth Cavendish!* It sounded so right, and deep in her bones Bess honestly believed she was destined to become the wife of William Cavendish.

Late that night, before she went to bed, Bess decided to write home and tell them all about her visit to Chelsea Palace as the guest of Lady Frances Grey. Bess was a prolific letter writer, who had already written to her mother and Aunt Marcy about the Greys, but now that she had met Princess Elizabeth and visited Hampton Court Palace, she couldn't wait to put it all down on paper.

Bess wrote several paragraphs and then paused with the quill end between her teeth. Should she tell them about William Cavendish? She was dying to describe him to her family and impress them with the importance of his position in the king's treasury. But once she mentioned his name, they would immediately write back to ask if she and William had made wedding plans. Bess thought perhaps she had better wait until she had something definite to tell them.

In her decisive hand she wrote: *Chelsea Palace rises above the Thames like a glittering, fairy-tale castle, filled with royal treasures preserved through the centuries. I have a great passion for London and its magnificent noble houses, where I have met many gentlemen from Court circles. My ambition is set on making a good marriage, and I intend to have a great household of my own, where you can come to stay. I wish with all my heart that you could visit these grand places with me, to see the Tudor courtiers bedecked in velvets and jewels, to listen to the music as it floats down from the minstrels' galleries and be waited upon by the liveried footmen. For me, it is like a dream come true. I long to share with you all the wonders of this glorious city, and vow that someday I shall!*

She pictured Derbyshire in her mind's eye. It was much farther north than London, with a harsher climate. It was probably already cold at home. Though she loved Derbyshire and missed it, she was happy to be in London. It was the center of the universe, and the magnificent Tudor Court was the jewel at that center. As she finished her letter and snuffed her candles, she couldn't believe how lucky she was to be a part of it.

The following day was a busy one for Bess. She packed for Lady Zouche and her daughters because they were returning to London on the morrow. In the afternoon, when the ladies retired for a nap, Bess seized the opportunity to go for a walk and explore the wealthy village of Chelsea.

She strolled slowly past Syon House, owned by the Earl of Warwick, and marveled that she had actually met one of his sons, Robin Dudley. She couldn't remember how many there were, but she knew Warwick had a large brood. She studied Syon House with a critical eye. Built from dark gray stone, it was huge and square, but that's all that could be said for it. The house was downright ugly. If she had Warwick's money, she would have built something beautiful as well as functional. Why didn't people use a little imagination when they built a house that would be a lasting monument down through the centuries?

Bess followed a footpath down to the river, watching a pair of swans glide along past the bank. They were such regal birds, these royal swans, and far more numerous here in Chelsea than in the city of London. Through the trees Bess glimpsed another imposing mansion and quickened her steps when she heard the sound of laughter from the rolling lawns that dipped down to the Thames.

As she emerged from behind a huge stand

of fuchsia rhododendrons, Bess realized that she had intruded upon some boys who were swimming naked in the river. Two of the young lads squealed when they saw a female, and they dashed to grab towels and shirts to cover their nakedness, then ran laughing and shrieking up toward the mansion.

Bess stood rooted to the spot. Because of the boys she had failed to notice the young man who was lying on the grassy bank sunning himself. It was George Talbot. He was stark naked! Bess immediately realized that this must be Shrewsbury House and the males were the Talbot brothers.

"Mistress *Hard*-wick." He emphasized her surname in a suggestive way that made her blush profusely, yet Talbot was not the slightest bit embarrassed to display himself nude before her. In a leisurely manner he stood up to face her, making no effort to cover himself with his towel.

Shrewsbury's heir had the piercing glance of an eagle. In his dark face his ice blue eyes were startling. Bess decided not to retreat with an apology, because the arrogant look he threw her was a direct challenge.

"You are trespassing," he said coldly.

"Forgive us our trespasses, Lord God Almighty!"

"Blasphemous as well as insolent."

"Servants don't know their places these days." Bess lifted her chin aggressively.

"You are right. Your attitude should be respectful in the presence of your betters."

Bess was blazing mad. She tossed her head and swept him from head to foot with a glare. "I have no betters, and respect must be earned."

"Look your fill." His eyes mocked her, dared her.

Slowly, Bess let her glance slide across his hirsute chest, then down his belly to his groin. Suddenly, his phallus thickened and hardened and stood out rigid from his lithe body.

"Do you like what you see?" he drawled confidently.

Bess was stunned. She had never seen a naked male before, let alone one with a jutting arousal. "You look like a river rat," she disparaged.

"Vixen!"

"Knave! Fool! Black devil!"

"Hell's teeth, you don't even swear well."

Bess took a deep breath and spat, "Whoreson!"

"Bravo, you have a temper worthy of a lady."

"I *am* a lady, Talbot!"

"Never in a million years; your breasts are too big, Mistress Tits."

"A pox upon you," cursed Bess, turning on her heel and leaving. It was the second day in a row he had made her retreat, and she hated him for it.

That night there was a terrible thunder and lightning storm, and Bess was up half the night comforting the Zouche girls. Even the placid Frances Grey became upset when her daughters, Jane and Catherine, screamed with hysterics and cried that it was the end of the world. Dawn arrived to prove them wrong, but it *was* the end of summer. The temperature plummeted, and the north wind stripped the beautiful gardens of Chelsea with a vengeance.

On the barge ride back to London, Margaret Zouche praised Bess's forethought in packing warm cloaks for them. "We would perish out on this river today, Bess, if it wasn't for your efficiency. I never had anyone who planned so well. I warrant you could pack up an entire household in a day."

When they arrived home Lady Zouche ordered that all the fires be lighted and set the cook to preparing some hearty soup to warm the cockles of the travelers' hearts.

A letter from Derbyshire had arrived for Bess in her absence, but she slipped it into her pocket to read in privacy when all her household tasks had been completed. In no time at all she had unpacked for Lady Margaret and her daughters and found time to check up on her young friend Robert Barlow. Bess was distressed to find that the page had caught cold and was coughing his head off. "Rob, when did this happen?"

"I only started coughing today, Bess. The house got so cold, and the butler refused to order the fires lit until her ladyship arrived."

"Bloody servants need a flogging. When I

have servants of my own, I won't countenance high-handedness. Before you go to bed tonight I'll bring you a posset. One my aunt Marcy taught me to make with sack and milk and herbs."

It had been a long day, and when Bess finally climbed the stairs to her chamber, she could hear Robert's racking cough from up in his attic room. She went back down to the kitchens to get some camphor grease from the medicinal cupboard. Then she climbed to the attic and rubbed the youth's chest and back with the concoction.

He pulled his flannel nightshirt on over his head and sat on the side of the bed. "I love you, Bess," Robert Barlow whispered.

"I love you too, Rob. Get under the covers and keep warm. Let's hope you feel better tomorrow."

When she was finally in her own chamber, Bess took out the precious letter from home and broke the seal. It was from her older sister, Jane, and Bess was surprised at the news.

Dearest Bess:
I am to be married soon to Godfrey Boswell, who comes from Gunthwaite in Yorkshire. He is a farmer who has leased land from your friend Robert Barlow's family. I wasn't sure at first, but Godfrey is in need of a wife, and conditions here at home grow desperate. Our stepfather, Ralph Leche, has also been farming land he leased

from the Barlows, because Arthur Barlow
has been too ill to farm it himself. But Ralph
has fallen behind in the rent, and Mother is
worried to death. Once I am married I will
be one less mouth to feed. To help out, Aunt
Marcy has been cooking for the Leches at
Chatsworth, and some days the food she
brings home is the only thing the children
have to eat. Mother sends her love. We miss
you and thank heaven that you found such a
fortunate position in London. Your life
sounds like a fairy tale.
                    Love—Jane

Bess put the letter down and felt a terrible
wave of guilt wash over her. Her parents were
in debt, and Jane was sacrificing herself on a
farmer named Boswell, while she herself was
in love with a man from the Royal Court.
She had just returned from Chelsea, where she
had actually spoken with Princess Elizabeth
Tudor. Jane was right—her life was like a
fairy tale!

SIX

The weather stayed cold all month, and the
wind whipped down the streets of London,
making whirlwinds of leaves, dust, and debris.
Bess gave Robert Barlow the warm muffler that
her aunt Marcy had knitted, but it didn't
prevent his cough from turning into bronchitis.

Bess took over the page's duties and did her best to nurse him with hot soup and chest rubs, but eventually she had no option but to speak with Lady Zouche. "Ma'am, I don't wish to alarm you, but Robert is quite ill. It's more than just a cough, I'm afraid."

"Oh, dear, it's such a heavy responsibility to take these young people into service to give them a start in life. Sometimes it works out well, as in your case, Bess, but often the youngsters are more trouble than they are worth. You are very good with herbs and such, can't you dose him with something?"

"I've made him possets and rubbed him with camphor, but it hasn't helped. Lady Margaret, I think he needs a doctor."

"Heaven forbid, you don't think it could be plague?" she cried in alarm.

"The weather is too cold for the plague, but he could have some other contagion."

"I'll send for the doctor, and in the meantime keep him isolated upstairs, well away from the girls."

When Dr. Belgrave arrived, Bess escorted him up to Robert Barlow's attic room while Lady Zouche hovered at the door to the tiny chamber. The boy's fair cheeks showed two bright red spots of fever, and Belgrave tapped his chest and examined his sputum. The doctor produced some packets of fever powder and instructed Bess to administer them with water. Then he turned to the woman at the door. "A word with you in private, if I may, Lady Zouche."

Margaret escorted the doctor down the stairs to her own private sitting room and closed the door. Bess went down immediately and put her ear to the keyhole.

"The boy is from Derbyshire, Doctor; I employ him as a page. He's always had a delicate look about him."

"Hmmph." Belgrave cleared his throat. "He's fevered at the moment, but the powders I left should take care of that. However"—he cleared his throat once again—"in my learned opinion, the boy suffers from a chronic distemper of the lungs. He won't make old bones, and I strongly suggest you get rid of him."

"Oh, dear, oh, dear." Lady Margaret wrung her hands. "You don't think he could pass it on to me or my daughters, do you, Doctor?"

"We have made great strides in medical science in this century, Lady Zouche, but the truth is we still don't know enough about these illnesses. He could recover, of course, but he'll always be a weakling. Better to be safe than sorry."

Bess ran back upstairs; she had heard more than she wanted to know. Poor Robert, whatever would become of him? She was so thankful she hadn't told him that his father was too ill to work his own fields. What was the point in adding worry to his woes?

Within a couple of days Robert Barlow's fever abated, but the youth looked far from well when Lady Zouche summoned him and Bess to her sitting room. Though he was only fifteen, he had shot up like a gangly weed this past year and he towered above Bess's five feet, three inches.

Since Bess had heard the doctor advise Lady Zouche to get rid of Robert, she knew he was going to be sent home, and she braced herself to help her young friend through his dismissal.

Margaret Zouche did not get too close, and her face was set in a rigid mask of determination. "Master Barlow, I am thankful your fever has been cured, but Dr. Belgrave believes you should be home with your family in Derbyshire." She withdrew a letter from her pocket. "I have written to your mother explaining to her that you are returning home. I will send you by my own coach, and I will ask Bess to accompany you."

The look on Robert's face turned to relief; the look on Bess's face was pure astonishment. She realized she should have seen it coming, but she hadn't. Who else was there to nurse the semi-invalid and see that he arrived home alive? Bess saw that Lady Zouche was awaiting her compliance. One part of her selfishly wanted to refuse. When William Cavendish returned to London, Bess wanted to be here to welcome him. A glance at Robert Barlow's face melted her hard heart. "I will accompany Master Barlow, my lady."

"Good, good. I've arranged for you to start out tomorrow. Bess will soon have your belongings packed up." Lady Margaret dismissed him from her thoughts and turned to Bess. "It will give you a chance to visit with your family, but then you must come straight back to me. By that time Christmas will be only a month away, and you know the preparations that will entail."

Bess smiled, relieved that Lady Zouche found her services indispensable. "Oh, indeed I do, Lady Margaret."

Before she began packing, Bess dashed off a note to her family in Derbyshire, telling them she was accompanying Robert Barlow home because of his ill health. The post would arrive at least a day before she would, giving them notice of her impending arrival. Bess wanted to write to Cavendish, but she had no address for him. She knew that Lady Frances Grey would pass a letter to him but decided against it in case Lady Zouche found out she was writing to Cavendish and dismissed her. If luck was with her, Bess could be back in London by the time Rogue Cavendish returned from Dover. She smiled a secret smile and made a wish that absence would make his heart grow fonder.

The next morning, with their baggage tied on top of the carriage, Bess and Robert Barlow set off for Dunstable, the first stop on their journey to Derbyshire. Earlier she had filled a brass foot warmer with hot coals, which she now placed beneath Robert's feet, then tucked the lap robe about him.

It was slow going until London was left behind, but there were so many places of interest to see from the coach windows that time did not lag. Once they were in the countryside, Bess kept up a running conversation, and Robert was content to leave his book unread as he sat back listening to her and watching her with adoring eyes.

After an intense coughing spell, Bess felt his forehead to assure herself Robert was not fevered. He captured her hand and smiled at her, seemingly happy to be wrapped in the private cocoon of the coach with her. Then he closed his eyes and drifted off to sleep, clutching her hand possessively.

As he slept, Bess allowed her glance to roam over him. He was a beautiful youth, with the fine complexion of an English rose and a shock of thick, fair hair. A year ago, when Bess had arrived at the Zouches, he hadn't been any taller than she; now he was so tall and slim he towered over her.

Surely the doctor was wrong when he said Rob wouldn't make old bones, Bess thought with a frown. He'll recover, she reassured herself. His mother will nurse him back to health! But then she remembered Jane's letter telling her that Robert's father was too ill to work his land. Rob's mother, poor lady, was going to have her hands full.

The posting inn at Dunstable did not have rooms available next to each other, so Bess told the Zouche coachman to pay for only two. When he raised his eyebrows, Bess was affronted. "How the devil could you think such a thing?" she demanded. "Master Barlow has been so ill, I dare not leave him alone all night." To Bess, Rob Barlow was a boy, while she was a woman full-grown.

They dined on lamb and barley stew with hot crusty bread, followed by a pear tart with clotted cream. She ordered that a fire be lighted in the room she and Rob would share but found she had to pay for it herself. While she doled out her carefully hoarded money, she paid for a tot of brandy at the same time. When Robert had eaten his fill, Bess bade him go up and get into bed. When she entered the chamber ten minutes later, carrying the brandy, she warmed it at the fire, poured a little into her palm, and she rubbed Rob's back and chest. Then she made him drink the rest.

"Thank you for nursing me so well, Bess. I'd rather be here with you tonight than any- where else in the world," he said worshipfully.

"What rubbish," she scoffed, but as she sat before the crackling fire, she had to admit it was a cozy place to be on such a bleak, cold night. Soon the fire and the brandy worked their magic and put Rob to sleep. When Bess heard his heavy breathing, she removed her gown and slipped beneath the covers on the trundle bed at the foot of Robert's.

The next day, as they lumbered through the countryside from Dunstable to Northampton, Bess entertained Robert with stories about

Christmas. Then they sang some merry songs to pass the time, and when Robert became short of breath, she carried on alone, filling the bumpy coach with her rich voice.

The inn that night could accommodate them with adjoining rooms, but when Bess stoked his fire and tucked him into bed, Robert begged, "Please don't leave. Stay with me, Bess."

"I'll leave the adjoining door open—I'm a light sleeper; I'll hear you if you need me."

"I need you now, Bess," Robert avowed. "I can't bear it when you're not close by me."

She sat down on the bed and took his hand.

"I'm going to die, Bess," he said hollowly.

"Oh, no, Rob, no. Push those fears away. I heard Dr. Belgrave say you would recover."

He smiled at her, for once feeling much older than his beautiful companion. "When you're with me I'm not afraid of anything."

Bess sat holding his hand until he slept, then she, too, curled up on the bed and fell asleep. She roused in the night, and by the light from the fire, she knew Rob was awake and watching her with worshipful eyes.

"I love you, Bess," he whispered.

"You love me because you are grateful to me, Rob."

He shook his head. "No, I mean I have fallen in love with you."

Bess felt slightly alarmed. "You are only fifteen, too young to be in love."

"Age has naught to do with it. I'm so lucky to have found you."

Bess patted his hand. "Go back to sleep; tomorrow will be an exhausting day."

Bess's prediction proved true. Now that they were so far north, the bone-chilling cold entered the coach, and the pair huddled together to share their body warmth. When they came to the River Trent, the coach and horses had to be transported across by ferry, which took a considerable amount of time.

Now that they were nearing their own county, the coalfields of Nottingham disappeared and were replaced by the moors and peaks of Derbyshire's limestone uplands, filled with tors, fells, and stone-walled fields. Both the Barlows and the Hardwicks lived in Baslow village, where the Derwent widened from a mountain stream into a broad and beautiful river.

The Zouche coachman lifted down Robert Barlow's baggage and was prepared to wait for Bess, but the light was fast disappearing from the late-afternoon sky, so she bade him drop off her small trunk at the Leche house and told him she would walk home from the Barlow farm. Bess knew the coachman had been told to proceed to Ashby-de-la-Zouche and await her return to London in a couple of days.

Robert's mother, amazed at how much he'd grown, seemed pleased to have her eldest son home, if only to unburden her troubles. Bess now wished that she had prepared Rob for his father's ill health.

"I cannot believe Lady Zouche dismissed you because of a cough, Robert."

"It isn't just a cough, Mistress Barlow," Bess interposed. "Rob has been very ill. The doctor says he has a chronic distemper."

"He looks well enough to me. Now, your father is another matter entirely. All hope for recovery is gone. I have to nurse him night and day."

Robert looked stricken. "Bess exaggerates my condition, Mother. I'll be able to help you with things now that I'm home."

"In more ways than one," Mistress Barlow said enigmatically, casting a speculative eye over Bess Hardwick.

"Where is Father?"

"I've set up his bed in the front parlor; he'll never be able to go upstairs again."

Bess suddenly felt in the way. "My family will be expecting me, Mistress Barlow, but I'll call tomorrow to see if there's aught you need."

"Yes, we'll likely see you tomorrow—there's business to discuss. Your mother will explain."

Bess said good night to Robert, knowing he needed his bed after his exhausting day but was unable to voice the thought to his mother. She walked down the lane, past the Barlow fields and through the tiny village to the house that her stepfather, Ralph Leche, leased from his father, Sir Francis.

When she opened the garden gate, the front door flew open and her mother and sister Jane hurried outside to enfold her in warm embraces. "Darling, darling, it's so good to see you after fifteen long months! We had your letter yesterday, but Robert's mother got Lady Zouche's letter two days past, so we knew you were coming."

Inside, her little half-sisters stared at Bess in awe. "Let's have a look at the fine lady you have become," Aunt Marcy cried, taking her woolen shawl.

Bess pirouetted for them all, displaying the elegant gray gown she had been given by Lady Margaret. Her mother handed her a mug of hot mutton broth and made a place for her beside the hearth. In that moment Bess was overjoyed to be at home. "Where are James and Ralph?" Bess immediately saw a look pass between Jane and her mother and saw, too, Aunt Marcy's mouth harden in disapproval.

"Ralph's gone to fetch James from Edensor."

"From the *alehouse* in Edensor," Aunt Marcy interjected.

"Let's not speak of it tonight, Marcella. Let's not spoil Bess's homecoming."

"It seems to me that now is the perfect time to speak of it, while the men are out."

"Tell me," Bess insisted, searching their faces.

Elizabeth Hardwick shooed her three younger daughters upstairs to bed, then said, "James has a tendency to drink too much. It's all because Hardwick won't be his for another three years yet. It's hard working for wages when someone else reaps the profits from James's own five hundred acres."

"In two years he'll be a drunken sot, unable

to make a go of Hardwick, if he keeps it up," Marcella said bluntly.

"Does he not help Ralph farm the Barlow lands?"

"Yes, but the crops were so poor this year, there have been no profits," Elizabeth declared.

"Profits?" Marcella scoffed. "Ralph is so far behind in his rent, the Barlows are threatening him with imprisonment in the Fleet!"

"Oh, no," Bess cried. "I had no idea you were in such dire straits." She brightened. "I have some money I won at cards with Lady Frances Grey. Tomorrow I'll take it over to Mistress Barlow. She is in a terrible mess herself at the moment with both her husband and son ill."

"Arthur Barlow is dying," Marcella said baldly. No one in the room doubted her word; Aunt Marcy treated many sick people with her herbal medicines and knew the unmistakable signs of death.

"How much money do you have, Bess?" her mother asked doubtfully.

"Almost two pounds; I spent a shilling at the inn."

"That's amazing," Elizabeth said faintly, exchanging another look with Marcella.

"So, Jane, you're to be married. I'm so happy for you," Bess said warmly, giving her sister a hug. "When is the wedding?"

"The first of December. Oh, Bess, I'm so glad you'll be here for the ceremony," Jane cried.

"Oh, I cannot stay until December. I'd love to see you wed, Jane, but Lady Zouche needs me back for the Christmas preparations."

Jane looked down at her hands, and again Elizabeth and Marcella exchanged a glance. Before any more could be said, Ralph and James arrived, and for the rest of the evening Bess had the impression that the women of her family hadn't quite said all that they wanted to say before the men came home.

At bedtime Jane shared her bed with Bess, and the two sisters whispered and laughed together as they had done all the years they were growing up.

"Your clothes are so elegant, Bess. I've never seen anything so fine as the gown you are wearing."

"You must have it—or better yet, choose whichever one you like best." She threw open the lid of her trunk to reveal the other two dresses she had brought.

Jane sat on the bed, mesmerized. "You would really give me one?"

"Of course."

When Jane stroked the green velvet, Bess held her breath. That particular gown evoked thrilling memories of the hunt with Cavendish.

"I won't take the green—it's your color—but I'd love the purple."

Bess picked it up and shook out the folds. "I wore this when I went to Hampton Court Palace and met Princess Elizabeth. We were both in purple, and the resemblance between us was uncanny. The only difference was that I had breasts, while she was flat as a board, but she's young yet."

Jane's eyes flooded with tears. "Oh, Bess,

your life was so exciting, you shouldn't have come back."

"What rubbish! I wouldn't give up this chance to be here for anything."

In the morning, however, when her mother and aunt awaited her on a united front, Jane's words suddenly made sense.

At the kitchen table Bess poured herself a cup of milk and took a hearty bite of bread and cheese. The food stuck in her throat as she heard her mother's words. "Bess, we have a plan. Our affairs are inextricably tied to the Barlows', and the way out of both families' troubles is for you to marry Robert."

Bess laughed, but there was little mirth in it. "What are you talking about?"

Marcella took over the conversation. "Arthur Barlow is going to die, and since Robert is a minor, the Court of Wards will take the Barlow farm and lands until he is twenty-one. That's six long years away."

It will be a miracle if Rob sees twenty-one, Bess thought sadly.

"If Robert is a married man when he inherits, it puts a different complexion on things. The Court of Wards cannot touch a bride's portion, for one thing. That is a one-third value of the estate. When an underage heir is a married man, all falls into confusion and the Court is often more lenient."

"I cannot marry Robert; he's just a boy!" Bess said, outraged.

"He's fifteen, a year past the age of legal consent for a man," Marcella pointed out gently.

"No, no! The Barlows must get a lawyer to draw up a will for Arthur, leaving the farm and land to be administered by trustees." Bess repeated what Cavendish had told her. "It will be *legally* protected."

"Mistress Barlow cannot afford lawyers, and who in the world could be trusted to leave land to? Bess, darling, it breaks my heart to ask you to give up your ambitions and make this great sacrifice to help your family. I know how grand your dream is, but it is just wishful thinking, my love. I beg you to be practical," said Marcella.

"We've talked at length with Mistress Barlow, and she agrees not to press charges for the money Ralph owes, if you agree to the marriage, Bess," her mother said quietly.

"But I told you, I'll give her the money."

"Bess, the debt is twice as much as you have."

When a shilling represented a week's wages, Bess suddenly realized the seriousness of their debt. "What about Ralph's father? Can't Ralph get the money from Sir Francis?" she asked desperately.

"The Leches are so hard-pressed for money, they are trying to sell Chatsworth. Their land holdings are vast, running all the way from Bakewell to Chesterfield, but most of it is useless wild moorland."

"I'll speak with Mistress Barlow today. I'll persuade her not to press charges," Bess said adamantly. "Marriage is out of the question!"

"Bess, it is high time you were wed. You've had a whole year in London and still have no prospects."

"I do have a prospect, I do!" Bess was vehement. "He's an important man of the Court—one of the king's auditors."

She saw their pitying, skeptical looks. "I shall write to him immediately," she vowed desperately.

Marcella felt torn in half at Bess's desperation. She wished with all her heart that another way could be found to aid her sister and her husband. Marcella touched Elizabeth's arm, and they withdrew to a corner of the kitchen for a hurried consultation. Then her aunt came to Bess and put a comforting arm about her shoulders. "Write your letter, child. I hope and pray you get the answer you are wishing for. If your knight in shining armor comes to your rescue, or sends a written proposal offering for you, your parents will consider him. But he'd better hurry up," she admonished gently. "Time is running out for the Barlows and for us."

SEVEN

William Cavendish knew he had done an exemplary job in Dover. He had curbed his impatience to return to London, firmly setting duty before pleasure, because of his driving ambition. Upon his return he went immediately to Court to make his report to Treasurer Paulet and learned that his ambition had served him well.

"I have good news for you, Cavendish. King Henry is most satisfied with the work you have done at the monasteries. He has you in mind for another such post and asked to speak with you the moment you returned."

Paulet hinted at preferment of some sort, and William was flattered and eager for an audience with the king. William did not take time to change his clothes but went directly to the Presence Chamber, where after a short wait he was ushered into the king's Privy Chamber.

He could smell Henry's ulcerated leg the moment he entered the room, in spite of the perfumed royal body, and put aside his concern for his own travel stains.

"Cavendish!" Henry beamed graciously. "We are not unmindful of the competent job you have done month after month."

Cavendish bowed, also with grace. "Your Majesty, I thank you."

"We have need of your services, further afield. The post we have in mind will be a shade more difficult perhaps, but we feel you have the qualities necessary to bring all to completion."

"Your Majesty, I will do my utmost to see that it is so." William knew the qualities Henry spoke of were energy and a certain ruthlessness.

Henry's small eyes seemed to diminish to

pinholes in his fleshy face, and William held his breath as he wondered what the devil was coming.

"Ireland!" Henry spat.

Cavendish let out his breath. *Christ Almighty, I will need to be a magician to deal with the bloody Irish monasteries!* But nevertheless he was highly flattered that the king thought him capable of such a task. "Ireland," William repeated. "As you say, Your Majesty, a shade more difficult, but I relish a challenge."

"Just so, man, just so! And we will not be ungrateful in this matter. You will be amply rewarded for any results."

Henry, truer words were never uttered!

As the king approached to take his hand, Cavendish pinched his nostrils and held his breath. Then he kissed Henry's rings.

"Thank you, Sire, you do me great honor."

Before Cavendish went to his own residence, he stopped off at Suffolk House to share his news with his friend, Henry Grey.

"I don't know whether to congratulate you or commiserate with you," Henry said wryly. "There are some bloody religious fanatics in Ireland, old man."

William laughed. "The Irish are all fanatics, religious or otherwise, and since half the English orders I've dealt with were overrun with Irish monks and nuns, I don't believe I'll encounter anything I can't handle."

"Well, better you than me. When do you go?"

"Immediately. Paulet says I'll be gone at least a year, perhaps two."

"Two years in Ireland? That's a bloody life sentence! Let's hope there's a title in this for you."

"My thoughts exactly."

"Well, come to us before you leave. Frances will be beside herself."

"Who's taking my name in vain?" Frances asked, sweeping into the salon. "If you are going to be made *Sir* William Cavendish, I'd better work on Henry to elevate me from a marquess to a duchess," Frances drawled.

"She listens at keyholes," Henry explained.

"He's telling the truth, that's how I knew it was you, Rogue. I have a letter for you." She pulled the envelope from her ample bosom and handed it to him. "It's from your ravishing redhead, darling; obviously she missed you sorely."

William took the letter and frowned when he noted it was postmarked Derbyshire. He felt annoyance that Bess had run home. He'd fully expected her to be here awaiting his return. Disappointment washed over him. "Thank you, Frances. I'm going to miss you both."

"Not half so much as I shall miss you, Rogue," Frances said, sighing heavily. "Who's going to keep my husband occupied while I go about my indiscretions?"

William clipped her close and bade them good-bye, promising to spend an evening with them before he departed for Ireland.

The envelope inside his doublet was burning a hole in his chest. When he arrived home he handed his horse to a groom and, before he left the stable, opened Bess's letter.

My Dearest William:
Lady Zouche asked me to accompany Master Robert Barlow home to Derbyshire because he became ill. I now find myself in dire circumstances and cannot extricate myself from them without your help.
Sadly, Robert's father is dying, and to protect the farm our families are making plans for my marriage to young Rob Barlow.
William, I am determined to wed none but you!
I cannot expect you to come all this way but ask that you reply immediately, confirming that you care for me and that we are pledged to each other.
I would not beg for your help if there were any other course open to me. Please hurry, my time is running out.
Yours alone,
Mistress Elizabeth Hardwick
(Bess)

One sentence jumped out at him from the page:

William, I am determined to wed none but you!

God's death, how could she possibly be that innocent? Cavendish had taken it for granted that Bess knew he was already married. She was begging him for help, and a protective urge rose up in him. Perhaps he could take her to Ireland with him. He stuffed the letter back inside his doublet. He had other pressing matters to attend to, and it would be later in the day before he could pen a reply.

The moment Cavendish opened the front door, his daughter, Catherine, was there to greet him warmly.

"Cathy, how are you, my sweetheart?" He swung her into the air in a huge bear hug.

"I'm well, Father, but Eliza has been poorly again."

"Don't be sad, sweetheart; Eliza won't change. I know she isn't robust, but I've come to suspect she rather enjoys her days in bed."

Twelve-year-old Catherine flushed with relief. "Oh, I felt so guilty because I suspected the same thing."

William Cavendish found it ironic that he had wed Eliza Parris to care for his motherless daughter, and almost from the beginning she had been the one who demanded care. Cavendish felt no guilt for not dancing attendance on Eliza. It had been a marriage of convenience, and she had never been much of a wife to him. He had provided her with a lovely house and dozens of servants, then looked elsewhere for his pleasure.

James Cromp had brought his luggage home

hours ago, and when William entered his bedchamber, James had arranged hot water for his bath and laid out fresh garments.

William set Bess's letter beside his bed, and as he did so a vivid picture of her flashed into his mind. The dark eyes, so direct, her full lips, flaming hair, and luscious breasts formed an image that had been with him the entire time he had been in Dover. He heaved a sigh as he removed his clothes.

William found Eliza in her sitting room wrapped in a lap rug, sipping a tisane of chamomile. "I'm home," he announced cheerfully, dismissing the two maids hovering about his wife.

"I couldn't fail to know you were home, William. Your voice is so loud it rattles the dishes, and when you stride about in your riding boots, the floorboards tremble."

He bit back a caustic remark that she wouldn't have to put up with him much longer and, instead, set his back to the mantel and said, "I have been given a new post by the Crown, Eliza. It necessitates my traveling to Ireland for a year."

She blinked rapidly as she digested how this would affect her. "I don't mind your going, William, but your daughter, Catherine, is getting to an age where she could become restless and precocious and need watching constantly. The responsibility is too heavy for me in my condition."

"I have no intention of leaving Cathy here with you." *I don't want my child stifled, and that's just what she will be if I leave her here, entombed with you.* "Since Catherine is espoused to Lord Cobham's son, I will arrange for her to join his household until she and young Thomas are old enough to be married in more than name."

"An excellent arrangement. Thank you for your consideration, William. Would you put more coal on the fire before you go?"

William complied, wondering how on earth she could breathe in such suffocating heat.

He dispatched a note to Henry Brooke, Lord Cobham, to arrange a meeting later in the day, then sought out his daughter so they could spend a few hours together.

Cavendish enjoyed himself immensely. He and Cathy laughed away the afternoon as he indulged her every whim, buying her a harness with silver bells, for her palfrey, and a new fur cloak and hood.

"I would simply love a little neck ruff. Will you buy me one, Father?"

The image of Bess was conjured full blown, and it was brought home to him that Mistress Elizabeth Hardwick was only four years older than his little girl.

Later that night in the seclusion of his bed-chamber, he took up his quill to reply to Bess's letter. During the afternoon hours with his daughter, William Cavendish's perspective had altered. It was wrong of him to seduce a girl who was barely sixteen years of age. The kindest thing he could do for Bess was to let her have her honorable marriage.

Bess had been up at the crack of dawn each morning, avidly awaiting the post from London. Her stomach was in knots from apprehension. What if William didn't get her letter? What if he got it but didn't bother to reply? A hundred what-ifs chased each other through her mercurial thoughts as day by day her dread increased.

She had visited the Barlows on two occasions at the urging of her mother, but though Bess was deeply concerned about Rob's health, she couldn't bear to listen to Mistress Barlow urging her to the marriage and issuing veiled threats about having her stepfather imprisoned for debt.

Bess spent time with her sisters and younger half-sisters, though after Lady Zouche's spacious London house, it seemed they were living on top of one another. Ralph Leche and her brother, James, had little farming to do now that December approached, but they busied themselves going into the forest to cut wood for the fires.

Finally, the long-awaited post arrived. Bess looked down at the envelope bearing William's bold script, and as her heart leapt with joy, she kissed the letter fervently. She ran upstairs and sat on the bed she shared with Jane. Holding her breath, she tore open the envelope and unfolded the letter.

My Dearest Bess:
   *Please believe me when I tell you that I
never had any intention to hurt you. I am
deeply honored and flattered that you desire
me for your husband, but I swear to you that
I thought you knew I already had a wife.*

Bess stopped reading as the words swam
together. *A wife? No, no, how can that be?* The
news stunned her as if she had been given a
death blow. Slowly, she read the words again.
She was not mistaken. *I thought you knew I
already had a wife.* Bess's heart constricted. *No!
Noooo!*
The letter fluttered to the bed as she wrapped
her arms about her body and began to rock back
and forth. A deep sorrow engulfed her. Tears
she could not stay spilled down her cheeks and
dropped upon the parchment. She sobbed on
until she was breathless and her bodice was
soaked with tears. Sadness seeped along her
veins and into her bones. With nerveless fingers
she reached for the letter and read further.

   *The king is sending me to Ireland to
survey Church property, newly seized by the
Crown, and I shall be there for at least a
year. You could accompany me only as my
mistress, so I urge you to make an honorable
marriage in Derbyshire.*
               William Cavendish

The letter slipped from her fingers, and in
a trance she went downstairs, walked out the

front door, and didn't stop until she came to a sturdy elm tree. Bess wrapped her arms about the smooth gray trunk as if she were willing its strength to enter her body. Then all of a sudden her sorrow turned to anger. She smote the tree with her fists and began to curse.

"Knave, bastard, whoreson...ravisher of virgins! I hate you, Rogue Cavendish! I *hate* you!"

If he had been before her, she would have killed him with her bare hands. She was in such a passionate rage, she wished she were a goddess with a fistful of thunderbolts to hurl.

Inside, they watched through the window, clearly hearing her screaming and cursing. "Can't we help her?" Jane asked in anguish.

Her mother shook her head. "There's nothing we can do until the storm has blown itself out."

Bess remained outdoors, away from everyone. As dusk began to fall, Jane said, "She'll freeze; she has no cloak."

Aunt Marcy patted her shoulder. "Bess's blood is too hot to freeze. Her passionate nature will always stand her in good stead. She gets everything out of her system in one fell swoop."

Bess didn't come inside until it was full dark, then shortly after, she went upstairs to bed. Bess heard Jane come into the room, felt her climb softly into bed beside her, then eventually heard her sister's breathing change as it quieted in sleep. Bess lay for hours, wanting the oblivion of sleep, until finally, sheer exhaustion crept over her.

Bess awakened, terrified. The room was empty, stripped bare. She ran downstairs and found the bailiffs carrying off everything she possessed in the world. She begged, pleaded, and cried, all to no avail. Outside, her family's meager belongings were being piled on a cart. They had been put out of their house and had nowhere to go. Fear washed over her in great waves. Panic choked her. When she turned around, the cart was gone, her family was gone, even Hardwick Manor had vanished. Bess had lost everything she had in the world. The terror mounted until it engulfed her; the waves of fear almost drowned her. The hollow, empty feeling inside her belly was like ravenous hunger, only worse. She was overwhelmed with helplessness, hopelessness.

"Bess, Bess, wake up! You are screaming... you are having a nightmare."

Bess opened her eyes and clutched Jane with trembling hands. "I was back at Hardwick again!"

"Was it the same nightmare you always used to have?"

Bess nodded. It was just a dream, she reminded herself. It was over, thank God, but the hollow, empty feeling inside her belly remained.

Bess was late coming downstairs the next morning. She had barely set foot in the kitchen when she heard a frantic knock on the door and a gray-faced Robert Barlow was ushered into the room.

"It's Father. He's much worse...we think he's dying."

"Sit down, Rob. You are ill; you are white as a ghost." Bess was alarmed at his lack of breath.

"I must go to Edensor for Reverend Rufus."

Mistress Hardwick took matters into her own hands. "No, James will fetch the reverend. We must all hurry back to your house. We will be needed."

Her mother and stepfather, Marcella, and Jane set out at once. Robert lingered behind, waiting for Bess. "I'm so sorry, Rob," she said helplessly.

He looked at her, his blue eyes beseeching. "Bess, will you marry me?"

She couldn't reply; her tongue was stuck to the roof of her mouth. *I don't want this marriage! It will ruin all my chances.... It will ruin my life!*

"It won't be a lifetime sentence, Bess.... I have only a few years left."

"Don't say that, Robert, please—"

"I'm not afraid to die, at least not when you're with me. I love you, Bess. Will you do me the honor of becoming my wife?"

What could she say? How could she hurt him as cruelly as she had been hurt? "I...I'll think about it, Rob."

He squeezed her hand and smiled with renewed hope.

When Robert and Bess arrived, Arthur Barlow was sinking quickly. The death rattle could be heard in his labored breathing, yet incredibly Mistress Barlow was going hammer and tongs at Ralph Leche. "If you don't make her go through with this marriage, I swear I'll have you in the Fleet for the debt you owe us!"

"Stop, please! Have you no sense of decency?" Bess cried.

"Decency? There's little that's decent about the Hardwicks! Your father and brother have taken wicked advantage of me. While my man has lay dying, they've had the use of our land with no intention of paying for it! And you, Bess Hardwick, you're too selfish to help us in our time of need!"

Robert took her arm. "Mother, stop. Bess is the most unselfish girl in the world. I love her."

The Reverend Rufus arrived with James Hardwick, which put a stop to Mistress Barlow's accusations. He went to the bedside, then came back to the group. "If I am to perform a marriage, it must be with Arthur Barlow's consent, and the union must be *in the life of his father* because Robert is a minor. Mistress Hardwick, Mistress Barlow, you know all this; we have discussed it at length."

All eyes swung to Bess. She realized that she held her family's fate in the palm of her hand. Then she looked at Robert, who was mutely begging her. Bess was suddenly furious. As usual, everything fell on her shoulders; everyone in the room was weak, forcing her to be strong and decisive. "I want it in writing that you won't press charges against Ralph Leche."

Reverend Rufus said, "There's no time; Arthur is dying. All that can be written out later."

Bess stood her ground. "Unless I get a signed paper, there will be no marriage!"

There was an undignified scramble for paper and pen. Bess got her signed paper, as well as a document setting out her bride's portion of one third of the Barlow estate's income, should her husband predecease her.

Arthur Barlow breathed his last before the vows were completed, but all present chose to pretend otherwise. When Bess whispered, "I will," she felt completely numb. Surely this wasn't really happening to her. Everything seemed totally unreal!

She looked at Rob across the corpse of his father and suddenly saw that he was near collapse. She straightened her shoulders and addressed her mother-in-law with blazing eyes.

"Excuse me, please. I'm going to put my husband to bed where he belongs."

EIGHT

In spite of the fact that Robert Barlow had told Bess he was not afraid to die, he *was* afraid after witnessing how ravaged his father had become before he took his last breath. Yet he had not lied overmuch. With Bess beside him the ordeal would be less frightening. Though his mother would not accept it, Robert feared he suffered from the same malady as his father. It was a chronic distemper of the lungs that steadily debilitated the body until the coughing spasms brought forth black-blooded sputum, which was disgustingly foul.

It was a fateful day for Robert Barlow; not only had he lost his father to death, he had gained his heart's desire. Tumultuous emotions warred within him, taking him to the brink of collapse. Gratitude toward Bess almost undid him as she helped him up the stairs to his bedchamber.

Robert was thankful it was a spacious, comfortable room with a fireplace, since from now on it would have to accommodate two. He sat on the bed, exhausted, drained of every drop of his energy. As if Bess knew exactly how he felt, she began to undress him. When she knelt to remove his boots, he felt humbled. Tears flooded his eyes as he looked down upon her beloved red head.

On a sob he asked, "Bess, how can this be the unhappiest, yet the happiest day of my life?"

Bess rose, sat on the bed beside him, and gathered him into her arms. "Rob, we have *fateful days* when both good and bad things can happen…things that alter our lives. There is absolutely nothing more you can do for your father, he's in God's hands." You, however, are in my hands, she thought with silent resolution. "I want you to rest and regain your strength." She finished undressing him in her capable manner, tucked the covers about him, then restoked the fire.

"Bess, don't leave me."

She came back to the bed and once more enfolded him against her breast. Suddenly, he couldn't hold it in any longer. He began to sob out his heart, and Bess held him tightly, giving him her strength, her comfort, and her love.

When Robert slept, Bess went downstairs. It was midafternoon and her family was still there. Marcella had helped to wash and lay out Arthur Barlow, and Ralph and James had gone to the barn to milk the Barlow cows. Jane slipped her hand into Bess's and squeezed. Meanwhile, Reverend Rufus was making arrangements with the widow for Arthur Barlow's burial.

They stopped talking as Mistress Barlow stared at Bess with hard eyes. " 'Tis indecent—you couldn't wait to get him into bed!"

Bess was shocked at her implication. She looked directly into her mother-in-law's eyes. "Robert is ill. I shall do my best to nurse him back to health. I would like your cooperation."

Marcella, who had been holding her tongue for hours, declared, "Bess is right. You will be burying your son alongside his father unless you open your eyes." She turned to Bess's mother. "I'll go back and see that the girls get their supper."

"I'll come with you," Bess said. "I must get my things."

"We'll all go; I think Mistress Barlow needs a little peace and quiet," Elizabeth Hardwick said firmly.

When they arrived home Bess immediately went upstairs to pack. Rogue Cavendish's letter still lay on the bedside table. Bess snatched it up and tore it in half, then thought better of destroying it completely and placed it at the bottom of her trunk.

She folded her clothes, then, as an afterthought, picked up her long-forgotten doll Esmeralda, who had been passed on to her younger sisters. She realized the doll was a representation of herself. She had named her Lady Ponsonby, hoping someday to become a titled lady in her own right. How naive she had been. Bess put the doll into the trunk, closed the lid, and stared down at it. Everything she owned in the world was in that chest.

Her mother slipped into the room. "Bess, how can I ever, ever thank you? You are so kind and unselfish, I can't believe it."

I'm not! I'm the most selfish female in the world. Thank God you cannot hear my thoughts. "Don't ever lose that paper Mistress Barlow signed. She can never press charges against Ralph so long as you have it safe in your possession!"

Marcella entered the bedroom as her mother left. "Bess, what can I say, child? You won't get much comfort out of this marriage, except knowing you've given Elizabeth and Ralph peace of mind."

"It is Robert who needs comfort."

"And you will give it to him, in full measure." Marcella drew her close and kissed her brow. "My dearest Bess, sometimes our destinies are played out in strange ways.... All things come at their appointed time. You are so young, you have your whole life before you. Perhaps if you give now, someday you will attain your heart's desire."

Bess Barlow now had a mission. She set about restoring her young husband's health and making his life more pleasant. She demanded an extra room next to their bedchamber and turned it into a comfortable sitting room. She spent most of her time with Robert, except for attending her sister Jane's wedding and a weekly visit with her family. She prepared his meals, rubbed his chest, dosed him with herbal possets, and amused him to keep his spirits from flagging.

Bess became everything to Robert: mother, nurse, friend, companion, everything except wife. He never attempted to consummate their marriage, and Bess told herself that it was

113

because Robert was younger than she and his body was not yet physically mature. Although Rob was tall, he was extremely thin and underdeveloped in muscle and other male attributes.

Bess realized that she would never have known this if she had not seen that bold devil, George Talbot, stark naked by the River Thames last summer. She could not help but make a comparison between the two young men. Never would she have believed that two males of approximately the same age could be so physically disparate, if she had not seen them with her own eyes!

Talbot's arms and shoulders were sleekly muscled, as were his slim hips. Dark hair covered his chest. She remembered that his legs—and thighs too—had bulged with muscles. But it was what had risen up from between those thighs that left an indelible impression on her innocence. It had been her first encounter with a naked, aroused male.

Remembering the way the devil had enjoyed shocking her, Bess shuddered. How very thankful she was that her fair young husband represented no threat whatsoever to her. Robert worshiped Bess in every way; he was simply not robust enough to consummate the marriage, and in a way Bess felt relieved that it was so.

It was no secret that Robert adored his beautiful wife, and as a result his mother became excessively jealous. She spoke spitefully to Bess but was careful not to antagonize her daughter-in-law too far. There was something intimidating about the redheaded young woman who was responsible for safeguarding the Barlow estate.

When the Court of Wards had stepped in, they hadn't been able to touch Bess's marriage portion, which consisted of one third of the estate, and the remaining two thirds in question became secure when Godfrey Boswell, Jane's new husband, bought Robert Barlow's wardship.

Robert's health remained poor all winter, but when spring arrived it began to improve. By May he was able to accompany his wife on short rides, and they attended the wedding of Bess's younger sister, Alice, to Francis Leche of Chatsworth, who was the nephew of her stepfather, Ralph. They rested their horses on the summit of the hill before descending to Chatsworth. "Rob, that is the most beautiful piece of land I've ever seen in my life," Bess declared, filling her lungs with spring air as if it were the elixir of life.

Chatsworth was green and lush, and the River Derwent circled to the west like a glittering, silver ribbon, while Sherwood Forest lay close on the east. "I often came up here when I was a little girl and pretended that someday I would build a fairy-tale castle down there."

"Poor Bess. You had dreams of being a princess, but instead of Prince Charming, you got me."

She glanced up at him, thinking that his face and thick fair hair were worthy of a prince. If only he were stronger, she thought poignantly. "Save your pity. I have no doubt you will be the handsomest young man at the wedding," she assured him. If only he were older, much, much older, she wished with a resigned sigh.

That night, when they returned home from the wedding, the romance of the occasion stayed with them. When she joined Rob in bed, Bess was not surprised to feel his arms slip about her. He loved to hold her and look at her and stroke her hair. She knew it gave him untold pleasure, and it was no unpleasant thing for Bess to be so sweetly cherished by her young husband.

"Alice was a beautiful bride and Chatsworth such a perfect setting for a wedding." Bess sighed.

"She's not nearly as beautiful as you, my darling. You make my heart sing, Bess; can you hear it?" Rob was so much taller than Bess that her cheek rested against his heart.

Her arms went about him, and she lamented his thinness. "You must try to eat more, Rob. Are you never hungry?"

"I'm hungry for you. Bess, you are still a bride, still a virgin. I want to make you my wife tonight. May I kiss you, sweetheart? I won't kiss you on the mouth, Bess, I don't want you to catch my sickness. I love you too much to ever harm you."

Bess kissed him, very close to his mouth. She bloomed with health and was not afraid of contact with her young husband. He was both stronger and older than when they had wed,

116

and she wondered what it would be like to lose her virginity. A tremulous smile touched the corner of her mouth as she recalled how passionately she had protected that virginity from a determined Rogue Cavendish.

Encouraged, Robert covered her face with kisses. He adored his beautiful wife with all his heart and soul and was suddenly filled with an overwhelming physical desire to love her with his body as well. For the very first time he stroked her breasts and pressed his lips worshipfully to her firm flesh. More excited than he had ever been in his life, he felt his arousal start. As it brushed against her soft thigh, Rob moaned from the wave of pure pleasure that washed over his entire body.

Dear God, at long last he was a man, and he was about to achieve his heart's desire of making a woman of the beautiful girl who was his wife. With trembling hands he lifted off her short bed shift and devoured her luscious young body with his eyes. "You are so lovely, you take my breath away—literally."

Rob was panting heavily, and Bess knew a moment of alarm. Perhaps he wasn't strong enough to make love to her. She wondered wildly what she could do to help him. Would it be easier if she made love to him? She cursed her inexperience, wishing she had knowledge of the mysteries of sex. Then with the innate wisdom of women that had come down through the ages from Eve, she knew she could not wound his masculine pride by assuming the dominant role of aggressor. She would have to lie passive and compliant and let him do the taking. A man must slay the dragon outside his own cave, or he was not a man.

He pulled her against him, and she experienced the strange yet pleasant sensation of warm, naked flesh pressing against the length of her body. When she felt his manhood stirring against her, Bess opened her thighs in sweet invitation and was completely surprised by Rob's reaction. He violently rubbed himself against her mons, then cried out as he was overtaken by a spasm that made his entire body go rigid. With great gasps of what sounded like tormented pleasure, he spent himself, then collapsed, sprawling half upon the bed, half upon Bess.

"I'm sorry, I'm so sorry...I couldn't stop myself."

"Rob, it's all right. It didn't hurt at all," she assured him, but her words caused him to groan as if still in torment. Bess felt a wet stickiness on her thigh and wondered if this was the virgin blood people always whispered about. Yet how could there be blood without pain? This mating business was all very strange, she thought. Rumor had it that men were driven to it, thinking of little else. She decided that the sex act must have a greater impact on men than it did on women. Bess brushed the damp fair hair from Rob's brow and laid a tender hand upon his cheek.

"I love you, Bess; you are too kind and generous. I can't put into words the glory and the ecstasy you made me feel. Next time, sweetheart, I promise to do better." He fell asleep within minutes, totally exhausted from his first sexual experience.

Bess lay in his arms for a long time, listening to Robert's contented breathing. Her maturing body vaguely yearned for something more. She didn't understand exactly what it was she wanted, but the sex act had somehow disappointed her. After years of whispers, innuendos, winks, and bawdy jests, Bess had expected something earth-shattering and cataclysmic. Not the mild little encounter she had shared with her husband.

An hour later a hungry, demanding mouth took total possession of her. Even in her sleep she wondered how on earth her husband had grown so muscular and strong. She pressed against the hard, powerful body of the man who held her immobile, and reveled in the desire that was building steadily in her woman's core. Her arousal became so intense, she wanted to scream. His mouth was hard and she *loved* it, his arms were like steel bands, holding her imprisoned against him, and she *loved* it.

"When I'm done with you, you'll never be the same again," a deep voice promised, and Bess longed with all her heart that it would be so! His mouth and his powerful hands aroused her to madness. When the dark figure rose above her, poised to pierce her with his fearsome weapon, she was actually writhing in need, begging him to take her. Her blood was on fire, her breasts tingling with anticipation, her belly taut with lust, her woman's center aching to be filled with her lover's manroot. His passion fueled her passion until it consumed them and a cry was torn from her throat. Yes! Yes! This is what making love was all about! Taking all; yielding all; enjoying the exquisite pleasure to its last drop.

Suddenly, Bess awoke, the dream still starkly vivid in every erotic detail. He was there in the bed with her. She could see him and feel him and taste him. The memory of Rogue Cavendish had overtaken her so completely it felt as if he had stolen into her bed during the night. She blushed scarlet as she recalled the wildfire his touch had aroused in her. *Damn you, Cavendish, damn you to hellfire!*

As the summer months progressed, Robert often attempted to make love to her but always with the same unsatisfactory result. Bess dreamed more and more frequently of Rogue Cavendish. Shame and anger always followed when she awoke, and she added this to the score she would one day settle with the hated seducer.

The first winds of autumn brought a racking cough to Robert. No matter how much Bess coddled him, his condition did not improve. By October, in fact, he was worse. Rob's energy was at low ebb, and Bess knew how ill he felt sometimes. He never complained; he suffered in silence and always had a smile for her.

Robert was content to sit with a book, his other passion besides his beautiful wife. While he read the classics and poetry, Bess stayed beside him, usually embroidering. One evening in early November, as they sat before the fire, he said, "We've been married almost a year, and I want you to know it's been the happiest year of my life."

"Rob, what a lovely thing to say, thank you. This tapestry I'm working on will mark our anniversary." She held it up to show him the fairy-tale castle.

"Is that me on the white horse?" he asked in disbelief.

"Yes, you are the prince and I am the princess. I just have to embroider our entwined initials above the date and it will be finished."

"You are so clever, sweetheart."

"Rubbish, you are the clever one. You read philosophy and poetry, and you even taught yourself French and Italian."

Suddenly, Robert was gripped by a coughing spasm that wouldn't stop. Bess's eyes widened in alarm as he began to cough up blood. When it was over she bathed him and got him into bed, then she sat beside him and talked softly in an effort to calm him and calm herself.

"I'm going to start making Christmas presents. I thought I'd embroider a pair of cushions for your mother. I've been making sketches of Barlow Hall."

Robert watched her with haunted eyes. "We won't have another year together, Bess."

"Don't talk like that, please, Rob."

But as December dawned, Bess acknowledged to herself that this time Robert's condition was serious. When she next visited her family and they invited her and Robert for the Christmas festivities, she told them she was extremely worried about her young husband's health and that perhaps they should stay quietly at home.

Christmas week was a busy, festive time in the country, with much visiting and socializing. When snow began to fall the day before Christmas Eve, the children were overjoyed. Robert's younger brothers and sisters dragged out the cutter from the barn and went off on a sleigh ride. With Robert's arms encircling Bess, they watched from their upstairs windows, vicariously enjoying the fun the young Barlows were having.

On Christmas Eve it was traditional for everyone in the nearby villages to congregate at the church for a communal supper, then at midnight the Reverend Rufus held a joyous carol service. In the early evening Mistress Barlow bid Robert and Bess a happy Christmas, then climbed into the cutter with her other children and headed to the Edensor church.

After they left, Bess found the big house unusually quiet. She gazed through the window at the thickening snowflakes and pushed away a sense of loneliness.

"You are pensive tonight, Bess," Robert said quietly.

"No, no, of course I'm not," Bess vigorously

denied, poking at the fire until it blazed cheerfully.

"I'm sorry you have to miss all the fun, sweetheart."

"Nonsense! We'll make our own fun. We can exchange our Christmas presents, and I have some malmsey I've been keeping for a special occasion."

They retrieved the gifts they had hidden for each other, then Bess poured them wine. Robert opened his first. It was a book cover she had embroidered in brilliant Spanish silks with his name on it. In the bottom corner their initials were entwined.

"It is beautiful, like you, Bess. Everything you do is beautiful."

She gave him a radiant smile and opened the gift he handed her. It was a silver letter opener wrought with a stag's head. "Oh, wherever did you get it, Rob?"

"It was my grandfather's. He left it to me."

"But you must treasure it. Why are you giving it to me?"

He squeezed her hand. "Soon I won't need it; I want you to have it."

"Don't talk like that, Rob. You're always worse in the wintertime. When spring comes we'll ride out again—"

His long fingers brushed her lips to silence her. "Bess, I need to speak of these things. You always stop me, thinking you are being kind, but, sweetheart, let me talk. I hold it inside and I have to let it out."

She sat still and waited apprehensively.

Robert indicated the tapestry of the fairy-tale castle hanging on the wall.

"I'll never ride over the hill with you again to look at Chatsworth, but, Bess, you must go. Never let your dreams die."

Bess swallowed past the lump in her throat. Tonight he didn't sound like a boy, he sounded old and wise beyond his years.

"You made my life so very happy, Bess; please have no remorse that I will die. My only regret is that I couldn't give you a child. You will make a wonderful mother, Bess."

Her throat ached so much she couldn't speak, but she shook her head in denial.

"*Yes!* You will go on without me! You have such a passion for life, you must marry again and have the children we didn't. Promise me!"

"Rob—" It came out on a sob.

"You have to live for both of us. It's all right, Bess. I feel quite euphoric most of the time. I don't suffer overmuch."

Bess didn't know what *euphoric* meant—she didn't read as much as Robert—but she put her arms about him and held him tightly. "Let me help you to bed," she insisted, doubly determined to nurse him back to better health.

Robert reached into the drawer of the bedside table. "I have made a will, Bess. No, listen to me, this is very important. Poor Godfrey Boswell, your sister Jane's husband who bought my wardship, will lose all his investment of one hundred marks when I die, because my younger brother, George, is next in line." Robert paused, gasping to catch his breath, and Bess tenderly stroked his back.

"At least the Court of Wards cannot touch your marriage portion. Darling Bess, it is so little reward for all you have given me. But the court will seize the other two thirds because George is a minor. In my will I have named Godfrey Boswell as trustee so George's wardship cannot be resold."

"I understand, Rob." Bess took the paper and kissed his brow. She watched him drink his malmsey and then drift off to sleep. Bess took her glass to the window and looked with unseeing eyes at the silent, snow-blanketed landscape. She had to face the truth. In her heart she knew that Robert would not live many more months, no matter how devotedly she nursed him. Pity for her young husband welled up inside her and threatened to overwhelm her. She felt wretchedly guilty also. How many times had she stood at this window feeling trapped like a wild bird, madly beating its wings against its cage?

She didn't know how long she stood at the window, but eventually she began to shiver and went to build up the fire. It began to smoke, and she opened the flue in the chimney so the smoke wouldn't fill the room.

In the bed behind her, Robert awoke and began to cough. Blaming herself for causing his discomfort, she said, "I'm so sorry, I made the fire smoke. I'll get you a drink."

The water made him choke, and the coughing spasm deepened. Bess knew what to expect, it had happened before. She ran for a clean linen towel and held it ready for the bloody sputum. But all of a sudden the towel she was holding became drenched in bright red blood, and to Bess's horror she realized that Robert was hemorrhaging.

Panic rose up in her. For a moment it seemed to stop, and Robert lay back, exhausted. She squeezed his hand and felt him squeeze back, but then the blood poured out again, and this time there was no stopping it.

Bess sat stunned, still holding Robert's hand. The bed looked like a slaughterhouse where the thin, pale body of her husband lay lifeless.

NINE

The moment Bess became a widow, all her pent-up energy surged to the fore in a great torrent. It was as if she had been living in a cage for over a year and suddenly the door had been opened. Only a week after Robert's funeral, Bess began to ride out over the countryside in spite of the bitter cold weather and Mistress Barlow's thin-lipped disapproval. Bess ignored her objections. Now that she was a widow, she had no one to answer to but herself. The wonderful feeling of freedom she experienced acted as a countervailing force to the sadness she felt at having lost Robert, whom she'd never truly viewed as her husband but had certainly considered her friend.

Because her husband had predeceased her, her marriage portion entitled her to one third of the Barlow farm. As the new year dawned, Bess felt like a different woman from the naive sixteen-year-old who had been coerced into marriage fourteen long months ago. On her next birthday she would be eighteen, but she felt a maturity far beyond her years.

Bess made a resolution that never again would she allow herself to be victimized or to let others decide her fate. From now on, she vowed, she'd command her own destiny. She had no idea that her resolute determination would be put to the test almost immediately.

In February the Court of Wards swooped down on the Barlow property to take it in wardship for George Barlow. Bess was at home when the Court's representative paid them a visit with his sheaf of legal papers and his superior, paternalistic attitude.

"Mistress Barlow?" he inquired, taking the best chair in the parlor.

Bess replied, "This is Mistress Arthur Barlow, and I am Mistress Robert Barlow."

Her mother-in-law said sharply, "There is no need for you to be present, Bess. Barlow Manor has nothing to do with you."

Bess was affronted and took the offensive immediately. "Actually, it has everything to do with me, since it belonged to my husband

and my marriage portion entitles me to one third of the income."

"That is a lie! My son was a minor when he wed you, and my husband died before he could give his consent to the marriage."

Bess was outraged at the lie. Robert's mother was trying to cheat her of what was legally hers.

"Ladies, ladies, there is no need for unpleasantries. This is simply a formality. Since George Barlow is a minor, the Court will take the Barlow house and lands into wardship until the boy is of age."

Bess shot to her feet, her eyes blazing. "The *bloody* Court will do no such thing! I have a legal document, *signed by my husband's father,* entitling me to my one-third bride's portion. I also have my husband's will, leaving the other two thirds of the Barlow farm to a trustee."

"I know of no such will; where is it?" Mistress Barlow demanded.

"The legal documents are at my mother's home for safekeeping. If you would care to return tomorrow, sir, I will produce them for you. I bid you good day."

Livid at the younger woman's high-handedness, the man gathered up his papers and departed. The minute the door closed, the two women confronted each other.

"You know damned well the marriage was just a ploy to keep us from losing the farm. I'll *never* let you have a third of the income!"

"*You,* madam, own nothing here. Robert suffered your presence here out of the goodness of his heart," Bess pointed out. "I get one third of the income, and your son, George, owns the rest. Robert appointed my brother-in-law to hold it in trust for George. When I was six years old, I learned that the world owed me nothing and that I would have to stand firmly on my own two feet. Now it is time for you to learn that lesson. I will fight you and I will fight the Court of Wards for what is legally mine. And let me warn you, I will fight with no holds barred and use every means within my power!"

Bess swept upstairs to pack her belongings. When she was done, anger gave her the strength to haul her heavy trunk downstairs. With her head held high, Bess announced regally, "I shall return tomorrow with my legal documents *and* my legal witnesses. Good-bye and good riddance to you, madam."

Bess felt only relief as she left Barlow Hall. She could no longer tolerate living with Robert's mother, now that he was gone. In her heart London was calling to her once again, but first she would fight for the monetary compensation to which she was legally entitled.

When Bess arrived at her mother's, all welcomed her with open arms, and since her two sisters were now married, she was given a small bedroom of her own. A message was dispatched to Jane and her husband, Godfrey Boswell, who came immediately.

"What in the world can the woman hope to gain by denying your marriage portion to the official from the Court of Wards?" Bess's mother asked. "Surely she doesn't want the entire farm to be held until young George Barlow is twenty-one?"

Bess's aunt Marcy announced, "I have the answer! I have heard that Mistress Barlow has found herself a man—one who intends to buy George's wardship—and the pair of them are not satisfied with only two thirds."

Godfrey Boswell spoke up. "Robert's will made me trustee. I am legally in charge of the Barlow farm until George comes of age."

The following day the entire family accompanied Bess to confront the Court of Ward's official. When he demanded that Bess turn over her legal document concerning her marriage portion along with Robert's will, she adamantly refused. Finally, she agreed to make him exact copies of the documents, and he left, telling them he would take the matter under advisement and the administration would have to sort it all out before the matter could be settled.

When three months had passed and Bess had heard nothing, she began to realize her marriage jointure was firmly enmeshed in the legal machinery of the Court of Wards and she would never get her settlement so long as it was the subject of legal wrangling.

As she lay in bed one night, the words of

130

William Cavendish came back to her: *You should have had a lawyer. They are costly, but worth every penny. The side with the better lawyer* always *wins.* Bess suddenly realized she needed the services of a lawyer, but without money she knew none would take her case.

The next morning Bess saddled her horse and rode out in the warm May sunshine. The hedgerows were awash with wildflowers, and as she left the village behind, she saw that the Derbyshire dales were dotted with sheep and new lambs. Bess knew she was going to her favorite place in the world.

She drew rein on the summit of the hill that overlooked Chatsworth. *I got up early so I could taste the day. Up here the air is crisp and clear, like fine wine, and the view is forever!* Bess had been convinced that here in the rarefied air she would be able to think better and decide what she must do. *If it's going to be, it's up to me.* Bess had never had anything handed to her in her life, and she wasn't afraid to fight for what she wanted.

Gradually, an idea stole to her. She needed power behind her, and who was the most powerful man in the north of England? The Earl of Shrewsbury, of course! He was the lord lieutenant of Derbyshire, and his magnificent Sheffield Castle was only a dozen miles north of this very spot. The idea was an audacious one, but Bess knew she had never been short of audacity!

It was June before Francis Talbot, Fifth Earl of Shrewsbury, was in residence at Sheffield Castle. But Bess had not wasted her time since her decision to pay a visit to the lord lieutenant of Derbyshire. She and her aunt Marcy had refurbished the elegant gray taffeta gown that Lady Margaret Zouche had given her. They took the billowing sleeves and embroidered them with violets. Then Bess took the scissors and altered the high neckline so that it was low and square-cut, to show off her breasts. Marcella took the piece of taffeta and fashioned a stomacher, also embroidered with violets, to emphasize Bess's tiny waistline. When it was done, the dress was quite showy, but its gray and mauve were quite acceptable mourning colors. Bess considered having Ralph Leche or her brother accompany her, then decided against it. A woman alone just might appeal to the earl's chivalry.

Bess rode down the long avenue of century-old oaks that led to the grounds of Sheffield Castle. It sat in an eight-acre park, and she stared in disbelief at the number of gardeners she counted. The vast lawns were manicured, the ornamental bushes clipped neatly, and the flower beds were laid out with a precise symmetry. Bess sighed with longing. Just so would she want the grounds of her own estate to look.

When she reached the stone courtyard that

led to the long row of stables, two grooms approached her, one to take her mount, the other to assist her from the saddle. Bess removed her hooded cloak that had protected her hair and her gown from the dust of the roads. Then she rolled it up and tucked it into her saddlebags. Before she took out her package of precious documents, she brushed her glorious red hair until it crackled. The grooms stood gaping at her, but Bess forced herself to blithely ignore them, reminding herself that that was how the nobility treated servants.

Sheffield's size alone was intimidating. It was so enormous, it easily contained over two hundred rooms. The arched doorway to the castle was flanked by uniformed guards, and beyond them Bess could see footmen in the entrance hall. Their blue liveries sparked her imagination, and she decided on the spot that when she had her own footmen she would put them in blue and silver.

When the majordomo approached to ask her business, she told him, "I'm here to see the Earl of Shrewsbury."

"That would be impossible, madam," he replied stiffly. "His lordship is not receiving today."

Bess drew herself up and lifted her chin. Though the majordomo was an imposing figure, she refused to be intimidated by him. "I must insist—I am here on a most important matter."

"Would that be a personal matter or a business matter, madam?" he asked impassively.

"It is a business matter," she stated emphatically.

"Then you wish to see his lordship's secretary, Thomas Baldwin, who looks after all the earl's business affairs."

Bess held her tongue. The man was too rigid to bend even slightly. The majordomo led her to a carved settle in a reception room off the entrance hall and told her to wait. After a half hour Master Baldwin put in an appearance. He had a scholarly look about him, with a sharp, pointed face and ink-stained fingers, and Bess hoped he would be more reasonable than the majordomo. Such was not the case, however. Baldwin refused to let her speak with Shrewsbury and insisted she lay her business before him instead. With a sinking heart she explained her predicament to the earl's secretary, who answered in a condescending manner.

"Madam, have you any idea how many supplicants come begging assistance daily from the Earl of Shrewsbury? 'Tis impossible to accommodate the constituents of three entire counties."

A spark of anger ignited in Bess. "I refuse to leave until I have seen the earl!"

The heavy front door banged, and an extremely tall, dark young man in riding attire strode past the door of the reception room. Within thirty seconds he came back to get a second look at the woman with Baldwin. George Talbot advanced into the room, slapping a riding crop into the palm of his hand.

"Well, I'll be damned, if it isn't Mistress Elizabeth Hardwick." He pronounced her name with the emphasis on the last syllable to provoke her.

"If I get my wish, you *will* be damned, and my name happens to be Mistress Elizabeth *Barlow*," she said imperiously.

His eyes narrowed as they swept down over her luscious breasts and tiny waist. "So, you're now a married woman, with experience of the marriage bed. Hell's teeth, I'll bet you know a trick or two, Vixen!"

Bess's black eyes flashed with fury. "I am a widow, you uncouth lout; show a little respect!"

"Still teaching me manners? Splendor of God, it wouldn't surprise me if you could teach me other things as well, and while we're at it, there's a couple of things I'd like to teach you."

Thomas Baldwin stepped away from the couple, who seemed to be on intimate, though extremely antagonistic terms.

"As an earl's son, someone must have tried to make a gentleman of you, but it is obvious that they failed miserably."

Talbot ignored her assessment of him. With his riding crop, he flicked a red curl that sat upon her shoulder. "Is that color real?" he drawled.

"Everything about me is real, including my temper!" Bess knew she was ruining her chances for help from the noble Talbots, but she simply couldn't control her tongue.

"Vixen!" he taunted.

She watched his eyes slide down her body and come to rest below the stomacher. Suddenly, Bess knew he was undressing her with his eyes. The flat of her hand delivered a stinging slap to his cheek.

His powerful hands shot out to clasp her about the waist and lift her from the carpet. If Baldwin hadn't been in the room with them, Bess knew that Talbot would have tried to ravish her. Slowly, he set her feet back to the floor and murmured, "You owe me for that, Vixen, and someday I'm going to collect." He walked across the room to the secretary and spoke low.

Though Bess could not hear their words, she imagined the terrible things that were being said about her. Angry tears of frustration sprang to her eyes, and she fought them back with sheer determination.

The two men spoke at length before young Talbot departed and Baldwin returned to her. She thought she would be dismissed immediately and was surprised when he asked to see her legal documents. She gave them to him and sat back down on the settle while he examined them carefully.

When he left, Talbot immediately sought his father and found him at his massive desk in the library, signing letters and documents that had been prepared by his secretary.

"Father, there's a young woman downstairs asking to speak with you."

"Not another petitioner? Have Baldwin attend her," the earl directed.

"He is with her now, but as a favor to me, Father, I ask that you see her personally."

The earl's eyebrows elevated and bristled as he laid down his quill and gave his heir a piercing look. "The only possible interest you could have in a young woman is a prurient one!"

George Talbot ignored his father's accusation. "She's a young widow from Hardwick, close-by in Derbyshire. Her family are farmers, the salt of the earth, as you are fond of saying. She's being cheated out of her jointure."

"Then she needs a lawyer," the earl said dismissively.

"Of course she needs a bloody lawyer, but she's a penniless young widow who has come to you for help."

"Why me? Is it because you're bedding her? Is this some sort of blackmail?"

"No, sir, it isn't. I met her in London. Her reputation is above reproach; she's an acquaintance of Princess Elizabeth."

"Why the devil didn't you say so?" Although the king's youngest daughter was a distant third in the line of succession and sometimes referred to as illegitimate, the remote possibility existed that someday she could rule England. The earl scribbled a note to Thomas Baldwin and summoned a footman to deliver it.

"Thank you, Father. All it will cost you is five minutes of your time."

When the footman presented the silver salver to Baldwin, he took up the note upon it and bade Mistress Barlow to follow him. As she walked through the passageways of Sheffield Castle and ascended the great staircase, Bess stared in awe at the magnificent furnishings. The Talbots were the wealthiest peers in the realm, and they lived in splendor.

When Baldwin ushered her into the vast library and she realized she was in the presence of the great Earl of Shrewsbury, she sank into a graceful curtsy.

"My lord, this is Mistress Elizabeth Barlow, who has been recently widowed. Her marriage portion is being considered by the Court of Wards, and I've tried to explain there is naught to be done but wait for their decision. There really is no need to trouble yourself with this matter."

"Thank you, Baldwin. I'd prefer that Mistress Barlow tell me all in her own words." Francis Talbot, Fifth Earl of Shrewsbury, was captivated by the beautiful young woman before him. No wonder his son had lost his head over her. Shrewsbury listened, mesmerized, as she told her story. She spoke passionately, her flaming hair crackling about her shoulders and her gray taffeta rustling seductively with her every movement. As the curves of her firm young breasts rose from the square neckline of her gown, Shrewsbury sighed, wishing he were twenty years younger. She was that rare creature: a true man's woman.

The earl examined her documents and, when they appeared legal, realized it would cost him nothing to help her. A simple letter to a Derbyshire man of law, eager to gain the patronage of the Earl of Shrewsbury, would do the trick.

Bess arrived home, flush with her victory. She hadn't the least notion that she had the hated George Talbot to thank for her interview with the lord lieutenant of Derbyshire.

Within a fortnight Bess was summoned to the chambers of Messrs. Fulk and Entwistle, the county's most prominent lawyers. Within a month they petitioned the Court of Wards, and within four months they had a monetary settlement for her.

"Ten pounds?" Bess repeated the amount of money they had for her with amazement.

Messrs. Fulk and Entwistle, thinking she was indignant, hastened to reassure her. "That is only a partial settlement, but we agreed to accept it until the true amount can be tallied, and of course the value of your jointure will go up each and every year."

Bess was overjoyed. She had never really expected the Court of Wards to concede her anything. Rogue Cavendish had been right; the side with the better lawyer would *always* win!

"My dear sirs, you are truly amazing, and I thank you from the bottom of my heart." Her thoughts were darting about like quicksilver. "Since you have dealt so well with the Court of Wards and achieved such favorable results, I would like you to handle another matter for me. My brother, James, is heir to Hardwick Manor, which has been held in wardship for nearly a dozen years. James is almost twenty, only a year from coming of age. Now that I have money, why can't I buy his wardship for the final year, so that our family can take back ownership of Hardwick's lands and manor?"

Fulk and Entwistle were impressed with the young woman's determination, and since the lord lieutenant of Derbyshire had asked them to aid her, they would do what she asked. "We will look into the matter immediately, Mistress Barlow. It seems a sensible course to pursue, 'though we must warn you that these wardship cases often take months."

Eight months later Bess stood in front of the half-timbered house where she had been born. She spoke to it, never doubting that Hardwick Manor could hear and understand every word. "I told you I would be back to claim you. We'll never let you go again; you will belong to the Hardwicks forever. Mother is back with my little sisters, and Aunt Marcy is going to lay out a herb garden. My brother, James, has a new bride, Elizabeth Draycott. From now on all your rooms will be filled with love and, soon, the laughter of children once again. I'm returning to London today, but this isn't good-bye. I'll be back...I promise you!"

PART TWO

WIFE AND MOTHER
LONDON 1546

❖

Had we but world enough, and time,
This coyness, lady, were no crime.
We would sit down, and think which way
To walk, and pass our long love's day.

ANDREW MARVELL

TEN

As Bess stepped from the Zouche carriage and looked up at the tall town house, the two and a half years she had been gone from London melted away like magic. Margaret Zouche looked exactly the same, although her daughters had certainly grown.

"Oh, Bess, my dear, you look all grown up. I'm so very sorry you were widowed at such a young age. I feel I had a hand in the unhappiness that befell you."

"Lady Zouche, you were not responsible in any way," Bess said kindly, but she had counted on Margaret Zouche's conscience to facilitate her return to London and reinstate her in the household. In the time that Bess had been gone, Lady Zouche had acquired a half dozen new servants and did not really have room for more, but Bess was willing to resume her position of unpaid companion, so how could Margaret refuse?

"So much happened during your long absence from London. The king took another wife—Catherine Parr, a widow in her thirties. Can you credit it? King Henry has had six wives!"

The king had married before Bess left London, but she did not correct Lady Zouche.

"Yes, it was the talk of Derbyshire, and I was able to fill my family in on all the fascinating gossip about her, thanks to Lady Frances Grey."

"Because the plague was rampant in London,

the Greys spent the entire summer at their country house, Bradgate. It's not too great a distance from Ashby-de-la-Zouche, and I finally got to see it."

"What is Bradgate like?" Bess asked raptly.

"It isn't a country house at all, it's a red-brick palace! It even has a moat and ramparts, though they are only for ornament, not fortification. It is set in acres of orchards and pleasure gardens." Margaret rattled on, "Speaking of Frances, she tells me that our dear friend, William Cavendish, returned from Ireland last month and the king has knighted him for his services to the Crown during the last two years. *Sir* William is so much in demand these days, I haven't had a chance to see him yet to congratulate him. The London hostesses are already inundating him with invitations this season."

Bess felt her heart constrict with pain the moment she heard his name, then her mouth went dry. *So, the damned rogue got his title after all!* She was surprised that the mere mention of his name could cause her emotional turmoil when she thought herself quite indifferent to him after all this time. She examined her feelings more closely, asking herself exactly what she felt for Cavendish. The answer came back quickly. She felt anger and betrayal; he had hurt her deeply and she longed to hurt him back and take her revenge.

"Cavendish is a married man," Bess said primly, then wondered why she had stated the obvious.

"Perhaps not for long. 'Tis rumored his wife is ailing. Mark my words, if he ever does become a widower again, he will be the catch of the season."

Bess lifted her chin defiantly. "I don't even recall what Cavendish looks like."

"Ah, my dear, you will soon have an opportunity to refresh your memory. Lady Frances has invited us to Suffolk House next week. 'Tis the first big ball of the season. She threw one last October, and it was such a success, Frances has decided to make it an annual event. You must come, of course; Frances will be delighted to see you again. It's a stylish affair; all the ladies are to be in white and all the men in black. I want your unique ideas about what to wear, Bess; there isn't much time."

Bess was suddenly in her glory. "We'll come up with something spectacular, Lady Zouche." Bess, of course, was referring to her own attire for the ball. I'll show him! she vowed silently.

With the help of Margaret Zouche's two full-time seamstresses, Bess turned her employer into a swan and her two young daughters into cygnets. Since the young girls were never permitted to wear anything but white dresses, it wasn't difficult to achieve a swanlike effect. The trick was in the details. Close-fitting, white feathered headdresses with matching fans were all that was required to turn the Zouches into graceful, gliding, fairy-tale creatures. Or so Bess convinced them as they preened before the mirrors in the sewing room.

Bess had no difficulty finding a discarded white dress in the Zouche wardrobe, and she worked over it an entire night, enlarging the tight white satin bodice so that it molded her luscious, upthrust breasts. She used the only thing she had—black satin mourning ribbon—but the striped effect she created was startlingly sophisticated. She found an exquisite lace ruff that had yellowed with age and a faded ostrich-feather fan and cleverly dyed them black. At the first ball of the season, not only would she stand out from all the women in white, but they would not be able to fault her choice of black accessories, because they symbolized her widowhood.

"Well, stab me with a bodkin!" Lady Frances said, clasping Bess to her ample bosom, then holding her at arm's length so she could appraise the ravishing redhead in the vivid black and white. "You always were a clever girl. God, how I've missed you. Most of the females I know are dull as bloody ditchwater! You are the only one who dared to disobey my edict of white!"

Bess laughed with delight. "I don't care to follow trends, I prefer to set them. Why did you choose white, Lady Frances?"

"So I'd have something to laugh at, of course. None of the jades at court have worn white since they were brides, and most didn't have the right to wear it even then! And having the men wear black is simple revenge for their flamboyancy. They strut about in scarlet and gold putting us women in the shade."

"None could ever put you in the shade, Lady Frances."

"Nor you, Bess. I'm glad you're back in London, where you belong. Widows are bringing a high price on the auction block these days," Frances said, referring to Queen Catherine Parr, "but don't wed the first man who asks you; have a little fun first."

Bess brought up her fan to conceal her smile as Lady Zouche approached. She would have little enough fun in Margaret's household. Frances rolled her eyes at Bess and whispered, "I love her dearly, but she's so damned straitlaced. Margaret, darling, your geese have finally turned into swans!"

Although the Greys' ball boasted a dozen countesses and a duchess or two, it was Bess who drew every eye. When Frances was questioned about her guest with the glorious red hair, she glossed over the fact that she was an unpaid servant and gave out the information that she was a widow of independent means.

Bess's first dancing partner was Lord Suffolk, Frances Grey's young brother. She had always thought of him as a boy, but the way he squeezed her hand and stared hungrily at her breasts made her realize he was growing up quickly. When the dance ended, Bess steered the youth in the direction of his sister's husband.

Henry Grey lifted Bess from her deep curtsy

and drew her hand to his lips. "My dear, it is so good to see you back in London. Please accept my heartfelt condolences."

"Thank you, Lord Dorset."

"It's Henry," he said quietly.

"Henry," she said softly, wondering if Frances knew how lucky she was in her choice of a husband.

"Here is someone who desires an introduction. May I present Sir John Thynne, who is also from Derbyshire? Sir John...Mistress Elizabeth Barlow."

"Mistress Elizabeth, I am delighted. I understand you are a Hardwick?"

Bess examined the man before her and liked what she saw. He was perhaps thirty, but the tight brown curls falling over his forehead made him boyishly attractive. She summed him up in a trice by observing his speech, manner, hands, and his honest green eyes. She decided he was kind, intelligent, hardworking, and, above all, sincere. In short, he was excellent husband material.

"Sir John, do you know the Hardwicks?"

"I have never had the pleasure until now, but I am very familiar with Hardwick Manor. Houses are a hobby of mine."

"Oh, I, too, have a great passion for houses, Sir John; the subject absolutely fascinates me."

"I have just started building a house in Brentford."

"I've been there! Isn't it on the river before you get to Hampton Court Palace?"

"Yes. Dudley's Syon House is close by my property."

"Build something beautiful, Sir John. Such a lovely setting deserves a worthy jewel." She lifted her fan and spoke confidentially. "Though it's very imposing, I thought Syon the ugliest house I'd ever seen."

Sir John laughed. "Then that is something else we have in common." Within minutes they were fast friends, as if they had known each other all their lives.

Sir William Cavendish arrived late on purpose. The only reason he was even attending the ball was that he had given Frances his word that he would at least show his face. Since he had been knighted for his service to the Crown, he had high expectations of being appointed treasurer of the Royal Chamber. To achieve his ambition required a place where he could entertain, and the Greys had generously made Suffolk House open to him day or night since he had returned from Ireland.

Sir William avoided the Great Chamber, where the crush of dancers was measuring its steps to corantos and lavoltas, and headed directly to the gambling salon, where a man could indulge his twin vices of gambling and drinking at the same time.

"Oh, no, you don't, you damned rogue!" Frances tapped him sharply with her fan. "Rule number one: No skulking past the ball-room."

"I make my own rules," he told her bluntly, then relented and grinned at her. "I suppose it is bloody bad form not to dance with my hostess."

Frances tucked her arm beneath his and guided him back toward the Great Chamber. "Don't think you're getting off that lightly, you wretched swine. I've a room filled with dowagers, duchesses, and debutantes simply dying for dancing partners."

He swept her into a coranto, grimacing at the roiling sea of white gowns. "Good God, they all look like unmade beds!"

"Any you'd care to sleep in?"

"Not a dowager, duchess, or debutante," he assured her flatly.

With great cunning Frances maneuvered their dance steps so that he could not fail to see Bess, who stood out so dramatically from the crowd. "Are you sure I cannot tempt you with a widow?"

Cavendish stopped dancing. He stood as if rooted to the floor, staring at the beauteous redhead who was having an animated conversation with his friend John Thynne. "Excuse me, Frances," he said absently, and walked directly to the object of his desire.

As the tall figure loomed beside him, John Thynne looked up, recognition lighting his face. "William! Congratulations are in order."

"Sir John," Cavendish murmured without looking at him. His entire attention was focused upon the female standing next to his friend. "Bess." His deep voice made a caress of her name.

Bess looked at him blankly, then allowed a tiny frown of puzzlement to crease her brow. "Do I know you, sir?"

John Thynne, ever affable, rushed in. "Permit me to introduce you. Mistress Elizabeth Barlow, this is my good friend Sir William Cavendish, newly knighted by the king."

Bess forced herself to remain outwardly cool and calm, though she felt her very blood rush hotly through her veins at the nearness of him. It had been two and a half years since she had laid eyes on him, yet he made her feel exactly the same, damn him! He looked rugged and vital, and now that he had been knighted, she'd warrant he'd be even more cocksure of himself. She was determined to show him her indifference.

Bess plied her fan languidly. "What an honor. How proud your wife must be," she said politely. "Is she here tonight?"

Cavendish saw how her eyes glittered and knew she was punishing him. "My wife is ailing," he said shortly. To John he said, "Mistress Elizabeth and I met over two years ago, when we were both last in London."

Bess pretended to search her mind. "Surely I would have remembered you? Yet you seem a complete stranger to me. Well, 'tis of little consequence. If we did meet, I have completely forgotten you."

Rogue Cavendish ground his teeth. Just then the musicians struck up the introduction to a galliard. "Do you care to dance, mistress?"

"Indeed, I love to dance. Sir John, would you partner me?"

As Bess swept off in his friend's arms, Cavendish wanted to throw her across his knee and give her a good spanking. He returned to Frances, who had been standing on the sidelines, enjoying the byplay.

Frances shrugged, not even trying to mask her amusement. "What can you do? He has such an advantage over you."

"You think so?" Cavendish said dangerously.

"Sir John is a bachelor."

"Sir John can piss off!"

"I love a cockfight!" Frances exclaimed.

Cavendish strode onto the dance floor and unceremoniously tapped Sir John Thynne on the shoulder. "Excuse me, John."

Surprised, yet suddenly realizing there was more between Bess and Cavendish than met the eye, Sir John stepped aside with grace.

While Bess strove with every bit of her willpower to appear cool and unaffected by Rogue Cavendish's proximity, on the inside her emotions were running amok. The only reason she hadn't fainted dead away at the sight of him was that she had been expecting to meet him at the ball tonight and had steeled herself for the encounter.

Even so, the moment she heard his deep voice caressing her name, she had experienced a deep sensation of pleasure. The tension of forcing herself to appear indifferent to him while they conversed had taken its toll. She suddenly realized her fingernails were cutting deeply into her palms each time she spoke. Damn him to hellfire; why did he have this compelling effect on her?

Bess braced herself for the moment his hands would touch her body during the dance. But she was not prepared for the devastation he wrought. The heat from his hands felt as if it were scalding her through her clothes. Her blood seemed to turn into liquid flame and run along her veins like wildfire. Her breasts tingled, her nipples peaked painfully, her belly went taut with longing, and she could feel her pulse quicken between her legs.

Half-closing her eyes, Bess swayed toward him as if in a mating dance. Then his powerful hands were on her waist, his thumbs brushing the underside of her breasts, as he lifted her high in the galliard. Time seemed to stand still, and Bess wanted to throw back her head and laugh, perhaps even scream with arousal. She longed to do something wanton, like pull his hair and bite him in a frenzy of passion. Bess did none of these things. It was pure rage that saved her. How *dare* he abandon her, then come back into her life and within minutes make her feel this way?

As Cavendish swung her back to the floor and she felt the polished parquet beneath her toes, Bess cried out with pain. "Oh, dear, I've twisted my ankle! I am so sorry that I cannot continue, Sir William, please excuse me." She had every intention of walking away from him without so much as a limp, but Cavendish thwarted her intent. He gently lifted her up into his arms and gallantly carried her to a chair at the side of the dance floor. He knelt before her and tenderly examined her ankle. Was he really concerned, or was the rogue aware of her ploy and using it so he could touch and caress her?

"It's fine now; you may leave me." She prayed he could not hear how loudly her heart was hammering.

"Bess, it's wonderful to see you again. You are even more beautiful than I remember. It's been so long; can't we find a spot that is more private so we can talk?"

He is attempting to charm and seduce me already. I must get away from him. With relief she saw John Thynne approaching with a concerned look on his face.

"Are you all right, Mistress Barlow?"

"I shall be if you will lend me your arm, sir, and help me find our hostess. I mustn't trouble Sir William any further." Bess dismissed him and walked pridefully off on the other man's arm.

Cavendish prowled the rooms at Suffolk House, looking for Frances. He was in a dangerous mood and had decided that come hell or high water he would make Bess listen to reason. He knew he couldn't do it in public and would need an accomplice to get her alone. When he spotted his best friend, he assumed Henry would aid and abet him. He didn't expect an argument.

"I won't trick Bess into being alone with you; I'm her friend too. I always feel the urge to protect her when you're about."

"Protect her from what?" Cavendish demanded.

"Your lust! You behave like a rampant stallion around Bess."

"She's no longer a sixteen-year-old virgin, Henry; she's a *widow*, for Christ's sake!"

"Frances and I are very fond of her."

"Frances my arse! You're half in love with Bess yourself; admit it."

"At least I don't have seduction in mind."

Rogue Cavendish suddenly saw the humor in the situation and began to laugh. "One little wench has us all jumping through hoops."

Henry grinned. "Perhaps you've met your match at long last."

Cavendish returned to the Great Chamber and sought out Lady Zouche. "Margaret, you're in fine feather tonight."

"Sir William, I'm so happy to be able to congratulate you on your knighthood. It is long overdue."

"My sentiments exactly, Margaret. I hear that Mistress Hardwick has returned to your household."

"She's Mistress Barlow now. Widowed, you know. So very sad. My household is overcrowded with servants, but how could I refuse her a place under the circumstances?"

William fought the urge to strike her. The

woman had Bess's services twenty-four hours a day, and she had them free of charge. "Would you tell her that Lady Frances needs her upstairs?"

Half an hour later, when Bess entered Frances Grey's sitting room on the third level, she found William Cavendish pacing the floor. Abruptly, Bess turned on her heel to leave.

He beat her to the door, slammed it, and leaned his full weight against it. "We have to talk, Bess."

"Indeed?" She arched one of her dark brows as she waved her black fan in front of her face.

He searched his mind, wondering where to begin. His marriage was the sticking point between them, so he knew he must begin there. "Bess, I swear to you that I thought you knew I was married. It was common knowledge; everyone in London knew."

"Indeed?" Bess continued to wave her fan languidly, apparently indifferent to his words.

"What the devil do you expect? I'm thirty-nine, more than twenty years older than you!"

"Indeed?" Bess stifled a yawn behind the black ostrich feathers.

William clenched his fists and prayed for patience. "I was left a widower with a young daughter. I wed Eliza Parris to give my child a mother and to sire a son. It wasn't until after we were wed that I learned she had a history of miscarriage that left her barren. We've always had separate bedchambers and led completely separate lives."

"Indeed?" Bess said coolly.

"Put that bloody fan down and stop this ridiculous act of indifference!" William snatched the fan from her fingers and flung it to the floor.

She raised her chin, her eyes glittering dangerously. "Whatever makes you think it an act?" she drawled.

"Because you're punishing me, and you wouldn't feel the need to inflict pain on me if you were indifferent!"

Bess flew at him and raked his face. "Bastard! Whoreson! Ravisher of virgins!"

He grabbed her hands and forced them behind her back. His arms were around her now and he arched her body forward against his. "Little bitch," he murmured. "I warrant you know just how magnificent you look when you are in a temper."

Tears of utter rage filled her eyes, and her lips began to tremble. "Damn you, Cavendish, damn you to hellfire!"

"Too late, Bess. The king's work has already done that." He brought his mouth down over hers and kissed her deeply, thoroughly.

Bess's temper flared higher, and she pulled away from him. Now she had to fight herself as well as him. "Ravisher!" she accused.

"I wish to God I *had* taken your maidenhead that day in the forest, and I wish I'd taken you to Ireland as my mistress. Instead, I did the noble thing and urged you to make that honorable marriage that was so bloody important to you. I cared about you so deeply, my conscience wouldn't allow me to despoil you."

"Your conscience?" Bess laughed in his face. "Don't you dare speak to me of conscience, Rogue Cavendish! You concealed not one but two wives from me, to say nothing of a daughter. You told me when you returned from Dover you'd have a question to ask me about a permanent relationship. You said you wanted us to be together. I was so young and naive, I thought you were going to ask me to marry you. But you knew that was impossible. You had every intention of seducing me! Rogue Cavendish, you have no conscience!"

"Not from this moment on I haven't, my beauty."

"Oooh!" Bess pounded her fists against his chest and burst into sobs. William swung her up into his arms and carried her to a love seat before the fire. He sat down with his arms still about her and cradled her in his lap. Without a word he removed her lovely black lace ruff and brushed his lips against her throat. Then he threaded his fingers through her hair and kissed her gently, soothingly. "You are still in mourning; when did your husband die, Bess?"

"A year ago Christmas Eve," she whispered. "He was too young to die."

"Were you in love with him?" he asked possessively.

"He loved me too much...he adored me. Rob was younger than I was.... He was ill, weak; I had to be the strong one. I'm very wicked.... I felt as if I was just marking time until I could return to London," she confessed.

"Bess, listen to me. In almost every relationship one loves more than the other, and the one who loves is the lucky one, the happy one. If Robert loved you, then he must have been happy."

"Oh, he was...even though he knew he was dying, he was happy."

"Then you can have no regrets. The past is over and done; the future lies before us. I would like to take up where we left off. You and I are well-matched. It is very rare for a man and a woman to love equally, but we could be such a couple. Bess, will you let me take care of you? Will you let me buy you a little house in London? Will you let me love you?"

Bess sat perched upon his knee, her head at war with her heart. She suspected she was in danger of falling in love with Rogue Cavendish all over again. The sight of him made her faint, his voice made her quiver, his touch made her burn. He was so strong; how wonderful it would be to be able to be weak for once. Yet she knew if she became his mistress, that would be all she would amount to in this world. And Bess wanted more. Bess wanted it all, and her ambitious dreams would not allow her to accept less. She picked up the lace ruff and slowly fastened it about her neck.

"You haven't given me your answer, sweetheart." He looked sure of himself, quite confident she would do as he wished. His eyes looked at her possessively.

159

She looked at him with tears still clinging to her lashes. "My answer is no, William. I want more."

ELEVEN

Within the month Sir William Cavendish was appointed treasurer of the King's Chamber, and because he was so familiar with both church and royal lands across the whole of England, he was appointed to the Court of General Surveyors. He reported directly to the powerful lord high treasurer, William Paulet, who had just been made Marquess of Winchester, a rank below duke but above every earl in the land.

Cavendish and Wily Winchester now controlled the purse strings of the entire nation and were besieged by the nobility for favors, patronage, and appointments, for which they were well-paid. The highest and most ambitious in the land now curried favor with Sir William Cavendish, and he realized the next post he must attain in his upward climb to power was that of privy councillor.

His time was no longer his own. Although he now had a secretary and a huge staff of clerks, he spent endless hours at Court and had rooms at Whitehall, where he spent most nights. His only respite was with his friends the Greys at Suffolk House, just a short distance from Whitehall down the Strand, where he could escape for a few hours. Although it was impossible to see Bess often, since she worked for Lady Zouche and lived in her household, she was never out of his thoughts. Her sparkling vision rose ever before him, always irresistibly radiant. She was easily the most attractive female he'd ever seen. He pictured every detail—her dark eyes flashing and her breasts heaving quickly. Sometimes she became so intense she actually quivered. Bess was a natural coquette without even knowing it. Whenever she gave him that level look without a trace of flirtation, it held him in thrall.

All his life, by hard work, boldness, and ruthless determination, Cavendish had achieved every goal that he desired. And now he desired Bess, for what good was such heady success without someone to share it with? The fact that Bess had refused to become his mistress did not deter him in the least. To William it was quite simple and straightforward. He wanted her. He would have her.

It was close on midnight when he arrived at Suffolk House, but the lights were ablaze and he knew he would find Frances Grey still playing cards or backgammon.

"Rogue! I'm bored to death. Please save my life by throwing me a tidbit of Court gossip." Frances dismissed her yawning ladies-in-waiting, who were thankful to escape to bed.

"Well, let's see, our good friend William Parr has finally been granted his divorce, and Elizabeth Brooke is up to her pretty eyes in wedding plans."

"Well, I'll be damned! It seems that nothing is impossible for Parr since his sister became queen! First he's made Marquess of Northampton, and now he's rid himself of an aging wife. Actually, I'll be double damned! How the devil did you learn of it before I did?"

"My daughter, Catherine, is espoused to Elizabeth Brooke's brother, Thomas. It so happens I visited her today at Lord and Lady Cobham's."

"I had forgot Catherine no longer lives at home. I warrant she's far happier in the Cobham household. Why don't you take a page from Parr's book and divorce that wretched Eliza Parris?"

"When I was in Ireland, I had made up my mind to do just that, but when I returned, Eliza's doctor took me aside and told me she has a malady that is almost always fatal. Divorce seemed a shabby thing to do under the circumstances."

"And why cover yourself with the scandal of divorce when the angel of death is about to grant your dearest wish?"

Completely used to her cynical irreverence, he rebuked her only lightly. "Frances, my dear, is nothing sacred to you?"

"Very bloody little, I'm afraid." Her eyes swept over him with speculation. *So the rumor that she is dying is true! He'll have to fight off the women. Heigh-ho, they'll be scratching out each*

*other's eyes to become the next Lady Cavendish.
How utterly divine that I'll have a front-row
seat!*

Cavendish picked up her plump hand and
toyed absently with her fingers for a moment.
"Darling Frances, I need yet another favor from
you. I would like you to make Bess one of your
ladies-in-waiting."

Her eyes widened with comprehension.
"Why on earth didn't I think of it before?
She's exactly what I need to banish my
boredom. My latest ladies have less wit than
head lice."

"How much do you pay your ladies?"

"Five pounds a year, I believe."

"Offer her ten; I'll give you the money. I want
her to be able to dress well."

"You'll do no such thing! What is money to
a Tudor? Whatever gowns she wants will be
provided by the Royal Wardrobe. Harry's
purse pays for every garment at Suffolk House,
from the servants' liveries to the nursemaids'
corsets."

"Mmm, as treasurer I'd better look into
such extravagance," he said with a grin, happy
that she was amenable to his suggestion.

"You can look into my underdrawers if it
makes you happy, darling, just don't expect
me to exercise restraint. Intemperance is my
middle name."

"Nay, Frances, you are not intemperate, you
are most generous, and I love you dearly for
it," he said before he kissed her hand.

Bess was ecstatic when Frances Grey offered her the position of lady-in-waiting; she could hardly believe her great good fortune. Margaret Zouche did not stand in Bess's way of advancement and reluctantly let her go to Suffolk House immediately.

Frances took the greatest delight in giving Bess a spacious suite of rooms, complete with bedchamber, sitting room, and its own dressing room. It was in another wing entirely from the chambers of her other ladies, and the sheer luxury of the furnishings momentarily stunned Bess. But within days she adapted to her elegant surroundings as if she had been born at Suffolk House.

New gowns were the first item on the agenda, and Lady Frances decided that she along with Bess would have an entirely new wardrobe. They spent endless hours discussing style, choosing colors, and selecting material. Bess knew exactly what suited her best and had a flair for the dramatic, which she was free to indulge for the first time in her life. While Frances needed darker shades to minimize her full figure and contrast with her blond hair, Bess chose the bold jewel tones of sapphire, amethyst, turquoise, and emerald. She indulged herself with black taffeta petticoats that rustled deliciously, black lace stockings, and satin high-heeled slippers that made her feel quite wanton.

Bess was so regal that the servants ran to do her bidding and the noble guests who streamed through Suffolk House treated her as an equal, since it was clear to everyone that she and the Marchioness of Dorset had become intimate friends. Bess had no real duties, so she was free to study and learn exactly how Suffolk House was run and to acquire the skills necessary to entertain on a lavish scale. She had boundless energy; all that was expected of her was to help Lady Frances entertain until midnight almost every night of the week, then rouse her in the mornings with a cup of chocolate accompanied by a generous serving of the latest gossip.

Bess entered the luxurious bedchamber of Lady Frances and drew back the heavy brocade drapes. "Good morning." She set the tray with the porcelain cups and saucers and the jug of steaming chocolate on the bedside table.

"God's balls, surely it's still the middle of the night!" Frances protested. "Go away!"

Bess ignored her protests. "It's almost ten; you'll sleep the day away, and you asked me to remind you that you had a special dinner party to plan this morning."

"Lud, how do you put up with me?" She picked up a hand mirror and stuck out her tongue. "My mouth tastes like I've been licking the bottom of the parrot cage."

Bess handed her a cup of chocolate and sat down on the wide bed. "Lady Frances, I don't know how to thank you for everything

165

you've done for me. I am so very grateful—"

"Rubbish, I'm the one who's grateful. Bess, we deal so comfortably together. I'm not the least ashamed of letting you share all my tawdry secrets, because I know I can count on your discretion. I have a new groom I'm absolutely panting for—he's such a big young brute! You will accompany us when we go riding and make sure we are not disturbed. I need absolute privacy while he gives me equestrian lessons."

Bess laughed, thinking Frances was simply being her outrageous self and trying to shock her.

"And of course I'll make sure you are not disturbed when you entertain a lover. Speaking of Rogue Cavendish brings me to the dinner party we must plan."

The smile left Bess's face and was replaced by a blush. "Cavendish isn't my lover."

Frances stared at her in utter amazement. "You clever girl! You've put the ultimate price on your favors as Anne Boleyn did. No bedding without a wedding! How in the name of God have you managed to hold that rampant stallion at bay? Or for that matter, how do you control your own lust, darling? I know I can't!"

It suddenly dawned on Bess that lust was exactly what she felt when Cavendish touched her. "I refuse to play the whore."

"Darling, we're all whores under the skin, whether we give ourselves by calculation or by desire. It's just that some of us demand a higher price than others. You are quite clever to demand marriage when you know he'll be widowed shortly. Just don't let any other woman steal your candy. While you're pushing him off with one hand, be sure to keep him hot for you with the other. Remember that the steps to the mating dance are advance as well as retreat. I told you years ago that cock-teasing was the surest method of trapping a husband; I'm most flattered you are taking my advice."

It's not like that! Bess protested silently, then her innate honesty came to the fore. It's exactly like that! she admitted to herself with a blush.

"This dinner for Sir William could be as important for you as it is for him, if you have ambitions to become Lady Cavendish."

Bess did not deny her ambition. Instead, she stopped protesting and listened carefully.

"To become a privy councillor, Sir William must have the approval and backing of the other privy councillors—hence the dinner party. Since the lord high treasurer, William Paulet, is William's patron, he'll be amenable, as will his friend Parr, and of course William Herbert, Earl of Pembroke."

It was suddenly brought home to Bess just how important marriage was at the Tudor Court. One of Parr's sisters had become queen by marrying King Henry, while Parr's other sister had long been Countess of Pembroke by marrying William Herbert. Parr himself was about to wed Elizabeth Brooke, daughter of Lord Cobham, while Elizabeth's brother, Thomas, was espoused to Cavendish's daughter.

"Will you invite the wives to the dinner party?"

"Yes, indeed, Bess. The influence of a wife is quite often the driving force behind an important man. Take Privy Councillor Edward Seymour, Earl of Hertford. He made Ann Stanhope his countess. I hate her with a passion! She is a rabid bitch—jealous, avaricious, grasping—in short, just the kind of woman an ambitious man needs. Be extremely wary of her, Bess. On the other hand you need not worry about John Dudley's wife, Lady Warwick, or William Herbert's wife, Lady Pembroke, for they already know you from your visit to Chelsea."

"It sounds like even a simple dinner party can be filled with intrigue and back-stabbing. Perhaps I shouldn't attend," Bess said doubtfully.

"If you wish to be a successful player at the Tudor Court, you cannot be fainthearted. A woman with your brains and beauty could be an invaluable aid in Cavendish's climb to the ivory tower. You must partner him if you want the highest in the land to think of you and Cavendish as a couple."

"That is the last thing I want! My reputation would be ruined, for they all know he's a married man. Besides that, it would drive away any other suitors."

"Then I shall seat you next to someone

else at dinner. Let's see, the Earl of Shrewsbury is a widower and will need a partner."

"I've met the Earl of Shrewsbury. He was most kind to me when I appealed to him for help."

"Then we shall seat you next to him so that you can appeal to him again. He's an unknown factor. Since he's one of the few men in England who doesn't need money, he may not back William. Be sure to wear a gown that shows off your lovely breasts. Older men are notoriously ruttish."

That evening, as Bess walked through the Long Gallery with Frances Grey's brother, Lord Suffolk, who was escorting her to supper, she came face to face with Rogue Cavendish, who had just walked down the Strand from Whitehall.

"Bess, will you take supper with me?"

"Won't you join Lord Suffolk and me?" she invited graciously.

Cavendish fixed young Suffolk with a challenging glance. "Lord Dorset is looking for you."

Since Suffolk was no match for the masterful Cavendish, the youth excused himself.

"That was rather high-handed," Bess accused.

"Damned pup, always hanging after you. I want us to be alone."

"We certainly won't be alone in the dining hall."

"Dining hall?" he scoffed. "We'll take supper in your rooms, where we won't be disturbed."

"We could very easily be disturbed. You forget that I am lady-in-waiting to Frances, and she may need me."

"Hell's teeth, don't be so naive," he said, thoroughly amused. "When you are with me, Frances wouldn't dream of disturbing us. I'll order us some supper and join you upstairs shortly."

"You know where my rooms are?" Bess asked, mildly surprised.

"I should; I selected them for you."

As Bess watched him stride away down the Long Gallery, his words floated about her. Then she remembered Lady Frances's words from this morning: *I'll make sure you are not disturbed when you entertain a lover.* A suspicion came full-blown into her mind. The pair of them were in collusion. She had been brought to Suffolk House at Cavendish's bidding. Purely for the rogue's convenience! Blazing anger almost consumed her.

As Bess paced about her chambers, she practiced the things she would say to him. Tonight would be the showdown. Tonight she would take her revenge for the hurt he had inflicted on her two long years ago. He was nothing but a rake who was still plotting her seduction. Well, tonight was the night that *Sir Bloody William* would meet his match!

Bess went down on her knees before her trunk and searched its contents until she found the infamous letter he had sent her. She stuffed the two halves into the bosom of her new gown, arming herself for the battle that was to come. When a low knock came, she flew to the door and flung it wide. "You scurvy bastard!"

The tall footman holding the heavy tray begged her pardon. The pageboy carrying the flagon of wine gave her an impish grin. "Put them over there," she ordered loftily, refusing to show the slightest chagrin. Cavendish arrived before the servants departed, which prevented Bess from hurling a passionate curse at his head.

She watched in utter amazement as he coolly closed the door and turned the key in the lock. "You look magnificent tonight, my beauty."

"No doubt that's because I'm in a towering rage," she said silkily.

"No doubt." His dark eyes filled with amusement, and her temper flared higher because he looked so devilishly pleased with himself.

"Tell me, *Sir William,* just when was it that you and Lady Frances decided I would become your mistress? I don't recall being consulted in the matter."

"Damn it, Bess, I'm trying to court you. I couldn't run round to the Zouches' and woo you under Margaret's long, prudish nose."

"But Frances won't blink an eye at your lechery. How very convenient for you. Perhaps she's always allowed you to bring your whores to Suffolk House?"

"Bess, stop this! You know damned well I don't want you for my whore."

"That, sir, is a barefaced lie! If I agreed you'd make me your whore this very night. You are not free to make me your wife, so whore it must be!"

"Bess, there's a world of difference between a mistress and a whore, as well you know."

Bess was on the verge of tears. Never once had he told her he loved her, never once had he told her he wanted her for his wife. She allowed her temper to explode. It was the only thing that kept her tears at bay. "There's no difference! Both accept payment for sexual favors! You have compromised me by bringing me to Suffolk House. Damn you! Damn you! I refuse to stay here under these circumstances!"

"Bess, stop being ridiculous; you know you're better off here at Suffolk House."

Though Bess knew it very well, she raved on at him, cataloguing all her grievances against him. Rogue masked the amusement in his eyes and allowed her to get it all out of her system. She stormed on, her hands on her hips, tossing her flaming hair.

When she began to pant from her exertions, it aroused a towering lust in him. Truly, she was the most beautiful, passionate creature he had ever seen. He was mesmerized, watching her work herself up to a climax. She didn't know it, but she needed a damned good fucking.

Rogue pulled her gently into his arms and

brushed the damp hair from her temples. "Are you finished, sweetheart?"

She was breathless. "I've barely started!"

He tightened his arms so that her breasts were crushed against his hard chest. "I have a present for you." He reached into his doublet and took out a flat velvet jewel case. Then he heard the crackle of parchment inside her gown. "What's that?"

"It's the last present you gave me, you knave!"

When he quirked an eyebrow, she reached down between her breasts, pulled out the torn letter, and thrust it at him. "Rogue Cavendish, once upon a time I trusted you completely. When the entire world was against me, I wrote to you, begging for your help. I put my entire faith in you, and you let me down. When I got your letter, I couldn't believe it. I wanted to die!" Tears flooded her eyes in spite of her resolve.

He took the letter and read the words he had penned. "What did you do?"

"I coped!"

"How?"

"I got angry!" Suddenly she was laughing through her tears. Anger always seemed to be her most reliable refuge, and she was finding comfort in it once again.

He swept her up into his arms, high against his heart, and carried her to a deep cushioned chair before the fire. "Bess, I adore you. I swear on my life I'll never let you down again. Give me a second chance—give me your love and your trust once more, and in return I will strive to give you everything you've ever wanted."

She gave him a level look. "Even if I decided to let you court me, I would never commit adultery with you."

He ground his teeth in frustration. "Why won't you sleep with me?" he demanded.

"Because you'd give me a baby, of course, and I won't be shamed in the eyes of the world!"

His deep laugh rolled over her. "Bess, you are absolutely priceless! I've never seen a woman so ripe for loving, yet your practical, shrewd head rules your heart and your body. Well, at least we are honest with each other, which is more than most couples are. I'll wait until you're ready to give yourself to me. I let you go once—I'll be damned if I'll do it again!"

"Do you promise that you won't try to seduce me anymore?"

"Of course I'll try to seduce you, but I will stalk you patiently till I have you secure. In any case, we won't have to wait long; my wife is dying—"

Bess quickly put her fingers over his lips to silence him. "Never, never wish for her death, William. Your conscience would plague you forever."

"I have no conscience," he said sardonically.

"But I have! I couldn't live with myself if my happiness depended upon another woman's misfortune."

"I'll never speak of her again. Our time together is too precious to waste on unhappy thoughts. Life is for living, and laughing, and loving. Open your present."

Bess gasped with appreciation at the sheer beauty of the amethyst necklace. "I can't accept this," she said, running a finger over the sparkling stones.

"You can and you will. I'm a rich man, Bess. Don't deny me the pleasure of giving you things I know you long for. I enjoy being generous. I want to give you the whole world." He took the necklace, fastened it about her throat, then kissed her nape, which was usually hidden beneath her glorious hair.

"You are trying to seduce me!" Bess accused. She was no longer blazing mad at him, but she had no intention of giving in to him, or even forgiving him.

"Mea culpa, sweetheart, but I'll allow you to have supper before I demand my reward."

She saw that his eyes were alight with wicked amusement. "You are a damned rogue!"

"There is almost nothing you can say about me, good or bad, that isn't true. Indeed, I am a rogue and a scoundrel, but that makes me devilishly attractive, don't you think?"

Bess decided that Cavendish was far too cocksure of himself and resolved to put him firmly in his place. She climbed from his knee and looked him directly in the eyes. "That may be true, Sir William, but you are not the only attractive man at Court. If you wish to become my suitor, you will have to join the line. If I receive an offer of marriage, I intend to consider it seriously."

Her words inflamed him. He had to crush down the urge to push her back on the rug and ravish her right here upon the floor, marking her as his forever. She was the most infuriating female he had ever encountered, but she was also the most intoxicating, and he was willing to bet that when he did finally make her his, the wait would be passionately rewarding.

TWELVE

The night of the dinner party, Bess chose a purple velvet gown with a low décolletage to show off her amethysts. The billowing bishop sleeves were slashed with rose-colored silk, and she knew she had never looked so splendid in her life.

"Undo these bloody corset strings and fasten them up looser, Bess," Lady Frances begged.

Bess obliged and helped her into a gown of deep crimson. As Frances opened a jewel coffer and selected rubies, Bess looked through the tall windows, excited as a small child who was attending her first party. The river was congested with the grand barges of their guests. She identified the Shrewsbury barge by its device: the great white Talbot hound. She also recognized Thomas Seymour's barge because it flew the flag of admiral of the fleet.

Then she gasped as she recognized the royal barge.

"You didn't invite the king, did you?" Bess cried.

"Of course not. All attention must focus on Cavendish tonight."

"But there is no mistaking the green and white Tudor barge."

"I invited the Lady Elizabeth, my dearest cousin."

"Really? I wonder if the princess will remember me."

"Elizabeth Tudor forgets nothing. I love her dearly, but never slight her, Bess, or she will hold the grudge to her dying day." Frances applied bright red lip rouge, then stood up and shook out her petticoats. "Now, remember, tonight Sir William and I are the host and hostess, while Henry will be your escort until you are seated at dinner. He's an expert at putting the proper name and title to a face, so be guided by Henry if you are unsure. We'll stand at the doors of the grand salon to greet the first guests, but I have learned it's best not to have a formal receiving line as they do at Court functions. The pecking order changes constantly, and tonight I wish to offend no one."

Henry Grey strolled in from his dressing room. "Dearest Frances, you cannot resist offending people. It's your only vice."

Frances rolled her eyes at Bess. "Little he knows!"

Henry smiled good-naturedly at Bess. "See what I mean? She doesn't even know when she's doing it. Are you lovely ladies ready to go down?"

When Cavendish saw Bess, the look of appreciation that warmed his eyes told her not only how beautiful she looked but how special she was to him. Apprehension made her mouth dry. More than anything in the world she wanted to acquit herself well tonight. She longed to be an asset, rather than a liability to him, but she was only a farmer's daughter out of her depth in a room awash with nobility.

She lifted her chin. *You are Bess of Hardwick— just as good, if not better, than any in the land!* She straightened to her full height of five foot three inches and forced a brilliant smile to her lips. Then Henry Grey was introducing her to people, and she somehow found her tongue and acknowledged them. The names seemed to go in one ear and straight out the other, until Bess took a firm grip on herself and focused her attention.

"I'd like you to meet William Parr, Marquess of Northampton, and his bride-to-be, Lady Elizabeth Brooke."

Lud, there are so many Williams and Elizabeths that I shall never keep them straight. Then she realized this was the queen's brother and therefore one of the most important men in the land.

William Parr cocked an eyebrow at his friend Henry Grey. "So this is *she?* Splendor of God, she's spectacular! No wonder Rogue has kept her under wraps until tonight."

Bess blinked rapidly as she realized the queen's brother was extolling her beauty. That she had no rank mattered little to him. She was a desirable woman; he was a man. His response was immediate, and so was hers: They liked each other on sight.

Behind them came Lord and Lady Cobham. "I have you and Sir William on the guest list for the wedding; do say you'll come," Lady Cobham urged Bess, who then realized these were the parents of Elizabeth Brooke. She was annoyed that Cavendish's friends thought of them as a couple. *Has the damned rogue told them I'm his mistress?* From the corner of her eye, Bess caught sight of a beautiful dark-haired girl who was kissing Cavendish. She stiffened immediately and stared hard at her rival, preparing to do battle. The young woman laughed up at William with worshipful eyes, and Bess ground her teeth when he laughed back in a most familiar fashion. As the female made her curtsy to Henry Grey, Bess was shocked at how young she appeared.

"May I present Catherine Cavendish, Sir William's daughter, and her espoused husband, Thomas Brooke?"

"I've been longing to meet you," the young woman said to Bess. "Father has told me how special you are to him."

A tender smile suffused Bess's face, and a wave of relief swept over her as she realized that the lovely laughing girl was William's daughter. Catherine was the spitting image of him.

"I'm so nervous," Cathy confided. "This is my first formal dinner party."

Bess's heart went out to her. "Don't be nervous, darling. You look so grown up. I know your father is very proud of you. As well he should be." Bess suddenly felt very mature, and her confidence soared.

There was a flurry of attention as all eyes were drawn to a tall, slim figure gowned in white. The Lady Elizabeth Tudor with two attendants came forward regally. She acknowledged Cavendish with a cool nod but gave Lady Frances a kiss of greeting, and Bess heard the princess say, "Thank you, Frances, for inviting me. I shall not forget your kindness." Then her eyes were on Bess, eagerly acknowledging their friendship before all those present.

Bess sank into a curtsy, and Elizabeth immediately raised her and swept her aside so they could speak privately. "Is there somewhere we can talk? After dinner?"

"Of course. I have my own suite of rooms, Your Grace." Bess was amazed at how tall Elizabeth was. Slim as a reed, she still had no breasts to speak of, but she carried herself like a queen, and her mass of fine-spun, red-gold hair was like a cloak of light about her narrow shoulders. Though Bess knew that the princess was very young, her demeanor and poise were that of a sophisticated court lady, worldly-wise beyond her years. Only the excitement glittering in her amber eyes, which she could not suppress, betrayed her tender years.

The Lady Elizabeth, who was accompanied by a lady-in-waiting and Sir William St. Loe, her own personal captain of the guard, spoke softly to Bess before she rejoined them. "When I give you the signal, we'll give my attendants the slip and go upstairs to your private chambers." The princess then moved off to greet the Dudleys and the Herberts, who stood high in the Tudor pecking order.

The guests were now arriving en masse, and Frances Grey decided she had stood at the entrance long enough and it was time for everyone to mingle. She took Cavendish by the arm and signaled the liveried footmen to offer the guests wine before they went in to dinner.

As an elderly nobleman approached Bess, Henry Grey bowed formally. "Allow me to present—"

"The lady and I need no introduction, Dorset; we are already acquainted."

Bess sank down in a graceful curtsy, stunned that the powerful earl had recognized her. "Lord Shrewsbury, I owe you a great debt of gratitude."

Shrewsbury's shrewd eyes twinkled. "I take it the legal matter was settled in your favor, Mistress Barlow?"

"Indeed it was, my lord, and I thank you from the bottom of my heart."

The Fifth Earl of Shrewsbury raised Bess up and gallantly kissed her fingers. "It was my pleasure. It's not often a man of my age can *serve* a beautiful young woman and make her happy."

The double entendre showed a ribald wit,

and Bess's low, sultry laugh told him she appreciated it. "I believe we are dinner partners tonight, my lord, so once again you will make me happy," Bess said, taking his arm.

"Then I warrant I'll be the envy of every red-blooded male in the room. This is my daughter-in-law, Lady Gertrude Talbot, and my son, whom I believe you've already met."

Startled, Bess looked up into George Talbot's ice blue eyes and found them undressing her. He wore an expensive black velvet tunic and a heavy gold chain studded with Persian sapphires that matched his eyes. His dark hair curled about his collar, longer than the current fashion set by the king. She looked away quickly to keep herself from uttering a biting retort that would perhaps alienate the powerful Earl of Shrewsbury. Her glance fell on Talbot's wife, and she immediately saw that the plain-faced girl was breeding. Bess blushed as Robin Dudley's words from years ago rushed back to her: *He'll be an old man by the time he gets some!*

She glanced quickly at the tall, dark, arrogant Talbot and saw that he had read her mind. The corner of his sensual mouth quirked, and Bess's blush deepened.

"We meet again, Mistress Elizabeth Barlow." He used her widowed name. "How are you faring?"

"I am well, my lord."

His appreciative glance lifted from her gown to her face, lingering on her mouth, then her eyes. "Blooming, in fact. London suits you, mistress. It is a place that rewards ambition."

To cover her embarrassment Bess spoke to Gertrude. "I am delighted to meet you. The Lady Elizabeth has always spoken so highly of you, my lady." The princess had done no such thing, of course. She said they had shackled George to the wealthy Earl of Rutland's daughter, Gertrude, to safeguard the Talbot fortune! Bess examined the young woman closely. She had such a petulant look on her face that Bess felt sorry for the child she was carrying.

After dinner Lady Frances encouraged the guests to talk and wander freely about Suffolk House. There was to be no masque or entertainment to distract those invited, but she provided strolling musicians and card tables, since many a deal had been struck while gambling.

Bess found Frances and Cavendish conversing with Henry Grey and William Parr. "The dinner seemed to be a great success. Is all going well?"

"I believe it's in the bag, darling. The only one we couldn't manipulate was Shrewsbury, but you are such a clever girl, you have him eating out of your hand."

"I think he's attracted to me," Bess confided in a whisper. Each of the three men ran appreciative eyes over her low-cut gown and luscious perfumed breasts, then exchanged knowing glances.

"I wonder why?" asked the queen's brother with a perfectly straight face.

Bess gasped as a pair of strong arms slipped about her waist and she was pulled back against a hard male body.

"Trust you three to monopolize the most seductive woman in the room. I insist you share her; isn't that what friends are for?"

Bess swiftly extracted herself from the admiral's bold embrace and instinctively moved closer to Cavendish.

"A friend doesn't poach on a man's private preserve, Thomas," Cavendish warned.

Bess was suddenly furious. She was no man's private preserve, and the moment she was alone with Cavendish she would tell him so.

"Of course he does," Tom Seymour said, laughing. "In the hunt all partridge are fair game."

Fury almost choked Bess. She guarded her virtue scrupulously, yet here was Tom Seymour speaking as if she were a strumpet. "Not all quarry are easy game, my lord."

Seymour bowed his golden head gallantly. "Forgive me? There is just something about vivid redheads that makes other women seem colorless drabs."

"Curse you for a damned knave, Thomas!" Lady Frances struck him with her fan, pretending to take offense, and everyone laughed as the moment's tension melted away.

Thomas became serious, something he seldom did. "I'll use my influence with the king to appoint you to the privy council, William, if in return you use your influence with the other members to get me appointed also."

Bess listened intently to the methods these courtiers used to further their ambition. She soaked up everything like a sponge, sensing that the lessons she was learning would prove invaluable. When she glanced across the room and intercepted the Lady Elizabeth's signal, all seemed unreal for a moment. Was she actually here, a lady-in-waiting to the king's niece, rubbing shoulders with the queen's brother, fending off advances from the king's brother-in-law, and secretly conspiring with a royal princess?

Bess suddenly smiled. It seemed that anything she wanted was within her grasp. Perhaps all she had to do was reach out her hands and the world would be hers! Bess nodded her head in the direction of the grand salon and slipped away from the others, confident that Elizabeth Tudor would follow her lead.

When Bess closed the door of her private suite, the princess looked about the chamber with glittering amber eyes. "Did you know that my father leased Suffolk House for my mother before they were married, so they could be lovers here? It's only a few steps down the Strand from Whitehall. I picture her awaiting him in bed night after night. I was most likely conceived here! I wonder how many times he made love to her before he planted me inside her?"

Bess was momentarily shocked at Elizabeth's avid interest in the scandalous sexual encounters of her parents. "Suffolk House has a fascinating history."

"That is patently obvious. I didn't come up here to exchange platitudes. I want to know what it feels like to be bedded!"

"Why are you asking me, Your Grace?"

"Because since we last met you have been wedded, bedded, and widowed! Prithee, who the hell else can I ask?"

"My husband was even younger than I, and he was ill." Bess suddenly felt ashamed of her ignorance. She was covered with shame that, although she had been a bride, she had little experience of the marital rites.

"Curse you, Bess Hardwick, we swore a pledge to trust in ourselves and trust each other—*no matter what!*"

"Your Grace, I swear I would tell you if I knew. I have never breathed it to a living soul, but my marriage was not consummated!"

Elizabeth stared at Bess, completely incredulous. "Your husband never fucked you?" Her brows drew together in consternation. "What about Cavendish?"

Splendor of God, there it was again, the implication that she and Cavendish were lovers. "We have never sinned. Sir William is a married man."

"That doesn't stop men; it certainly never stopped my father!"

"It stops me," Bess said quietly.

"Hell's teeth, I could shake you!"

Bess's humor reasserted itself. "So could Rogue Cavendish."

Elizabeth joined in her laughter. "Oh, Bess, are you in love? Does your pulse race madly when you see him? Do you dream about him ravishing you? Does your blood rush through your veins like wildfire when he draws close, and do you want to scream with excitement when he touches you?"

"Aye, I'm in love, or at least lust," Bess said slowly, "and so are you."

"Ah, God, 'tis more than love, 'tis a divine madness! Has he ever kissed your breasts? Have you been naked together?"

Bess watched with alarm as Elizabeth became aroused. Her eyes glittered gold and she was panting with desire. Bess knew exactly what was happening to the princess, because it happened to herself when she longed for Rogue Cavendish.

"Has he taught you how to masturbate to safely pleasure yourselves?"

Bess had never heard the word before, but she knew it must be something prurient and erotic. "My God, you once told me you had learned caution. Who is it you are in love with?"

Elizabeth laughed. "I have enough caution not to divulge his name, even to you. I should have known that you and I, being so similar, are at exactly the same place at the same time on the mysterious road to womanhood."

"Nay, we are not, Your Grace. I am five years older than you—you should not even know about these things. Is it Robin Dudley who has tainted your innocence?"

"Robin is a callow youth," Elizabeth said with scorn. "I am in love with an older man of the world. I have chosen him for my husband. There, I've said it! You are the only one in the universe who knows my secret. Bess, swear on your life that the moment Cavendish takes your virginity and you become lovers, you will come and tell me what it is like. I have no one else I can ask, and I shall die if I don't soon find out!"

"Your Grace, promise me you will do nothing reckless at such a tender age; it could ruin your life!"

"I may be five years younger in actual age, but I am five hundred years older in wisdom. We will go down now." Elizabeth Tudor spoke so regally, Bess had no choice but to obey. The royal princess would not be lectured; she made it crystal clear she would do exactly as she wished.

As Bess rejoined Lady Frances she was on the horns of a dilemma and pondered what she should do. If the king's daughter was being compromised by some unscrupulous courtier, was it not Bess's duty to report it before the princess was ruined? Yet, on the other hand, when Elizabeth had confided in her as a trusted friend, how could she betray her? Bess weighed the alternatives and found them both unsatisfactory.

"What does *masturbate* mean?" Bess asked softly.

"God's balls, for a widow you are woefully ignorant. It is when you take a man in hand, which they all need from time to time." Frances waved her fan toward an aging earl. "He's too old, and yon fairy fellow is too limp-wristed to masturbate." Frances roared with laughter at her own wit.

Bess changed the subject. "I shouldn't have come. Everyone thinks of Cavendish and me as a couple, even though they all know he's a married man."

"They all know he's about to become a widower, and they see that he has already chosen someone to be the next Lady Cavendish, who is capable of becoming his social and intellectual equal. All are impressed and immensely relieved."

Cavendish, accompanied by the Earl of Shrewsbury, joined them. "I shall take my leave of you lovely ladies, and thank you for the invitation, Lady Frances," the earl said. "I cannot remember when I had a more stimulating dinner partner. Cavendish, I shall see you at Whitehall next week."

Bess rewarded the earl with a radiant smile and a curtsy. Suddenly she felt someone staring at her and lifted her eyes to meet George Talbot's. For a brief moment his gaze was predatory, as if given the chance he would devour her. Then he smiled as if the two of them shared a secret. "It was my pleasure to find you here at Suffolk House, mistress. Perhaps our paths will cross again in the near future."

Not if I can help it! Bess returned his smile. "None of us knows what the future holds."

"May fortune follow you." His tone was far too intimate.

Bess lowered her lashes. "And you, my lord."

Before the Talbots were barely out of earshot, Frances commented, "Did you see that whey-faced Gertrude was wearing a rope of the famous Talbot pearls? Young Talbot soon got his mare in foal once he got her to bed."

"She has such a haughty air, her face would crack if she smiled. I feel sorry for her," Bess murmured.

"You must be mad. When Shrewsbury sticks his spoon in the wall, Gertrude will become a countess and her husband will inherit a king's ransom. The Talbots have ten times the wealth of the Tudors, to say nothing of at least eight more ropes of priceless pearls in their jewel coffers."

"I much prefer my amethysts," Bess declared, suddenly glad that the highest in the land linked her with William. This time she saw the hunger in Cavendish's eyes and loved the strange sexual power it made her feel.

One by one the guests began to take their leave. A gentleman approached Bess and bowed elegantly. "Permit me to introduce myself, madam. I am St. Loe, captain of the guard to the Lady Elizabeth. I am afraid I cannot find her, and the royal barge is ready to depart."

Bess smiled at him. "She has given you the slip."

"Yes, madam. Something she delights in doing."

"Perhaps you should guard her more carefully," Bess hinted with concern.

"Lady Elizabeth hates being monitored with a passion. She has little freedom and even less privacy. I try to guard her without being intrusive."

"I think I know where she might be, my lord. I will relay your message to Her Grace."

Bess hurried through the grand salon and up the staircase that led to her own private suite. As the door swung open, Elizabeth and Thomas Seymour sprang apart.

"You intrude!"

"Forgive me," Bess declared, trying to mask the shock that must have registered on her face. "Your captain of the guard asked me to inform you that the royal barge is ready to depart."

"Then let it depart!" Elizabeth looked ready to defy the world. "The admiral will escort me safely home aboard his own barge."

The golden god opened his mouth to admonish the princess, who was his niece by marriage. "Elizabeth, that would not be wise." He stroked her hair with a possessive hand. "Be a good girl." Tom Seymour looked Bess directly in the eye, then gave her a suggestive wink of conspiracy. "We are all friends here, who know the value of discretion."

Seymour departed, and the two young women faced each other like protagonists ready to fight. Elizabeth, who had the palest of skins, was flushed and her eyes were fever-bright. Suddenly, the blood left her cheeks and her haughty stare became beseeching.

"Can I truly trust you, Bess Hardwick?"

She supposed to Elizabeth she would always be Bess Hardwick. In that moment Bess's heart went out to her. Elizabeth Tudor had no one in the world in whom she could place her trust. Bess sank to the carpet, her skirts forming a pool of deep purple.

"Your Grace, you can trust me with your life—*no matter what!*"

Elizabeth sagged with relief and came forward with outstretched hands. As their fingers clasped tightly, she said, "Someday I shall repay your loyalty to me. I have never forgotten that you were the one to warn me of Catherine Parr's ambition to become queen."

"Is she a dreadful stepmother?" Bess asked with compassion.

"She would be, had I not learned to manipulate her. We have learned to give each other what we need. She lets me stay at Court, and in return I make her look like a devoted stepmother. I translate French into English for her and English prayers into Latin, making her look both educated and pious. In return she has made it possible for me to have my own tutors. She is working on my father to have my sister, Mary, and me declared legitimate again, so she has her uses."

"Does she exercise great influence over the king?"

"Yes, but not by sexual congress, as she thought before they were wed. She is more nurse than lover these days; my father's temper is intolerable. He is a selfish, monstrous tyrant, and Catherine has aged ten years in as many months trying to appease him. Like all his other wives, she is afraid of him."

"You cannot appease a tyrant," Bess said quietly.

"Exactly! Thank God I don't need to." A wild peal of laughter escaped Elizabeth. "I have Catherine to do it for me!"

THIRTEEN

Cavendish expected to escort Bess to the wedding of William Parr and Elizabeth Brooke, but she refused him. "It is all right to court me in private, but certainly not in public. I shall accompany the Greys," Bess told him firmly.

Although William Parr was the queen's brother, because of the divorce scandal the wedding had to be a private one rather than a lavish Court affair.

"The bride looks lovely," Bess murmured to Frances, wishing it were her own wedding.

"Elizabeth Brooke has a very shrewd head on her shoulders. Today, not only did she become Marchioness of Northampton, but the clever little jade made herself sister-in-law to the Queen of England. How's that for sleeping your way to the top?"

Bess's low, sultry laugh caught the attention

of the bride's eldest brother, Harry, heir to the Cobham title and fortune. He begged an introduction, then danced attendance on her throughout the celebration. Young Harry Brooke suddenly decided he was in the market for a wife, and the vivacious flame-haired widow made his blood thicken in his veins.

Cavendish seethed quietly as he sat with his daughter, Cathy, who was espoused to Harry Brooke's younger brother, Thomas. As Bess and Harry danced down the length of the ballroom, Cathy said, "You have acquired marvelous taste in ladies, Father. I liked her the moment I saw her."

"She had the same effect on me, sweetheart." William recalled the first time he laid eyes on her from the Suffolk House terrace, and suddenly he wanted to choke his friend Harry Brooke.

"Why don't you ask Bess to dance?"

"Last time she left me standing in the middle of the dance floor, and the little hellcat wouldn't hesitate to do it again."

A short time later Bess danced the galliard in the arms of Sir John Thynne. The couple were engrossed in deep conversation, seemingly oblivious to anyone else in the room. "Who is that gentleman? He looks familiar," Cathy asked.

"Too bloody familiar," Cavendish muttered. "He is my good friend John Thynne, Lord Edward Seymour's property agent. He's building his own country house at Brentford."

"I hope he isn't looking for a wife," Cathy said innocently.

Cavendish shot to his feet. "Come, sweetheart, I'll introduce you to him." When the dance ended, Sir William greeted Sir John warmly. "John, may I present my daughter, Mistress Catherine Cavendish. She's betrothed to young Thomas Brooke, but I'm sure he won't object if Cathy dances with you."

As Sir John, ever the gentleman, bowed to his friend's daughter, Cathy and Bess exchanged a highly amused glance. When the music started, Sir John murmured politely, "Would you do me the honor, mistress?"

Sir William bowed formally to Bess and solemnly echoed the question. "Would you do me the honor, mistress?"

Bess bit an amused lip. "I thought older men preferred to sit on the sidelines. Still, it is a coranto, a rather staid measure. I don't suppose you'll do yourself an injury."

"When you danced the galliard, you gave a shocking display of petticoats and lace stockings."

For once Rogue Cavendish didn't seem amused, so Bess tried to make him laugh. "Isn't that the whole point of the galliard, to titillate? John is stronger than he looks; I wondered if he'd be up to it."

"He was *up*, all right, as was every other male who looked at you. I thought your breasts were going to fall out of that low-cut gown!"

"Is that what your eyes were riveted upon?" She gave him a dazzling smile. "Your jealousy would be flattering if it weren't so ridiculous. All we spoke of were houses."

"A subject that stirs your passion! Did he invite you to Brentford?"

"As a matter of fact he did."

"And did you accept?" he asked dangerously.

Bess lifted her chin. "As a matter of fact I did." The music stopped. "Excuse me, Sir William. I promised Harry Brooke the next dance."

The hour was late by the time the raucous bedding of the newlyweds was celebrated, and at last the guests, flown with wine, began to take their noisy leave. As Bess and Henry helped an unsteady Frances climb up into the Greys' coach, she felt a pair of powerful arms seize her from behind in the darkness. Before she could cry out, Bess found herself being lifted into a carriage emblazoned with the Cavendish stags. With blazing eyes she watched Rogue Cavendish slide in beside her and slam the door closed. He was not his usual laughing self, and Bess should have been warned by his dark mood. Instead, her temper flashed.

"Is this an abduction? Will you carry me off and rape me?" she challenged.

"God's bones, you invite rape!"

She flew at him, intending to rake his face with her fingernails. He caught her wrists and held them tight as iron manacles. "Stop acting like a common trollop, or I'll take you over my knee."

"Stop acting as if you own me, for you don't!"

"Splendor of God, it's time I put my brand on you!" He dragged her into his arms and crushed her mouth with his.

Bess bit down on his lip and had the satisfaction of hearing him utter a filthy curse. He did not allow her to free herself from his embrace, however.

"You led those men on to make shameful advances today!"

"There is nothing shameful about them. Their intentions are perfectly honorable. Both have marriage in mind; they are that kind of men."

"*I* am that kind of man!"

Bess knew he was consumed with jealousy. It was the closest he had come to promising her marriage, and she reveled in the feeling of power it gave her.

"I have marked you for mine, and I won't allow other men to fondle you." This time his mouth was so possessive and demanding, Bess opened her lips with a pleasurable little sigh and allowed his tongue to ravish her.

His hot mouth trailed down her throat, and his lips traced the curves of her breasts where they swelled from her gown. Then suddenly he had her breasts bared, cradling them in the palms of his big hands as his tongue curled about a taut nipple and drew it into his mouth like a cherry.

Bess cried out at the unbelievable sensations he was arousing in her. Her blood was on fire and she went wild, offering him her other breast to feast upon.

"Have you any idea what you do to me?" His deep voice was hoarse and ragged.

"Tell me," she invited huskily.

"Rather, I'll show you." He took her fingers and drew them to his swollen groin. He was too big to cup in one hand, and Bess eagerly brought up her other hand to cover his hardness. The moment she touched him, his phallus thrust forward. He lifted her skirt and slid his hand boldly up her leg. When he touched the bare flesh on the inside of her thigh where her stocking ended, Bess shuddered involuntarily.

"Don't, William! I'm still virgin."

"What the devil are you talking about?" he growled.

"My husband was only a boy, William; I'm not sure the marriage was consummated properly. In any case I still *feel* virgin."

"Bess, you never cease to amaze me!" William was momentarily stunned, then he became skeptical. "Are you sure this isn't just the wine talking?"

Bess wished she hadn't mentioned her virginity. "I confess I've had far too much to drink, and it has made me behave shamelessly. Fortunately, I know you won't take advantage of me."

The carriage jolted to a stop, and William withdrew his hand as a liveried Suffolk House footman opened the carriage door. Cavendish blocked the servant's view to give Bess a chance to pull her bodice up over her naked breasts, then he climbed out and turned to lift Bess to the ground.

The Greys' coach pulled up beside them, and Henry climbed out. "Bess, my dear, would you help me with Frances? She's a little unsteady."

"I'm not unsteady; I'm randy as a nanny goat. Weddings always have that effect on me! How about you two?" Frances winked owlishly at Bess and William.

As the footman stood at attention, pretending to be both blind and deaf, the humor of the situation struck them and they began to laugh. "She's right," William whispered in Bess's ear. "I'm randy as a billy goat. I'd better sleep at Court tonight."

"Henry, I need a good bedding, and Bess, I need you to get me out of these bloody corsets!" Frances declared at the top of her lungs.

The winter season proved to be the busiest in years. November 1546 did not have enough nights to accommodate all the masques, balls, and entertainments in which the nobility wished to indulge.

Cavendish had to journey to Canterbury before winter made the roads impassable. His prime occupation was ferreting out the wealth of the religious orders, which they were adept at hiding. In his absence Bess had many would-be suitors, who vied with each other to partner her when she attended masques thrown by the Dudleys or the Herberts. Yet none of them captured her heart or had the physically devastating effect on her that

Cavendish wrought, and by the time he returned in early December, Bess was counting the days.

When Cavendish arrived at Suffolk House, Frances invited him to dine and asked him to join them at Hertford House in Cannon Row. "Edward Seymour and his delightful countess are giving a play tonight to honor the king and queen. I wouldn't miss it; I need a good laugh."

"I don't believe it's a comedy, my dear," Henry ventured.

"Don't be obtuse, Henry, it isn't the play that will amuse me but the maneuvering of that rabid bitch, Ann!"

"I thank you for dinner, Frances, but I believe I will forego the play." He had just come from an interview with His Majesty. Cavendish sat across from Bess, devouring her with his eyes. He could have been eating roast dog for all the attention he paid to his food.

Bess was gowned in pale lavender velvet slashed with silver. She wore the amethysts he had given her, and she knew it pleased him. Bess watched his eyes linger on her half-exposed breasts, then rise hungrily to her mouth. As she watched him she sensed that he wanted to tell her something in private. Suddenly, she didn't want to attend the play she had been looking forward to all week. When dinner was over Bess pressed her fingers to her temples. "I have the headache; perhaps I shouldn't attend the play either."

Lady Frances stood and shook out her voluminous midnight-blue skirts. "Of course you shouldn't, darling." Frances lifted an arched brow at Cavendish. "Rogue has an infallible cure for the headache—something about putting your head between your legs, or was it putting his head between your legs—anyway, it's something delightfully ingenious."

"Frances, you're bloody incorrigible!" Henry rebuked, hurrying her from the room before she said something even more outrageous.

As Cavendish followed Bess up the gilt staircase, he was afforded a glimpse of heliotrope petticoats and stockings. For a moment he was stunned at the outrageously bold color of her underclothes. Such garments were obviously not meant to be hidden but displayed for some man's eyes. Immediately jealous as fire, he wondered whom Bess had been seeing in his absence or, more to the point, whom had she intended to meet tonight?

The moment they entered her private rooms, Cavendish locked the door. When Bess opened her mouth to protest, he said, "You need to be kept under lock and key, I'd say, by the look of your undergarments."

"What in the world are you talking about?"

He grabbed her hand and pulled her before her mirror. "In that pale lavender and silver you look sweet and innocent as an angel." He lifted her skirt to reveal her ankles. "But beneath the gown, you are dressed like a harlot!"

Determined not to lose her temper the

moment they were alone together, she laughed up at him in the mirror. "And have you much experience with harlots, Sir Cavendish?"

He groaned and slid possessive arms about her. "Did you go to Brentford?"

"Of course." Bess saw no reason to lie.

"And?"

"It's going to be lovely. Sir John has a feel for houses."

"To hell with houses! Did he feel you, that's what I want to know? Or did you hold him off with that fictitious virginity tale?"

Her temper flew up the chimney. Bess spun around from the mirror to face him. "Sir John Thynne is a gentleman, which is more than I can say for you!"

Cavendish made a rude noise. "You forget he's a friend of mine." He refused to believe that she preferred Thynne to himself. "It's his great country house that attracts you, isn't it? Is that what you want, Bess?"

She drew back her hand to slap his arrogant face, but he seized her arm and pulled her roughly into his embrace. Panting furiously, she said, "I gave up an evening in the company of the King of England to be with you tonight. I must be mad!"

"I smell better than Henry Tudor." Rogue's mouth came down on hers in a kiss that branded her as his. He lifted his mouth a fraction from her lips and murmured, "I just came from an interview with him."

"The king?" Suddenly her eyes widened with anticipation.

"He just confirmed my seat on the privy council."

"William!" Bess's arms went up around his neck, and he lifted her from her feet and swung her about the room. "Who else knows?"

"No one but you, Bess. You are the first."

Her heart melted with joy. "Why didn't you tell me right away, instead of accusing me of dalliance? I swear you provoke my temper apurpose."

"Perhaps I do. Anger arouses your passion." He slid his arm beneath her knees and lifted her high so that the pale lavender velvet fell back, revealing her legs.

"You'll ruin my new gown!"

"Then let me remove it. You're longing to show off your harlot's undergarments anyway."

"They are perfectly respectable!"

"Then show me." As he kissed her, his knowing fingers unfastened the back of her gown, and when he set her feet to the carpet, her dress fell in a pool about her.

Bess gasped and scooped up the precious gown to cover herself. "You are far too experienced with women to suit me, Rogue Cavendish."

"Bess, my sweet, you are a widow," he reminded her.

"But I told you I'm—" Bess bit her lip, knowing he didn't believe her.

He pried the dress from her fingers and laid it carefully across a chair. "Then you should be thankful that I am experienced," he said softly. "I know how to give pleasure

203

without any risk to you." He carried her to the love seat before the fire and sat down with her in his lap. His eyes were alight with devilry. "I brought you a present. All you have to do is find it."

Her eyes searched his face and then his person. She smiled as her fingers unfastened his doublet and she reached inside. He shrugged out of it, and as Bess ran her hands over his fine linen shirt, he murmured, "Lower."

Her eyes dropped to the bulge between his legs. "You devil!"

He held her fast as she struggled to escape. "I'm teasing you, sweetheart. It's right here." He reached inside his shirt and placed a small velvet box in her hand.

Bess lifted the lid and gasped with delight. It was a ring set with a large amethyst surrounded by diamonds. "Oh, it's the most precious thing I've ever owned. William, I don't know what to say."

He slipped the ring onto her middle finger. "Then say it with kisses." He eased her back against the cushions and came over her in the dominant position. Bess offered up her mouth to him, letting him take what he wanted, what she wanted. She had no idea that his kisses would arouse an insatiable hunger in herself that must be quenched.

He unfastened the tiny busk she wore to cup and mold her breasts, and they spilled into his hands like ripe little melons. "Tell me these belong to me and no other man!" he demanded. His hot mouth laved the upper curves with kisses, then his tongue came out to lick and tease the rose-pink tips until they grew erect.

Bess loved the strange but deeply pleasurable sensations that suffused her body. His powerful hands and mouth made her wild with desire. Her passion began to mount so quickly, it alarmed her. As his fingers went to her waist to undo the tapes of her petticoat, she clutched at his hands to stay them before he stripped her naked. "I don't want to be nude!"

Her gasps told him that indeed she did, so long as he took all the responsibility. "You won't be nude; I'll let you keep on your stockings for propriety's sake."

Bess couldn't contain her mirth at the absurdity of his words, but when she lay before him clad only in heliotrope lace stockings that bared her creamy thighs and exposed her high mons topped with red-gold curls, the intense anticipation of what he would do to her banished her laughter.

His dark eyes licked over her flesh like a candle flame. "You have no idea how many times I've pictured you like this, but you are even lovelier than I dreamed." He looked at her with such adoration, he knew it would make her feel both beautiful and highly excited. When he finally reached out to touch the red curls, Bess gasped, "No!"

His fingers paused above her mons. "Yes!" he insisted, though his hand was not yet touching her. "Nature gave you a voluptuous body, Bess. I want you to enjoy it." His hand descended upon her and he held it there, giving her a chance to get used to his touch. Then he slowly pressed a fingertip against her woman's center.

Bess cried out, arching her back, inviting yet denying his bold advances.

He encouraged her, "Cry out your passion, sweetheart; it will give us both pleasure. I'm going to stroke you until your bud unfurls its petals. I'm going to make you bloom like a flower drenched with dew."

His words lured her in to taking the first tentative steps that would initiate her into the mystical, sensual rites of womanhood. His fingertip made slow circles around her sensitive flesh until it became moist. "I feel it pouting like a sulky child demanding more," he whispered.

Bess made little inarticulate cries as her pleasure mounted. Heat leapt from his fingertip, scalding her with a brand of excitement she'd never experienced before. Sensations like threads of fire spread up into her belly, and her breasts tingled deliciously.

"Hold your bud tightly closed until it's ready to burst open," he instructed, leaning forward and putting his mouth close to her ear.

The intimacy of his touching her on such a forbidden part of her body made her feel most wanton, yet incredibly she didn't want him to stop. Reclining before him with her legs apart rendered her completely vulnerable to his demands, yet she felt wickedly insatiable. Bess moaned and writhed as the threads of fire tightened. She gripped his free hand and brought it to her mouth, kissing then sucking on his fingers.

Suddenly, she felt her taut bud erupt, and then she felt herself bloom, unfurling hotly, darkly. Her woman's center felt as exotic as an orchid, drenched with diamond drops of dew. Bess cried out and bit his hand in a little frenzy of passion.

When his fingers felt her wetness, he gently slid one up inside her and, unbelievably, he encountered the barrier of her hymen. "My darling girl, you were telling me the truth!" William was stunned, then joy rose up in him, filling his heart with the fiercest love he had ever known.

Bess was enthralled with the erotic reaction of her body. It seemed inconceivable that a man's touch could bring such exquisite pleasure. "I was woefully ignorant," she murmured in wonder.

Cavendish enfolded her in his arms. "I want you to learn all your carnal knowledge from me." He'd never wanted to possess anyone or anything as much as he wanted Bess, but his craving was tempered by an overwhelming desire to protect her. He knew that she had crossed a vitally important threshold by allowing him to touch her intimately and bring her sexual pleasure. It showed that she was willing to put her trust in him. Not completely, of course, not yet, but enough to allow her strong sex drive to overcome her natural caution.

Shrewdly, he knew he must not abuse that

trust. He could not unleash the savage desire that had ridden him so long. He must exercise an iron self-control over his fierce hunger to ravish her and instead concentrate on giving her the pleasure without risk that he had promised.

He cupped her face in his hands and brought her mouth up to his. "You are so lovely, you stop the breath in my throat and slow the blood in my veins." He kissed her with great reverence, showing her how precious she was to him. Then he deepened the kiss and began to arouse her with his tongue.

Bess couldn't get enough of his kisses. His mouth was by turns soft and coaxing, then hard and demanding. She gave him back kiss for kiss, matching his ardor, yielding to his ravishing, which unleashed a ferocity that was both wild and sensual.

His powerful hands stroked down the length of her back, then up again, slipping around to caress her full, luscious breasts. "Let me show you what you look like in your amethysts and lace stockings."

Bess had forgotten she was still wearing them, and when he carried her to the mirror and placed her before it, she was shocked at her reflection. Her flaming hair was wildly disheveled, and she had never seen her naked breasts adorned with amethysts as if they belonged to some pagan goddess. The heliotrope stockings contrasted so vividly with her pale thighs and blazing mons that Bess blushed at the erotic vision staring back at her from the mirror.

She gasped as he went down on his knees before her, cupped her bare bottom with his hands, and brought her close to his mouth. He covered her creamy thighs with kisses, then blew softly upon her curls to separate them. The tip of his tongue unerringly found the bud at the top of her cleft, and he began to make love to her with his mouth.

Before Bess could protest, she became highly aroused and stared mesmerized into the mirror. She watched her fingers thread through his hair to hold his head to her hot center and saw her body arch with the unbelievable pleasure he gave her. A deep, sultry laugh escaped from her lips as she remembered what Frances had said. Unbelievably, Rogue's head was between her legs!

Bess cried his name over and over when she reached climax. She was unable to stand and slid down on her knees, sagged into his arms, and buried her face against his chest. When the room stopped spinning, she drew back and looked into his eyes.

"Am I very wicked?" she whispered.

"Bess, my darling, you are the most innocent yet the most passionate woman I have ever known."

A shocking thought suddenly struck her: *This is what the princess was talking about. My God, this is what the admiral is doing with Elizabeth!*

FOURTEEN

The Holy Days of Christmas were upon them before they knew it. The Greys moved their entire household to Chelsea, as Lady Frances declared that Christmas was for children and she wanted to bring Lady Jane from Hampton Court Palace to spend this time with her parents and her sister, Catherine.

"I'll be glad when Christmas is over," Frances sighed, "and we can enjoy ourselves at the New Year's celebrations. I remember in the good old days, when the king finally rid himself of that religious fanatic, Catherine of Aragon, and was in hot pursuit of Anne, Christmas was spectacular fun. We celebrated with such racy abandon and merriment that the entire Court never slept and was intoxicated for all twelve days!"

Bess closed her eyes as the painful memories of last Christmas washed over her. During the year of her marriage to Rob, the days had seemed endless, yet looking back she realized they had passed in the blinking of an eye. When Bess lifted her lashes and saw herself surrounded by the luxury of Chelsea Palace, she put the bittersweet past behind her. The year 1546 had begun with such deep despair for her, yet it had gone on to be incredibly good to her. Bess offered up a fervent prayer of thanks. If fortune continued to smile upon her, 1547 promised to be the best ever!

Bess knew she wouldn't see much of Rogue this month, as the privy council sat every day, either at Whitehall or at Baynard's Castle, nearby in the Strand. Baynard's Castle was the magnificent abode of William Herbert, Earl of Pembroke, whose countess was sister to Queen Catherine Parr. But Bess decided this was most fortunate. Their relationship had become dangerously intimate, and a figurative step back to cool off would be best. She, too, would be busy accompanying the Greys, who would be dividing the Holy Days between Chelsea and Hampton Court.

On the short barge ride upriver, the air was freezing. Henry Grey's glance moved from Frances, huddled in furs, over to Bess, who wore only a woolen cloak. "Aren't you cold, my dear?"

She smiled up at him. "Nay, milord, I'm far too excited about visiting Hampton Court Palace. This time I intend to have a good look at the king, the queen, Prince Edward, and Princess Mary."

"Brace yourself for disappointment, darling," Frances warned dryly. "The Tudors are an unpalatable lot."

Young Catherine Grey, wearing a little fur cape, shivered, and Bess pulled her close to keep her warm.

"Lady Mary is nothing like the Lady Elizabeth, even though they are sisters—rather like Lady Jane and myself."

"You, my poppet, take after your mother," Bess told her. "Do you miss your sister Jane?"

Catherine put her lips to Bess's ear. "Even though she's too prim and proper to piss, I do miss her sometimes."

Bess laughed and hugged her close. As the barge pulled in at the Hampton landing, a picture of Elizabeth in Tom Seymour's arms flew into her mind, and with her newfound knowledge of sexuality, Bess wondered how she would be able to look Elizabeth in the eye.

As it happened, the moment Elizabeth welcomed the Greys, she turned questioning amber eyes on Bess and, as she kissed her cheek in greeting, whispered, "Do you still have your hymen?"

Bess blushed and whispered back, "Yes! Do you still have yours?"

"Unfortunately, my answer would have to be in the affirmative," Lady Elizabeth said without lowering her voice. "Do let us hurry from the vicinity of the chapel before I'm coerced into attending Mass with the hypocrites. Oh, Lud, speak of the devil!"

As two ladies and their female attendants approached down the Long Gallery, Elizabeth swept to the floor in a graceful curtsy. Bess, Lady Frances, and little Catherine Grey all followed suit.

"Your Royal Highness, Lady Mary, may I present Mistress Elizabeth Hardwick?" The Lady Elizabeth's demeanor was regal.

Bess stared in disbelief at the two middle-aged women whom Elizabeth addressed. Since Queen Catherine Parr had had three husbands and numerous lovers, Bess had expected her to be an alluring courtesan. Instead, she saw a prim and proper figure who could have been mistaken for a respectable vicar's wife. "Your Royal Highness," Bess murmured.

The Lady Mary was an even greater shock to her. Bess had always imagined the princess to be young and fair, but she was neither. Mary was a little, dumpy, thirty-year-old spinster, with graying hair escaping from her starched cap. "Lady Mary," Bess murmured.

The two royal ladies clutched their bibles and stared back at the vivid creature in peacock-blue velvet. Bess sensed immediately that the Lady Mary disliked her on sight. She watched her eyes flick over both her and Elizabeth with disapproval, as if to say: *Birds of a feather!* Finally, the royal ladies turned their attention to Lady Frances and little Catherine, greeting them warmly.

Elizabeth gave them a direct lie. "I was on my way to join you at Mass, but Cousin Frances has asked me to take her to Father. I beg you to excuse me today."

"That was a narrow escape," Frances said with her usual irreverence. "The queen looks worn out; what the hell has Harry been doing to her? Not his husbandly duty, by the look of her."

"I cannot believe that was your sister," Bess said softly.

"Neither can I," Elizabeth said dryly.

"Looks like a bloody suet pudding," Frances declared. "Why doesn't she get that hair dyed, instead of eating pickled bibles!"

"Come to my apartments so we may be private!" Elizabeth commanded Bess.

"That's it, run off and leave me to the wrath of your father," Frances complained.

"There's hardly a man breathing you couldn't handle, sweet coz."

"Well, there certainly isn't a hard man breathing I couldn't handle. Run along and have fun. I'll be in Lady Jane's apartments if you're looking for me."

The Lady Elizabeth's rooms were elegantly appointed, reflecting her innate good taste. As they passed through the chambers, Bess saw that many of the walls were covered with shelves of books, and there was a writing desk in almost every room, reflecting Elizabeth's thirst for knowledge and love of reading and writing. There were also bolts on most of the doors, reminding Bess that the princess was an obsessively private person. Elizabeth had four ladies-in-waiting in her household, but none of them was in evidence save a large, motherly-looking woman, who sat in a cushioned window alcove, plying her needle.

"This is Mistress Cat Ashley. She used to be my nurse but is now head lady. This is Bess Hardwick, the friend I told you about. She is lady to my cousin Frances."

"Another redhead—may the good Lord save us!" Mistress Ashley's eyes twinkled with mischief.

"Ashcat is privy to all my secrets. She is the only one in the world I trust entirely. I'm taking Bess into the inner sanctum; don't let *anyone* disturb us."

It was as if they passed from one world into another. The chamber was large and lined with Murano mirrors. Hundreds of candles set in crystal chandeliers hung from the ceiling, ready to light up the room when darkness fell. At the moment sunshine streamed in through the long leaded windows.

The chamber boasted many musical instruments: fiddles, lutes, a harpsichord, and a pair of virginals. The princess took Bess into the adjoining dressing room. Bess's eyes widened in astonishment. At least two dozen magnificent gowns hung in splendor. Some were elaborately embroidered with gold thread, while others were encrusted with brilliant beads.

Hanging beside the dresses were a half dozen fantastic costumes, suitable for masques. There were wigs of every style and color, high-heeled slippers, undergarments, and a great casket of jewelry. There was also a dressing table laden with creams, perfumes, and pots of makeup.

"I cannot wear any of these garments at Court, because I am continually censured, but they cannot stop me from owning them and adorning myself in private. Sometimes I dress up and dance until dawn in my mirrored chamber." Elizabeth pulled out two gowns. "Look at these."

One was black satin, the other black velvet with trailing angel sleeves lined with silver tissue. Both were designed in the shocking French style, with the bodice cut low enough to reveal a female's nipples and to show off precious jewels. The gowns were highly inappropriate for a young lady, and Bess opened her mouth to remark upon their unsuitability.

"These were my mother's!" Elizabeth whispered.

Bess touched the gowns with awe. "They are exquisite; how did you get them?"

"Cat Ashley married my mother's cousin. They secretly managed to save some of her things for me. I have more hidden at Hatfield."

Bess touched a glossy black wig. "Do you ever disguise yourself?"

Elizabeth laughed and arched a plucked brow. "How did you guess?"

"It is what I would do if I were watched day and night," Bess admitted.

"Once I even disguised myself as a boy," Elizabeth confided. "It greatly amused him."

Bess knew Elizabeth was speaking of the admiral, and she was afraid for her. She felt compelled to caution her. "You cannot meet him here?" In spite of the locks on the doors and his reckless nature, surely this was impossible.

"Nay. Always outdoors. The gardens have numerous bowers, I rode and hunted in the forest when the weather permitted, and now that winter is here, the river will always be at hand."

The admiral had ships of every size, as well as his barge on the Thames. Under cover of darkness she could slip aboard, Bess realized. "Your Grace—" Bess hesitated. She knew how Elizabeth hated being told what to do and how at all costs would do as she pleased. Bess continued, choosing her words carefully, using her own situation to caution her friend. "I, too, am in love with an older man, who has sworn there will be no risk to me. Yet even so I will not allow him to consummate our union until he is free to wed me. The consequences would ruin my reputation—yet *my* reputation is as nothing when compared with yours. Your father would run mad. The consequences for you *and* your lover would be disastrous! Your Grace, please let us pledge, here and now, that we will not yield our virginity until we wed!"

A loud scratching sounded on the locked door. Like a hissing swan, the princess glided to the door and raged, "I told you none was to disturb us!"

"Your Grace, you are summoned by His Majesty."

"Peste!"

Elizabeth carefully locked the door behind them with a key she wore on a chain about her neck. She led Bess into her bedchamber, where two of her ladies awaited her with a fresh white gown and rose water to bathe her hands and face. "Hurry, hurry!" she ordered impatiently.

Bess suddenly realized that Elizabeth was afraid of her father, the king, just as was every other female who'd ever been close to him. Bess felt a wave of relief. Fear of her all-powerful father would keep her virgin more surely than all the pledges in the world!

The royal page led the way to the king's privy chambers and stopped outside one of Henry's private dining rooms. Elizabeth was white with relief. "Thank God, we are only summoned to dine."

Inside the chamber those who had been invited to luncheon with His Majesty stood talking and laughing while they awaited the king's exalted presence. Bess took a tentative step in the direction of Lady Frances, who was talking with her daughter, little Lady Jane Grey. Elizabeth put out a hand to stop her. "I don't want to waste my time with the little dog turd when the Dudleys are here."

Three well-made young men were gathered about a fair-haired boy who looked about nine. "This is my brother, Prince Edward.... Your Grace, may I present my friend, Bess Hardwick."

Once more Bess was taken off-guard. The slightly built boy had the face of a saint. How on earth could this be ruddy King Hal's son? Bess curtsied low and saw that the young heir to the throne studiously avoided looking at her breasts. Not so the Dudley brothers, who couldn't keep their eyes off them.

"You remember Cock Robin?" Elizabeth asked. "He certainly remembers you, or parts thereof."

"Mistress Hardwick." Robin's eyes were a warm dark brown, glossy as chestnuts.

Bess smiled and said softly, "It is Barlow....
I am a widow."

"Hardwick is easier to remember," Elizabeth asserted.

Robin Dudley laughed. "George Talbot did make your name unforgettable." As Bess blushed becomingly, he introduced his brothers. "This is Ambrose and Guildford." Both were well-built youths with pink cheeks and golden hair.

Robin gets his swarthy good looks from his mother, Nan, Bess thought as she pictured the attractive Countess of Warwick.

"Are you invited to the New Year's costume ball?" Ambrose Dudley asked Bess, licking his lips in anticipation.

"Yes, she is, but Bess will be disguised to protect her from uncouth louts like you," Elizabeth informed him.

"I'll be able to see through her disguise," Ambrose boasted, staring at her breasts.

"Stop trying to see through her gown, you jackanapes!" Elizabeth cuffed him on the ear.

Bess was not offended. The Dudley brothers were all younger than she, and their youthful lust didn't threaten her at all.

When the Lady Mary arrived, Bess curtsied to her. Elizabeth did not, however, and Mary threw her a look of disdain before joining Frances and Lady Jane. Mary and Elizabeth loathe and detest each other! Bess realized. Then Queen Catherine Parr arrived, accompanied by Henry Grey. Trust Henry to do the proper thing, Bess thought. This time Elizabeth sank to the floor with all the other ladies, while the young men, including the heir to the throne, bowed low.

Finally, King Henry arrived, and all in the room made their abject obeisance. When he bade them rise, it was the signal for everyone to take their place at table in strict order of rank. Next to the queen came the heir, then the Lady Mary and the Lady Elizabeth. Frances Grey sat on the king's left, then her daughters, Lady Jane and Lady Catherine, and then their father, Lord Henry Grey. He smiled at Bess and indicated that she should sit beside him. It was fortunate he did so, for Bess had seemed rooted to the floor at the sight of King Henry Tudor.

Never in her life had Bess seen such an imposing figure. His vast bulk clearly showed that he was grossly overweight. On top of this, he was swollen and bloated, making his stomach bulge obscenely below his huge barrel chest. The king's face, once ruddy, was now purple, pouched, and puffy. An expression of discontent marred it further. His neck was nonexistent. He did not walk but lumbered forward, dragging a huge bandaged leg. His gentlemen followed at a safe distance.

Judas! No wonder Rogue Cavendish was insulted when I mistook him for the king when we first met!

King Henry's garments were resplendent. He wore a ruffled silk shirt beneath a heavily embroidered velvet doublet whose sleeves were slashed with scarlet and gold, then overall came a sleeveless brocade coat. Across his chest sat a massive gold chain with an emerald the size of a duck egg. Its weight would have brought a slighter man to his knees. Henry Tudor did not wear a crown; he did not need to. Instead, he wore a plumed velvet cap adorned with another emerald, surrounded by diamonds.

Catherine Parr hurried forward to assist him. "Where the devil have you been? The queen's place is beside her king!" he roared.

"Your Grace, forgive me, I attended Mass with the Lady Mary."

Henry shot his elder daughter a venomous look, then threw himself into a high, carved chair and lifted his hand to indicate that everyone might now be seated.

Bess shuddered, imagining his hands upon her. His fingers looked like fat sausages, albeit they were adorned with more than a dozen jeweled rings.

A hushed silence blanketed the room as Henry Tudor spoke. "Some of you will be leaving us to spend the Holy Days of Christmas with your families." He paused, looked around the room, then with feigned bluffness continued, "When you return, Christmas will give way to the feasts and revels of the New Year and Twelfth Night. We will celebrate together." The short speech gave the king's subjects permission to leave Court and, more importantly, permission to return.

Now that the king had spoken, all were

free to resume their conversations. Elizabeth immediately turned her back upon her sister, Mary, and began talking to Robin Dudley on her other side. Frances Grey waited until the king's food taster sipped the wine, then she raised her goblet. "Merry Christmas, Harry."

Henry Tudor was in a decidedly peevish mood, and he had monstrous reason to be, he told himself. His vigorous youth and virility were gone. Age crept upon him as insidiously as the foul ulcer crept up his leg. What he wouldn't give to ride his great stallion again or, better yet, ride a woman!

He fingered his codpiece with disgust. What good was a weapon that remained flaccid no matter what stimulation his wife applied? *Might as well cut the useless thing off!* He had been so proud of it once—its inordinate size, its staying power. His beady eyes slid to Catherine Parr. Mayhap it was *her* fault? She was hardly a woman to inspire lust.

His eyes lifted to the holly and ivy Christmas decorations and he winced, recalling a far better time. Besides Frances, only one other woman had dared call him Harry. *Anne!* Her beauty and her laughter still haunted him. Christmas had been their special time. It was after the Christmas revels that Anne had first yielded herself to him, and with such abandon. She had been insatiable for him through Twelfth Night, enticing him to bed her a half dozen times a day, so that before their first month was ended, his seed had taken root and begun to ripen in her fecund body. Exactly nine months later Anne had given birth to Elizabeth.

Henry's eyes were drawn to his red-haired daughter. She was haughty and proud, as her mother had once been. He wondered if she, too, were a witch. Anne had certainly bewitched him! The Christmas following their daughter's birth, Anne had lured him to duplicate their excessive coupling so she could give him a son. It was not her fault she had lost him. He remembered her silken body with bitter regret. Anne was the only woman he'd ever loved, and those about her were so jealous they had maneuvered her downfall. Never for a moment did Henry blame himself.

He sighed heavily. The only pleasure left to him was food, and even that had its price. He washed down a mouthful of venison with a goblet of golden Rhenish wine and massaged the pain in his belly until he produced a massive belch.

"That was well brought up, Harry, even if you weren't!"

My sister's daughter Frances is the only woman in the world who dares speak her mind to me. Anne used to do that. How I miss her, he thought morosely. He wondered if she was laughing at him from above. Nay, more likely she was cursing him for declaring her daughter illegitimate. He looked hard at all his children now. Only Elizabeth had his stamp on her. Her brilliant hair proclaimed her Harry Tudor's daughter. In that instant he vowed to change his will and restore her title of *princess*, which would put her back in the line of succession. Anne's child was just as fit to inherit his crown as any of his other wives' children, perhaps more fit.

His eyes roamed the table and came to rest upon another red-haired female, who was having an animated conversation with Henry Grey. He felt his groin stir slightly. "One of your ladies?" he asked Frances.

"Aye, Bess Hardwick is also my dear friend."

"A spirited filly. Is your husband riding her?"

Frances rolled with laughter. "He'd better not be! Sir William Cavendish would have his balls!"

FIFTEEN

At Chelsea, Lady Frances and her daughters were in the gallery, surrounded by sewing women. Bess sat in an arched bay window making sketches of the costumes being considered for the New Year's masque at Hampton Court.

"I need something to cover my bulk, and let me warn you I wouldn't be caught dead dressed as a shepherdess," Frances said.

"What about a medieval lady?" Bess made a quick design of a wimple.

"Well that's certainly better than Botticelli's Venus, though that would be perfect for you, Bess, with your red hair."

Bess looked uncertain. "I believe masks and disguises lend themselves to licentious behavior. The flimsy dress of a goddess might invite unwanted advances."

"I've got it! Oh, my idea is so sly, you will love it. I shall wear the black habit of a mother superior, and you can be my novitiate in white."

"That *is* deliciously, wickedly sly." *It will send a message to all that I am chaste and to William that I intend to remain so!*

"I want to be a butterfly," Catherine piped up.

"Then so you shall." Bess sketched a costume whose sleeves were delicate, fluttering wings.

"I think Jane should be a bookworm," Catherine whispered.

"You have inherited your mother's sly wit, my poppet."

The Greys went by carriage from Chelsea to Hampton. Long-suffering Henry, going along with his wife's religious theme, had agreed to be a friar.

"When Rogue learned you'd browbeaten me into being Friar Tuck, I suggested he be Robin Hood. He told me where I could go, rather rudely. Said he'd wear his black riding leathers."

"Well I think Robin Hood was a clever suggestion, since Cavendish steals from the poor to give to the rich! Bess, where is my eye mask? I don't wish to be recognized."

"Then you will have to keep your mouth shut, Frances, my dear," Henry warned. "Your caustic tongue will be your undoing."

"I'll be defrocked...God willing!"

Hampton Court had been turned into a fairy-tale palace. Hundreds of torches and thousands of candles illuminated the chambers decorated with holly, mistletoe, gilded cherubs, and archangels. The crush of revelers filled the rooms and galleries to overflowing. Frances elbowed her way through musicians, liveried servants carrying trays of wine and marchpane, and merrymakers disguised in elaborate costumes.

There was a huge dais set up at the end of the Long Gallery for the king and queen and the royal family. Frances had Bess bent double with laughter at her witticisms. "I can't believe how bloody apt these costumes are. Look at that turban! The king thinks he's the Sultan of Baghdad, and if any man had a harem, it's Harry!"

"Isn't that the admiral dressed as a pirate?" Bess asked, unable to contain her amusement.

"You'd think he'd have more brains than to advertise his piracy. He's the biggest looter on the high seas."

Bess looked in vain for the Lady Elizabeth and concluded that she was too well-disguised to be recognized. She accepted an invitation to dance with a crusader and learned that it was Lord Thomas Darcy, a rich and noble bachelor who was much sought after. When an antlered stag turned out to be Guildford Dudley, Robin's brother, Bess couldn't stop laughing.

"I'm devastated," he murmured. "You're covered from your temples to your toes. I'd hoped for something much more revealing."

"How did you recognize me?" Bess demanded.

"I undressed you with my eyes, of course."

"Knave!" Bess jabbed him with the cross that hung about her neck.

"Stop acting like an animal," Robin Dudley admonished his brother. Costumed as the king of beasts, Robin wore a magnificent lion's mane, topped by a crown. His brother Ambrose was a wolf.

"Where is the Lady Elizabeth?" Bess asked.

"Still upstairs, trying to raise her courage."

"Surely her costume cannot be that outrageous?"

"Wait and see," Robin said, laughing.

"What disguise did Father decide on?" Ambrose asked.

"I have no idea," Robin said, "but I warrant he'll be up on the dais with the king. Let's go and look."

Bess saw with amusement that the Lady Mary was dressed as a simple shepherdess. How Frances would mock her! Suddenly, like a play being acted out for the audience, the shepherdess lost control of her long crook. She made a grab for it that resulted in its hooking the Sultan of Baghdad's turban. The sultan cursed and, when he reached to retrieve it, inadvertently jabbed the other end of the crook into his bad leg.

Henry Tudor roared with pain, and the shepherdess began to cry. Queen Catherine Parr, wearing a medieval wimple, rushed forward to assess the damage. She received the brunt of Henry's rage and bore it with great fortitude. It was decided that the king would retire from the revels, and Lord John Dudley and Lord Edward Seymour helped the wounded monarch to bed.

Within minutes of her father's departure, Elizabeth put in her appearance. It took Bess awhile to realize that the half-clad female in the blond wig was indeed the princess.

"Don't you recognize me? I'm Circe, who transformed men into beasts."

Bess looked from the girl wearing only a golden wisp of material, which exposed the nipples on her small, high breasts, to the grinning Dudley brothers.

"Your Grace, you are courting scandal," Bess said in a low voice.

"We can't all be nuns! Besides, no one will recognize me."

"*I* recognize you." The Lady Mary looked outraged. "I am ashamed to call you sister. Your mother wore that costume when she was my father's concubine!"

"You bitch—my mother was his *queen!*"

Mary Tudor's poisonous glance fell on Bess. "How dare you mock me and the Catholic

Church with your blasphemous attire? The king shall hear of this."

"At this moment my poor wounded father wishes you in hell alongside your mother!" Elizabeth spat.

Robin Dudley grabbed Elizabeth around the waist and forcibly moved her away.

Bess was upset. Elizabeth was acting recklessly, and she herself should have had more good sense than to dress up in religious attire. Her cheeks were burning, the room was overheated, and her novitiate's habit was stifling. Bess needed fresh air and made her way toward the doors that led to a balcony.

With relief she saw the man clad in black riding leathers coming toward her. The only concession to a costume that he wore was a slouch hat and a black eye mask.

"Rogue, where have you been? I need some air."

He took her hand and led her out onto the balcony. "What's amiss, my little nun?"

"Lud, I should never have worn this novitiate's robe. I thought I was being clever, showing you I would remain chaste, but I have outraged Princess Mary."

"Hush." He cupped her face in his hands and bent his head to capture her lips.

Bess yielded her mouth and melted against him, feeling secure in the circle of his powerful arms. "Oh, I wish you weren't wed to another."

"So do I," he murmured against her lips.

Bess began to shiver. The winter night was extremely cold, and after the warmth of the crowded rooms, she was suddenly covered with gooseflesh. "I'm freezing," she said, taking his hand and drawing him back through the French doors.

Across the Long Gallery Bess caught sight of another man in black riding leathers. Her eyes widened in disbelief as she recognized that it was William Cavendish. In dismay she swung around to look at her escort. Now she realized that he was taller than William and had wider shoulders. "Who the devil are you?" she demanded furiously.

He grinned down at her. "Don't worry, Vixen, even I wouldn't violate a nun." Then he walked away.

Cavendish saw her and cut through the crowd. "Was that George Talbot in riding leathers?"

"Yes! He makes me want to spew!" Bess said passionately.

"Don't swallow your rosary beads, sweetheart. Whatever has upset you?"

"Oh, Rogue, please take me home. I'm having a miserable time."

"Come on, then. It isn't yet midnight, and I want to give you your New Year's gift." He put his arm about her to keep her warm as they ran across the courtyard to his carriage. He lifted her inside, climbed in after her, then drew her back into his arms. Her lips were cold as ice when he kissed her, but his mouth soon warmed them.

"I know what will make you hot," he whispered.

"No, Rogue, please," Bess protested.

"I'm teasing you! Here, open this."

Bess removed the lid from a large box and gasped with delight. The light from the courtyard torches reflected on the sheen of silver-fox pelts. She lifted the fur cloak and saw that it was lined with amethyst velvet. Bess pulled it around her immediately and blew upon the silvery fur, reveling in its luxury. "I love it! It's the first fur I've ever owned."

"It won't be the last," he promised.

She lifted her lips for his kiss.

"Happy New Year, Bess."

"Happy New Year, William." She snuggled against him, and as the carriage started to move, she proceeded to tell him of the evening's disasters. Soon he had her laughing, and she realized that one of the things she loved about him was that he saw the amusing side of every situation. Suddenly, she didn't want to go back to Suffolk House. She wanted to stay in the safe, warm cocoon of the carriage and watch the new year dawn.

Rogue sighed. He had hoped the fur would persuade her to relent and put an end to their celibacy. Resignedly, he instructed his driver to take them to Richmond Hill with its spectacular view, where they could watch the sunrise over the Thames Valley and welcome in the dawning of the brand new year of 1547.

It was the last week of January before Cavendish saw Bess again. He'd had to go into Hertfordshire on the Crown's business, to inquire into disputed leases of the Abbey of St. Albans. In addition to his secretary, he took his team of surveyors, because the lands and property owned by St. Albans were vast, much of it leased out in an effort to keep the Church coffers filled. The Church lands extended as far as Northaw, which boasted a lovely country manor house where Sir William and his men were given hospitality.

Whenever he was away from London, Bess was never far from William's thoughts. He knew he had rivals who were free to offer her the security of marriage, and he wished he had the means to bind her more closely. As he surveyed the Northaw manor house, Cavendish wondered if he had found the solution to his dilemma. Gifts of jewels and furs had certainly not been the answer.

He recalled the day they met and how she was incensed that her home had been taken away when she was a child and how she longed to have a house of her own. William remembered her words exactly: *Don't laugh at me, sir. I shall have my own household!*

The more he thought about it, the more convinced he was. Bess had never given herself to him because she needed the security of marriage. She had suffered insecurity all her life and needed a safe haven. Perhaps that was even part of the reason she was attracted to him. He was an older man with a certain wealth and power and was experienced in the ways of the world.

Cavendish decided to do nothing until Bess had seen Northaw for herself. If she fell in love with it, he would find the means of acquiring it for the two of them.

Cavendish arrived at Suffolk House in time to dine with the Greys. Thomas Seymour was also there, giving them the news that the king had finally appointed him to the privy council. The meal was extremely merry, with many toasts of congratulations.

By the time dinner was over, it was apparent to the admiral that Bess had not divulged his dalliance with Elizabeth to either the Greys or Cavendish, and he was relieved. Thomas kissed Bess's hand with gratitude and murmured, "I am so pleased that we are friends who know the value of discretion." He turned to Cavendish and placed Bess's hand in his. "You are a lucky man, William. The lady refuses to be seduced, though I have tried my damnedest."

William steered Bess to the relative privacy of a drawing room. "Have you had much chance to ride lately?"

She hoped he wasn't questioning with whom she had ridden. "We rode every day at Chelsea, though we seldom went farther than the park. I miss my long rides over the Derbyshire fells and moors."

"Would you like to ride out with me, Bess?"

"Why, I would love it!" Her dark, almond-shape eyes took on an excited sparkle.

"I'd like you to come to St. Albans. I'm handling a dispute over the abbey's land leases. It's a long ride, about eighteen miles," he warned.

Bess suddenly looked uncertain.

"Is that too far in this brisk weather?"

"No, no, it isn't that, Rogue." She gave him a level look and told him honestly how she felt. "I don't relish watching you crush a religious order beneath the heel of your jackboot, even if it is by the king's order."

"Bess, sweetheart, I can't believe you know so little about me. I don't use bullying tactics; I use the golden spur."

She looked at him blankly.

"Little innocent. The golden spur is a bribe. It's what makes me so successful at what I do. It's the oil that smooths away the difficulties in every negotiation I undertake."

"Surely you are not telling me that priests and nuns take bribes?"

"Of course not!" The amusement came back into his eyes. "The abbots and abbesses at the heads of these orders, however, are a different breed. Dealing with them successfully requires a deft touch; I succeed at what I do, where many others have failed."

Bess laughed. "You are a damned rogue!"

"Come with me and I'll show you how I go about my business."

The excitement was back in her eyes. "I'll be ready at dawn!"

"Treasury business keeps me in London tomorrow; the following day will be better."

He slipped his arm about her and hugged her close. "I'm glad to see you are so eager for new experiences."

Bess blushed, knowing this was another step in the mating dance.

Two days later the small riding party was blessed with late January sunshine on their ride to St. Albans. William's secretary, Robert Bestnay, accompanied them. They took the main road north, and the city of London soon gave way to the patchwork fields of the gentle countryside.

Cavendish was delighted that Bess easily kept pace with him. His job had always entailed long hours in the saddle, and he was inured to arduous journeys. The previous day he had arranged to have a wagonload of choice victuals, game birds, and French wines sent to the Abbot of St. Albans to ensure them a warm welcome. He took Bess directly to Northaw so he could gauge her reaction before he began his negotiations.

In the walled courtyard he lifted her from the saddle and led her through the studded doors of the country manor house. "I want you to tell me what you think of this place."

Bess stripped off her riding gloves and went into the large hall, where the blazing fire was a welcome sight. As she warmed her hands, her eyes roamed the large chamber with appreciation. Its ceiling was vaulted with carved oak beams, and the tables and benches were carved from matching dark oak. There were two parlors off the hall, one for private dining and one for sitting. Both had linenfold paneling and beautifully carved fireplaces. Behind them was a huge kitchen, gleaming with copper utensils.

Even the staircase was a thing of beauty, curving upward from its ancient, carved newel post. On the second floor were eight bedchambers, whose leaded casement windows looked down onto the gardens.

William came up behind Bess as she looked out a window that faced west. "Those are the Chiltern Hills." He took her hand and led her into a bedchamber with an eastern view. "Over there, perhaps four miles away, is the Lady Elizabeth's Hatfield."

"Really? I wonder how she could ever bear to leave such lovely countryside." Bess sighed and leaned back against him. "This is such a perfect house; I am quite envious of whoever owns it. Why is it vacant?"

"The Abbey of St. Albans leased it out, but the rent wasn't paid, so the lease is in dispute at the moment."

"What a pity; a house like this should be lived in and cherished," she said wistfully.

He turned her to face him and ran his fingertip along her cheekbone. "Bess, could you be happy here?"

She drew in a swift breath, and he saw her eyes fill with eager questions. Before she could voice any of them, he covered her mouth with his in a kiss that marked her as belonging to him alone. He captured her hand again, laughing down at her as he saw her eyes dart possessively about the chamber. "Come with me and listen quietly while I secure Northaw as our country manor."

At the abbey Bess met the abbot, and Sir William did not correct the churchman when he welcomed her as Lady Cavendish. With amused eyes William watched her blush. Over lunch Bess sat quietly sipping her malmsey as William and his secretary, Robert Bestnay, conducted business with a swiftness that took her breath away.

"As you know, Sir Abbot, I am commissioned by the Crown for the dissolution and surrender of religious houses. When I came last week, I was prepared to do just that. I surveyed the lands and took an inventory of the contents of the abbey and its properties, and technically all that remains to be done is transfer the property to the Crown."

When the abbot threw him a desperate look, William commiserated with him. "Religion is the overriding problem of our times, my friend, but the Throne and the Court are staunchly Protestant, and as a result the Catholic cause must suffer."

"Can we at least try to recover the rents owed to us on our leases?"

"I'm afraid you owe that money to the Crown also. It amounts to quite a considerable sum." Cavendish signaled Robert Bestnay, who showed the abbot the tally. The look on the abbot's face turned from desperate to hopeless.

"Somehow this doesn't seem fair," Cavendish said gravely. "Since I am given considerable leeway in these matters, I could give you a year's grace while you try to recuperate some of your losses"—William paused until hope returned to the abbot's face, then he continued—"though I am well aware how seldom these debts are ever collected." The abbot looked hopeless once more.

William gave the impression that he was wrestling with his conscience. "I'll tell you what. Write out new leases renting all of St. Alban's lands and properties to the Crown for one year. I shall see that those rents are paid to you personally. When the leases expire after one year, St. Albans will revert to the Crown."

"The rents will be paid to me personally?" the abbot repeated, not quite believing his good fortune.

"You have my guarantee, Sir Abbot." William turned to his secretary. "How much is owed on the Northaw manor house, Bestnay?"

"Sixty pounds, Sir William."

"If you give me the deed to the Northaw property so its ownership can be transferred immediately, I will give you the money owed on it this very day."

The abbot broke out in a relieved sweat. "Sir William, how can I ever thank you?"

"There is no need for that, my good man. I just want you to feel that the Crown has dealt fairly with you."

On the ride back to London, the afternoon shadows lengthened and Bess drew her silver-fox cloak more closely about her. "Rogue, explain to me exactly what you did back there and exactly how such a thing can be legal."

"You look chilled, sweetheart. Come ride with me and I'll warm you."

Bess gave the reins of her horse to Robert Bestnay, and Rogue lifted her before him. He slipped his arm possessively about her, and she snuggled back against the warmth of his broad chest. His wide shoulders, clad in black leathers, blocked the cool wind, and he put his lips against her ear. "Whether the means I used are legal troubles neither myself nor Henry Tudor."

"You don't intend to register the deed for Northaw in your own name?" Bess whispered the question. Surely he would not dare do such a thing.

"It will be my fee for annexing the Abbey of St. Albans to the Crown, with the abbot's full agreement."

"Rogue, will Northaw truly be yours?" she asked in awe.

He slipped his hand inside her fur to cup her breast. "I'll register it in my name, but it will be ours."

An intense thrill shot through her, and he felt her nipple harden through the fabric of her riding habit.

His teeth nipped her ear. "It will be our country home when we are married."

It was the first time he had said the words. Finally, he had promised to wed her! Bess wanted to fling her arms about him and kiss him until they were both senseless, but they were not alone. Instead, she rubbed her bottom against his groin and felt him swell inside the leather riding pants.

"You are torturing me, and well you know it."

Her sultry laugh rang out.

When they arrived at Suffolk House, it was after dark. Cavendish dismounted and lifted Bess from the saddle. During the last few miles his desire to make love to her had mounted like a rising tide. "I need to bathe and change, but then I'm coming back." He was not asking her permission. He was warning her of his resolute intent.

More than anything in the world, Bess wanted to be alone with him. They had been in the company of others all day. Whitehall, where he had rooms, was practically next door, and she knew they would be able to be together in the privacy of her chambers within the hour. She lifted her face, wanting his kiss yet knowing it was impossible. "Hurry!" she whispered.

By the time William returned, she was bathed, scented, and wearing a simple morning dress of pale green. She had ordered them a late supper, which the footman brought up just as Cavendish arrived.

The moment the footman left, Bess went into William's arms. They kissed and whispered, then kissed again, inseparable now that they were at last alone. Both were insatiable for the kisses they had been denied all day.

He lifted her against his heart and carried her to the love seat before the fire. "Bess, I'm so much in love with you. I swear I've never felt this way before."

She needed him to pledge his love to her. She lifted her arms about his neck and melted against him, feeling completely secure for the first time since she had lost her father.

His kisses deepened and grew rough with his mounting desire, until Bess was weak with longing. His strong fingers splayed through her hair and held her captive for his mouth's ravishing. His lips traced a hot trail, seeking the pulse points on her temple, behind her ear, and at the base of her throat. Her scent filled his nostrils, making them flare with carnal desire, and his insistent hands slid her dress from her shoulders, freeing her breasts for his mouth's pleasure. Heat leapt between them, arousing a smoldering need that cried out to be quenched.

The food lay forgotten as William, refusing to be denied any longer, picked her up and carried her purposefully into the bedchamber. He sat her on the high bed and with sure hands removed her gown. When he saw she wore nothing beneath it, he knew she had anticipated that he would make love to her tonight.

As Bess lay before him in naked splendor, the breath caught in his throat. He stood gazing down at her. Nature had fashioned her for lovemaking, and at last she was ready to yield. He was so hard, his arousal so fierce, that he ached. His possessive gaze touched her everywhere, and his fingertips followed, stroking the sleek, satiny flesh that curved and swelled so enticingly.

Bess felt consumed by desire and was impatient for William to remove his clothes so that at last they could lie naked together. Quivering with need, she came up from the bed to offer him her mouth. When she felt his tongue delve deeply into her mouth, she couldn't keep from moaning at the intense pang of sensual need that flooded through her body. As her lips trailed down his corded throat, her fingers unfastened his shirt so that her mouth could trail kisses down his chest. When her lips found the pelt of auburn hair, she longed to feel its crispness brush against her naked breasts. She pressed her lips and tongue against his belly and cupped his arousal, wanting to free it so she could see it, and touch it, and learn its mysteries.

"Take off your clothes for me; I want to see you naked and feel you against me. Are you as hot as I am?" she panted. "Feel how I burn!" She took his hand and stroked it down her body from her breast to the inside of her thigh.

"You will be even hotter inside. Let me show you." His hand took her fingers and he pressed one into her scalding sheath.

Bess moaned. "I am in a fever for you."

Her words inflamed him. He could feel his blood surging and pounding; his own heartbeat was deafening inside his ears. Then slowly, unbelievably, he realized that someone was knocking on the outer door.

Bess came up from the bed. "What was that?"

William cursed. "How dare they disturb us."

Bess covered her nakedness with the bedcover as William strode angrily to the door and, without unlocking it, demanded, "Who is it?"

"It's Henry, I'm afraid."

William reluctantly unlocked the door and opened it to his friend.

"The king is dead."

"*What?*" Cavendish wondered if he had heard right.

"King Henry has just died at Hampton. We must go immediately."

SIXTEEN

Cavendish went to Hampton alone, while Bess accompanied the Greys. Sir William's position immediately turned from rock solid to precarious, along with that of every other man at Court who wielded power. Frances and Henry were on firmer ground. She was a Tudor, and their daughter, Lady Jane, would marry Edward, who was now the King of England rather than simply the heir to the throne.

By the time they arrived, every noble in London, including Archbishop Cranmer and his churchmen, had gathered at the palace. A pall had already fallen over the entire place, making the atmosphere grave and hushed. The courtiers, both men and women, were shocked and caught unawares at the sudden turn of events. While the Greys went immediately to seek out their daughter and the nine-year-old boy who had just become King of England, Bess went straight to the Lady Elizabeth's apartments.

When she knocked, Bess had to give her name and was kept waiting for several minutes before she was admitted. She was escorted to Elizabeth's bedchamber, where her ladies were adorning her in black. Bess sank to the carpet. "Your Grace, I am so sorry for your terrible loss."

Two of the ladies were weeping openly, while Elizabeth stood motionless, more deathly pale than Bess had ever seen her. "Are you faint?" she asked in alarm.

Elizabeth looked at her ladies. "Leave us."

They obeyed her only because they had no choice. The moment they were alone, Bess closed the gap between them and took Elizabeth's hands.

"I can't believe it. I can't believe it," Elizabeth whispered.

"Come and sit down," Bess urged.

Elizabeth resisted stiffly. "I'm not faint, I'm giddy...with relief. I'm free at last, I can't believe it. I have an uncontrollable urge to laugh, but I know I must not," she confessed. "I loved my father, but I hated him too!" she hissed. "Can you understand? He was the tyrant who murdered my mother, and yet I am proud that his Tudor blood flows through my veins."

"I understand completely; love and hate are but two sides of the same coin. Can you compose yourself enough to face everyone, to receive condolences, to mourn your father, and make your obeisance to your brother, Edward?"

With head high and back as straight and stiff as a ramrod, she said, "I am Elizabeth Tudor. I can face *anything*. Call my ladies."

The boy king was flanked by his Seymour uncles, Edward and Thomas. It appeared from the first moment of his reign that they were determined to set themselves up as a bulwark between the boy and the entire world.

Bess stood beside Lady Frances as they watched Elizabeth approach her young brother. It was the Seymours who gave her permission to draw close, and suddenly Bess felt afraid for Elizabeth. It wasn't little Edward who would now rule but the powerful Seymours. The very last appointment King Henry had bestowed was on Thomas Seymour when he became a member of the privy council, only four days past. Bess clenched her fists impotently. Who would keep the admiral's dalliance with Elizabeth in check, now that her all-powerful father was dead?

A few days later, when the late king's will was read, many people were amazed yet happy that he had restored his daughters to the succession. Bess was overjoyed that her friend was no longer the Lady Elizabeth. From now on she would be accorded her rightful title of Princess Elizabeth!

In the weeks that followed, Bess saw little of Cavendish. She fully understood that he had to remain at Court to secure his position in the new reign of King Edward the VI. The Greys stayed at Chelsea, bringing Lady Jane there from Hampton, during the long, drawn-out mourning for the late king.

The coronation for the boy-king was kept as simple as possible, with a short procession to Westminster Abbey, the usual interminable religious crowning ceremony, followed by a not overly lavish celebration, all supposedly in deference to the king's tender age, but which in reality had more to do with keeping the coffers filled.

Henry Grey brought messages from Cavendish to Bess, and it was Henry they relied on for news of what was happening at Court. As soon as his nephew was crowned, Lord Edward Seymour and his countess, Ann, moved into Hampton to be with the boy-king day and night, and by mid-February King Edward had given his uncle the dukedom of Somerset and appointed him lord protector. This put the privy council in an uproar, because they had expected to rule as a Council of Regency.

It was rumored that Thomas Seymour objected to his brother's outright manipulation of the little king, so at the direction of the lord protector, Thomas was elevated from admiral to lord high admiral and was created Baron Sudely to silence his objections.

Young King Edward was making new appointments almost daily. With the approval of the protector and the privy council, William Cecil, a brilliant young secretary of the Court, was appointed to the post of king's personal secretary. Then King Edward, at the prompting of Cecil and Edward Seymour, asked for an audit of the late king's treasury. Paulet and Cavendish and their treasury clerks worked diligently, sometimes feverishly, day and night over this accounting. It was a vast undertaking, and both knew the books must be in perfect order when they were presented for scrutiny.

At Chelsea, Lady Frances took personal offense at Seymour's insufferable high-handedness. "It is that bastard Edward Seymour who is demanding an accounting of the treasury. He had better not start investigating my bills! On top of that he has made his rabid bitch of a wife, Ann Seymour, a duchess! For Christ's sake, Henry, we must do something!"

"What *can* we do, my dear?" Henry asked doubtfully.

"If you think I'm going to sit here at Chelsea on my fat arse while Edward and Ann Seymour aggrandize themselves playing king and queen, you are sadly mistaken. At their own peril they are overlooking my God-given rights as a Tudor! Bess, pack immediately. Lady Jane goes back to Hampton this very day, and I shall camp in the king's bloody bedchamber until he makes *me* a duchess!"

At Hampton Court Palace, Catherine Parr was in full mourning. It was quickly brought home to her that she was no longer Queen of England, but a much less powerful queen dowager. Edward Seymour was already putting subtle pressure on her to move from Hampton because it now belonged to young King Edward. Seymour had been less subtle toward Princess Mary. Because she practiced the Catholic faith, he persecuted her unmercifully, insisting that everyone at Hampton must practice the Reformed Protestant faith. Deeply offended, Princess Mary haughtily removed her household to her own country estate of Beaulieu.

Lady Frances and little Lady Jane were dressed in identical black mourning when they arrived at Hampton. Bess wore a gray taffeta with tiny white ruffles at its high neck. They found the young king talking earnestly with his sister Elizabeth, but when he saw Lady Jane Grey, Edward's face lit up with happiness. Frances Grey missed nothing. Her daughter would have no difficulty at all persuading the king to make her parents a duke and duchess.

Princess Elizabeth, also gowned in gray, withdrew and beckoned Bess to follow her. As the two red-haired young women walked down the Long Gallery, Bess could see that Elizabeth was trying to suppress great excitement. "What is it, Your Grace? Has something happened?"

"Something is *about* to happen. I dare not

say what; it is a secret," Elizabeth whispered.

Bess guessed immediately that it concerned Thomas Seymour, for the princess was obsessed with him.

"Suffice it to say that shortly, everyone will be in for a great surprise." Elizabeth looked at Bess coyly. "How does your own affair of the heart progress?"

"It doesn't," Bess said flatly. "Sir William is completely occupied at Whitehall with treasury business."

"We'll both have to be patient, something that doesn't sit well with either of us. And I absolutely hate these prim mourning dresses, but my brother won't hear of allowing me to wear anything save black and gray. Poor little devil has been brought up so straightly. He actually looked happy to see the little dog turd."

"He seems to have much in common with Lady Jane, Your Grace."

"They are like two peas from the same pod." Elizabeth's eyes slid toward Bess. "Rather like us."

At the end of May the audit of the treasury was complete, and early in June, Paulet was reconfirmed as lord high treasurer and Cavendish as treasurer of the king's chamber. They kept their posts not just because they handled the money of the realm, but because they did such an outstanding job collecting that money. Both were members of the privy council and received a vote of confidence from their fellow members.

Cavendish stole a couple of hours from Whitehall to dine with the Greys, who were back at Suffolk House celebrating their own good news. Their other guests were Lord and Lady Herbert, William Parr and his wife, and Thomas Seymour. All the men were members of the privy council except Henry Grey, who was always careful to show no political ambition.

Cavendish kissed Frances and, when they sat down to dine, proposed a toast to the new Duke and Duchess of Suffolk. Bess and Cavendish couldn't keep their eyes from each other. His forced absence had created a hunger in both of them that could hardly be satisfied beneath the watchful eyes of others. But under the circumstances it was impossible for them to withdraw to Bess's private chambers.

Thomas Seymour, the newly appointed lord high admiral, held forth on the necessity of increasing the navy to a formidable force of ten thousand.

"Necessity?" William Herbert, Earl of Pembroke, asked, puzzled.

Frances laughed. "The necessity is to increase Tom's power. He has to do something to counter the power of his odious brother Edward and that insatiable wife of his!"

Her guests all joined in her laughter, for Edward Seymour had ridden roughshod over his fellow councillors. Bess watched Thomas with speculative eyes. Not only was he vain and arrogant, he, too, was insatiably ambitious. She wanted to say something to Cavendish, to warn him in some way.

When the meal was over and the company moved to a drawing room, William sought out Bess. "I've been starving for the sight of you."

"Oh, William, I am so happy that you are confirmed as treasurer of the new king's chamber."

He drew her hand to his lips in a formal kiss. "Who the devil else could do the job?" he murmured, unable to hide the wry amusement in his eyes. "The trouble is, I have to go to Evesham and Bordesley Abbeys in Warwickshire."

Bess's dark eyes looked into his wistfully. "How long will you be gone?"

"Not an hour longer than is absolutely necessary," he pledged, squeezing her hand, telling her how much he would miss her.

Bess confided in a near whisper, "I may be wrong, but I think the admiral has ambitions to marry Elizabeth."

"You're not wrong. He's been told to forget it; it's absolutely impossible." William shook his head. "Don't speak of it."

Bess was relieved. It would put an end to the dangerous liaison. Yet she felt sorry for Elizabeth, who imagined herself in love with the swaggering devil.

The talk had turned to country homes. "Have you had a chance to visit Sudely yet?" Frances asked Thomas.

"Nay, it is in Gloucestershire, built of mellowed Cotswold stone and reputed to have a magnificent banqueting hall."

"We shall be going to Bradgate for the summer. Where does the time go? Only another month and we shall be packing up here."

Bess said to William, "Try to get back before we leave for Bradgate." She had been looking forward to seeing Bradgate in Leicestershire and visiting with her family in the next county, but suddenly the only place she wanted to go was Northaw.

Frances looked over at them and winked knowingly. "You are all invited to Bradgate to stay as long as you wish. William, you must promise to come and keep Henry company."

Sir William was the first to leave, and Lady Herbert waited until Thomas Seymour had also departed before she told Frances—in strictest confidence, of course—what her sister Catherine Parr, Queen Dowager, had divulged.

"That wretched Edward Seymour, self-styled protector of our king, wants the queen out of Hampton Court."

Frances didn't give a tinker's damn for Catherine Parr, who had managed to put three elderly husbands in their graves, until Anne Herbert mentioned the word *Chelsea*. "Chelsea?" Frances cried in outrage. "He had the audacity to suggest she move her household to Chelsea Palace? *My* Chelsea? Bess, get my smelling salts."

In spite of the fact that Frances declared Catherine Parr would reside at Chelsea *over her dead body,* she began to remove the furniture, paintings, and household items that belonged to the Greys, as well as everything else that took her fancy. With the aid of Bess and her other ladies, they spent almost a fortnight packing up clothes, linens, silver, bed hangings, and curtains. Some of the items were marked for Dorset House or Suffolk House, but Frances decided the bulk of the furnishings would go north to Bradgate.

Frances, Duchess of Suffolk, then made a formal protest to the privy council, pointing out that she had had the use of Chelsea Palace for many years. Surely, with all the palaces owned by the Crown, another residence could be found for the queen dowager.

"I have decided to sit tight and delay going to Bradgate," Frances told Bess. "The moment I leave London, they will descend upon Chelsea like bloody vultures!"

"If they do they will find that the carcass has been picked clean," Bess remarked candidly.

Frances laughed heartily. "Possession is nine tenths of the law, remember that."

In spite of Frances Grey's protest, Chelsea Palace was declared the official residence of Catherine Parr, Queen Dowager. And since she was stepmother to Elizabeth, it was decided that the princess would go with her. Now

Frances really had a dilemma on her hands. Would she allow her daughter, Lady Jane, to reside with the queen dowager, or would she bring her home? It was clear she could not remain at Hampton Court Palace, which was turning into a male bastion for the bachelor king.

"The bloody lord protector has won!" Frances cried angrily. "It is clear he intends to isolate the little king from everyone he loves. Edward Seymour is removing anyone who might influence him: his stepmother, his sister, and my daughter. It is clear that his rabid bitch of a wife is advising him every step of the way!"

Since Frances had been outmaneuvered, she decided that Lady Jane Grey would indeed reside at Chelsea with the queen dowager and Princess Elizabeth. Frances, Bess, and a cluster of servants descended upon Hampton to move Lady Jane and her furnishings from one residence to the other.

Princess Elizabeth was in the middle of her own move, and Bess could steal only a moment alone with her. "Are you upset about moving to Chelsea, Your Grace?"

"No!" Elizabeth whispered. Suppressed excitement turned her amber eyes to glittering gold. "We'll be free of their watchful eyes; we'll be able to see each other every day at Chelsea!"

Bess was stunned. Didn't she know the admiral had been refused permission to marry her?

"I must go, Bess. Come and visit me at Chelsea."

At the end of the month, Bess received a note from Cavendish marked *Private*. She opened the envelope and read the short message with a slight frown.

> *My Dearest Bess:*
>   *I have news. I will come after midnight when we can be private.*
>   *W.*

Her imagination conjured dozens of reasons for the secrecy. Was the news about Princess Elizabeth, Tom Seymour, the Greys? Or did it have to do with treasury business or his position therein? Was it about the privy council and some decision they had taken? The mystery baffled her.

In the late afternoon Bess gathered spring flowers from the gardens at Suffolk House, filling vases with lovely white lilies, purple lilac, and heavily scented hawthorne. She waited until after the evening meal to bathe and put on one of William's favorite gowns to help fill the hours until midnight.

At last the knock she had been waiting for came. She opened the door and flew into his arms. "Whatever is it?"

He enfolded her against him and kissed her hair. "Bess, my wife died today."

She stared up at him in disbelief. It was the

one thing she had never thought of. "William." Her arms tightened about him.

"We must not be seen together for a decent interval; the gossips would crucify you," he said intensely. "But I want to be with you. Will you come to Northaw for a few days, where we can be away from prying eyes?"

"Oh, yes, William. I love you so much." She hid her face against his chest to hide her tears. They were not tears of sorrow, may God forgive her, they were tears of joy.

"We cannot go together; we shall have to meet there. The funeral is the day after tomorrow. I'll come the next day."

"Do Frances and Henry know?"

He shook his head. "We'll go and tell them together."

Hand in hand they made their way to the west wing, where the Greys had their private suite. Frances opened to their knock and admitted them, then her hand flew to her throat. "There's been another death!"

"Yes, my wife," William acknowledged.

"Oh, thank God," Frances said with an exaggerated sigh of relief. "Henry, pour us all some brandy, darling."

"The burial is arranged for the day after tomorrow."

"We'll be there, as will the rest of the Court, but Bess should disappear for a few days."

"I'm going to Northaw. I'll ride there tomorrow."

"You'll do no such thing. You'll go in a carriage," Frances insisted.

"Thank you, Frances." William kissed her hand.

"An unmarked carriage, with a discreet driver and a guard," Henry interjected.

"Bess, would you like Cecily to go with you? She considers herself your maid, darling."

"Thank you, but I'd rather go alone," Bess said as a blush dusted her cheekbones.

"Northaw has a small staff of servants," William said, squeezing Bess's hand and watching her blush deepen.

On the drive to Northaw, Bess carefully went over the things she had packed to make sure that in her excitement she hadn't forgotten anything. Long trained to pack up entire households, she decided to take bed linen, food, and wine. In her head Bess also went over the things she would say to the staff of Northaw. Because she had been a servant, she knew how they wished to be treated.

The moment she arrived Bess asked the housekeeper, Mistress Bagshaw, to assemble the servants. The indoor staff consisted of the housekeeper-cook, a pantryman, a footman, and two housemaids. She discerned immediately that Mistress Bagshaw ruled the roost and knew if she won her over, the others would follow.

"I have been asked by Sir William Cavendish, the new owner of Northaw, to prepare the house for his arrival. I am Mistress Elizabeth Barlow from Suffolk House, where Sir William spends his time when he is not at Court. I realize how difficult it is to serve a new master." Bess looked directly at Mistress Bagshaw. "I will help you all I can and beg that you will help me. I understand you do not know how Sir William likes his household run. Neither do I." Bess smiled. "We shall learn together. Thank you very much."

She repeated her little speech for the outdoor servants, the gamekeeper, the stableman, and the grounds keeper, then she returned to the carriage to speak to the coachman and his guard.

"A Mistress Bagshaw is in charge here; please defer to her in all things. There are ample chambers on the third floor. Ask for anything you need. Thank you for a safe and pleasant journey."

Bess, with Mistress Bagshaw at her side, soon set the maids to dusting and polishing. The food and wine were turned over to the pantryman, and the mounds of fresh bed linen carried upstairs to the second floor.

She chose a spacious bedchamber with long windows that looked out over the garden and the Chiltern Hills. She stripped the big bed down to its feather mattress, then used the bed steps to reach the dusty curtains. When all was removed Bess flung open the windows and bade the maids give the chamber a thorough cleaning.

When the room was spotless, Bess made up the bed with fresh linen, a soft woolen blanket, and a green velvet bedcover. Then the footman helped her hang her own matching bed-curtains. By the time the chamber was finished, the afternoon shadows were lengthening.

"Thank you, we'll do the second bed-chamber tomorrow. I'll unpack my own trunk," she told the maids. "Go and help Mistress Bagshaw in the kitchen." To the housekeeper she said, "I'll just have a light supper of fruit and cheese—and perhaps a little of that delicious soup I smell."

On the day that William was to arrive, Bess filled Northaw with flowers from the gardens. She gave Mistress Bagshaw a detailed menu for dinner, then spoke to the footman. "Sir William will most likely bring his own manservant, James Cromp, but could you please scrub out the wooden bathtub upstairs and make sure there is ample hot water ready? Sir William will wish to bathe and shave when he arrives."

Bess tried to control her excitement, but as the hours ticked by she found she could not. It would have been easier to hold back the tide than the happiness that was building inside her. In the early afternoon she bathed and changed into a pale green gown that she knew was one of his favorites. She brushed her heavy mass of red-gold hair until it crackled and touched all her pulse points with the scent of April violets.

Some inner sense told her he was here, and already breathless and giddy, Bess flew down the stairs and out the front door of Northaw just in time to see him arrive. Astride the black stallion, his great horsemanship was evident, and she knew he was aware of the splendid figure he cut. As Bess watched him dismount, a dozen emotions swam together, threatening to engulf her. As well as elation and excitement, uncertainty made her feel shy and tongue-tied. What would he say to her—what would she say to him?

Then suddenly she was in his arms, his lips whispering against her ear, "Why aren't you in bed?" Then his deep laughter rang out, and she saw the teasing amusement in his eyes and knew why she loved him so much.

No longer tongue-tied, her sultry laugh matched his. "You are a damned rogue!"

SEVENTEEN

The servants gathered inside the front entrance to greet Sir William. To give him an opportunity to speak to them in private, Bess led James Cromp upstairs and showed him where to put William's luggage.

"James, I see no need for formality between us, since you will be privy to all our secrets," Bess said with her usual candor. "I've ordered plenty of hot water, and there is a huge wooden bathtub in the next bedchamber."

"Thank you, ma'am." He started to unpack and hung Cavendish's clothes in the wardrobe beside hers. He glanced at the fireplace. "Would you like a fire lit tonight?"

"Yes, after dinner. It got quite cool last

night when the sun went down." Bess blushed, thinking her bed would not likely be cold tonight.

Cavendish came bounding up the stairs. As he entered the room, she saw his eyes sweep about the spacious chamber she had chosen for them. He nodded his approval.

"I just love the house," she said breathlessly.

He gathered her in his arms, unmindful of James's presence. "And I just love you." Bess closed her eyes as he kissed her, not quite believing that at last their time had come.

He kissed her again. "Let me get the stink of London off me."

Bess and William had dinner alone in the private dining parlor off the hall. Northaw's only footman served them. The beefsteak was cooked perfectly, the vegetables tender, the Yorkshire pudding crisp. Bess was proud of her menu; she had planned it with a man's hearty appetite in mind.

William lifted his wine goblet. "I toast the loveliest lady in England tonight." Then he quaffed deeply. "This claret is extremely good. I had no idea Northaw had anything in its wine cellars."

"It doesn't." Bess laughed softly. "I brought the wine."

"I always knew you were a very clever girl. What other surprises do you have for me?" he asked with a rakish smile.

"Faith, my lord, 'tis the other way about. What surprises do you have for me?"

His deep laugh rolled across the table. "Sweetheart, don't tell me you're apprehensive?"

"A little," she admitted breathlessly.

His whole heart went out to her. He came around the table and lifted her into his lap.

"William, the servants," she protested softly.

"They won't mind a bit. I told them I was raising their wages."

"But that's almost a bribe."

"No, love, it is exactly a bribe. The golden spur works every time. Watch, we'll have them eating out of our hands."

"You're unconscionable."

"I know." He brushed the backs of his fingers across her cheek. "What do you want for dessert?"

"Strawberries, of course!"

"I'll feed them to you." He dipped a red berry in sugar and lifted it to her lips. Her tongue came out to lick off the sugar before she took the strawberry into her mouth. His eyes showed his adoration as his desire mounted. "Luscious," he murmured, touching his lips to hers. He repeated the ritual of strawberry and kiss until she was laughing helplessly.

"No more," she said breathlessly.

"No more strawberries or no more kisses?" he teased.

"Come into the garden and I'll show you where they're grown."

He quirked an eyebrow at her, then realized

that perhaps she needed a little more time before they went upstairs.

Outside, dusk had fallen as they strolled hand in hand along the overgrown garden paths. Night-scented flowers filled the cooling air with their intoxicating perfume. Bess was about to tell him all her plans for the garden when he drew her into the deep shadows and took her into his arms. Her breasts heaved quickly, and she began to shiver with the intensity of her feelings. When he kissed her, her response was fierce, telling him that though she might be apprehensive, her desire was fast becoming greater than her trepidation.

His lips brushed the bright tendrils at her temple. "Bess, I've waited so long."

She took his hand and drew him toward the house. Her heart was hammering. It was true, she had made him wait forever, but now that their time had come, she vowed she would love him with every pulse in her body.

When they entered Northaw there were no servants in evidence, but they were beyond caring. They climbed the stairs with their arms entwined about each other, unwilling and unable to conceal their passionate desire any longer. If any had seen them, they would have known the pair were about to become lovers.

Before their heavy bedchamber door swung closed, he enfolded her in his powerful arms, then claimed her mouth with his in a kiss that was possessive and demanding and would never be denied again. Her lips parted at his insistence, and his tongue invaded the hot, sweet cave of her mouth, exploring with strokes and thrusts until she shivered at the intensity of her arousal.

Her delicious shivers prompted him to draw her closer to the fire before he began to undress her. His hands were knowing and sure as he unfastened her gown and lifted it off. Bess undid the tapes of her petticoat herself and stepped out of it, leaving herself clad in only a short shift and her stockings.

William gathered her to him again, and she felt the heat of his hands through the thin material that both revealed and concealed her curves. "Your body was fashioned to give a man pleasure." His possessive hands fondled her breasts, and he dipped his head to kiss, then tongue her nipples through the delicate fabric. The clinging wet material turned transparent, so that the bright pink tips of her breasts were now temptingly visible. His eyes told her of the inner excitement the sight of her body brought him.

Every glance, every touch heightened her arousal and made her hands bold enough to go inside his doublet to unfasten his shirt. "William, I want to look at you and touch you in the same way." When he shrugged out of his doublet and removed his shirt, Bess's dark eyes drank in his male splendor. She had never seen him unclothed, and she thrilled at the realization that his wide chest and powerful shoulders had nothing to do with the padded doublets that were the fashion.

"Oh," she gasped, as she ran her hand over his sleek muscles. "You're so hard."

He took her hand and brushed it across his groin. "Hard as marble."

"Let me see!" she demanded, as a hunger for the sight of him gnawed inside her belly.

William stripped off his clothes and stood before her completely nude.

"Oh, my God," she murmured with breathless admiration. His cock was so dominant, it was a full minute before she could take her eyes from it. Then she saw the other things that made the male so different from the female.

His hips were narrow, but his thighs bulged with muscles, which had no doubt developed from long hours in the saddle. She reached out inquisitive fingers to trace a sinew and watched in fascination as his shaft reared and bucked as if demonstrating the brute force it possessed.

Bess gazed at him in wonder, her eyes slowly sliding up his magnificent male body. "You look like your stallion."

"That's exactly how I feel—rampant!"

"Now I understand.... My God, how ignorant I was. Now I see how difficult it must have been to control your raging need. I understand your haste."

"I was in a hurry, Bess, but I'll never be in a hurry again, sweetheart. Slowly. I'll savor you slowly." He drew her closer to his body and thrust his phallus against her soft belly.

Her back was to the fire, and he inched up her shift until her bottom was bared. The flames heated her naked flesh, arousing her further. Bess pulled the front of her shift up above her thighs, then she rubbed herself against him. "Mmmm, that feels so good."

He kissed her eyelids. "Foreplay with you is like being in paradise."

Bess thought it a lovely word. "Why, because I'm a virgin?"

He cupped her hot bottom cheeks. "That's part of it, knowing this is the first time you'll be fully aroused, knowing I'm the first to breach all your defenses. But a year from now, when you'll be anything but virgin, foreplay will still be like paradise. Your body is so lush, Bess, and your inborn sensuality so potent, nothing will stop it once I've awakened it."

She rubbed her cheek across his dark auburn chest hair and nipped at his nipple with her teeth. "If you light a fire in me, you'll have to douse it."

"Oh, I'll certainly try, sweetheart, but I suspect it will be more than a fire. It will be a conflagration." He laughed down at her, then lifted off her shift and flung it into the air with a flourish. She was now clad in white lace stockings, held up by ribbon garters. "Those are the sauciest garters I've ever seen. Walk about for me, so I can get the full effect."

"You rogue, what do you mean?"

He rolled his eyes in ecstasy, making her laugh. "There's something so titillating about red curls and green ribbons. I can't describe it.... Walk over for me and look in the mirror."

Bess went to the mirror and blushed pink

at her wanton reflection. Her high mons was covered by a profusion of red-gold curls, while on either side a green ribbon decorated her thighs. Bess liked the naughty picture she made. He'd had her stripped down to her stockings once before, and she remembered vividly what he'd done to her that night. Only this time he didn't have to stop! This time she would let him play out his erotic games to their wicked conclusion! Bess cupped her breasts and admired them in the mirror.

He growled low in his throat and pounced. With one arm about her back, the other beneath her knees, he swept her up, raising her mons until it was high enough for him to kiss. Bess arched provocatively, then squealed as he buried his tongue in her, carrying her to the high bed before he withdrew it.

"Lie back," he murmured.

As she did so, Bess lifted her hair so that it spread over the green cover in silken splendor. He knelt on the bed and gazed down at her. "Open your legs for me so I can look at you," he said huskily.

Bess lifted her legs and placed a small foot on each of his shoulders. The tip of her tongue came out to lick her lips. "Would you help me remove my stockings, sir?"

William reached down her leg and slowly drew off a lace stocking and garter. Then he brought the dainty bare foot to his mouth for a kiss. Bess curled her toes in pleasure, allowing him a peek at her pink cleft as his hands slipped off the other stocking.

Her teasing, wanton behavior told him she was becoming highly aroused and that she was inviting him to make love to her. But William didn't want this deflowering to be painful. If he gauged her sensuality right, she had a long way to go yet before she was in full-blown arousal. He would wait until she was begging and writhing in white-hot need, so that all she would experience when he mounted her was pure sexual pleasure.

He stretched out beside her on the bed, then came up over her in the dominant position and pulled her into a fierce embrace. One of the most beautiful things about her was her mouth, and he knew he'd never have enough of it. He splayed his fingers into her hair and lowered his mouth, molding his lips and his body to hers as she lay captive beneath him.

At first his kisses were tender and melting, then they turned sensual as his tongue delved deep, tasting her honeyed sweetness and tempting her tongue to duel with his in a play of love that felt like hot, sliding silk. These kisses aroused a ferocious hunger that became rough and elemental in their intensity. Her full breasts were crushed against the hard, sleek muscles of his chest, the hair on his chest abrading her nipples, turning them to diamond-hard jewels.

Now he traced the outline of her mouth with the tip of his tongue, licking her full, sensual lower lip, then sucking it into his mouth as if it were a ripe strawberry. A flame ignited between them, burning their mouths with a smoldering, savage heat that made their blood surge and pound wildly until raw moans of passion erupted from their throats.

William rolled to his back and took her with him, so that now it was Bess who was in the dominant position. She gazed down at him, smoky-eyed, then with feverish hands and mouth explored his body and his maleness to the full. She cupped and stroked and rubbed and kissed and licked every naked inch of his muscle-hard body. Never had he experienced such a splendidly uninhibited female in his life. Then, suddenly, she wrapped her legs about his thigh and began to ride it, raking his flesh with her nails and panting, "Rogue, Rogue, please."

He stroked the inside of her thighs to loosen their grip on him, then he took her down to the bed and rose above her, suddenly looking ruthless and completely masterful. She needed him to be in full control. She needed him to dominate her completely so she could yield to him. And he became everything she needed.

He positioned himself so that the head of his phallus touched her cleft, then he thrust inside her sheath with a steady pressure that did not falter at the barrier but thrust through it until he was anchored deep. She was so tight, a hot shudder jolted through his body, then slowly, with long, drugging strokes, he began to make her his.

Never in her wildest imaginings had Bess ever dreamed anything could be so powerful and cataclysmic. At first there was pain, but she didn't fight it, she welcomed it, relished it, loving the fullness and instinctively knowing the pleasure would drown everything with exquisite liquid tremors.

He knew when her passion suddenly soared above every other sensation, for she began to writhe and arch her body and her legs slid high about his back, holding him captive until her ravishing was complete. She craved more kisses, then, when even they weren't enough, she slid her scalding mouth down the powerful column of his neck and she began to bite his shoulder.

He felt his seed almost start two or three times from the silken torment, but with an iron will he stroked deep and strong, knowing the surging wave was building inside her as surely as it built inside himself. He urged her on with raw whispers of love, taking untold pleasure in her cries of passion. Then, suddenly, she screamed and clung to him tightly, and a cry was torn from his own throat, as miraculously they climaxed together.

Each felt the throbbing and pulsing of the other as they were fused together in this fierce mating that allowed them to unleash all the pent-up desire that had been building for years. They were unable to move for long minutes as they lay entwined, their heartbeats thudding against each other, conjoined as if they were one being.

Bess mourned the loss of his weight when he lifted himself from her body, but he slipped his strong arms about her and gathered her close, gazing down at her with love. She was luminous in the candlelight, her flaming hair gloriously disheveled from his loving. Her creamy thighs bore the tiny drops of blood and pearly semen that proclaimed her lost innocence. Bess was soft with surfeit and languorously put her arms about his neck.

"I didn't know," she murmured in wonder. "I had no idea it was like that."

He smoothed damp tendrils from her forehead. "My love, it is seldom like that. Only for a special few is it earth-shattering."

Bess felt soft and small and exceedingly feminine. She loved the smell of his male-scented skin, loved the salty taste of him that lingered on her tongue. She loved the heavy languor that came with being sated; she even loved the heady, musky smell of sex that floated in the air.

The corners of her mouth lifted. She had found her perfect mate. He was so strong and virile and dominant that she could be weak and helpless if she so chose. Yet he was so much a man that if she felt like being assertive and opinionated and bossy, it didn't threaten him, it amused him.

She lifted her mouth to his. "Rogue Cavendish, I have lost my heart to you."

He grinned down at her and patted her thighs with a corner of the snowy sheet. "By the look of things you've lost more than your heart tonight. Any regrets, beauty?"

Bess stretched like a sensual cat with a bellyful of cream. "My innocence? I didn't lose it; I flung it away with great abandon. My only regret is that you didn't make love to me sooner," she said dreamily.

"I'll make up for that, never fear. God, how long I've wanted you in bed beside me. All night. To have you fall asleep in my arms, to awaken you with a kiss, makes me the luckiest man alive." He lifted her between the sheets and tucked the blanket about her. She curled beside him and closed her eyes. He curved an arm about her and cupped a breast, glorying in the lush weight of it. Safe inside their warm cocoon, her body and her senses replete with love, Bess slowly drifted off in blissful slumber.

In the middle of the night, William awoke and found the place beside him empty. His eyes were drawn to the flickering fire in the hearth and he saw Bess standing before it, her beautiful body bathed in the fire glow.

"Are you all right, love?" He slipped from the bed and covered the distance between them.

Her face was radiant. "I'm so happy—I just couldn't sleep."

He moved behind her and cupped her shoulders, drawing her back against him. "That's excess energy—sexual energy." He shuddered as her bottom brushed across his groin. His hands moved down from her shoulders to cup her breasts, and he felt her quivering response. "The firelight loves you as I do. It touches you everywhere, making you glow, making you hot." His fingers traced her rib cage and stroked across her belly, then they threaded through the fiery curls atop her mons and he rubbed his palm against her.

Bess turned to face him and went on tiptoe to slide her arms about his neck. With a low moan she said fiercely, "I don't think I'll ever be able to sleep again."

"I know what you need." His voice was like dark velvet. "Will you let me burn off all this delicious sexual energy?"

She nodded her consent and gasped as he lifted her onto his marble-hard manroot. With his hands beneath her bottom cheeks, he moved purposely toward the high bed. "I'll make you sleep."

Just after dawn Bess opened her eyes and stretched sensuously. William, in black leather pants and linen shirt, came to the bed. "Sweetheart, I wanted to surprise you. I'm on my way to buy you a mount so we can ride together. I thought I'd be back before you awakened."

He dipped his head to kiss her and she came up on her knees to him, a naked supplicant, sliding her arms about his neck. "Take me with you. Teach me how to buy a horse. Let me do the bargaining."

His hands stroked her back and she opened her mouth, inviting his deep kiss. His fingers slid into the cleft between her buttocks and she immediately arched against his arousal. His eyes brimmed with amusement. "You already know how to get exactly what you want."

The tip of her pink tongue came out to trace his lips, and her fingers undid the buttons of his shirt. "Give me another lesson; I want to learn everything."

He lifted her from the bed and she wrapped her legs around him. "We are so alike; we both have ravenous appetites when we awaken."

"Will you slake my hunger and thirst?" she teased.

"Will you slake mine?" he demanded intensely, his lids heavy with desire.

"Each and every morning," she vowed.

An hour later, as Bess lay sprawled across him on the floor before the ashes of the burned-out fire, William stirred. "You need a bath. You have my male scent all over your lovely body." He sniffed her with lusty appreciation and rolled his eyes heavenward to make her laugh. "I wonder if that bathtub is large enough for two?"

As they rode from St. Albans, heading back to Northaw, Bess patted the glossy neck of the black mare he had just bought her. "I'm sorry I called you a scabby old jade," she crooned into the filly's ear. "That was just a bargaining tactic."

Cavendish grinned at her. "I honestly thought you fancied the white palfrey."

Bess grinned back. "Aye, and so did the old horse thief, but I had my eye on the black all along. We can put her to your stallion and add to our stable at Northaw."

He didn't hide his amusement at her ambitious plans. On the ride to St. Albans, as she'd sat before him in the saddle, she had told him of her ideas to improve the house, redesign the garden, and now she was starting on the stable. She tossed her head at his laughter. "I'll show you!"

"I bet you will." His eyes swept over her possessively. "Just don't show any other man. St. Loe couldn't keep his eyes off you."

"I almost fainted when Elizabeth's captain of the guard rode in."

"St. Loe was buying horses for Hatfield. It's a small world, Bess. For your sake we have to be discreet for a while."

"I know we shouldn't be together yet."

He couldn't bear the look of guilt that clouded her eyes. "Come on, I'll race you!"

"What stakes?"

"I'll think of something—I'll tell you in bed tonight."

"Cocksure devil!" Bess kept abreast of him, hoping he was too gallant to trounce her unmercifully. When the gate to the Northaw property came into view, she recklessly darted her mare in front of his stallion, causing him to rein in, causing him to lose the race.

He grabbed her bridle. "I should take you across my knee."

"A dangerous position—I might bite."

He rubbed his shoulder. "You do bite."

By the time the evening meal was over and darkness descended, the lovers were in a fever of longing to be alone. As the minutes dragged by, they seemed like hours. Cavendish thought he could get some of his paperwork done before they retired, but he finally got up from the desk, abandoning all pretense at concentration. He went to the sideboard and restlessly picked up a flagon of wine.

"Would you bring that upstairs, Sir William?" Bess asked sweetly as Mistress Bagshaw came into the room to draw the drapes.

"Of course." His eyes glittered as he watched Bess climb the stairs as innocently as a nun going to vespers. He followed her immediately and secured the door. "Hell's teeth, the woman couldn't keep a straight face. *Sir William* indeed."

"She doesn't suspect a thing," Bess insisted stubbornly. "She helped me prepare separate bedchambers."

"And what do you suppose she thought when she changed our sheets today?"

Bess thought it over for a second. "Who cares? I'll race you to bed!" She kicked off her slippers and stripped off her stockings. She began to laugh as she struggled with the fastenings of her gown and watched him fling off his shirt and reach for his boots. She was naked before he was and ran up the bed steps and did a little victory dance. With a yell of triumph, he launched himself at her and they rolled together into the big featherbed.

Bess reached up and grabbed his hair, shuddering with the intensity of her feelings. "Rogue, I want to make love all night!"

He couldn't stop laughing at her. "Do you

hear that, Mistress Bagshaw, she wants to fu—"

Bess covered his mouth with her hand to silence him. "You devil," she whispered. "I'll never let you bed me again. Well," she amended, "at least not until you pour me some wine."

EIGHTEEN

In the bed Bess sat cradled between William's legs, a most comfortable position for talking and sipping wine from the loving cup they shared. Though her body felt replete, her mind was already anticipating and dreading the hour they would have to part. "When must you leave?"

She felt his lips glide down her neck, then felt his warm breath fan her shoulder. "Tomorrow. Bess, it will be for only a short time, then we can be together always."

"As soon as I get back, come to me at Suffolk House."

"I shouldn't. I want to protect you from gossip; it can be so vicious. If it was known we were already cohabiting, we could be accused of taking a hand in my wife's death."

"No one would believe such a thing!" she said, outraged.

"The Court thrives on gossip. Did you not hear the rumor that Catherine Parr poisoned the king?"

Bess turned onto her stomach so she could look up at him. "If I'd been wed to Harry, I, too, would have poisoned him." Her sultry laugh rang out.

He kissed her to stop her treasonous words. "Never say that outside this bed."

Bess suddenly sobered. "What if St. Loe spreads it about the Court that we were here together?"

"Sir William St. Loe is a gentleman or he wouldn't have been chosen to guard Elizabeth. He would never besmirch a lady's reputation."

"It doesn't seem fair that Elizabeth cannot have the man she loves."

"Tom Seymour wants only the power she can give him."

"How do you know he doesn't love her madly?"

"Because he asked the council for permission to wed either princess—Elizabeth or Mary."

Bess was deeply shocked. "My God, how could he? Both the princess and Seymour know about us."

"Don't fret, my love; they'll all know soon enough."

"Most of them already know. Frances is probably making wedding plans."

"Well, I think we should wait a month before we are seen openly together."

"A month?" she wailed. "Two weeks— promise me you will come to me in a fortnight!"

He gathered her close, stroking her beautiful hair. "A fortnight, I promise—if I can hold out that long."

The following day neither of them could bear to part, so they stole an extra night together. But despite the powerful strength of their feelings for each other, they could not hold back the dawn. Like a loving wife and dutiful chatelaine, Bess was up and dressed in time to break their fast together and to see William and James Cromp depart for London.

Uncaring of who observed them, Cavendish swept her into his arms in the courtyard. "I have a hundred things awaiting my attention, sweetheart. Thank you for these precious days at Northaw. I adore you, Bess."

She was devastated at the parting but kept her emotions hidden from him. She gave him a brilliant smile as he took the reins from Cromp and swung into the saddle. Bess stood waving until he was out of sight, feeling utterly forlorn. Then she realized how ridiculous she was. She was no longer a girl, she was a woman, the luckiest in the world, with a lifetime of happiness beforeher.

Bess swept up the steps into Northaw, thinking of at least a dozen things she must accomplish before she packed for London. By the time she reached the servants' hall she was already humming a merry tune.

"Bess, thank God you are back. I've been trying to pack for Bradgate, but I make such a bollix of everything. You will restore order from chaos. What the hellfire I'll do without you, I'll never know. When is the wedding, by the way?"

Henry protested vigorously. "For Christ's sake, Frances, the woman's corpse isn't cold yet!"

Frances waved her hand dismissively. " 'Tis the fashion for widows to remarry quickly, and Bess has been a widow for over two years."

"But Cavendish hasn't been a widower. The funeral was only four days ago!"

"Five, but who's counting?" Frances drawled.

As it turned out, a fortnight later it was Bess who was counting. Her monthly courses were late, and because she had been regular as clockwork since she'd turned twelve, she suspected that she had conceived.

She pushed the frightening thought away, immersed herself in the enormous task of sorting out what things were to go to Bradgate, and wished desperately that William would show up at Suffolk House.

When July turned into August, Bess began to panic. She casually asked Henry to pass a message to William that she would like to see him.

"Haven't seen him since the funeral. Strange." He looked at her with concern. "I'll ferret him out."

As soon as Bess had all of the pictures and furniture for Bradgate crated and labeled, she set to work packing for Lady Frances and

Lady Catherine. That night she sat and wrote out long lists of inventory to occupy her hands and her mind.

The following day Henry sought her out. "I spoke to Paulet yesterday; it seems William is away on the king's business—Oxford and Abingdon Abbey."

Bess was somewhat relieved that he had not gone farther afield. Still, Oxford was almost sixty miles from London.

"God, men are all alike—off tomcatting, no doubt, sowing his wild oats as a bachelor," Frances teased.

Bess blushed furiously. Cavendish had certainly been sowing his oats, damn the rogue to hellfire. But she wasn't worried about other women, thank God. She could hold her own against any woman breathing. What did worry her was his possible aversion to marriage. Her overwrought mind went over everything he'd done, every word he'd uttered at Northaw.

He had told her he adored her and that they would be together always, and she believed him. He had loved her passionately, day and night, and taught her passion too, but he had not asked her to marry him. Bess had taken marriage for granted when she agreed to go to Northaw. She should have pinned him down to the specifics about a wedding—where and, more importantly, when?

Bess had no one to blame but herself. She had run to his arms, to his bed, blindly, eagerly, and, yes, shamelessly! She assured herself over and over that all would be well and that William would come on the morrow. But William did not come. The weather turned extremely wet. It poured down every day, and Bess told herself this was delaying his return.

Frances fretted over the weather. "The summer will be gone before we even get to Bradgate. We are usually up there by now."

"The baggage carts would have bogged down in the rutted roads if we'd left earlier," Bess pointed out. She was not anxious to leave London before William's return.

"You are right. Bess, I have a dilemma. I don't know whether to leave Jane at Chelsea with the queen or take her with us to Bradgate. I worry about plague in the hot weather."

"Chelsea should be safe; even though it's close to London, it's surrounded by countryside."

"We'll go to Chelsea tomorrow and let Jane decide for herself," Frances declared.

Abiding by her daughter's wishes, Frances brought Lady Jane and her ladies back to Suffolk House. They would all set out on the journey to Bradgate, Leceistershire, on the morrow. Tonight the Greys would bid goodbye to their closest friends at their last dinner party of the season.

John Dudley and his countess were there, as were William Herbert and his countess, who was sister to the queen. As they were going in to dinner, William Herbert smiled at Bess. "Won't Cavendish be joining us tonight, my dear?"

"I—I believe he's away on the king's business, my lord," Bess replied vaguely.

Lady Herbert cut in, "Nay, he returned from Oxford long since; he dined with us at my brother Parr's two nights back."

Bess felt stabbed to the heart. She could not believe her beloved had returned to London without coming to see her or sending a note. The blood drained from her face as she realized his actions must be deliberate; William was avoiding her. As if she were in a trance, Bess sought out Frances. "I haven't finished my packing; will you excuse me tonight?"

Once she gained her own rooms, Bess flung herself onto the bed and began to cry. She missed William so much, her heart ached. Without William she felt utterly alone. Abandoned. She told herself that was ridiculous; how could he abandon her when he loved her? Bess sat up and swiped impatiently at her tears as a tiny spark of anger ignited within her. She knew where he lived; she would send a message to summon him immediately!

Nay! The very last thing she would ever do was send him another letter of supplication. Her pride was too great to ever humiliate herself in that way again. She'd die first! Bess picked up a flacon of perfume from beside the bed and hurled it across the chamber.

She began to pace the room like a tigress, seeking a way to vent her rage. Not only was she angry at Cavendish, she was furious at herself. She had gone to him of her own free will, knowing the risk involved. Now that he'd had his way with her, he had tossed her aside. She would have to face the shame and humiliation of bearing his bastard!

She stopped pacing and put shielding hands to her belly. Thank God she was leaving London tomorrow; she couldn't face a scandal. On the way to Bradgate perhaps she would find the courage to tell Frances, or failing that she could go home to her family. Both options were anathema to her. She clenched impotent fists, and decided to keep the shameful secret to herself. Bess was afraid and shockingly vulnerable and insecure. She did not know what she would do and resolutely pushed the decision away, but she knew that somehow, someway, she would have to find a way to cope.

Three carriages, four wagons, and a dozen pack-horses made up the Greys' entourage. Lady Jane and her ladies had their own carriage, and Lady Catherine insisted on taking the dogs in the carriage in which she was traveling.

"Take the parrot with you, Henry," Frances directed. He eyed the yapping dogs and came to a swift decision. "I'm riding!" He set the cage on the seat beside his wife. "You'll have to look after your own bloody parrot, Frances."

"Men! Apart from bed sport, what use are they?" As the carriage bowled along the Great North Road, Frances settled in for a long gossip. "Bess, you missed all the juicy gossip last night. In a way I'm glad I'm leaving London. If what I am about to tell you turns out to be true, there will be such an uproar, we could all be dragged into it. Lady Herbert told me—in strictest confidence, of course—that our friend Tom Seymour frequents Chelsea day and night!"

Bess stiffened. Hell's teeth, gossip spread faster than the plague! How foolish Elizabeth was to think she could keep his visits secret.

"I must admit I love a whiff of scandal, but Anne Herbert has a nose for it like a bloodhound." Frances lowered her voice confidentially, and Bess braced herself to hear the rumor about Elizabeth.

"She suspects that Catherine Parr and Seymour are secretly wed!"

Nooo! The denial screamed through Bess's brain. She was rocked with disbelief.

Bess closed her eyes. Dear God, could any man plot such perfidy? Bess's mind recoiled from the evil thought, yet still it persisted. Denied marriage to one, would he wed the other so he could live with *both,* have congress with *both*?

Bess felt sick, yet she dare not display symptoms of nausea before Lady Frances. The Court was a cesspool of scandalous gossip. Bess did not want it to touch her or her baby. "I don't believe it," she said quietly.

"I do! Thomas is so insatiably ambitious, he would risk anything to gain more power than his brother Edward. Since he cannot have

Harry's daughter, he'll settle for Harry's widow!"

"Why do men take whatever they want?"

Frances laughed. "Because women let them."

And there is my answer, Bess thought dispassionately.

NINETEEN

During the second week of August, Bess was kept busy uncrating, unpacking, and rearranging the furnishings at Bradgate. The modern red-brick palace was massive, with twenty bedchambers, so there was plenty of space to accommodate the pieces Frances had purloined from Chelsea.

Bess took a chamber high in the east wing, away from the family, where guests were usually accommodated. Because she was kept constantly busy, the days flew by swiftly, but her nights were almost unendurable. Alone in her bed, her body ached for William, and it took hours before she could fall asleep. Then, when she did sleep, her dreams were filled with his laughing face and his powerful body. She loved him and hated him at the same time. She silently cursed him, reviled him, and condemned him, yet all the while she longed for him.

Bradgate was set among orchards and pleasure gardens, with ornamental bridges across a trout stream, a wishing well, huge shade trees, and a long terrace filled with cushioned chairs. As Bess sat in the garden in the sun-filled August afternoons, she kept putting off making a decision about what to do. She went over and over her options, knowing her mind was running in circles that accomplished absolutely nothing. She knew the time had come when she must face facts.

She thought about ridding herself of the child and recoiled from that course of action. Yet Bess knew that in order to keep her position with the Greys, she would have to give up the child in one manner or another. She could have her baby in secret and pay to have it brought up in the country. Or she could swallow her pride and go home. Her family would help her; she could leave the child with them, where she knew it would be loved and where she could see it from time to time.

Suddenly Bess knew her pride wasn't the sticking point. It was her towering ambition that was making her decision so difficult. Her hands went to her belly. This wasn't her baby's fault. A fierce protectiveness gripped her. She loved it with a passion. Her child was part of her, mayhap the best part! She knew they were inseparable. She could no more farm it out than she could get rid of it. She realized that she was just as ambitious for her child as she was for herself.

She had achieved so much, climbing the social ladder one rung at a time, and just as she was about to reach her goal, fate had snatched away the ladder. For the second time all she had worked for in London would be lost. Her glorious plan for the future lay in ruin, and she would be plummeted back to where she had started. Well, she had survived before, and she would survive again, Bess told herself fiercely.

Her energy was so sapped, it was an effort for Bess to get up out of her chair. She had become so lethargic, she felt as if she were dragging one foot after the other. Somehow she managed to get through dinner, but as she sat playing cards with Frances and her guests, Bess began to yawn her head off. She felt so weary that all she wanted was to escape into blissful sleep.

Frances laughed at her. " 'Tis this country air, darling; it is positively soporific. You've lost every single hand, Bess. Do retire and get some sleep."

In her chamber Bess undressed slowly, opened the window wide, and climbed into bed. Tonight she was so drained, she fell asleep almost immediately.

Bess awakened, terrified. The room was empty, stripped bare. She ran downstairs and found the bailiffs carrying off everything she possessed in the world. She begged, pleaded, and cried, all to no avail. Outside, her meager belongings were being piled on a cart. She had been put out of the house and had nowhere to go. Fear washed over her in great waves. Panic choked her. When she turned around, the cart was gone, the Greys were gone, even Bradgate had vanished. Bess had lost everything she had in the world. The terror mounted until it engulfed her, the waves of fear almost drowned her. The hollow, empty feeling inside her belly was like ravenous hunger, only worse; her baby was gone! She was overwhelmed with help-lessness, hopelessness.

Bess sat up in bed, awakened by her own scream. The darkness closed in about her, ter-rifying her. Her hand flew to her belly in a pro-tective gesture, then with trembling fingers she lit the bedside candles. Relief washed over her; everything was as it should be. It was only the old recurring nightmare. She drew up her knees and put her head down, waiting for her heart to stop hammering, waiting for the fear to go away.

Bess lifted her head as her door slowly opened. Her heart slammed against her ribs as Cavendish came in. Was she still dreaming? A great tide of anger swept through her, dousing her fear. "Get out! How dare you enter my chamber? Get out, you swine!" She looked for something to throw at him, and her hand closed about the candelabra.

He saw her intent and closed the distance between them. "Bess, it's me, it's William."

"I know who it is, for Christ's sake; only you would have the bare-faced gall!"

"What the devil is the matter?" he demanded, reaching out a comforting hand to stroke her hair.

Bess jerked her head away. "Don't touch me!" she cried.

Cavendish stood staring down at her. What in God's name had made her change her mind? It could only be the age difference. She was barely nineteen, while he would never see his fortieth birthday again.

"It is the middle of August!" she flung at him. "I haven't seen you since the last day of June! Once I yielded to you, you abandoned me!" She was panting with fury.

"Abandoned you? My own love, how could you think such an absurd thought? Surely, you never doubted me, Bess? I swore on my life I would never let you down again. I thought our trust in each other was absolute. It has been only seven weeks—hardly a decent mourning period, and I've been so busy, the days have flown past. I sold the old house and bought you a new one from our friend William Parr. I assumed you and Frances would be up to your eyes in plans."

"Plans?" Bess said angrily.

"You have such definite ideas about the way you want things. You have a mind of your own and so much strength of purpose, I didn't dare make wedding plans for you."

"You never once asked me to wed you!" she accused.

"Well, I'm asking you now. Would you like a festive Christmas wedding, sweetheart?"

"Christmas?" Bess was so dismayed, she slapped his face and burst into tears.

He took her into his arms and held her close. "Bess, what's wrong?"

"I'm having a baby," she whispered.

His powerful arms tightened around her. "Oh, my precious love, no wonder you feel abandoned." He rocked her gently and stroked her hair. He always thought of her as so self-assured, yet beneath her confident facade she was a mass of insecurities. He drew aside the covers. "Come on, get dressed."

"Why?" She pulled away.

"We're going to get married."

"I wouldn't marry you, Rogue Cavendish, if you were the last man breathing!" Bess said stubbornly.

"You will do as I bid!"

"It's the middle of the night!" she protested.

"What in the world of God does that have to do with anything? We'll rouse the bloody priest out of his bed and give Frances something to talk about. Now, are you going to get dressed or will I carry you down in your shift?"

Rogue's eyes were filled with such a teasing light, Bess knew he was capable of doing such a thing. She padded to the wardrobe. "Whatever shall I wear? I want to look beautiful."

"You always look beautiful." He had more good sense than to suggest what a woman should wear. "Hurry, I'll be back for you very shortly," he warned.

Bess chose a cream silk gown whose sleeves were slashed with jade. She pulled on stockings and fastened them with jade garters. Gone was her lethargy; suddenly, she was bursting with energy and her heart was singing. When Frances arrived Bess apologized for the late hour.

"It's only two o'clock; I hadn't gone to bed

yet. I've brought Cecily to do your hair. Everyone in London will be foaming at the mouth to have missed this. Cavendish is a madman; what on earth is his hurry?"

"I'll tell you what's the hurry," William said from the doorway. Bess threw him such a desperate glance, his heart went out to her. "She's refused me again. No bedding without a wedding—what's a lusty man to do?"

Bess suddenly realized that it was August 20, the same date she had been evicted from Hardwick. A lump came into her throat. This was her fateful day, when either bad or good things could happen—things that would alter her life. She smiled through her tears and gave William her hand.

By the time they made their way to the chapel, Henry and the priest were awaiting them. Bess was surprised to find the seats filled with the Grey's noble guests. Sir John Port, who had recently been knighted at the young king's coronation, and his wife, Lady Port, were there, along with her family, the Fitzherberts. Also present was Sir John's daughter and her husband, the Earl of Huntingdon, and their friends the Earl and Countess of Westmorland. Bess was amazed that William was on intimate terms with so many noble families and shrewdly guessed that it must be because of his position in the treasury.

As Bess stood beside William to exchange their vows, she felt that her heart might burst with joy. When William slipped a diamond wedding ring onto her third finger, all her doubts about his wanting to make her his wife disappeared forever. When they were pronounced man and wife, and Bess realized that at last she was Lady Cavendish, she was giddy with happiness.

The company hurried back to the hall, showering the newlyweds with rose petals that some enterprising guest had plucked from the gardens. When they arrived, the musicians were already playing their instruments and Bradgate's liveried servants were rushing about, providing food and wine for the celebration.

They danced until the sun came up, then William picked up his bride and carried her off to a hastily prepared bridal suite, where William firmly closed and locked the door, depriving the avid guests of the bedding they had been anticipating.

"My darling, when I told you to get dressed, I didn't mean for you to put on so many layers."

"Did you expect to find me naked beneath my gown?"

"That's how I pictured you," he said thickly, trying to undo the fastenings of her petticoat.

"In the chapel?" She pretended to be shocked.

"I would have laid you naked on the altar if we'd been alone. I've been starving for you."

She brushed her breasts against him and decided to tease him. "But it's been only seven weeks; you told me yourself the days had flown past." She danced away from him and left him holding her petticoat.

"The nights were sheer torture!" He came after her.

"Torture? You don't know the meaning of the word. Shall I teach you?" She inched up her shift, giving him a tantalizing glimpse of red-gold curls, then let it fall again.

"Cockteaser!"

The corners of her mouth went up. "I'm going to tease your cock until you beg."

He threw her a wicked grin and began to fling off his clothes. He stood naked before her in rampant splendor. "I suspect you are hot for me." He lunged toward her and caught her. His hand dipped beneath the hem of her shift and a finger deftly stroked her cleft. "Scalding-hot and wet"—he licked his finger—"my little honeypot."

She eluded him, but instead of running away, she walked a direct path to the big bed, while he watched her from beneath lids heavy with desire. Bess reclined against the pillows. "Do you like honey?" Her voice was sultry. She dipped her finger into her own honeypot and touched her nipples with the sweetness.

She was so splendidly uninhibited, William found her allure impossible to resist; it was impossible for him to leave her untasted. He came to the bed and rose above her, hungrily feasting his eyes where his mouth would follow. He knew he would love her all his days. He could hardly believe that at last the prize was his. Not only was Bess beautiful, sensual, and passionate, she was also clever, witty, and shrewd. He vowed that he would devote himself to her and love her enough to banish her insecurities and turn her into the confident woman she pretended to be. They remained in seclusion for two whole days and nights before Rogue Cavendish could bear to share her with anyone else.

Bess couldn't wait to take William to Derbyshire and show him off to her family.

"Why don't we surprise them?" William suggested.

"I wouldn't dare descend upon them with anyone as grand as Sir William Cavendish without giving them fair warning."

"Me, grand?" he teased. "You are the grand lady."

"Oh, I know," Bess said happily.

Since William loved hunting and the game was plentiful in Leicestershire, the Greys arranged a hunt for their guests. Bess accompanied William for the first couple of hours, then retired back to Bradgate to write a letter to her mother. With a flourish, she signed *Lady Elizabeth Cavendish,* flushing with pride as she gazed down at her new signature for the first time.

They traveled to Derbyshire in William's big black carriage with the Cavendish stags emblazoned upon it. William insisted she couldn't go home empty-handed, so they made their first stop in the city of Leicester, where Bess indulged her love of shopping and bought presents for everyone in her family.

William had never in his life seen a family so excited as Bess's when the newlyweds arrived at Hardwick Manor. He soon realized that Bess was as special to them as she was to him. To his great consternation they were deeply in awe of him, and he had to set about making them feel at ease in his company.

Aunt Marcella Linaker was the exception, of course. She had never been in awe of any man breathing, and William won her over immediately. Soon his laughter echoed through the lovely but shabby manor house, and his easygoing ways encouraged Bess's family to seek out and enjoy his company.

William's manservant, James Cromp, had to share a bedroom with the coach driver, and the only one available was next to Bess and William's chamber. When they retired Bess put her finger to her lips and pointed to the wall. "I know James is privy to some of our secrets, but I don't want your servants to hear every shocking detail of our lovemaking. You'll have to behave yourself."

"Me?" he teased. "My lovemaking is always circumspect. You're the one who will have to behave, Lady Cavendish."

She went into his arms and bit his earlobe. "Well, I won't behave; I'll just go about the whole thing silently." She was a constant source of delight and amusement to her new husband, and he adored her.

The Hardwick farm covered five hundred

acres, and as they rode about it, William pointed out to her many improvements that could be made and various ways of making extra money, such as enclosing some of the moors for sheep runs. Bess hung on her husband's every word, for no man in England knew more about land and property and few had his eye for money-making opportunities. That night she passed the advice on to her brother, James, hoping against hope he would become a better businessman and make Hardwick start to pay.

The following day they planned a visit to the Leches. Bess's sister Alice, married to Francis Leche and living at Chatsworth, was expecting her first child. Bess told her family they could use the Cavendish coach, because she and William were going to ride to Chatsworth.

She had told William long ago about her favorite place in the world, and when they drew rein at the top of the fell and looked down on Chatsworth, William understood why she was so enamored of it. It was truly a spectacular piece of land, encircled by the gentle River Derwent, a small, fertile Eden set down amidst the high peaks and wild moors of Derbyshire countryside. It was the perfect, ideal landscape seen in classical paintings.

William watched her face as she gazed down, enraptured. He recognized the hungry look; she got it when she looked at him sometimes. "The house is in the wrong place." He pointed his riding crop. "It should be over there."

Bess looked at him in wonder. "That's exactly right! Oh, William, we are so alike in our thinking. This piece of land deserves a magnificent palace-of-a-house. The outer park should stretch all the way into Sherwood Forest and be filled with deer and pheasant. The inner gardens should be formal and stately, with waterways and fountains. Such grandeur and order set in the midst of this howling wilderness would stagger the senses!"

The rapt look of longing on her face staggered William's senses. He dismounted and held up his arms to her. "I want to make love to you."

Bess asked no questions. She knew he felt the passion she experienced over Chatsworth and that he wanted to be a part of it. She came down to him in a flurry of petticoats. "How fortunate I'm wearing green, and the best part is we don't have to behave ourselves out here. We can cry our pleasure to the highest peaks."

Bess couldn't wait to return to London and begin her new life. She made her mother, aunt, and sisters promise to visit her. Cavendish helped James Cromp load their luggage so that Bess could say her good-byes in private. Her mother embraced her. "Bess, you have so much courage. Marcella was right when she insisted you were the one who must go to London."

Bess wiped away a tear. Courage? If only they knew how terrified she had been just a short time ago. "William is my strength."

Marcella shook her head. "No, Bess, the strength and the courage are yours. You knew what you wanted, and you went after it. You set your goal so high, and now you have achieved it."

Bess embraced her aunt Marcy. "Nay, I've only just begun."

The London house that Cavendish bought from William Parr was in Newgate Street, not far from St. Paul's Cathedral. When they arrived and William took her on a tour, Bess was surprised to find many of the rooms empty.

"I want you to start fresh. This is your house, Bess, and I want you to furnish it with things that will please you. You'll have to start by hiring your own staff. You are completely in charge here. You will also have to keep your own accounts; I'm far too busy with the accounts of the treasury."

She flung her arms about his neck and went up on tiptoe to kiss him. "Thank you, William; I swear I won't disappoint you."

Bess immediately threw herself into making her new household a rival of those of the Greys and the Dudleys. The seaport of London had the treasures of the world to choose from, and Cavendish gave her carte blanche to purchase whatever she fancied. She began interviewing servants the first day and decided to keep on two men who already worked for her husband, Francis Whitfield and Timothy Pusey. She hired a cook and a cook's assistant, as well as housemaids and footmen. She decided she needed a full-time seamstress to fashion her clothes and was lucky enough to find a woman who also did exquisite embroidery. Bess sketched out the scenes she wanted for a pair of wall hangings and set the woman to work immediately.

By the end of the first week, Bess had a staff of twelve servants. This was in addition to James Cromp, William's valet, and his secretary, Robert Bestnay, whom Bess kept close beside her all week to record every expenditure. Bestnay showed her how to prepare a set of household account books, which she kept meticulously, and at the end of each day she signed *Elizabeth Cavendish* with a great flourish.

They went to Northaw for the autumn hunting and stayed until Christmas, entertaining all their friends. Bess took great delight in her role as hostess and, after a full day's hunt, presided over the gaming room, where they played cards and gambled into the night. But Bess also took a great interest in the estate's administration.

It had languished in Church hands and had not kept pace with current methods of management. William showed her how to increase the rents and revenues by enclosing commons and wasteland on which their tenant farmers could now graze extra herds of cattle and flocks of sheep.

William also put the Northaw property in both their names and taught Bess how to convey property to trustees and back again to them jointly to establish indisputable title to their lands. "I am much older than you, Bess, so if we hold our property jointly, it will be yours when I die, and there will be no question of wardship for our children. And speaking of children, my darling, when are you going to divulge your deep, dark secret to our friends?"

He was sitting before the roaring fire, and she climbed into his lap. "William, don't you dare to breathe a word of it!"

His hand slipped to her belly, which was hardly mounded in spite of her being in her sixth month. "But I'm so damned proud of it. I want to exercise my bragging rights."

"I'll tell them at New Year's," she said loftily.

But when New Year's came, Bess changed her mind. They had been invited to spend the revels at Chelsea, where Thomas Seymour was determined to entertain the king and Court with a lavish celebration, complete with the traditional masked costume ball. When the crowds were at their greatest, the admiral announced that his new wife, Dowager Queen Catherine, was with child.

Princess Elizabeth, standing next to Bess, clenched her fists so tightly, her nails cut into her palms. "That's disgusting! Men love nothing better than to shout their virility to the world. Strutting about, displaying their codpieces like cocksure, cock-proud boys!"

Her words wrung Bess's heart. Elizabeth had idolized and loved Tom Seymour since she was a little girl and would no doubt have given her soul to be wed to him.

Elizabeth's envious eyes swept over Bess's costumed figure. "Next it will be you who is swollen with child, displaying your belly like a symbol of womanhood."

Bess knew she could not tell her. She would not add to her friend's misery for all the Crown jewels.

Finally, in mid-February, when she and William were dining at Suffolk House, Bess took great delight in telling Frances and Henry that she was going to have a baby.

Frances raised her glass to William. "Well, that didn't take long, you randy devil."

William's eyes danced with amusement. Frances had no idea.

"How far along are you?" Frances inquired, her speculative eyes roaming over Bess's expanding midsection.

"I'm not really sure," Bess said vaguely. "Perhaps five months."

William choked on his wine. The little minx had conceived seven and a half months ago. Henry clapped him on the back and offered his heartiest congratulations.

"You wretch, why didn't you tell me sooner?" Frances demanded.

"Well, I was going to tell you at New Year's, but when the admiral made his grandiose announcement, I found it rather vulgar and William thought we should be more discreet."

Cavendish choked once more.

"You look absolutely blooming."

"I've never felt better." It was the first truthful statement she'd uttered since she sat down to dinner.

"From what her sister tells me, Catherine Parr is suffering for her sins. She's sick every day; in fact she's been ill since the moment of conception."

Bess had such a tender heart when someone was ill. She invariably felt guilty because she enjoyed robust health. "Poor lady. Having a baby should be a happy time."

"The woman is crowding forty; she's far too old to be having her first child."

Henry changed the subject. He knew Frances would never utter a kind word for the woman who had usurped Chelsea. "Would you like a girl or a boy?"

"A girl," William said without hesitation, "a little redhead exactly like Bess."

"Whoever would have thought the dissolute Rogue Cavendish would turn into a fatuous fool?" Frances drawled.

The corners of Bess's mouth went up. "If it's a girl we shall call her Frances, and if it's a boy we'll name him Henry."

"You don't have to do that," Henry protested, though he was highly flattered.

"Speak for yourself, Henry. My goddaughter should certainly be called Frances," his wife hinted broadly.

"Now who's being a fatuous fool?" her husband teased.

That night William sat on the edge of the ornate bed and undressed Bess. He stood her between his thighs and caressed her belly. Her skin was so taut and smooth it looked like ivory satin, and her breasts were lush and full. "You are so beautiful." The light from the fire played across her flesh, turning her skin to glowing amber. He traced kisses across the lovely outward curve of her belly.

"Do you really want a girl, William?"

"Yes, a beautiful little liar like her mother." His hands slipped around her and cupped her buttocks. "Bess, you are always honest to a fault. Why the devil did you lie to Frances?"

"I don't want them counting on their fingers and whispering behind their hands about me," she cried passionately. "I want no scandal attached to the name of Cavendish. We'll leave the scandal to the bloody Tudors!"

"But, my darling, they will know when you go into labor," he pointed out gently.

"No, they will not!" she insisted stubbornly. "Next month I shall go into seclusion at Northaw, and no one in London will know what date I am delivered."

His eyes brimmed with amusement. "You are so willful and stubborn."

"Qualities that arouse you, I see."

"I'm sorry, sweetheart, I can't help it—you're so ripe and luscious."

"Don't be sorry; I want you to make love to

304

me!" She slipped down between his muscled thighs and touched her lips to his arousal, then took him into her mouth.

"Don't, you know I'll spill, then what will you do?"

"But you are too careful—you are afraid to put your weight on me."

"Come on, you know there are other ways to take your pleasure." He pulled the red silk curtains about them and stretched out supine upon the bed. "You enjoy being on top sometimes. Mount me and ride me. This way you will be able to take as much of me or as little of me as you can. You will be in control."

"You don't like to give up control." Bess straddled him.

"Tonight I will. I'll be putty in your hands."

"Marble in my hands." Her voice was sultry as she reached out to toy with him. Then she sank down upon him slowly, sheathing him inch by delicious inch until he was seated to the hilt. She splayed her hands against his hips and slowly lifted until he was almost fully withdrawn, then she sank down upon him, making him groan with a hunger of his own.

He could feel the brush of her thighs and her bottom against his groin. When she bent her head to look down at him, her flaming hair cascaded down, whispering across the muscles of his chest and his rib cage. His hands came up to caress her body, and her luscious breasts spilled into his palms.

She eased into a tantalizing rhythm that inflamed him. As she slid sleekly around him, he wanted to thrust hard and deep but held himself in check, allowing her to lead the way.

"Watch this," she whispered.

As Bess began to increase her speed and her undulations became intensely erotic, the red silk walls about them began to flutter and ripple in the breeze she created with her gyrations. Then she began to ride him like a stallion, and the crimson silk flew like victory banners streaming past them as she galloped to her goal.

He was reeling with need as fire snaked through his groin, and he thrust wildly until they exploded together, shuddering out their release.

Bess finally wrote home to tell her family that she and William were expecting a child, and her favorite sister Jane came to be with her. The moment Jane arrived, Bess moved her household to Northaw, and William took Jane aside the following day.

"Bess will never admit it, but the baby was conceived before we were married. She could go into labor at any time now. Mistress Bagshaw's sister is a midwife and she's already here." He ran his fingers through his hair distractedly. "Jane, I'm worried to death about her."

Jane was only momentarily shocked. Bess did everything her own way. "I'll get her to bed. Don't worry, William, when Bess does something, she invariably does it well."

Jane's prophesy turned out to be true. The following afternoon Bess delivered a baby girl. Her daughter had not red hair, but the same shade of dark auburn as her father. The very next morning the proud mother was sitting up in bed, feeding her daughter, and looking radiantly beautiful. She told William her plans for the christening. "I want Frances and Henry Grey to be her godparents, but we won't ask them until June."

"But, darling, that is two months away. Babies are baptized within days, not months."

"There is no law about the time of baptism of which I'm aware!"

Again William took Jane aside. "Can you talk to her and persuade her she is being silly about this?"

Jane looked at him in surprise. "William, Bess isn't like other people, you must know that by now. When she makes up her mind about something, nothing and no one can persuade her otherwise."

As Bess decreed, little Frances Cavendish was christened in June with Henry Grey, Duke of Suffolk, standing as godfather. Frances Grey, Duchess of Suffolk, and her close friend Nan Dudley, Countess of Warwick, were the two exalted godmothers. This was a far-reaching choice since the Dudley's were politically powerful. A huge christening party followed at Northaw, where no one seemed to know or care that baby Frances was over two months old.

TWENTY

London, September 10, 1548

Dear Mother and Marcella:
I know you will have heard rumors about the explosive situation at Court, so I will bring you up to date. Protector Edward Seymour refused to hand over to Catherine Parr the jewels that King Henry left her, claiming they belonged to the new king. As a result Thomas Seymour made threats against his brother and suggested that he should be lord protector. As lord high admiral, Thomas has hired ten thousand men into the navy, and Edward Seymour is so fearful, he put Tom under surveillance.

Bess paused. She could not bring herself to tell them of the scandal that had exploded at Chelsea when Catherine Parr had caught her husband, Thomas Seymour, and Princess Elizabeth *in the act,* on the floor of Elizabeth's bedchamber!
Bess continued her letter on a sad note.

I am so sorry to tell you that four days after Catherine Parr was delivered of a baby girl, she died of childbed fever.

Bess lifted her pen once more, as her thoughts flew about like wild birds trapped in a cage. Had Seymour had a hand in his wife's death? Would the ambitious devil find a way to make Elizabeth his next wife?

It is rumored that the admiral is abusing his position by extorting bribes from vessels sailing to Ireland and that he condones piracy for a share of the loot.

Though Bess dare not put it in her letter, she knew Marcella would conclude that Seymour needed cash to mount a rebellion.

Princess Elizabeth has moved her household to her own palace of Hatfield, and Frances Grey has reclaimed Chelsea Palace as her daughter Lady Jane's official residence, since Jane will be queen when she marries young King Edward.
We will celebrate Christmas at Northaw and only wish you could be with us. I miss you sorely and promise to come for a visit in late spring when the weather permits.
All my love, Bess.

Events at Court moved forward so rapidly that Bess wrote home often, informing them of the political intrigue as it unfolded.

London, March 21, 1549

Dear Mother and Marcella:
By now you will know that in January Thomas Seymour was arrested. There was

*evidence that he obtained ten thousand
pounds from the mint by corrupt means. As
well, the protector swore that Thomas had
plotted a secret marriage with Elizabeth and
attempted to seize the king's majesty and
dispose of the privy council.*

*Within days Mistress Cat Ashley and
Master Parry, Elizabeth's cofferer, were taken
to the Tower for questioning, and the princess
was placed under house arrest at Hatfield,
where she was relentlessly interrogated for over
two months. In the end Elizabeth could save
only herself and her loyal servants. The protector persuaded the king to sign a bill of
attainder against the admiral, and yesterday
Thomas Seymour was sent to the block.*

Bess paused, remembering the horrendous
quarrel she and William had had. Because
he was a member of the privy council, he
knew that the protector was just waiting for
his brother Thomas Seymour to lift one finger
toward the king or his royal sister so he could
arrest him for treason. Bess had promised
William she would not breathe a word of
what he told her, then had ridden hell-for-
leather to Hatfield to warn Elizabeth. Cavendish
had been livid that she had betrayed his trust,
but when she begged him to forgive her, their
reunion was so fierce, Bess conceived again.

Bess continued her letter.

*On a happier note, I am delighted to tell
you that I am going to have another child.*

310

William and I are both hoping for a son, and after he is born we will come north for a visit.

All my love, Bess

There were those on the council and at Court who found what Edward Seymour had done to his brother abhorrent. Discontent over the protector's rule spread into the populace of England, and by autumn there was outright rebellion. John Dudley, Earl of Warwick, rode into Norfolk at the head of the army to subdue the revolt. He quelled the uprisings with little bloodshed, and when he returned to London, the council switched their allegiance to him. Edward Seymour was arrested, stripped of his power, and taken to the Tower.

The Cavendishes went to Northaw for the autumn hunting, where they entertained all their friends from Court. Bess learned that the young king did not enjoy robust health but was delicate and often sickly since his bout with smallpox. When she learned that Elizabeth had fallen into a decline over the death of Thomas Seymour, Bess resolved to try to pull her out of it.

When Bess arrived she was amazed to see that Hatfield was still shrouded in deepest mourning. When she saw Elizabeth lying silent in her bed, waxy as a corpse, Bess realized she was ill in her heart and soul. Fury rose up in Bess.

"This is an act that has gotten out of hand. You meant to punish everyone for taking the admiral, but you've gone too far and are punishing only yourself!"

Elizabeth leaned forward and put her head in her hands hopelessly. "Go away."

"He wasn't worth it!" Bess said vehemently. "Tom Seymour was Catherine Parr's lover, long before she ever wed your father. He urged her to the royal marriage."

"Liar," Elizabeth whispered.

"He wanted the power that a royal female could give him—any royal female would do. He asked the council for permission to wed you *or your sister Mary*. Ask anyone on the council." Bess let her cloak fall open to reveal that she was blooming with a child. "I am fulfilling my destiny, but you are throwing yours away! Someday you will be Her Royal Majesty, Queen Elizabeth of England."

"It can never be. They called me bastard and, now, whore."

"Go to Court and prove them wrong! John Dudley, Earl of Warwick, is in charge now. He will see that your brother welcomes you, and all will accord you the title, honor, and respect your position demands."

Elizabeth arose from her bed to pace the chamber. When she flung a book across the room, Bess knew Elizabeth had taken the first steps toward fulfilling her destiny.

Bess presented her husband with a son and heir, whom they named Henry. Their friends the Earl and Countess of Warwick were his godparents. In the spring William bought a bigger house on the river for his growing family, and while it was being made ready, they went to Derbyshire to show off the children to Bess's family.

At week's end they left the children with her mother and Aunt Marcella and rode out to look at Chatsworth. When they reached the top of the fell, Bess reined in to enjoy the view, but William didn't stop. He rode straight to the house and dismounted on the lawn. He leered at her wickedly. "Come and feel what I've got for you."

She never refused a dare—not one Cavendish threw at her. She dismounted, tossed back her flaming hair, and swaggered toward him with bravado. Her arms went up about his neck and she lifted her mouth to his. Halfway through the fierce kiss, she slipped her hands inside his doublet. When her fingers closed over metal, she pulled her mouth away. "What the devil is this?" She pulled out a heavy iron ring of keys.

"The keys to Chatsworth, my darling. I hope it gives you more pleasure than you've ever had before."

Bess stared at him blankly, not comprehending.

"I bought Chatsworth for you—it's yours."

"Splendor of God, Rogue Cavendish, you didn't!" Bess was stunned. He had just paid out a generous marriage settlement on his daughter and bought Bess a new house on the river. Where had the money come from to buy Chatsworth? Bess burst into tears.

He enfolded her in powerful arms, and in that moment Bess felt she needed his support more than ever before. "Now you can build your palace."

"Me?" Bess asked in a small voice, completely overwhelmed.

"It was your dream; now you can turn it into reality." He looked down at her and saw that her great dark eyes were filled with apprehension. "Sweetheart, what's wrong?"

"I'm afraid," she whispered. "Oh, William, I liked the dream.... It was so safe, so unreachable, forever in the distant future. But it's no longer in the future, it's here and now. It's too much, too soon. The reality of it strikes terror in my heart."

His big hand smoothed the fiery tendrils from her brow. "Come on," he said, untethering her horse and lifting her into the saddle. "Follow me."

Slowly, silently, they trekked back up the side of the steep fell until they gained the summit, then he held up his arms and lifted her down. He kept one arm about her as they gazed down at Chatsworth. "The very first time I met you, I asked if you'd like three houses. Your reply was so direct, so sure. 'Certainly, I would,' you said. You chided me for laughing at you and vowed you would have your own vast household. That very first day I knew I wanted you. I immediately sensed that your ambition matched mine."

Bess's mind flew back to her first year in London, and she relived her strong feelings.

She had been determined to become a great success and share in the world's riches. She had sworn it, vowed it, pledged it like an oath. Her future had lain before her with clarity. She wanted it all!

William hugged her close. "Since that day I have come to know just how much strength, courage, and determination you have. Your uncertainty is just foolish fancy—I have no doubts. You have the will and the energy to turn the dream of your 'palace of the peaks' into reality."

"William, what about the money it will take?"

"Money is the least of your worries; I can always get you money." He spoke with such authority, her fear was laid to rest.

"The house will go over there," she pointed. "Built entirely of stone, with great square turrets at each corner. I want an inner court-yard and another over there by the stables."

"It will be the most impressive house in Derbyshire."

"Of course it will! The servants will wear blue and silver livery."

William began to laugh.

Bess looked up at him shrewdly. "I know why you brought me up here. It all looks so much smaller and less intimidating from up here. Everything falls into perspective. I lived all my dreams and made all my plans from way up here. You brought me back so I would lose all my fear."

"Of course I didn't. I brought you up here

to make love to you. Now, where exactly was that spot again?"

"Oh, William, my heart is overflowing with love for you. This truly is one of the happiest days of my life."

Bess now divided her time between Chatsworth and London. They sold Northaw and the annexed Church lands. William also had acquired Church lands in Wales, which were too far away to properly administer, and a small holding in Shropshire. Through his high position in the augmentation office, he exchanged these lands for a large property in Doveridge on the River Dove, close to Chatsworth. Bess leased out its manor house, called Meadow-pleck, and they poured the money into building the new house at Chatsworth.

Their new land was valuable; it had both lead mines and great shallow seams of coal. Bess kept a meticulous accounting of earnings and expenditures, and Francis Whitfield, whom she appointed as her agent, took them to William in London.

Bess was an economical builder. The wood, stone, bricks, and mortar, as well as the lead for the windows and the roofs, were all provided from her own estates. Laborers worked for a pittance, and even craftsmen such as carpenters, plasterers, and stonemasons could be hired cheaply. As William had taught her to do at Northaw, she enclosed common land across the moors for sheep runs and marketed the wool.

The more that Bess accomplished, the more her energy and her confidence increased. She allowed William to keep his own servants in London and moved the rest of the household to Derbyshire. They lived in the old Chatsworth Manor while the new Chatsworth was being built. Her sister Jane came to live with her to help with the children; her aunt Marcy also came, and Bess immediately put her in charge of laying out a plan for the elaborate gardens she wanted.

Cavendish traveled north regularly, and whenever he came it was as if he and Bess were newlyweds. She presented him with another son, named William, exactly nine months to the day after he had given her the keys to Chatsworth.

Bess had never been happier in her life. Whenever she came to London, she went home with wagonloads of furnishings for the new house, which was gradually beginning to take shape. According to her plan she intended to finish one magnificent story completely, then, when money permitted, begin the second story. Sometimes Bess accompanied William when he went on official business to a northern priory or monastery. Since his job was to confiscate their hoarded treasures, Bess offered to buy for hard cash anything that took her fancy and that she could someday showcase at Chatsworth. She felt no guilt—the heads of these religious houses were glad to slip the money into their own pockets and keep their mouths shut.

In London, the young king developed a contagion of the lungs, and it became obvious to those close to him that he was wasting away. John Dudley, Earl of Warwick, and most of the council, who were staunchly Protestant, began to panic. Princess Mary, the dreaded Catholic, was next in line to the throne, and none of the men in power wanted her there.

In a desperate move Dudley banished Elizabeth to Hatfield, then had the dying king make out his will proclaiming Lady Jane Grey his successor and declaring his sisters Mary and Elizabeth illegitimate. The entire council knew that Dudley planned to wed his son Guildford to Lady Jane to keep the power in his hands.

Cavendish was appalled that his friends, Henry and Frances Grey, were willing to go along with this, and in early July they brought their fifteen-year-old daughter from Chelsea to the stronghold of the Tower, where she and Guildford were married in a hasty ceremony.

Bess was blissfully unaware of the tense situation in London, and that was exactly how Cavendish wanted it. Up in Derbyshire she could never be accused of being a party to the unlawful and disastrous plans that were being carried out.

Though the Earl of Warwick bound the council to secrecy, somehow word was sent to Princess Mary, and by the time young King

Edward took his last breath and Lady Jane Grey was proclaimed queen, Mary Tudor was rallying an army. Cavendish suspected it was his boss, Paulet, who had warned Mary, for he was the only Catholic on the council.

John Dudley once more rode out at the head of his army to capture Mary and defeat her forces. He met with no success, and it immediately became apparent that the people of England supported Princess Mary Tudor. To a man, the privy councillors knew they would be sent to the block if they did not immediately declare their support for Mary. On July 19, 1553, John Dudley was arrested and Mary Tudor was proclaimed Queen of England.

Events had taken place so swiftly that Lady Cavendish in Derbyshire learned all at once that the king was dead, Lady Jane Grey had been proclaimed queen for nine days, then Mary Tudor was proclaimed the rightful queen.

TWENTY-ONE

Bess packed immediately and set out for London, and it seemed to her that half the populace was also making its way to the capital for the crowning of England's new queen. By the time she arrived, the momentous month of July was drawing to a close, and when Cavendish saw that she had rushed to London, his heart sank.

In her usual forthright manner, Bess took the offensive immediately. "Why on earth did you keep me in the dark about the calamitous events that were occurring? You must have suspected for months what was in the wind!"

"Bess, I've hardly been to bed this month; the council has been in session day and night. Even if I'd had time to write, I wouldn't have dared commit anything to paper."

"The real reason is you didn't want me here meddling!"

"I didn't want you putting yourself in danger," he countered.

"I must go to Frances immediately."

"You will not," he said implacably. "Frances and Lady Catherine are safe at Suffolk House. Henry and Lady Jane are safe in the Tower."

"Safe for how long, with that dried-up religious fanatic on the throne?" Bess felt so frustrated, she burst into tears. "Dear God, I am so worried for them."

He took her shoulders in strong hands and forced her to listen. "It is Dudley who will have to pay the price. Frances is a royal Tudor, cousin to Queen Mary. She will keep her husband and daughter safe."

Bess wiped away her tears with a grimy hand. "I need a bath; the dust on the road nearly choked me. Oh, God, poor Nan Dudley."

"Order your bath," Cavendish said, coming to a decision. "Bess, we need to talk."

As his wife lay in the warm scented water, William sat on the edge of the wooden tub. "It is our own position we must worry about.

The council realized if we didn't proclaim Mary the rightful queen, we would all be sent to the block for treason."

Bess paled. "Oh, William, you could lose your position because of me. Mary dislikes me intensely."

"Bess, I could lose my position, but it won't be because of a petty personality conflict. Mary won't take kindly to a man who has dismantled the monasteries and religious houses across the country. She will no doubt start handing back all Church lands."

"Hell's teeth, you are right as always. Oh, how fortunate that we got rid of Northaw and put the money into Chatsworth."

In spite of the gravity of their situation, William laughed. "Christ, Bess, you are always so damned practical."

"And who taught me?"

"Well, I did do something expedient. Paulet and I pledged our own money to raise a force to aid Mary. I had to borrow seven hundred pounds, but that was exceedingly cheap insurance."

"She will keep Paulet as lord treasurer because he's Catholic."

"Yes, I'm hoping our close association will save me."

"William, I have a brilliant idea—we will turn Catholic! It will cost little to add a priest to our household."

"Don't you think that's a little too expedient?"

"No, it's a very wise thing to do. What does our religion matter if it safeguards our children and all they will inherit?" Her hand went protectively to her belly.

"Bess, you're not breeding again?"

"And if I am, whose fault would that be?" she flared.

"Christ, you're so fecund, all I have to do is look at you."

"You do a hell of a lot more than look at me, Rogue Cavendish."

He held up the towel for her. "Are you angry at me?"

"Not over the baby." She lifted her mouth to his for a hungry kiss. "Anyway, I'm not certain yet."

He wrapped her in the towel and lifted her from the water. "In that case I'd better take you to bed and make sure of it," he said with a devilish grin.

Both Bess and William thought it politic that she remain in London, at least for the new queen's coronation, which was being planned for August 3. Bess couldn't wait to see Elizabeth again and decided that before she returned north she would find a way to see Frances also.

Elizabeth traveled from Hatfield to meet her sister at Wanstead, join her procession, and escort the new queen into London. Along the way noble and commoner alike joined Princess Elizabeth's retinue, until her escort numbered about one thousand by the time she met Mary.

Mary noted that Elizabeth showed her every respect when she made her obeisance, but she did not trust the girl. And as Elizabeth rode directly behind the new queen, wearing virginal white, with her glorious red-gold hair cloaking her shoulders, Mary became sullenly jealous and wondered for whom exactly the populace was cheering so wildly.

The day after her state entrance and coronation, there was a reception at Whitehall that filled the Great Hall, the Guard Chamber, and the Presence Chamber, where all Queen Mary's loyal subjects came to bend the knee, to pledge to be her obedient servant, and to wish her God's blessing.

Lady Cavendish, resplendent in Tudor colors of green and white, made her curtsy. Queen Mary did not speak to her, but when her agate eyes flicked over her, Bess experienced an involuntary shudder. Shrewdly, Lady Cavendish retired from the Presence Chamber, leaving Sir William in the company of Treasurer Paulet.

Bess found Elizabeth in the Guard Chamber, surrounded by so many younger nobles, it looked as if she were holding her own Court.

"Lady Cavendish, walk with me."

The two striking redheads left the chamber to seek a more private place. Since Whitehall had over two thousand rooms, it was not difficult. "Your Grace, you look radiant."

"Today I am heir to the throne, but I have never been in a more dangerous position in my life. Robin Dudley is in the Tower—she holds his life in her hands!"

"Cavendish believes that all blame will be laid at John Dudley's feet and eventually she will pardon the others."

"I dare not plead his case; she hates me. She has supreme authority and will force me to Mass," Elizabeth hissed.

"Your Grace, for your own safety you must obey her in all things," Bess advised, fearing Elizabeth's disobedience.

"I must *seem* to obey her in all things. When she forces me to Mass I shall faint in the chapel, and that will send a signal to every Protestant in the realm that I attend under protest."

"Cavendish and I are going to outwardly conform."

"The venomous bitch is already spreading it about that I am not related to her by blood—that I am Mark Smeaton's by-blow!"

Bess took Elizabeth's hand and squeezed it. "Your Grace, no one seeing you can ever deny that you are Henry Tudor's daughter. People will know she is eaten alive with envy for your youth and your beauty. Your very aura is regal, and you draw every eye."

"Aye, that is the problem. As soon as I may, I shall withdraw to Hatfield, live quietly as a nun, and bide my time."

During the following week William and Bess discussed their future. His position with the treasury seemed safe at the moment, but as they had just seen, circumstances could change overnight.

"Derbyshire is a far safer place than London. Buying Chatsworth was the wisest thing you ever did, William."

"We should expand our holdings in the north. The Earl of Westmorland has eight thousand acres of good pastureland for sale, only a few miles from Chatsworth. It would make us the biggest landowners in Derbyshire—after Shrewsbury, of course."

"We cannot afford it!" Bess knew their expenditures were already greater than their income, for she kept a strict accounting of what they took in from their northern land holdings and what they paid out for the building of Chatsworth.

"I'll borrow the money from William Parr. My bribes of office will take care of the payments."

When Bess looked shocked, his eyes filled with amusement. "Don't be such a little hypocrite; when it comes to business you are quite capable of being ruthless. When you do the accounting, don't put down the interest we pay Parr on the loan. Usury is strictly against the law."

Almost immediately, marriage negotiations began between Queen Mary and Prince Philip of Spain. Bess hoped the marriage plans would occupy all the queen's thoughts and she would not waste her time plotting revenge. Bess heaved a great sigh of relief when Cavendish proved to be right about Lady Frances Grey's influence with her cousin, the queen. Henry Grey was released from the Tower by paying a heavy fine, and before Bess returned north she and William went by barge to Suffolk House to visit their old friends.

Bess did not know it, but it was the last time that she would ever see Henry Grey. Within a year of his release, Henry became involved in a plot to depose Queen Mary and set Elizabeth on the throne. When the revolt was over, Mary had Grey beheaded and for good measure sent his daughter Lady Jane to the block as well.

Princess Elizabeth was taken to the Tower and interrogated about her role in the treasonous plot. Her life hung by a thread for three long months, then she was released and sent to Woodstock, under guard.

Bess agonized over the Greys' tragedy, and William felt impotent that he had been able to do nothing to aid his friend. Bess could not get Elizabeth out of her mind and worried for her constantly. Bess herself was so safe and insulated here in Derbyshire, she was covered with guilt because the Cavendish fortunes seemed to be on the rise. Not only had she added to her nursery each year, everything they touched prospered. Their vast landholdings earned them a great income, and two full stories of Chatsworth were now complete, right down to the exquisite plasterwork frescoes. Bess filled her new home with the treasures she had been accumulating for years and entertained the great noble families in the northern shires.

Bess hadn't the faintest idea that because of their close association with the Greys and her close friendship with Elizabeth, the Cavendishes were in Queen Mary's disfavor.

Stories of the splendor of Chatsworth began to reach the queen's ears. It was said that Lady Cavendish had furnished fourteen bedchambers en suite with matching drapes, bed hangings, and covers, and that she displayed no less than sixty pieces of magnificent tapestry on Chatsworth's walls. Rumor said the ostentatious house was fit to entertain a monarch, but no invitation was ever extended to Queen Mary. When she learned that Frances Grey and her daughter Catherine were welcome visitors, along with Nan Dudley, it was like a slap in the face. These women had been married to Mary's bitterest enemies, who had gone to the block for plotting treason against her.

Eventually, Cavendish began to hear whispers of the queen's displeasure. Moreover, her Catholic policies were unpopular, which she blamed on her advisers, and it was hinted that for political reasons she was going to rid herself of these officials. Sir William began to suspect that sooner or later she would remove him from the privy council.

William was determined to keep all this rumor and speculation from Bess. She worried about things unnecessarily, and he wanted only her happiness. He would not disturb her peace of mind for anything. She was a perfect wife, a loving, indulgent mother, a superb hostess, and a capable chatelaine and business partner, who, with the aid of her bailiffs, ran their northern landholdings smoothly and efficiently.

Cavendish was determined not to add to her burden; she had quite enough on her plate. Philosophically, William reasoned that if he was replaced on the privy council, it would not be the end of the world and he would be able to spend more time in Derbyshire with his family. When he received a letter from Chatsworth, telling him that Bess was ill, William's priorities fell into line in a hell of a hurry. He set his London worries aside and rushed home to Bess.

He rode through the tall iron gates of Chatsworth, oblivious to the magnificent formal gardens that usually gave him such pleasure. Jane and Marcella greeted him with anxious faces, but when William saw that Bess's mother was there, a knot of fear twisted his gut. He took the stairs three at a time, then paused to catch his breath and compose himself so Bess would not see his panic.

He opened the door softly and stepped quietly up to the big carved bed. She lay so pale and wan, painful anxiety rose up like a hand squeezing his heart and clutching his throat. He swallowed hard. "Bess, my own sweet love, it's me."

"Rogue," she whispered.

She always used his nickname as an endearment, and it almost undid him. He reached out to gently touch her brow and felt that she was feverish. The change in her appearance greatly alarmed him. Bess was always so vivid and vital, always laughing. When she played with the children she was a hoyden—so wildly disheveled, no one would have ever guessed she was old enough to be their mother. Then in the evenings she would transform herself into an elegant, fashionable hostess, so slyly witty she could hold court amid a roomful of high-born nobility. When they retired she would let down her glorious hair and become a passionate seductress, making him reel from the hot desire she kindled in him.

Bess clutched at him and William sat down on the side of the bed, realizing that she desperately wanted to tell him something.

"The children," she whispered.

"You want to see the children, darling?" He knew they would swarm all over the bed and he would have to keep them in check.

Bess shook her head as if she were impatient that he didn't understand. "Promise me that you will make good marriages for them, promise me!"

He wondered if she was delirious and stroked her brow, but she was not burning hot and her words seemed to be coherent. "I want titles for every one of them."

"Yes, love," he soothed, trying to calm her agitation.

She dug her nails into his hands. "Cavendish, promise me! Swear it!"

He suddenly realized that Bess thought she was going to die. Splendor of God, did she feel that ill? He was astounded that her thoughts were not for herself, but for their children. The lump in his throat threatened to choke him. He gathered her into his arms. "Bess, I swear it, but I also swear you are not going to die. I won't allow it! You are only in your twenties—you have a long life ahead of you. I need you, Bess, don't even think about leaving me." He strode to the door. "Marcella!" She was a spry old girl and arrived quickly. "Have you had the doctor?"

Marcella made a rude noise. "Aye, but after his bloodletting, I swore not to have him back."

"Have you given her something for her fever?" he asked desperately.

"Of course I have—I am an herbalist!"

"She is so agitated," he said distractedly.

"Bess will be all right now that you are here, Cavendish. You are her bulwark, her strength."

"I'll sit up with her tonight."

"Good. You are all that she needs."

William tenderly bathed his wife, then gently fed her more of the potion that Marcella had brewed. Then he carried a big chair to the side of the bed and prepared to guard her all night from the angel of death. He was not a religious man, but when she smiled at him and closed her eyes, he covered her hand, which was so precious to him, and began to pray. Bess was his shining light; she had brought a radiance he had never experienced into his life, where before there had often been darkness. Bess was his passion, his joy, his life.

At dawn Bess fell into a more peaceful sleep, and William levered his big frame from the chair and left the chamber for a moment so he could stretch his long limbs. The household was already awake, and William found Bess's mother, aunt, and sister gathered in the morning room.

"Bess is sleeping; she seems a little better."

Her mother went up immediately, but Marcella fixed him with a daunting stare. A more fainthearted man would have been intimidated.

"Cavendish"—there would be no deferential *Sir William* from this old war-horse— "she's had too many children in too few years. Her last babies were only eleven months apart. Curb yourself, man!"

Her words not only quelled him, they covered him with guilt.

When Marcella swept from the room, Jane was blushing to the roots of her hair. "Sir William, I beg you pay no heed to her. Bess was visiting a tenant farmer's wife who was sick with a pestilent fever. When the woman's children caught it, Bess helped nurse them."

"Thank you, Jane. Nevertheless, there is truth in Marcella's blunt words," William acknowledged guiltily.

Within two days Bess was vastly improved. The fever left as quickly as it came, and as soon as she began to eat, her energy returned. She took William on long walks around the acres of gardens, where long avenues of trees had been planted and where formal land-scaping had transformed surrounding meadows into herb gardens, lawns, stone-edged terraces, and parterres, where the flower beds formed intricate patterns. William drew up a plan to divert a small branch of the River Derwent to run through the gardens and form a trout stream that would cascade into a series of ornamental ponds. It was a safety measure so their lands would not be flooded in times when the river rose.

By the end of the week Bess rode out with William across their vast acres, which now included the villages of Baslow and Edensor. Their older children accompanied them on ponies—Francie, dark and laughing, the very image of her father, and their little sons with their red curly hair, exactly like their mother's. William offered up a prayer of thanks that Bess was so quickly recovered. He marveled at her stamina; watching her, it was impossible to believe she had ever been ill.

That night, in the privacy of their magnif-icent bedchamber, Bess became quite playful. She undressed very slowly, her movements calculated and lithe as a cat, then she donned a black silk night rail that clung to every lush curve of her body.

"What do you think of this? I quite like to wear silk next to my bare skin."

"It was clearly designed with seduction in mind," William replied, keeping a safe distance between them.

"Yes, black silk begs for seduction."

He turned his back and poured himself a goblet of Rhenish wine, trying to ignore the sultry tone of Bess's voice. "You'd better put on your bedgown—I don't want you to catch cold."

"I'm never cold," Bess purred. "Darling, pour me some malmsey."

"Malmsey makes you wanton."

Bess climbed onto the bed and began an undulating dance. "Mmm, it makes me sybaritic."

"Herbs in milk would be better for you," he said repressively.

Bess began to laugh. "Aunt Marcy has been feeding me borage, chamomile, and *clary,* for God's sake. Clary is so lust provoking, I'm going to crawl out of my skin if you don't take off your clothes and pay some pointed attention to me!"

"Bess, no more babies."

She stopped swaying. "What?"

"We have enough children. I don't want to ruin your glowing health by getting you pregnant every year."

Her eyes filled with amusement. "But

abstaining from sex would certainly ruin my glowing health."

He took a tentative step toward the bed, desire for her playing havoc with his good intentions. "I...I'll have to withdraw."

Bess fell down on the bed and rolled about, laughing helplessly.

"What's so bloody funny?"

"Ohmigod, you are, Rogue Cavendish! You could no more withdraw than you could abstain!" Bess kicked her legs in the air, convulsed with laughter.

William grabbed her ankles playfully and pulled her toward him. The silk nightgown climbed up her legs, exposing the fiery triangle at the apex of her white thighs. Her knees fell apart, luring him down to feast upon her. His powerful hands slipped beneath her bottom cheeks and he raised her to his mouth. His thrusting tongue soon found the tiny bud between her hot folds, and as she writhed and arched her beautiful body for him, he felt her woman's center flutter, then pulse, then explode in intense orgasm.

"Rogue, I need more," she implored, knowing the brief satisfaction would not be lasting.

"And I want to give you more," he growled.

"I want you inside me. I love to feel your weight and your power. I know you have a fierce desire for me, and I need to feel you unleash it. My body screams out for you to master it." Her words inflamed him, as she knew they would.

"What the hell am I going to do?" he demanded desperately.

The corners of her mouth went up in a seductive smile. "Fortunately, Marcella has prescribed an herb that prevents conception. It's called dragonwort, and she has a whole bed of the stuff growing in the herb garden."

William groaned with relief and stripped off his garments with all speed. Bess wasn't the only one with needs. He needed her thighs wrapped about him as he plunged inside her; he needed her moaning and frenzied beneath him. He needed to bring her release at the exact same time as he spent. Then he needed to hold her against him until she softened with surfeit.

TWENTY-TWO

When Cavendish returned to London, trouble awaited him. Lord Treasurer Paulet summoned him and told him that Queen Mary had ordered an audit of the queen's treasury.

"We have spies in our midst who have run to the queen with tales of discrepancies."

"I have held treasury offices for thirteen years without complaint," Cavendish said bluntly.

"I explained to Her Grace that your appointment carries a very low salary and that you are entitled to take profits. Nevertheless, she insists that your account books be opened for scrutiny."

"I can turn over the two books that are made up, but my clerks have a dozen more account books in rough that are not yet engrossed."

"I advise you to get the accounts in order immediately, William. I know from my own offices that private accounting gets mixed with official business, so get them sorted out as soon as you can."

The auditors came into Cavendish's treasury offices and began the slow process of digging out receipts and payments. It dragged on for weeks, and then months, going back over all the thirteen years he had held office.

Cavendish scrupulously kept it all from Bess and warned his clerks and his secretary, Bestnay, not to breathe a word of what was going on. But the pressure he was under, month after month, took its toll on William. Sometimes, after a fifteen-hour day, he suffered chest pain, and the only thing that eased it was wine.

When the auditors made their final report, it stated that there was a discrepancy of over five thousand pounds, and the lord treasurer had no choice but to demand an explanation from Cavendish that would satisfy the queen. Sir William defended his accounting by revealing that over the years many clerks had disappeared with money. He also said that he was owed money from the reigns of the two previous monarchs, which he collected when Mary came to the throne. Cavendish even produced personal receipts for the money he had paid to raise men to help Mary gain the throne.

At the beginning of August, William had not yet been charged, but he knew the possibility existed and consulted his London lawyers. Worn out with work and worry, he retired to Derbyshire to prepare a formal defense. Five thousand pounds was a vast sum of money, when an average wage was three pounds per annum.

William knew he must find a way to break the news to Bess. Cavendish hoped to successfully defend himself—if he was actually charged—and salvage his career, but it was only fair to warn Bess of the possibility that they could lose everything for which they had worked so hard.

Before he left London William bought his wife an anniversary present. It was a book with a gold filigree cover studded with ten rubies, which held two small portraits they had had painted the year before. He had promised to be home before the twentieth because Bess had a party planned.

When William arrived home on the eighteenth, Bess thought he looked exhausted. "Darling, are you feeling all right?"

William dismissed her anxieties. "The journey was tiring, all the better inns were filled, and I must have eaten something that disagreed with me."

Bess was in the midst of preparations for the anniversary party. In her usual thorough way she took a personal hand in every phase of the

337

planning, down to the finest details. Since it was mid-August she planned the celebration for outdoors in Chatsworth's incomparable formal gardens, but she wisely had a backup plan to have it in the magnificent twin galleries if it rained.

Bess decided it would be a perfect time to show off the Cavendish children, so when the invitations went out, she told the guests to bring along their own children. Of course, that meant they would have extra servants with them, and Bess made certain there would be food and accommodation for all.

Bess noticed that William drank a bottle of claret at supper, then during the evening he drank another. When she discovered him asleep in a chair, she realized just how tired he must be. Her face softened as she watched him sleep. She saw how much gray was in his once dark-auburn hair and was surprised that she had hardly noticed it until now. With a little shock she realized that he was fifty. The age difference had never mattered to them; William was so rugged and vital. But tonight, watching him sleep touched her heart with tenderness. Perhaps it was time that he slowed down a little.

August 20 dawned beautiful. Carriages began to arrive early in the day, and the Cavendishes were at the front door to greet their guests and give them a tour of the two completed stories of Chatsworth. Bess showed off her proudest possessions, which were her children. She and nine-year-old Francie were in identical summer gowns of white silk muslin. Her daughter carried a posy of pink rosebuds, while Bess wore a full-blown rose tucked into her low décolletage.

Her three little sons, Henry, William, and Charles, wore matching doublets and hose, with feathered caps atop their red curls, and her two baby daughters were in the charge of their nursemaids. Soon the grounds were ringing with the shouts of children as they raced about, chasing butterflies and soaking themselves in the fish ponds. Laughter filled the air as fashionably dressed ladies paraded about the lawns beneath their parasols, and men gathered in groups to discuss rents, horses, politics, war, and the shocking state of the realm.

All Bess's family were there, rubbing shoulders with the noble families of the north. Among the guests were the earls and countesses of Westmorland, Pembroke, and Huntingdon, as well as the Marquess of Northampton, Lady Port, the Nevilles, the Fitzherberts, the Pierreponts, and last, but certainly not least, the aging Earl of Shrewsbury. Bess had invited all the Talbots, not simply because they were the wealthiest and most powerful family in England, but because they were her closest neighbors and a lot of their landholdings ran together.

Bess hadn't seen the old earl since he had stood as godfather to one of her sons. When she saw him on the arm of his heir, George Talbot, she was shocked at how much he had aged. He was also totally deaf, so Bess swallowed her animosity toward his arrogant son and said, "Thank you so much for bringing him, Talbot. Your father was always so generous to me."

His dark eyes swept over her. "The Talbots are always generous to beautiful women, Lady Cavendish."

Bess ground her teeth. "Is Lady Talbot with you?" she asked pointedly.

"I'm afraid not. Gertrude has just presented me with another son."

"Congratulations, Lord Talbot. How many children do you have?" Bess asked politely.

"Six—the same number as you, Lady Cavendish."

Bess was momentarily startled. Surely he was too young to be the father of six children. Then she remembered that he was exactly the same age as herself, and if she could have six, then so could he.

Bess excused herself. It was time for the buffet to be set up, and as her liveried footmen carried out the huge silver trays laden with food and wine and fancy delicacies, she had never felt prouder in her life. The venison, lamb, veal, and game birds all came from their own land. The trout came from the Derwent, the fruit from their orchards, the cheeses and milk from their own dairy farms. Chatsworth even brewed its own beer. There wasn't a woman present who didn't covet Chatsworth; there wasn't a man who didn't covet its chatelaine.

In the afternoon the nursemaid brought

baby Mary to her mother. "I'm so sorry to bother you, ma'am, but she won't stop crying."

"Ellen, my children are never a bother to me. Give her to me; I'll soon rock her to sleep." Bess took her daughter in her arms and walked toward the sanctuary of the rose garden, which was separated by a walk of tall yews. When the baby felt herself pressed against her mother's ample bosom, she tried to suck. Bess laughed. "Oh, no, you don't; I weaned you weeks ago." She sat down on the edge of the stone fountain, and within a minute the child was asleep. Bess handed her back to her nurse, who gratefully carried her off. Bess closed her eyes with contentment, breathing in the heavenly fragrance of the roses.

George Talbot watched her from the yews. He overheard what she said to the nurse and was astounded that she breast-fed her babies. The thought was unbelievably arousing to him, but then everything about Bess Hardwick aroused him—it always had. Christ, he'd pay a thousand pounds for a glimpse of her suckling a child. It was ridiculous that sparks of animosity should fly between them every time they spoke. Talbot was determined to make a fresh start. He would try to behave himself and win her over. She was the most enticing challenge he'd ever encountered. He closed the distance between them before she opened her eyes.

"Lady Cavendish."

Bess lifted her lashes and looked up at the extremely tall dark man gazing down at her.

"Lord Talbot?" She said his name with a question that implied, *What do you want?*

"I would like us to be friends. We have known each other for a very long time, but we have not been friends."

Her brows arched. "And whose fault is that?" she demanded.

"I know the fault is mine, Lady Cavendish, and I wish to repair it." He hoped he sounded sincere.

Bess looked up at him. *No wonder he is arrogant. Not only is he heir to a princedom, he's the handsomest man I've ever seen—in a dark, devilish way, of course. Women must throw themselves at him.*

"I was such a callow youth, Lady Cavendish. Your beauty stunned me. I was totally infatuated. I treated you outrageously to make you notice me, but all I succeeded in doing was angering you."

Bess smiled. "I have a quick temper."

"I would like to think I have matured since those early days."

Bess's eyes filled with amusement. "So would I."

"Am I forgiven?" *Christ, did I really call her Mistress Tits?*

He hadn't actually apologized, just excused himself, but Bess knew he was not the kind of man who would ever say he was sorry. She decided to be gracious. She stood up, gave him a radiant smile, and reached out her hand.

Talbot didn't take it. Instead, he took the rose that nestled between her breasts.

The smile left her face, and her dark eyes flashed their fury. "The day we met I thought you an arrogant swine. You have not changed one iota—you are still an arrogant swine!"

"Vixen!" he taunted.

"Black devil!" Bess wanted to fly at him and scratch his eyes out. It was difficult to control the emotion he aroused in her, but she spun on her heel and ran from the rose garden before they had an open brawl.

Bess had so many other guests that it didn't take long for her anger to cool. She laughed at her reaction to George Talbot. He'd done nothing, really, except act like a typical male. She should have been flattered.

When the last carriage had left, the children were all put to bed, and the house restored to order, Bess and William ascended the grand staircase hand in hand. "It was a great triumph for you today, Bess. I'm so proud of you."

She leaned her head against him in an affectionate gesture. "I owe it all to you, William." When they reached the top of the staircase, Bess turned to survey her magnificent home. "It was absolutely perfect. Today I achieved everything I ever set out to do." She looked into his eyes. "You made all my dreams come true."

Cavendish knew she was completely happy tonight. He could not bring himself to destroy one small part of that happiness. Tomorrow would be soon enough. He waited until she was in bed before he gave her the present. She gasped with delight. "It's so precious.... I'll treasure it always."

William held her in his arms all night, savoring her love, dreading that on the morrow she would hate him.

Early the next morning, when William went into his office, he found all Bess's account books on his desk awaiting his signature of approval. Sick at heart he pushed them away, wishing his treasury accounts were as honest. He massaged the tightness in his chest and called Bess into his office. He made her sit down, then propped himself against the carved desk.

"Bess, I'm in trouble. The queen has ordered an audit of her treasury."

"That bitch! She is doing this because she hates me! How much time do you have?"

"It is over and done. They have been at it for months, scrutinizing every piece of paper my office has collected in the last thirteen years."

"You've been keeping this to yourself instead of sharing it with me," she accused. "No wonder you are so worn out!" She jumped to her feet, but with gentle hands he pressed her back down.

"There was no need to alarm you."

"But now there is?" The blood drained from her face.

"The auditor's final report claims there is a discrepancy in my accounts of over five thousand pounds."

"Five thousand pounds?" she repeated incredulously.

"Paulet seemed satisfied with my explanations, but I doubt the queen will be."

"Have you been charged yet?"

"No, but I fully expect to be. The queen wants to be rid of me. She is determined to replace all those about her in office. This is the means she will use."

Bess clenched her fists. "We'll fight her!"

"I contacted the lawyers, and I must now prepare my defense."

"I'll help you, William. I'm going back to London with you. This is no time for you to be alone."

Cavendish wanted to be sure she fully understood. "Bess, if I am not cleared of the charge and have to pay the five thousand, we will have to sell everything—Chatsworth, the London house."

"William, I don't care about Chatsworth, I care about you! My God, if you are not cleared of the charge, they could send you to prison!" She jumped up and wrapped her arms about him.

"You've not asked me if I'm guilty."

Bess laughed through her tears. "I don't need to ask, you are such a damned rogue!"

"Do you hate me?"

"Hate you? I am far more guilty than you. You merely diverted the funds; I am the one who spent them!"

Bess and William traveled to London the first week of September. They trusted each other implicitly and decided they were in this together. They had always had friends in the highest places, who would willingly have used their influence for them, but the friends they had cultivated were all staunch Protestants and were themselves in Catholic Mary's disfavor.

Bess accompanied William on his frequent visits to the lawyers, and she had her say. "Do you realize how much of our income is paid to you in lawyers' fees each year? It is more than we spend on building! And we have never begrudged you a penny of it."

"Lady Cavendish, we pledge to do our utmost."

"That is all I ask, gentlemen."

The formal charges were laid against Sir William Cavendish on October 1. One week later he went before the queen's judges in the Star Chamber with his secretary, Robert Bestnay, and his lawyers to answer the charges. He put forth his own defense, and then his lawyers asked for leniency because of his past loyalty and service to the Crown. They hoped to get the debt reduced to one thousand pounds.

The Queen's council owed their loyalty to Mary. Suffolk, Warwick, Somerset, and Seymour had all gone to the block, and the Earl of Shrewsbury was too old to be in London. It took fifteen long days before Cavendish was called to Court again. The waiting seemed endless, the pressure intolerable.

Finally, on October 23 he was called back. Cavendish was told that his defense was unacceptable to the queen. A quick consultation with his lawyers did him little good. They told him it was pointless to deny the charges and that his only recourse was to beg for mercy. He argued with them, but in the end he was forced into the humiliation of pleading guilty and throwing himself on the mercy of the court. His lawyers pleaded his case, saying that if Sir William was forced to repay the full amount, he would be ruined financially and he and his children would end their days in penury.

When he arrived home that night, William was in a rage. He cursed his lawyers for fools. He told Bess, "I was forced into a humiliating theatrical performance that got me absolutely nowhere."

Bess saved her curses for the queen, and William joined her, ranting and raving for hours. "After all the service I've given to the Crown, all the royal coffers I've filled, doing their dirty work for them, this is the thanks I get!"

"William, I don't care about the debt; I care about you!" It was inevitable that the Crown would recover the debt, but they had not handed down their punishment yet. Bess feared that William would be sent to prison. *He could even be sent to the block.* Bess pushed the terrifying thought away.

She did not fall asleep until the early hours of the morning.

Bess awoke, terrified. The room was empty, stripped bare. She ran downstairs and found the bailiffs carrying off everything she possessed in the world. Bess begged and pleaded and cried, all to no avail. Outside, her beautiful possessions were being piled on a cart. They had been put out of their house and had nowhere to go. Fear washed over her in great waves. Panic choked her. When she turned around, the cart was gone, her family was gone, and even Chatsworth had vanished. Bess had lost everything she had in the world. The suffocating terror mounted until it engulfed her, the waves of fear almost drowning her.

The hollow, empty feeling inside her belly was like a ravenous hunger, only worse: William was gone! She was overwhelmed with helplessness, hopelessness.

Bess shot up in bed, knowing she had had the old nightmare. William was not beside her, and the panic of the dream was all too real. Then she saw him across the room and knew immediately that something was wrong. He was clutching his chest and trying to pour himself some wine.

Bess sprang from the bed and ran to him. "William!" By the time she reached him, the pain had driven him to his knees. The goblet fell from his hand and the red wine spread across the carpet like blood. Bess cried out for James Cromp, who came running. "Help me get him to bed, James."

"It's easing," William gasped as he lay back against the pillows. "I'll be fine."

Bess threw on her bedgown and went to summon Robert Bestnay. "Get William's doctor as fast as you can."

When Dr. Turner arrived and examined his patient, he determined that Sir William had suffered a heart seizure. He gave him an opiate for the pain and warned him severely that he must rest.

Bess went downstairs with Turner. "Will he be all right?" she demanded frantically.

"Lady Cavendish, he must be kept quiet. This has been brought about by work and worry. If he does not have complete bed rest, he could suffer another heart seizure. I'll come again tomorrow."

Bess was thoroughly alarmed, but she was also determined to follow the doctor's orders. She called the staff of the London house together and gave them their orders.

William slept heavily through the entire day and into the night. He awoke about midnight and asked Bess to come into bed with him. She got up from the chair beside the bed and slipped beneath the covers. She put her arms about him and held him close. She did not want to transfer her panic to him.

Finally, he spoke to her in a calm voice. "Bess...my Bessie, I love and adore you. I am so very sorry to leave you in such a mess."

"William, you are not going to leave me, I won't let you!"

He smiled. How very like Bess to think she could order things the way she wanted. He knew he had been blessed the day he found her. He had taught her everything he knew about business. She had always had courage, but now she had confidence in herself as well. She was only twenty-nine years old—she had her whole life before her.

The next day Bess bathed him and fed him and forbade him to speak of their difficulties. By late afternoon she began to have a glimmer of hope that he would recover. In the evening he even teased her about being too bossy.

She went down to the kitchen to prepare him some soup laced with cream and wine. When she came back upstairs, she was furious to find him out of bed. Suddenly, William grabbed his chest and lurched forward. Bess screamed and ran to him. She knelt on the floor beside him and enfolded him in her arms. She held him until his body turned cold.

"No, William, no," she whispered with trembling lips. She shivered over and over, then her whole body began to shake uncontrollably, as she was convulsed by racking dry sobs. Bess stared at him in disbelief. "Don't leave me, William...I cannot go on without you."

PART THREE

THE ROYAL COURT
LONDON 1557

❖

There is a tide in the affairs of men,
which, taken at the flood, leads on to fortune;
Omitted, all the voyage of their life
Is bound in shallows and in miseries.

WILLIAM SHAKESPEARE

TWENTY-THREE

Bess was numb. She was as stunned as if a stone wall had collapsed on her. She could not feel, she could not think, she could not function in any way. This time, fate had dealt her a blow from which she would never recover.

Robert Bestnay and James Cromp joined ranks and did what needed to be done. They dispatched messages to Lady Cavendish's family immediately and gently coaxed her to tell them what funeral arrangements she wanted made.

Her mother, Marcella, and Jane arrived with all the children and their attendant nursemaids. They were alarmed when they saw Bess. She was silent and remote as if she were in a trance.

Sir William Cavendish was buried on Allhallows, the last day of October, at St. Botolph's, Aldgate. Bess thought it would please him to be laid to rest beside his mother and father and all the Cavendishes who had gone before him. She stood at the grave, veiled in black, holding the hand of her daughter Francie, who was so much like her father. His other children stood in a row beside them as his coffin was lowered into the cold ground, and the noble mourners who had come to pay their respects could not remember such a sad sight.

Sir John Thynne was the first to approach

Bess. Though he was now past forty, his tight brown curls still gave him a youthful appearance. As he looked at her, his green eyes filled with compassion. "Lady Cavendish—Bess, please accept my heartfelt condolences. If there is anything I can do to help you in any way whatsoever, I beg that you send word to me."

Bess stared at him as if she hadn't heard a word.

Frances Grey and Nan Dudley tried to comfort Bess. All three women were united in their hatred of Mary. Bess remained silent, rigid, and dry-eyed, and her friends were deeply concerned for her. As they gathered close about her, Bess stared at the two women and murmured, "I curse her."

During the next two weeks Bess did not speak, did not eat, and did not sleep. She had withdrawn to a place where no one could touch her, no one could hurt her again. Her heart had died with William, and she could not face the world without him. He was her bastion, her rock, her strength. William was more than her love, he was her very life. With him beside her she had conquered the world; without him she felt that she could not exist. Whenever her mother or Jane spoke to her, she did not answer, so they left her in peace and did their best to keep the children quiet.

Finally, Marcella went up to the master bedchamber to confront her. She found Bess lying on the great bed, carved with the Cavendish stags, staring up at the red silk canopy. "This nonsense cannot go on. You have abdicated your responsibilities, and it is time you came to grips with it all."

"You do not understand," Bess whispered.

"No, we do not. So you will have to get up off that bed, come downstairs, and talk to us."

Bess did not respond, but half an hour later she came quietly downstairs and joined the Hardwick women in the parlor. Wearily, she told them what William had gone through during the last months. Listlessly, she told them that the queen had ruined his career and that he owed the Crown over five thousand pounds. As she quietly told them of his insurmountable problems, her mother and Jane were shocked into silence by the amount of money owed.

"Queen Mary murdered him as surely as if she had plunged a dagger into his heart," Bess said softly.

Marcella demanded, "Aren't you going to get angry?"

My emotions are dead, Bess thought.

"So the queen wins! You are not even going to fight her!"

"You don't understand! William lost."

"Bess, you are the one who doesn't understand. William is dead. These problems are now *your* problems. Lying on your bed will not solve them. The five-thousand-pound debt is *your* debt. *You* must sell the land, *you* must pay off the debt. The legacy William left you is not Chatsworth, it is your Cavendish children."

Bess stood up all of a sudden. "I curse the bitch!" She ran to the front door, flung it open, and cried into the November wind, "I curse the bitch!"

The women exchanged relieved glances. Bess would be all right now that she had gotten angry.

The London house was on the Thames, the Cavendish barge moored at the water stairs. Bess went aboard and spoke to the bargeman. "Take me upriver, past Whitehall—I need the air."

She paced the deck without so much as a shawl. The fury erupting inside her kept her warm. Silently, Bess reviled the queen, heaping curses upon her head. Bess knew she was not alone in her hatred. Mary and the Spaniard she married had revived the practice of burning heretics at the stake, and her subjects condemned such evil and loathed her.

By the time Whitehall came into view, Bess had worked herself up to full pitch. Aloud she cried, "Bloody Mary! I'm going to fight you! Not one acre of Cavendish land will I part with! Not one acre! I will see you in your grave, you bitch!"

That night, in the privacy of her bedchamber, Bess cried for the first time. Her anger had opened the floodgates, and her other dammed-up emotions of anguish and sorrow came pouring forth.

Later, when the storm abated somewhat, she lay in the big bed with her hand upon William's pillow. "My love, when I had the fever and thought I might die, I made you swear that you would make great marriages for our children. Now I give the same pledge to you. I can do no less, William. You will always be with me in them. Help me to be strong."

Bess appointed Francis Whitfield as bailiff of Chatsworth; her sister Jane's husband would assist him. She put Timothy Pusey in charge of the lead and coal mines. She asked Robert Bestnay to become her secretary, and James Cromp, whom she trusted with her life, became her personal assistant.

Bess sent Cromp off with a letter to her old friend Sir John Thynne, who had attended the funeral and offered to do anything he could for her. Then, accompanied by Robert Bestnay, she paid a visit to the lawyers.

Bess made her position abundantly clear. "Gentlemen, you probably believe the simplest way out of my difficulties is for me to sell Chatsworth and my northern landholdings to pay what I owe the Crown. But I have no such intent! I am going to fight, and gentlemen, when I fight it is with no holds barred. I will use every means within my power. If it is humanly possible, I will not sell one acre to pay my debt to the Crown."

Bess had their full attention as she continued. "A bill to recover the five thousand will have to go through Parliament. I have dealt with the courts before and know how slow the process can be. It will be your job to see that the bill is delayed and delayed again. I don't care what it costs, and I don't care who you have to bribe. Cavendish taught me the effectiveness of the golden spur. I intend to put the London house up for sale today."

Bess knew that the only way to save her sanity was to keep busy. Within three months of her husband's death, Bess had sold the London house and packed up everything. From Sir John Thynne, Bess leased his house at Brentford and moved the children there the moment the London house was sold. It was on the Thames close by her friend Nan Dudley's Syon House. The quiet village near Chelsea would give her privacy from the Court but still allow her to be close enough to London to learn everything that was happening.

Bess's income from her tenant farmers and mines was three hundred pounds a year. Her London expenses equaled her income, so the building at Chatsworth came to a halt. Not one pound could be expended on workmen's wages or building materials. On top of this was the money she owed to Westmorland and to William Parr for the thousands of acres she and William had purchased from them.

Alone in her bed at night, she lay worrying about what would become of them all. She had shown a defiant face to the world, ordering the lawyers to use delaying tactics, but deep down inside she was realist enough to know the day of reckoning was inevitable. She feared that in the end Chatsworth and everything else she owned would have to be sacrificed. But at least her name had been on every legal document as co-owner. Bess had William to thank for the fact that she owned everything outright in her own name.

By keeping busy and expending all her energy, Bess got through the days. She played with the children, and she had learned to laugh again when she was with others, but the nights were something else entirely. She was so lonely she thought she would die of it. Her heart—and her body too—ached for him. She grew thin, and the emptiness inside her expanded instead of lessening, as day followed night and night followed day.

In late January Bess received a note from Frances Grey that read: *I have a surprise for you and Nan Dudley. Meet me tomorrow at Syon House.*

Both Bess and Nan were gowned in black silk when their friend Frances swept in wearing scarlet.

"Good God, you look like two old crows, sitting there in your widows' weeds. 'Tis time you threw off your mourning and took lovers!"

"Which is apparently what you have done," Bess said dryly.

"Ah, that is where you are completely wrong, darling. I took lovers long before I became a widow."

Nan Dudley was shocked. "You took a lover while your husband was alive?"

Frances's eyebrows arched. "And you didn't?"

"Duke Dudley gave me thirteen children; what the hell would I want with a lover?"

"Bess, surely you took lovers," Frances demanded.

"No, I never did, Frances. It was all I could do to keep Rogue Cavendish happy. He was a man of considerable appetite."

"Well, fortunately for me, I now have a husband of considerable appetite!" Frances waved her new wedding ring under their noses.

"You're married?" Nan asked in disbelief.

"To whom?" Bess questioned.

"To Adrian Stokes, darling, my master of horse."

Nan Dudley was speechless.

Bess said, "How old is he?"

"Twenty-one, darling. He has bright red hair, and you know what they say about redheads! I'm replete as a cat filled with cream."

"Aren't you afraid of Bloody Mary?" Bess demanded.

"She has forbidden me the Court, thank God; the place is like a tomb these days." Frances leaned forward and lowered her voice confidentially. "My daughter Catherine tells me the queen is ill. Her belly is swollen, but it isn't a child as she would have everyone believe. Her husband, Philip, has gone back to Spain. He's had enough of her false pregnancies!" Catherine had been made a lady-in-waiting to the queen as compensation for sending her sister, Lady Jane, to the block.

"I hope Mary rots!" Bess said with venom.

The three friends indulged in highly treasonous conversation for the rest of the afternoon. Before Frances left, however, their talk turned back to marriage. Both Bess and Nan kissed their friend and wished her every happiness.

"In a way I have to admire Frances. She doesn't give a fart what the world thinks of her. I'll always love her no matter what outrageous thing she does."

"Do you think there's any chance that the queen might be fatally ill?" Nan asked hopefully.

"Well, I certainly put a curse on her," Bess hissed.

"So did my sons." Nan sighed heavily. "The minute they were released, they went off to fight the war in France. The wretched queen declared war on France only at her husband's urging, to help Spain. It seems I never stop worrying over them."

"They were in the Tower so long, Nan. Who managed to get them released?"

"I think Elizabeth asked Cecil to help. He worked for my husband years ago. In fact, it was Duke Dudley who got young King Edward to appoint Cecil as principal secretary. Queen Mary didn't keep him on in that position, but he still has influence."

Bess sighed, remembering the caustic young man who had been a friend to her and William. Elizabeth had always trusted Cecil. Suddenly Bess wanted Elizabeth to know the rumor about the queen. It would give her a glimmer of hope. No one in the realm had more reason to hate Bloody Mary than Elizabeth did!

Bess told no one she was going to Hatfield, except the coach driver. When she was taken to Princess Elizabeth's private wing by attendants she had never seen before, Bess realized just how long it had been since she had visited. When the red-haired young women at last came face to face, Bess swept into a curtsy, then arose so they could study each other.

"I cannot believe it has been four years," Elizabeth said, putting a cautionary finger to her lips. Though Bess and Elizabeth had corresponded, they'd had to read between the lines. None of their private thoughts could be put down on paper. Whenever Bess had a child, she had told Elizabeth, who had written back to congratulate her, and when Sir William died, Elizabeth had sent her condolences.

Elizabeth took Bess into a private sitting room with a blazing fire. Bess kissed Cat Ashley, and that good woman took her embroidery and sat at the door as a watchdog so that the two friends might share their intimate thoughts.

"You are much thinner, Bess. Being widowed has robbed you of your lovely round curves."

"A part of me died with William, but you know what that is like, Your Grace."

"I do. But the sharp sorrow is tempered by poignancy and memories, even though they are bittersweet. I have learned there is something harder to bear than sorrow. It is fear—stark terror. When she sent me to the Tower, I did not believe I would come out alive.

Even when I was released and sent to Woodstock, I could not sleep for fear of a dagger in the night; I could not eat for fear of poison. Her spies are here at Hatfield."

Bess realized what Elizabeth said about fear was true. Bess herself had not lived a day without the terrifying emotion since William had told her of his trouble. "Your Grace, that is the reason I came. I wanted to ignite a tiny spark of hope." Bess lowered her voice. "Lady Catherine Grey told her mother that Mary is ill. She is grossly swollen, but not with child. Philip has gone back to Spain in disgust."

For a moment Elizabeth's amber eyes glittered gold. "She will never name me her successor. For months they have been trying to marry me to Spain, but so far I have eluded their trap." They talked on for two hours. Elizabeth told Bess how sick and tired she was of living a nun's life and wearing severe gray dresses every day of her life. Bess told Elizabeth of the massive burden of debt she owed the Crown and how she was struggling to hold on to what was hers.

Bess dared not stay longer in case she aroused suspicion. "I must go, Your Grace."

"Bess, you have given me hope that there is a light at the end of this very long tunnel. Promise you will come again if you hear anything—anything at all!"

On the drive back to Brentford, Bess felt good about her visit. If she could bring a little warmth, a bit of happiness, or a glimmer of hope to the ones who mattered in her life, it would help to fill the emptiness inside her.

One month inexorably followed another, and at the end of each one, Bess heaved a heartfelt sigh of relief that Parliament had not yet signed the bill to recover what she owed the Crown. It was an intimidating prospect to pit her will against the government, to pay regular visits to her lawyers and browbeat them to use every means in hope of delaying the day of reckoning.

In order to assure herself things were being run properly in the north, Bess made hurried visits to Derbyshire and took her mother back to Chatsworth as caretaker, to be in charge of the magnificent house that was all but closed down. In the carriage Bess's mother tried to give her daughter some advice.

"Bess, darling, you are so slim these days; you are working and worrying yourself into a decline. Don't you think it would be more sensible to sell Chatsworth and rid yourself of this massive burden of debt? Then you could marry a country squire and live in peace and comfort for the rest of your life."

Bess stared at her mother in horror. "A squire? A bloody country squire? Bite your tongue! I should hope my ambition would allow me to look higher than a squire! But in any case I shall never marry again!"

Back at Brentford Bess burned candles long into the night, balancing her income with her output and cutting corners to make ends meet. Her sons were growing so rapidly, none of their clothes fit them, and on top of that she had no choice but to find the money for tutors. She couldn't afford to send them off to school, and they were becoming little hellions without the strong influence of their father.

Late one June night Bess was surprised by a visitor. When she realized the well-built, handsome man was Robin Dudley, she took him upstairs to her private sitting room.

"Lady Cavendish, you are even more beautiful today than the first time I met you."

"My lord, I am almost thirty."

His dark brown eyes shone with amusement. "Never admit to more than twenty-seven; it is a perfect age for a woman."

Bess laughed. "All right, then, I won't." She sobered quickly. "You are back from France. Was it very bad?"

"It was a bloody, shameful, ignoble defeat. We lost Calais."

"I know. Mary's reign has been a disaster for everyone—for your family, for mine, and now for England."

"Lady Cavendish—Bess, I know I can trust you, but may I speak plainly and in confidence?"

"Robin, you may say anything to me."

"Have you seen Elizabeth?"

"Five months ago I took her the news that Mary was ill."

"I am longing to see her, but I dare not go yet. Will you visit her again and tell her that Mary is *incurably* ill? I cannot reveal my sources, but Mary is still refusing to name Elizabeth her successor. So when she dies it may mean civil war to put Elizabeth on the throne. But whatever it takes we will do it. Just tell her that the wheels have been set in motion. She will understand."

"That would take a great deal of money and troops."

"We have pledges of both." His eyes lifted and he glanced about the lovely room. "You lease this house from Sir John Thynne?"

"He is a dear friend of mine."

"He is a dear friend of Elizabeth also. He is a great landowner who has pledged his fortune. William Parr, another mutual friend, has secured a pledge of ten thousand troops from the captains who garrison Berwick."

Bess experienced a surge of euphoria. Was it really going to happen at long last?

This time Bess asked her friend Sir John Thynne to accompany her to Hatfield. Within days of their visit, Elizabeth received Count Feria, the Spanish ambassador, and this confirmed to her that her sister's reign was ending and they were desperately scrambling to secure Elizabeth's goodwill.

By August the road to Hatfield was thronged with crowds of well-wishers on their way to curry favor with the future Queen of England. By the look of things, there would be no need of civil war to put Elizabeth on the throne; the people were not even waiting until Mary was dead to switch their allegiance.

Though life at Hatfield changed drastically, Bess's life remained the same. Living quietly at Brentford, she endured a long, tense autumn, trying to live within her means and juggling her accounts. Bess knew she faced an uncertain future with insolvency staring her in the face. In the deep recesses of her mind, a tiny glimmer of hope flickered. If Queen Mary died and Elizabeth came to the throne, could the new monarch be persuaded to reduce the overwhelming Cavendish debt? But Mary did not die; she clung to life tenaciously, refusing to pass the Crown to a sister she hated.

At the end of September, Bess traveled up to Derbyshire before the harsh winter weather gripped the north. She had a large enterprise to oversee, disputes with tenant farmers to settle, leases of small manor houses to negotiate, land to drain and enclose, and a dozen other matters to discuss with her bailiffs. She tackled everything with a furious energy and strength of purpose, determined to be back home with the children before the anniversary of their father's death.

On October 25 Bess and her children held a commemorative service to honor the memory of their beloved father, and the following day Bess went by barge to London and took flowers to St. Botolph's. As she laid them on the grave, she said, "I cannot believe it has been only a year. Oh, my love, it has been the longest year of my life. Dear God, I don't know how I'm going to face another one."

As she knelt quietly, she felt a small measure of peace descend upon her, and her uncertainties melted away. Somehow she had survived and would find the strength to continue. Bess knew she had just as much courage, energy, and determination as she'd always had. The thing she missed was the joy in life. As she stood up a gust of wind whipped her skirts into the air, exposing her legs in their black lace stockings. Bess laughed quietly. "You are a damned rogue."

During the first week of November, London was abuzz with the news that Mary had finally named Elizabeth her successor, and the queen's servants went to Hatfield to inform Elizabeth.

Mary Tudor finally died on the seventeenth day of November. When Bess heard the news she burst into tears. They were neither tears of sorrow nor joy; they were tears of pure, unadulterated relief. "Elizabeth doesn't know yet," Bess said to Jane. "It will take hours for a courier to ride to Hatfield. I must pack and leave immediately; the road will be clogged with courtiers."

Bess opened her journal to record the momentous news, and as she wrote the date at the top of the page, a great shudder racked her body. "Dear God, it was exactly a year ago on this very date that I sailed upriver to Whitehall and cursed her." Bess clearly remembered the words she had hurled in passionate fury: *I will see you in your grave, you bitch!*

TWENTY-FOUR

The Great Hall of Hatfield Palace was packed with more people than it had ever held before. Bess knew almost everyone present. She stood laughing and talking with Robert Dudley and his beautiful sister Mary Sidney. Earlier she had received a kiss of greeting from Lord William Parr, Sir John Thynne, Sir Henry Brooke, William Herbert, the Earl of Pembroke, and a dozen other noblemen. Bess had forgotten she knew so many earls of the realm.

A pair of strong arms grabbed Bess from behind. She turned and cried out with delight. "Ambrose Dudley! God's feet, you were a pink-cheeked boy when last we met, and now you're an old man."

"You still look and *feel* like a young girl, my beauty."

Bess tapped him with her fan. "I'm almost"— she glanced at Robin—"I'm almost twenty-seven."

Robin threw back his head and laughed at the private joke. They were all giddy with excitement. Bess had stayed up half the night with Elizabeth and her ladies. "I shall never sleep again!" the radiant young queen had declared. "The lights in my palaces will burn all night, and I shall dance until dawn. No more rules to follow! I, and no one else in my realm, shall make the rules." Elizabeth stripped off her prim gray dress and threw it upon the fire. As it blazed up, her laughter held a hint of the hysteria she felt. "From this day forward my gowns will be magnificent and I shall change them a half dozen times a day."

Bess drawled, "I pity your poor ladies of the bedchamber." But completely understanding Elizabeth's intoxication, she prompted, "What about jewels?"

"God's feet, the Crown jewels now belong to me—and I shall wear every last one!"

Cat Ashley brought her a bedgown. "My lamb, you must get some sleep. Tomorrow you have to give your first address as queen."

Elizabeth turned and stared at her, then her glittering eyes looked at each one in turn. "By Christ's precious blood, no one will ever say *must* to me again. I will have no mistress, and I will have no master, for as long as I may live!"

As Bess stood with the Dudleys awaiting their new queen, she knew exactly what to expect of Elizabeth. She would be vain and demanding and imperious, but she had an unshakable belief in her destiny and would make a glorious monarch. She was more shrewd and clever than any man breathing, and devious too. Bess was certain that Elizabeth had been born to be queen.

"Where the devil is she?" Robin demanded impatiently.

Bess smiled up at him. "It gives her pleasure to keep us waiting."

At last Elizabeth made her appearance in the Great Hall, and the cheers were deafening. She did not hold up her hands to make them stop but stood basking in the tumultuous ovation. It lasted for a good half hour before the crowd stopped chanting, "Long live the queen." Only then did Elizabeth begin to speak. Her composure was extraordinary. She was in complete control.

"This is the doing of the Lord, and it is marvelous in our eyes. I owe my allegiance and my Crown to the people of England. The burden that has fallen upon me maketh me amazed, and I have chosen the most worthy men in the realm to help me carry this burden. Today I appoint Sir William Cecil as my principal secretary of state and head of my privy council.

"My other councillors will be William Parr, Marquess of Northampton, and the earls of Arundel, Bedford, Derby, Pembroke, and Shrewsbury. Others will be chosen in good time.

"I appoint Lord Robert Dudley as my master of horse. I appoint Sir William St. Loe as captain of the queen's guard. William Paulet, Marquess of Winchester, remains as lord treasurer, and I appoint Sir Nicholas Bacon as lord keeper of the great seal."

Bess was delighted. Bacon was Cecil's brother-in-law and a learned lawyer, who had been head of the Court of Augmentation. He had always accommodated the Cavendishes whenever William had wanted to exchange a piece of land.

Elizabeth continued, "I appoint Mistress Catherine Ashley as head lady-in-waiting and mistress of the robes. Today I appoint four new ladies-of-the-bedchamber: Lady Catherine Grey, Lady Mary Sidney, Lady Lettice Knollys, and Lady Elizabeth Cavendish."

Bess was stunned. Elizabeth had rewarded everyone Bess knew with an important appointment, but Bess herself had never once thought of an official place in Elizabeth's Court for herself! Bess wasn't even sure she wanted it. She had too much on her plate now; how would she juggle this appointment with all her other responsibilities? But of course Bess realized immediately that she could not turn it down. Doing so would be an unforgivable insult to Elizabeth. Bess was practical enough to understand that if she was ever to prosper again, it would be through royal patronage.

That evening, Bess was introduced to Lettice Knollys, who was the queen's Boleyn cousin. All the ladies Elizabeth had appointed thanked her profusely, then Bess summoned the courage to ask her first favor. "Your Majesty, may I return to Brentford to inform my family and see to my wardrobe?"

"Bess, your official duties won't begin until my coronation. By all means return home to see to your wardrobe. I already have my sewing women working day and night. When I enter London I have decided to wear royal purple velvet. I shall go straight to the Tower—to the Royal Apartments this time, of course. Cat's husband, John, is to be my master of the jewel house. It will take me a week to try on everything! We shall celebrate Christmas at my Palace of Westminster, and my coronation will take place in January, to symbolize a new year, a new reign."

The following morning Bess returned to Brentford. Elizabeth was intoxicated by her new power and busy from dawn to dusk making plans. Bess knew she would not be missed. Elizabeth had dreamed and fantasized for years about this moment. The last thing the new queen wanted was advice from another woman.

Jane and Aunt Marcy sat entranced as Bess told them what had gone on at Hatfield. "Elizabeth appointed me a lady-of-the-bedchamber. I wish she hadn't. How on earth will I manage everything? I will have to live at Westminster Palace and go with the Court wherever Queen Elizabeth chooses. You and the children will have to live here at Brentford."

Marcella clapped her hands. "It is exactly what you need, Bess. You belong at Court! You will thrive on being at the center of the universe. Elizabeth will gather about her the greatest men in the realm—where better to catch yourself a husband?"

"I will never marry again," Bess said firmly.

"I know better," Marcella contradicted.

Bess chose to ignore her prophesy. "I am not ambitious for myself, but my children are another matter entirely. My Court connections could be invaluable to them. Hell's teeth, if only I had money for their dowries."

"You need a rich, indulgent husband," Marcella pointed out. "Marriage is always the answer."

"You've managed to avoid it all your life," Bess said dryly.

"Ah, that is because I am not a man's woman. But you are, Bess, deny it how you will!"

"It is a bloody good thing I won't have to go into debt for new clothes. I have a wardrobe of magnificent gowns."

"Need I remind you they came from a rich and indulgent husband?" Marcella pressed.

"Cavendish did indulge me, shamelessly. I'll never love again. I gave William my whole heart, and when I pledged my love, it was forever. I could never feel that way about any other man."

Bess spent Christmas with her children at Brentford, then her barge was piled high with her lavish wardrobe of expensive garments and personal belongings as she embarked from Brentford to Westminster Palace in time for the New Year's revels.

Bess knew exactly what to expect at Court. As well as excitement and grandeur, there would be backbiting, petty jealousies, plotting, and mongering for power. All of them, including herself, were opportunists who would have to continually vie with each other to keep their place in the pecking order.

Bess was given chambers close to the Royal Apartments. She was well-pleased, for only a privileged few would have access to Elizabeth's private apartments, which lay beyond the Privy Chamber. Her two luxurious rooms were next to those assigned to Lord Dudley's sister, Mary Sidney, whom she had known for years.

Mary helped Bess hang her gowns in the commodious wardrobe. "Your clothes are beautiful; you have such exquisite taste. Which shall you wear tonight?"

"There is to be a ball tonight?" Bess asked faintly.

Mary laughed. "There is a ball every night, unless it is a masque or a play or a musical extravaganza. The New Year's Eve ball tomorrow night is a masquerade, but not just any costume will do. We are all to be gods and goddesses of mythology."

"That doesn't give me much time for a costume. Is Her Majesty to be Circe again?"

"Ah, no. The queen is to be Venus, and my dearest brother Robin is to be her Adonis." Mary rolled her eyes and they went off in peals of laughter.

Bess decided to wear her plainest gown tonight, since she had not yet discarded her mourning. Her dress was gray silk taffeta, and though it was plain it rustled and whispered mysteriously. She twisted her hair into a French knot and covered it with a snood encrusted with jet beads. By dressing soberly, Bess hoped to make a respectable impression. Everyone at Court must have heard of the Cavendish financial scandal, so she would hold her head high and remain on the sidelines. The last thing Bess wanted was for the Court to think she was manhunting.

The first man who asked her to dance was

Sir John Thynne. His green velvet doublet matched the color of his eyes.

"I'm hardly out of mourning, John. I don't feel right, dancing."

"Bess, my intentions are honorable. I would like leave to court you."

Bess was startled. He was wasting no time and was clearly hinting at marriage. Her massive debt of five thousand pounds was not a deterrent. "How is your building at Longleat coming along?" They both had a passion for building and could discuss plaster frescoes or carved paneling for hours on end, which she hoped would divert him from his wooing.

The next man who asked her to dance was Sir Henry Brooke, who had recently come into his title of Lord Cobham. "It is most kind of you to ask me, Lord Harry, but I am not dancing tonight."

"Kindness has nothing to do with it, Bess. I'm in the market for a bride."

Bess hoped that humor would divert him. "Harry, you've been in the market for a wife since your brother, Tom, married my husband's daughter, Cathy. Yet still you are unwed."

"That is because the lady I wanted was unavailable. Now she is free." He took her hand and pressed a fervent kiss upon it.

Bess firmly withdrew her fingers. "Your sister has just arrived; I must go and speak with her."

Lord Harry followed Bess as she went to greet his sister, Elizabeth, and her husband, William Parr. As Harry engaged his sister in conversation, Parr gave Bess a kiss upon her cheek and murmured, "There is never any need for you to be lonely, Bess, not while I am at Court."

Bess couldn't believe her ears. It was a proposition if ever she'd heard one! She did not want to offend him—she still owed him money for land purchases—but she wanted no sexual scandal attached to her name. "How could I possibly be lonely with dear friends like your wife, Elizabeth?" Bess asked sweetly.

The queen, escorted by Robin Dudley, made her entrance into the ballroom. She was gowned in gold tissue, cut exceedingly low in the neckline. The tight bodice of her gown was sewn all over with topaz jewels. All the ladies present sank down before her, and as she passed each one, Elizabeth raised them up.

As Bess came out of her curtsy, Elizabeth's eyes swept over her. "I burned all my gray gowns. I suggest you do the same."

"I beg to differ, madam," Robin Dudley said to the queen. "The gown gives Lady Cavendish a most sophisticated allure."

Elizabeth said to Bess, "Spoken by the man who can get a woman out of her clothes faster than any at Court."

Robin's bold eyes swept over the queen. "I haven't had much success in that direction lately, madam."

Elizabeth slapped him playfully with her fan, clearly enjoying the titillating banter. "Virtue is its own reward."

Robin took the queen's bejeweled fingers to

his lips. "Nay, madam, virtue is its own punishment."

The pair was engaged in open flirtation, and Bess knew that by tomorrow the Court would be abuzz with tales of Dudley's dalliance with the queen. Had Elizabeth chosen him because he was safely married, or was there an intense sexual attraction between them? Bess remembered what that felt like and was thankful it was something she herself would never experience again. A grand passion was all-consuming and far too emotional. She was a thirty-year-old widow and mother of six children, with a crushing financial burden hanging over her. She had no room in her life for such nonsense.

As Bess moved to the side of the dance floor, carefully observing everyone, she saw that dalliance seemed to preoccupy every man and woman present tonight. She was glad that that part of her life was over. Bess turned as she sensed eyes upon her. She was relieved to see that it was the Earl of Huntingdon from Derbyshire. Bess greeted him warmly, then wished she had not when his glance became speculative.

"I have been frankly worried for your well-being, my dear. A lady with no outlet for her natural needs becomes thin and irritable." He bent closer to her ear. "Coitus keeps a woman plump and content."

Bess glanced coldly at his wine cup. "Then I suggest you hurry north to your countess before she fades away—or puts horns on you." Bess moved away quickly, wishing she could retire, but protocol prevented her from leaving before the queen. She moved down the room toward the doors and found herself beside Sir William St. Loe.

"Lady Cavendish, I am deeply sorry for your loss."

"Thank you, my lord." He was the only man in the room decent enough to offer her sympathy. Cavendish had once told her St. Loe was a gentleman who would never besmirch a lady's reputation, and Bess was grateful for the respect he showed her. In fact, he was the only man in the room with whom she felt safe.

"Allow me to find you a chair, Lady Cavendish; Her Majesty will be dancing for hours."

Bess was grateful for his thoughtfulness as they sat down and began an easy conversation.

"Happily, the queen's circumstances have changed dramatically since last we met, Lady Cavendish. You restored her will to live and gave her the courage she needed." They were both intimates of Elizabeth, who had seen her at her worst.

"You, too, suffered the Tower."

"I considered it not only my duty, but my privilege."

Bess wondered if St. Loe was in love with Elizabeth. He had been in her household for many years and remained unmarried. But of course he had been chosen for the post because he was a polished gentleman with impeccable manners. He would never presume, unlike others. Bess's glance traveled down the room to Robin Dudley.

She smiled at St. Loe, curious about his age. He must be in his forties, yet he looked much the same as he always had. His closely clipped beard and mustache were graying, but other than that, he was still whipcord-slim with a proud military bearing.

"I am sorry your own circumstances are not as happy as the queen's tonight, Lady Cavendish. I sincerely hope fortune smiles upon you in the New Year."

Fortune? Is he alluding to my financial woes?

"Sir William, I almost dread the New Year coming."

"Ask the queen to help you, my lady. She can be most generous to those she trusts."

"I could not. There will be too many grasping hands, too many parasites at Court."

"You are special, my lady. I have no doubt that when the celebrations and the coronation are behind her, the queen will remember your plight."

Amen to that! Bess prayed fervently.

It was difficult for her to sleep in the strange bed, and Bess lay for hours thinking of the number of men who had made advances to her that night. Not once had her pulse raced, not one of them had made her heart beat faster. She was completely indifferent to the male sex. She doubted she would ever be attracted to a man again. The part inside a woman that responded to the male of the species was dead in her.

The New Year's masquerade was to be a lavish affair with five times as many guests as the previous night. The Great Hall, the Guard Chamber, and the Presence Chamber would be needed to accommodate the crowds.

Bess mentally reviewed the goddesses of mythology and pulled a face. She thought of Isis, goddess of the moon, but Lettice Knollys told her that was going to be her costume. Finally, Bess decided she would be Undine, the water nymph. Over an aqua-colored under-dress, she stitched floating green veils and wore a headdress with trailing iridescent strands of silver and green beads. They looked nothing like real seaweed, but surely goddesses were expected to be fantastical rather than realistic.

The chambers were so crowded with revelers that Bess soon became separated from Mary and Lettice. She declined so many dances, she lost count. Many of the costumes were so good, their owners must have planned them for weeks. Some were extremely clever, like Janus, the god of two faces, but others had absolutely nothing to do with mythology.

Bess was highly diverted, trying to guess who was behind the masks, which was difficult tonight because the chambers were filled with scores of French, Spanish, and Swedish envoys, all come to woo Queen Elizabeth into alliances of one kind or another.

A tall figure in a crimson silk devil's costume bowed before her and took her hand to lead her into the dance. Bess pulled back and refused, but the man in the satanic mask did not seem to understand the meaning of the word *no*. Bess saw his jet-black hair and assumed he was a Spaniard. It seemed easier to capitulate and dance with him rather than make a scene. Then slowly it dawned on her that a Catholic Spaniard would never dress as the devil.

"Who are you?" Bess puzzled.

"Can you not guess, my little nun?"

Bess remembered her nun's costume from years before and was gripped by a terrible suspicion. She reached up to pull down his mask and found Lord Talbot's glittering blue eyes laughing at her. Refusing to be goaded, she quickly snuffed out the spark she felt before it ignited her anger. "You need no mask to impersonate the devil. Your own face is exactly like Lucifer's," she said lightly.

"So I've been told," he drawled. His crimson doublet was in vivid contrast to his dark good looks. White teeth flashed in his swarthy, arrogant face.

As they bantered with each other, it finally dawned on Bess how extremely attractive he was. Talbot was a true aristocrat from an ancient, noble family, and it was evident in every line of his visage and figure. He appeared arrogant because he carried himself with a natural pride.

"I am delighted that Her Majesty chose

you as one of her ladies-of-the-bedchamber. Elizabeth's Court will be unsurpassed if she surrounds herself with ladies of beauty and wit."

Bess realized he was a polished courtier of thirty, far more charming and subtle than he had been as a youth. Yet he was still dark, dominant, and dangerous, a powerful combination that Bess realized was almost irresistible. "And should the gentlemen of the Court be witty or witless, my lord?"

Talbot laughed, clearly enjoying himself. "I assure you there will be no shortage of either kind of gentleman." His compelling gaze held hers. "Her Majesty is shrewd enough to surround herself with those who have proved their loyalty, as you have, Lady Cavendish."

As the music changed, Bess suddenly realized she was in the middle of the dance floor. When she made a move to leave, his hold tightened and she could not easily escape him. "I shouldn't be dancing, my lord, I'm in mourning."

"Costumed as a nymph of the sea, your siren song is irresistible. You've been widowed more than a year, Bess. Your mourning period is over."

"I'm not referring to the prescribed mourning period of a year. I'm talking about what is in my heart!"

He stared down at her with disbelief. Her aging husband had brought financial disaster upon her. "Cavendish was twenty years older than you. I always assumed you married him—"

"For his money?" She was suddenly furious. "Then the laugh was on me, wasn't it, milord devil?"

"That isn't what I meant at all. I humbly apologize, Bess. We have known each other so long, I spoke out of turn. Forgive me, I had no idea it was a love match."

"You've never been humble in your life," she flared. "Nor do you know what it's like to be in need."

"That's where you are entirely wrong, Vixen." My hunger for you is ravenous, he thought silently, hoping to mask the need that threatened to consume him.

Bess wondered if she had mistaken his meaning, but she was so angry she wanted to slap his face. When she realized what she had almost been goaded into doing in the middle of the dance floor, her temper flamed even higher. Suddenly her whole body was roiling with emotion. Her heart was pounding and every pulse was racing madly. Bess felt alive for the first time in fourteen months!

A cold wave of fear washed over her. Lord Talbot was so sexually attractive, she was responding to him against her will. "Peste take you, Talbot!" Bess turned and fled the Presence Chamber. She slowed as she reached the Great Hall, for out here the crowds were shoulder to shoulder. At the door she encountered Sir William St. Loe speaking with the guards he had posted.

"Lady Cavendish, may I join you?" he asked politely.

Bess took his arm as if he were her refuge. "Syntlo." She murmured the name the queen gave him. "I've been looking for you," she lied prettily.

TWENTY-FIVE

On New Year's Day George Talbot was ushered from the Privy Chamber into the queen's private rooms the moment he arrived. Elizabeth was sitting at one of her desks. "By God's precious blood, you took your own sweet time getting here, my Lord Talbot!"

He grinned at her. "It's lovely to see you too, madam. You make it sound as if you cannot manage without me."

"Well, I can! What the devil do I need you for now that I am queen?"

"Apart from my moneybags, I can't think of a thing." His grin was infuriating.

"Why would I need your moneybags?" she demanded imperiously.

"Because the treasury is bankrupt, because you have to pay for the war with France, the upcoming war with Scotland, and this bloody fancy coronation you are planning."

Elizabeth began to laugh. "You are an insolent hound, Talbot; you will never make a courtier, but God's death you speak the truth, Old Man. There won't even *be* a coronation unless we can find a Catholic bishop with enough guts to crown me."

"They've all refused?"

"Yes, plague take them!"

"I'll send immediately for Oglethorpe, Bishop of Carlisle."

"You think he'll be willing?"

"He had better be; he owes his living to Shrewsbury."

"Thank you, my lord, that's a blessed relief. Cecil was at his wit's end. How is Shrewsbury?"

"My father is frail. I'm acting lord lieutenant and acting chief justice, in the north. It's too much for him these days."

"I'm very sorry, George, but you'll have to take his place on the privy council as well. I have dismissed over forty councillors who served Mary. I need men I can trust."

"Stick the broom up my arse and I'll sweep the throne room too."

Elizabeth laughed. She liked a man whose salty vocabulary matched her own. "Oh, I know you are a rarity, George, and the most enterprising industrialist in the realm, but you couldn't run your vast financial empire without a competent staff to conduct business in your absence."

"That is only because I chose them, I trained them, and I rule them with an iron hand. I advise you to do the same, Your Majesty. Start out as you mean to carry on."

"At last you give me my due title, you hound. Does that mean you will pay for my coronation?"

"I will speak to Paulet," he conceded, without committing himself. "The treasury is in chaos, the coffers empty. His staff is completely incompetent, Your Majesty."

"I am keeping Paulet as lord treasurer only because he has held that post since my father appointed him, but I will take your advice and dismiss everyone else in the treasury. Is there anything else you would advise?"

"Lady Cavendish owes the Crown five thousand pounds. It would be most generous if you reduced her debt."

"But the treasury needs money, you said so yourself!"

"Your Majesty, Bess Hardwick is our friend. Cavendish not only left her a widow with six children, he left her in financial ruin. Her back is against the wall. Reduce her debt to a thousand pounds and I'll pay for your bloody fancy coronation." He knew Elizabeth down to her fingertips. He was quite aware that she would add the four thousand to the coronation bill, and that suited him well enough. Bess would never accept the money from him.

During the next two weeks, Bess was much relieved that Lord Talbot did not pursue her openly. Even in the Privy Chamber, where only intimates were allowed, he did not flirt with Bess or engage in titillating banter. He always addressed her as Lady Cavendish and showed her every respect.

But if he was masked at a ball or if he came upon her alone in a distant part of Westminster Palace, he behaved quite differently with her. His manner became intimate and intense. He closed the distance between them swiftly and took possession of her hand. Once he even touched her hair. Whenever she was poised for flight, he held her fast. "Bess, stop ignoring me; I don't dismiss so easily."

"What is it you want, Lord Talbot?" she demanded in desperation. It was the third time he had caught her in an empty chamber in as many days.

"I want to make love to you."

His words were so direct, they shocked her. His fierce blue eyes darkened with desire, and Bess felt her knees turn to water as she gazed up into his dark, handsome face. And then his mouth came down on hers in a kiss that was so demanding, she reeled from its impact and yielded her lips until he drank from them. She slowly came to her senses. "No!" she said against his mouth and brought her fists up to beat against his chest. It was so hard, she might have been pounding the stone walls of the palace. He was all male, rugged and virile—like Cavendish, Bess told herself wildly; that was the only reason she responded to him!

"Have you any idea of the violence of my feelings for you? Bess, you are like a fever in my blood!"

She was panting for breath, and his hot glance licked over her lush breasts as they rose and fell. She feared that any moment he would have her naked. "You are treating me like a whore!" she gasped in outrage.

He stared at her with disbelief; he was definitely not treating her like a whore. He had felt only indifference the rare times he had taken one. "Bess, I hold you in the highest regard.... My feelings for you are above reproach." He saw the look of panic and fear in her eyes and reluctantly released her. "Bess, the last thing I want is to make you afraid."

As he strode from the chamber, Bess knew she was afraid, all right. But it wasn't of the devastating Lord Talbot. Bess was afraid of herself, afraid of her blatant response to his virility, afraid of her own passionate nature!

After that incident Bess found that Talbot was no longer stalking her, but whenever they were thrown together in the same company, his dark gaze never left her, and when their eyes met he looked as if he would devour her. And even though he kept his distance, Bess found that she was not free of him. To her dismay she began to dream about him, and the dreams were blatantly erotic!

The frenzied nightly celebrations went on until dawn right up to the coronation. Then, on January 14, Elizabeth made a triumphant progress through the streets of London. It was an impressive cavalcade, with her guards, household officers, and peers of the realm all mounted on horseback, with Elizabeth herself riding in a canopied chariot. She wore a mantle of gold and silver tissue edged in ermine. Her ladies-in-waiting and ladies-of-the-bedchamber followed her, gowned in crimson velvet with gold-lined sleeves.

Along the route, upon platforms specially built for the occasion, magnificently costumed figures formed tableaux. Each had a crier who stepped forward as the queen approached and with rhymed couplets explained the significance of the scenes. It was cleverly planned to endear Elizabeth to the people. All along the way she received nosegays and flowers from the children and spoke to them sweetly, amid tumultuous cheers of "Long Live the Queen!"

The next day Elizabeth's coronation took place in Westminster Abbey. She sat before the high altar for a grueling five-hour ceremony where she was anointed, crowned, and given the ring that bound her to the people. Brass trumpets sounded as she was declared Queen of England. She then received homage from her lords of the realm, and finally Mass was celebrated.

Then Queen Elizabeth, carrying her scepter and orb, walked from the abbey down the long corridors to Westminster Hall for the coronation banquet. Elizabeth did not leave the hall until after midnight. Every man and woman at Court was literally exhausted. The queen, however, had made herself ill.

For the next fortnight Robin Dudley, Cecil, Talbot, St. Loe, Cat Ashley, and all her ladies hovered anxiously about Elizabeth's apartments and the Privy Chamber. Bess was convinced that all Elizabeth needed was rest. For an

entire month she had insatiably pursued pleasure, greedily snatching all that life now offered, like one who had been starved since childhood.

The queen's illness postponed the opening of Parliament, for which Bess was profoundly grateful. Until Parliament convened, the bill to recover the Cavendish debt could not be passed. Bess knew it would be only a short reprieve, but anything that lightened her heavy burden of worry was welcome.

On the first day of February, the queen arose from her bed with renewed vitality and determination. Her ladies knew Elizabeth was recovered when she treated them to a savage burst of profanity.

"By Christ's precious blood, I never closed my eyes last night. Some whoreson was crashing about directly above my apartments. I want his name so I can string him up by the balls." She waved an imperious hand. "Go and learn the dirty dog's name—he deserves to be housed in a kennel!"

Young Lettice Knollys blanched. "Me, Your Majesty?"

"No, not you, for Christ's sake! Lady Cavendish knows how to handle men; she has a temper that matches my own. Bess, I want you to rip up one side of the noisome bastard and down the other for the mad racket I was forced to endure."

Bess smiled her secret smile and picked up her skirts so she could hurry with ease to do the queen's bidding. When she arrived on the floor above, she bit her lip with amusement when she learned who occupied the chambers. Mary Sidney's husband, Henry, was housed up here, as well as Ambrose Dudley. His sister Kitty and the rest of the Dudley menagerie had been visiting last night. There was no way Bess was going to antagonize the favorite's family; Robin would have to lay down the law to his own unruly clan. Bess was headed toward the stairs when suddenly, out of nowhere, Talbot's tall shadow fell across her path.

"Bess, we have to talk."

"No! We have nothing to say to each other." Bess made a dash for the stairs. Her heart raced in panic. Dear Lord, it was like being stalked by a black panther. As she ran Bess turned her head to see if he followed and missed a step. She went tumbling down the staircase in a tangle of skirts and petticoats. She cried out as her ankle twisted painfully.

Talbot descended the steps three at a time. "God damn it, Bess, why did you run?" His arms were about her immediately, tenderly lifting her into his lap as he sat down on a step, his face filled with alarm, his heart filled with dread. "Are you all right?" he demanded, his voice roughened with apprehension.

"Splendor of God, I'll be far from all right if anyone sees me being cradled in a married man's lap. I'll have more than my ankle to worry about—my reputation will be blackened! Let me up."

Gently, he helped her to her feet and saw

that she could not bear her own weight. "I'll have to carry you."

"You'll do no such wicked thing, you lecherous swine; you've done enough! I am perfectly all right."

"Be silent," he ordered with authority. Lord Talbot was used to deference from everyone, and he certainly wasn't going to allow a woman to argue with him, especially not this maddening beauty he'd marked as his own. He swung her easily into his powerful arms and descended the rest of the stairs.

Bess sought refuge in anger. It was her only hope against his overwhelming masculinity. She dug her nails into the back of his hand cruelly. "You aren't just a devil," she panted furiously, "you are Lucifer himself!"

When Lord Talbot strode into the Privy Chamber carrying his pretty burden, the queen's eyes narrowed. "What the devil happened? Have you accosted her?"

Bess bit her lip. She was tempted to say, *Yes, he flung me down the stairs,* but she felt his hands tighten on her body in warning, and she did not dare. "No, Your Majesty, I twisted my ankle and Lord Talbot came to my rescue."

The queen studied the pair for a moment. This was the second time Talbot had cast himself in the role of knight errant to Lady Cavendish. Bess was certainly a tempting jade, a true man's woman. Even Robin wasn't immune to her allure. Perhaps it was time to get her safely married.

"She fell down the stairs, and her ankle is

badly swollen. She won't be any good to you for at least a week. I suggest you send her home to recuperate," Talbot advised.

Elizabeth saw the merit in his suggestion. If Bess remained at Court, the ladies would be running to wait on her instead of their queen. "Mary, pack her bag. Bess, I shall send for Syntlo and have him give you safe escort. But I want you back in a sennight."

An hour later, when Sir William St. Loe lifted Bess up in his arms to carry her to her barge, Lord Talbot fought the urge to smash the captain of the queen's guard in the face.

At Brentford, Syntlo set Lady Cavendish on the couch, and Aunt Marcy elevated Bess's ankle on a cushion. When Bess introduced Sir William to her children, her two eldest sons inundated him with questions about his office of captain of the queen's guard. They dragged him off to the stables to show him their horses and dogs, and when Syntlo asked them about their studies, they took him to the schoolroom and eagerly answered all his questions regarding the subjects their tutors were teaching them.

Sir William lingered all afternoon, and when Bess thanked him for bringing her safely home, he asked her if he could come again. "I envy you your sons, Lady Cavendish. They have such keen minds. Are you considering them for Eton?"

"Alas, there is no money for that, Syntlo, much to my sorrow."

"I beg your pardon, my lady, that was clumsy of me."

"Nonsense. I have no secrets from you, Sir William. I don't feel uncomfortable discussing my circumstances."

After he departed, Marcella brought her a posset of herbs to ease her discomfort. "William and Henry took to him like ducks to water. Instead of running about like wild men, they actually carried on an intelligent conversation. Those boys need a father, and it is your duty to provide them with one!"

All that week, away from the frenzied activities of Court, Bess had ample time to think. Her grief had undergone many stages. At first she had suffered total shock and isolation as she withdrew from the world. Then came sleeplessness, loss of appetite, guilt, and finally anger, all followed by acute anxiety over the ruinous debt she owed. It had been a powerless time, filled with such hopelessness, she felt she would go out of her mind.

Finally, when her intense sadness brought the torrent of tears every night, Bess experienced a dramatic emotional release. Her Court appointment had come at the right time. It had been a good and positive experience, and Bess knew she had no choice but to let go of her death hold on the past and focus on the future.

Her week at home was almost up, and because she had kept off her ankle, only a slight tenderness remained. Spring had come early, and the February sunshine slanting through the latticed windows lured Bess outdoors. The gardens were awash with crocus, tulips, and a sea of yellow daffodils. Francie and Jane carried cushions out to a garden lounge chair where Bess could look down the grassy bank and watch the swans gliding on the calm water of the river.

Bess could not afford to be completely idle. She had brought her account books outside and worked diligently bringing them up to date. Francie soon grew bored and begged Jane to come and pick strawberries for supper. Left alone, Bess soon tallied the accounts and made a list of food supplies that must be ordered.

There was no breeze, and the afternoon was warm. Bess looked down at her black velvet and decided that when she returned to Court, she would put away her mourning clothes. She fingered the gown; it was one of her very favorites, whose soft black sleeves were embroidered with bright golden leaves and acorns. Bess closed her eyes, feeling a measure of contentment steal over her.

When she lifted her lashes, she saw a wooden skiff gliding across the water to the bottom of her garden. She watched the man in it idly, and when he stepped from the boat and came up the grassy bank toward her, she was not the least bit surprised to see that it was Lord Talbot. Shrewsbury House was not a great distance from Brentford, and Bess realized that she had been half-expecting him.

"How are you feeling?"

"Rested." Bess recalled vividly another time when they had been in a garden by the river. Talbot had stood before her naked, proudly displaying himself. With a smile Bess remembered her outrage at his blatant arrogance. She also recalled every detail of his lithe sixteen-year-old body. He had stood six feet tall even in his youth, and his muscular torso had been covered by black hair. His compelling image, so virile and magnetic, had come to her when she had been married to young Rob Barlow, and lately it had come again in her dreams.

"Come for a row on the river." He neither asked nor ordered, he simply invited. "You'll be safe with me."

Bess knew she would not be safe, she would be in the gravest danger, but the moment had come for her to face up to his devilish attraction and her fear of it. She would never dispel it otherwise. "Why not? You'll have to carry me, though." She saw his body tense up and the desire flare in his eyes. She knew she was playing with fire.

He picked her up easily, as if she were thistledown, and strode down to the punt. Her body reacted to him the moment he touched her— nay, it had been before that. It had quivered the moment she sensed it was he on the river. He set her down gently, then climbed in facing her and took up the oars. He wore no doublet, only a black silk shirt, open at the throat. He rowed smoothly, with long strokes, and her mouth went dry at the sheer sensuality of her own thoughts. Beneath the silk she saw his supple muscles gather and ripple effortlessly.

There was something too intoxicating about his male power, and Bess forced her gaze away from him to look across the dappled sunlit water. The slow realization came that he had some purpose in mind. She felt almost mesmerized as she saw Shrewsbury House and knew that was where he was taking her. The boat glided to the water steps, and he jumped out to secure it.

"What are you doing?" she asked softly.

"Abducting you."

"You said I'd be safe with you."

"You knew I was lying, Bess."

"Yes." She could have taken refuge in anger, but that would have been taking the easy way out.

He came back into the punt, splayed his legs wide apart to balance himself, then lifted her high in his arms. As he strode into Shrewsbury House and headed purposefully for the stairs, there were no servants in evidence and Bess knew he had laid his plan carefully and issued his orders for privacy.

He took her into a spacious room she knew was his, and his alone. It was the most magnificently masculine chamber she had ever seen. The entire room was done in black and gold, a great deal of it real gold. The bed-curtains were black velvet, the matching bedcover was embroidered with an immense gold initial *S* that reminded her of a coiled serpent. The bed-posts were covered with beaten gold leaf. The walls were dull gold, the carpet thick and black. The fireplace looked like onyx with a heavy gold mantel. Solid gold chessmen marched across an onyx games table.

Talbot set Bess upon a deep window seat piled with black and gold pillows and stood gazing down at her. Bess realized her gown matched the room perfectly. It was uncanny, as if she had worn it especially for him. Everything in the chamber appealed to her flamboyant taste—especially its owner.

"Bess, I want to be your secret lover."

Oh, God, Bess thought, why couldn't there be just the two of them in the whole world? Why couldn't there be only this present time, with no past and no future?

"When I say *secret*, I mean *secret*. I won't flaunt you, I won't parade you about for decoration—though, God knows, you're the most decorative female I've ever seen. I have a dozen residences in the north. Just choose one and it will be ours alone. I will guarantee complete privacy. You may see me as often or as seldom as you wish."

Bess ran the tip of her tongue over dry lips and said carefully, "What makes you think I would agree to any of this?"

"Because I know you desire me. Not as much as I want you—that would be impossible. Bess, you are a woman of passion, and you know I could satisfy you as no other man ever has or ever will."

He was so cocksure, but Bess knew that's why she wanted him. He was all male, and he appealed to every one of her womanly senses. Bess wanted him to make love to her, all right, if only he could do it without making her his mistress. She remembered the first time he saw her; he'd said with youthful arrogance, *She's only a servant.* If she let him make love to her, he could say, *She's only a mistress,* and what would be the difference?

Bess looked at his beautiful, sensual mouth and took refuge in a lie. "You are wrong, Lord Talbot. I do not desire you; I feel completely indifferent."

His gaze smoldered. He was certain she lied. "A wager, Bess. Give me an hour to persuade you. If at the end of that time you are not *begging* me to make love to you, I'll let you go in peace."

It was a challenge she knew she could not refuse. She had to prove to him that she could indeed resist him, but even more she had to prove it to herself. "Why not?"

She watched him pick up a golden hourglass with black sand and turn it upside down. The window seat upon which she reclined was nearly as wide as a bed, and Bess thought he would immediately come down to her and take her in his arms, but he did not. Instead, he propped one booted foot on the ledge and leaned his weight on his raised knee.

His voice was husky. "Bess, I know you've had two husbands.... How many lovers have you had?"

"Only Cavendish," she answered truthfully.

His dark gaze studied her face. "Then you've never been loved by a man of your own age—a man in his prime. Jesus, you've no notion what our mating could be like. I'd want you in a sable bedgown with nothing beneath it. I'd carry you off at midnight on a black stallion and impale you right there in the saddle. I'd take you to one of my castles and lock us naked in its tower for a week and keep you at the peak of your arousal so that you would respond to my lightest touch." His voice became intense. "Always when I think of you, I see myself deep within you. I see your lips open and hear you cry out with passion as I sheathe myself to the hilt inside you." He reached down for her hands, holding them so close to his body, she could feel his heat leap into her fingers and race up her arms.

"Every night I would carry you to bed. The first coupling would be savage of necessity, the second so slow and sensual you would writhe for an hour, moaning and frenzied, until I brought you to climax. But the third time I would make real love to you, cherishing and worshiping you with my body until you dissolved in liquid tremors and yielded everything I ever wanted from you." His dark, erotic fantasies poured over her like wine, until she felt drunk with need.

Lord Talbot's mouth found hers, and Bess opened her lips in wanton invitation. The kiss was not savage, it was perfect. His mouth was firm and demanding, but not brutal. When the kiss deepened, he almost stole her senses. Bess expected to feel his hands upon her, undressing her, and she knew she would yield to him. What she felt was not love, it was pure lust. He was the most attractive and sexually arousing man she had ever encountered. Her breasts and belly ached with need. She wanted his hands and his mouth on her body, she wanted his long, thick, marble-hard manroot filling her emptiness, and, above all, she clamored to be taken by a man her own age.

"Please." Bess was suddenly horrified. Was that her voice begging? She did the only thing she knew would save her pride. She cried out her husband's name. "Please, William!"

She felt him go rigid at the insult, and she opened her eyes to watch the outrage on his face. But it was fleeting, gone in an instant, as his sensual mouth curved into a smile.

"Bess, you are so damned clever, and that is one of the reasons I am obsessed by you. It is part of your fatal allure."

"All right, my lord, I wasn't being honest with you, but I am now. I won't allow my heart to rule my head. I refuse to be any man's mistress. I am worth more than that."

"I am not any man, Bess. I am the wealthiest noble in the realm. I will give you anything, you only have to name it."

"Will you give me a wedding ring? Will you give me your name? Will you divorce your wife and marry me?"

Talbot was aghast. "Bess, I don't want you for a wife! Marriage is anathema to me! I've been wed since I was twelve. Wives are the dullest, most stupid and boring creatures on earth. Marriage is a death knell to love and pleasure."

"If that is how you feel about your wife, divorce shouldn't upset you overmuch. Many nobles have availed themselves of divorce— Edward Seymour, William Parr, even Henry Tudor."

"I am not a Tudor, I am a Talbot, and Talbots do not divorce." The air fairly crackled with his arrogance. "I would never disgrace my children."

Bess realized that, even if he had no wife, he would never marry her. He was a member of the upper aristocracy, while to him she would always be Bess Hardwick, a farmer's daughter. "I will not become your mistress, Lord Talbot. I would never disgrace *my* children. Your hour is up, milord; you had better take me home."

He bowed to her wishes. "All right, Vixen. Just remember, we always deeply regret the things we never do."

TWENTY-SIX

When Bess arrived back at Court, she was surprised to learn that Elizabeth had given Robin Dudley apartments that adjoined the queen's. The conspirators were waiting for Bess to return before he moved in.

Elizabeth asked Bess and Mary Sidney, Robin's sister, to attend her in her private sitting room. "I trust the ankle is healed well enough to allow you to dance, Lady Cavendish?"

"Yes, Your Majesty. It was most kind of you to let me go home for a few days."

"Perhaps you can go home more often if we work out a schedule that is mutually beneficial. I have so many ladies-in-waiting and ladies-of-the-bedchamber that I will not need you two in attendance through the day."

Bess and Mary exchanged a puzzled glance.

"The nights are another matter entirely. I want one or the other of you on duty every night, except Sunday of course. None of my other ladies will do. Each week I would like Bess on duty for three nights, and then Mary for the other three. The rest of the time you are free to do whatever you wish."

Bess thanked the queen profusely. It meant that for four days each week she would be able to be with her family at Brentford.

Elizabeth eyed her pale green gown with approval. "I am pleased to see you are no longer in mourning, Bess. It is time to start thinking about marriage. Mary here is wed, and I am being pressed on all sides to take a husband, so why should you be spared?"

"I am in no haste, Your Majesty," Bess said dryly.

The first night that Bess was on duty, the dancing ended early, just after midnight. The queen bade her courtiers good night in the Presence Chamber and withdrew with her ladies to the Privy Chamber, where only her intimates were allowed. Bess went through the anteroom to Elizabeth's private apartments and continued on into the queen's bedchamber. She drew the heavy drapes across the window and checked to make sure the queen had a supply of her favorite Alicante wine and water. She checked the supply of scented candles, then moved to the wardrobe to take out a furred bedgown. Bess opened a drawer and selected a nightdress of delicate white lawn embroidered with gold thread.

Suddenly, a man's arm slipped about Bess's waist, and the night rail was plucked from her fingers. "I'll do that, my sweet." She looked up into Robin Dudley's dark eyes, and he gave her a bold wink. "We need you on guard in the anteroom, Bess. We have very few friends we can trust."

She swept into a curtsy before the man and the woman in the shadows behind him, then, as if moving in a trance, she walked through

405

the apartment to the anteroom. It suddenly became clear why Elizabeth had insisted on either herself or Robin's sister attending her at night.

How naive she was to be surprised. Elizabeth allowed Robin to kiss her in full view of the Court, and their sexual attraction for each other was obvious. Why had she not guessed they were lovers? Bess sank into a chair and closed her ears to the whispering laughter that floated to her from within. If Elizabeth was being pressured to take a foreign husband for political purposes, why shouldn't she take what pleasure Robin could give her?

More and more Bess found herself in the company of the captain of the queen's guard. She was flattered that St. Loe seemed so fascinated by her and knew he was becoming enamored. He was the complete opposite of Cavendish, who had been a rugged, self-made man. The captain was a polished gentleman from an ancient and landed family of wealth.

One day in early summer, the queen asked her captain of the guard to attend her. Elizabeth did not beat about the bush, but came to her point directly. "My dear Syntlo, you are much in the company of Lady Cavendish these days."

Sir William flushed. "Your Majesty, if I have offended—"

She cut him off. "That depends upon whether your intentions are honorable or not."

"I hope I am an honorable man in all things, Your Majesty."

"I would not look unfavorably upon such a match. Since you are comtemplating marriage, I've decided to appoint you chief butler of England." If he wasn't contemplating marriage, her tone indicated that he should.

"Your gracious Majesty, I am honored by your trust in me."

Elizabeth said dryly, "You will need the money. Brides are expensive."

Sir William, on the horns of a dilemma, flushed again. Was the queen suggesting he wed Lady Cavendish so that he would pay off her massive debt to the Crown? He cleared his throat. "Your Majesty, the lady's debts are crippling—"

Elizabeth waved her hand imperiously. "I have decided to reduce her debt to one thousand pounds. Her services are indispensable."

St. Loe almost sagged with relief. Bess would be overjoyed at the news. She filled his every waking thought. He couldn't believe his good fortune. Not only had the queen appointed him to the highest post regarding her daily life and ritual, Elizabeth had given him leave to pursue his heart's desire.

"Would you be good enough to summon Lady Cavendish for me, Syntlo?"

Sir William found Bess on her way out of the palace. She had been on duty the last three nights and was on her way to Brentford. "Lady Cavendish, Her Majesty requests your presence."

Bess bit back a curse. She never swore in Sir William's presence; it was far too unladylike.

"After your audience it would give me great pleasure to escort you home, my lady. There is something I would like to ask you."

Bess felt a measure of panic begin to rise. She knew instinctively he was going to propose marriage, and her thoughts darted about, trying to think of some kind way to refuse him. Although she was fond of him and enjoyed his attention, Bess knew she would never love him, and he could never, ever replace Cavendish in her heart. "I welcome your safe escort, my lord." She would find the right words on the way to Brentford.

Bess went in to Elizabeth. Robin Dudley had not left the queen's chambers until four that morning, and after Bess had escorted him from the anteroom, Elizabeth had gone to bed for four hours. "Are you feeling well, Your Majesty?"

"I am feeling very well and extremely generous today, Bess. I believe I have found you the perfect husband."

"Your Majesty, I don't want a husband!" Bess blurted out.

"You may not want one, but you certainly need one. A respectable marriage to the right gentleman would raise your standing at Court. I have given Syntlo permission to court you."

"Your Majesty, I could never love another man after Cavendish."

"Piffle! What does love have to do with

marriage? A woman takes a husband for financial security and prestige. I have just appointed Syntlo chief butler of England. Surely you are ambitious, Bess. If not for yourself, then for your children?"

"Your Majesty, I would be lying if I told you I was not ambitious, but no man would be fool enough to take on a widow with six children, whose crippling debts are common knowledge."

"Ah, yes, Syntlo and I were just discussing your debt to the Crown." Elizabeth's eyes glittered.

Bess flushed darkly with shame.

"I have decided to reduce your debt to one thousand pounds. I told you I was feeling extremely generous today."

Bess felt the blood drain from her face. Had she heard right? She was dizzy with relief. After twenty long months of worry and anguish, the crushing burden of debt would be lifted. And obviously she had Sir William St. Loe to thank for it! Bess sank down before Elizabeth and kissed her beautiful beringed fingers. "Thank you from the bottom of my heart, Your Majesty."

Elizabeth looked down at her and experienced a stab of jealousy for Bess's lush beauty. Had Talbot enjoyed her body? Was that the reason he had blackmailed his queen into forgiving most of the debt? It was high time Bess was respectably married.

By the time Bess took her leave of Elizabeth, her mood was absolutely euphoric. She put the problem of the thousand pounds she still owed out of her mind. She would find some way to pay it off. Bess sought out Sir William immediately to thank him for the immense service he had just rendered her.

St. Loe laughed happily when he saw her glorious smile.

Bess could not restrain herself; she flung her arms about him. "Oh, thank you, thank you, Syntlo, you have saved my life!"

He flushed with pleasure. "Bess, I did nothing."

"I know better, my dear lord. The queen told me that you discussed my debt to the Crown with her."

"All I did was remind her that your debt was crippling," he assured her.

"It took such great courage to broach the subject and beard the lioness in her den. She has reduced it to one thousand pounds. I shall be in your debt forever, my lord. Oh, I can't wait to tell my family!"

"Come, it will give me the greatest pleasure in the world to take you home to them."

Aboard the barge, St. Loe sat beside her and took her hand. "Bess, I've never seen you look so radiant. The queen has given me leave to pay my addresses to you. If you would do me the honor of becoming my wife, I would consider it a privilege to take care of you."

She studied him openly. Had he really needed the queen's permission before he dare propose? Did Elizabeth dominate his life to such an extent? "You do me great honor, my lord. I swore I would never marry again. Will you give me a little time to consider your proposal, and can we still be good friends, no matter my answer?"

"Take all the time you need, my dearest heart."

When Bess told Jane and Marcella that her debt had been reduced, they knew their prayers had been answered, for there were times they had feared Bess would worry herself into an early grave. When Bess also told them that Sir William St. Loe had proposed to her, Jane was speechless. Marcella said bluntly, "I never believed you would bring such a refined nobleman up to scratch. It's the breasts—it's got to be the breasts—there is no other answer!"

"I'm going to tell him no," Bess said firmly.

"You must be mad, girl! He'll pay off your debts, he'll pay for the boys to go to Eton, he'll provide a dowry for Francie. The children need a father, even if you don't need a husband."

"It wouldn't be fair to him; my heart died with Rogue Cavendish."

"If Cavendish were here he would tell you to seize the moment, Bess. I wouldn't be surprised if Cavendish hadn't chosen St. Loe for you. It will be a giant step up in the world for your Cavendish children, and to top it all off, you will be able to start building at Chatsworth again. You know that a marriage should be a sound business arrangement. You've always used your head over your heart, and it's never let you down yet!"

For four days Bess seriously considered the marriage. It had so many advantages, and only one drawback: She was not in love; she could not make Syntlo happy. Then she remembered Rogue telling her once, *Bess, in almost every relationship one loves more than the other, and the one who loves is the lucky one, the happy one.*

Bess sighed. She owed Sir William St. Loe so much. He had made her almost debt-free and certainly worry-free. And the queen had made it plain that she wanted Bess to remarry, insisting that Syntlo was the perfect husband. Bess sighed again and made her decision. No one would be pleased with her answer—not her family, nor the queen, nor Sir William—but it was the only answer she could give.

When Bess returned to Court, she learned there was to be a masque that night. The theme was "The Forest," and Mary Sidney helped her with a costume. "With your red hair you will make a perfect vixen. I have a wonderful mask with pointed black ears, and I have a real foxtail too. You will make all the ladies mad with envy, for I warrant most of the men will be hunters."

When Bess arrived in the ballroom, she was not really in the mood for hijinks, because she knew she would have to face Syntlo and give him her answer. As she exchanged barbs with the Dudleys and the Parrs, she felt quite melancholy. Everywhere there were couples, and Bess seemed to be the only exception. Even the queen kept her possessive hand on Robin Dudley tonight.

Bess helped herself to a third cup of wine from a liveried footman and wandered along the gallery away from the dancers. Suddenly a man in a hunter's mask blocked her path. She knew who it was the moment his tall shadow fell across her.

"Is it true?" he demanded. His blue eyes glittered like ice through the slits in the mask.

Bess stared at him wide-eyed, wondering wildly how he knew.

Talbot's powerful hands took hold of her shoulders and he shook her. "Is it true?" he repeated. He did not even try to hide the fury he felt. "Did St. Loe propose marriage?"

Bess's anger flared hotly. How dare he stalk her continually, making it his business to know everything about her? "Do you find it so difficult to believe that a man wants me for his wife, rather than his mistress?"

"You set a high price on yourself! No bedding without a wedding!"

"Some men are willing to pay it."

"God damn you, Bess, you are doing this to spite me!"

"I am not—"

"I forbid it! Do you hear me, Vixen, I forbid it!"

"Forbid?" she cried passionately. "You black beast, you think you are God all-bloody-mighty, ordering the world and everyone in it!" The wine bloomed like a dark red rose in her breast.

"Be silent and listen to me!" he thundered.

"You autocratic swine—you love to be the all-powerful master! Well, let me tell you this much, sir, you won't master me. I shall marry whomever I please!"

"He's another old man! What the hell is the matter with you, Bess, that makes you wed these father figures?"

Bess gasped. She was about to fly at his face when she became aware of the attention they were attracting. She lowered her voice, trying to cloak herself in dignity. "St. Loe is a gentleman, something you will never be."

"You think marrying a gentleman will make you a lady?"

Her eyes blazed with triumph. "Yes, it will make me Lady Elizabeth St. Loe."

His voice lowered and he said with quiet resignation, "You will live to regret it, Vixen."

Bess walked briskly back to the ballroom, hoping no one had recognized her in the ridiculous mask. She slipped into an alcove, unpinned the foxtail from her derriere, and removed the face mask. When she emerged, the first person she saw was St. Loe. "William, I've been looking everywhere for you," she lied.

He smiled at her tenderly, hope shining in his eyes. "Does that mean your answer is yes?"

"Of course it is *yes*. Did you ever doubt it for a moment?"

"Oh, Bess...you've made me the happiest man on earth."

"Are congratulations in order?" an arch voice asked coyly.

Bess's mouth went dry and her heartbeat drummed in her ears as Syntlo answered the queen. "Your Majesty, the lady has just consented to be my wife."

As Lord Robert Dudley offered hearty congratulations, the queen announced to the room at large, "My dearest friend Lady Cavendish is about to be wed to my captain of the guard, Sir William St. Loe. The wedding shall be here at Court!"

Bess did not get off-duty until three in the morning. Back in her own chamber, she lay in bed, wishing for the oblivion of sleep to overtake her, but of course it proved elusive. At what point had she lost control of the situation? It was as if fate had taken her by the hand and snatched the decision away from her.

"Damn you to hellfire, Talbot!" she whispered, knowing if they hadn't had their near-brawl, she would have given St. Loe a very different answer. Bess shivered, still feeling his hands on her, reliving the intensity of his emotions. They had such passionate, clashing personalities, it was a wonder they hadn't murdered each other.

He had accused her of marrying father figures. Was there any truth to the charge? Bess, always brutally honest with herself, admitted that she had certainly looked up to Sir William Cavendish, and during the early years of their marriage, she had hung on his every word as he taught her how to buy land, how to run an estate, how to build Chatsworth and become a hardheaded businesswoman. And there was no way to deny that he had been more than twenty years her senior. But there had been a strong sexual attraction between them, and she had loved him with all her heart.

Bess examined her relationship with Sir William St. Loe. She was not in love with him, but her affection for him was genuine. It was her children who needed a father; she certainly did not. She was a competent woman, with intelligence, courage, and confidence. Talbot was wrong; she needed no father figure!

It would be a good marriage because she would make it so. Above all she vowed that she must never, ever regret it. She would not allow Talbot's prophecy to come true. Bess had made her decision for better or for worse.

Twenty-Seven

"**F**or better, for worse; for richer, for poorer; in sickness and in health; to love, cherish, and obey, till death us do part, according to God's holy ordinance; and thereto I plight thee my troth." Bess's voice rang out in the Queen's Chapel.

Sir William slipped the wedding ring on her third finger. "With this ring I thee wed, with my body I thee honor, and with all my worldly goods I thee endow."

The officiating priest intoned, "I pronounce that they be man and wife together, in the name of the Father, and of the Son, and of the Holy Ghost. Amen."

From the moment Bess was wed, she noticed that Lady St. Loe was treated differently than Lady Cavendish had been. Her status was suddenly elevated, and everyone at the wedding banquet treated her with a greater deference and respect, which secretly amused her.

Bess was inwardly dreading the moment when she would come face to face with Lord Talbot. How on earth would she be able to eat with his icy eyes upon her? What would she do when he insisted on dancing with the bride? And how in God's precious name would she be able to bestow a bridal kiss upon him before the assembly?

An hour into the reception, Bess heard the queen remark, "It is too bad Lord Talbot could not be with us this evening. He was called north; the Earl of Shrewsbury has been taken ill."

Bess felt suddenly weak with relief. She wondered if Talbot had withdrawn from the Court because he refused to acknowledge her marriage. Perhaps he was using his father's health as an excuse. She had a tender regard for the old earl and said a silent prayer that he was not really ill.

Finally, Bess knew she could relax a little and enjoy herself. However, because of her elevated status as Lady St. Loe, she felt she must be a little more reserved than she had been in the past. She cautioned herself not to drink too much wine and not to swear. She was beginning a new life, and she wanted her new husband to be proud of her.

It seemed the playful object of the guests was to keep the bride and groom apart, so William and Bess danced with everyone except each other until late into the night. When they were finally allowed to speak, Bess murmured with mischief brimming in her dark eyes, "Do you think they'll give us a bedding?"

Sir William turned beet red and said repressively, "I should hope they will do nothing so vulgar."

Bess sought out the Dudley brothers. "I need your help. I don't want a bedding; my lord thinks them vulgar."

"And so they are," Robin said, laughing. "That's the point!"

Ambrose Dudley winked at her. "Don't

you think I should come upstairs with you and show him how to go about the business?"

Robin drawled, "He's her third husband, for Christ's sake; Bess will show him how to go about the business!"

In the end it was Elizabeth who spared the newlyweds the indignity of a bedding. She allowed the couple to depart alone, and none of the other courtiers could leave the festivities until the queen decided to retire.

When Sir William St. Loe had been elevated to chief butler of England, he had exchanged his guard chambers for a luxuriously appointed apartment on the second floor of the palace, in the same exclusive wing as Cecil. Bess was delighted with their new accommodations, for most courtiers did not live in such comfort.

The door of the apartment was opened by Sir William's manservant, but when Bess did not step inside, her new husband looked at her uncertainly. Bess smiled and murmured, "It is customary for the groom to carry the bride over the threshold."

Syntlo laughed and lifted her up into his arms, and Bess felt his manhood rise and brush against her bottom cheeks. She put her lips against his ear and whispered, "Dismiss your man." Bess was not fearful or shy of what was to come, only wildly curious.

He set her feet to the carpet and inquired politely, "Did Lady St. Loe's things arrive, Greves?"

"Yes, my lord." Greves indicated her things were in the bedroom.

"Splendid. We won't need you again tonight; thank you, Greves."

Even when the servant withdrew, Bess thought Syntlo excessively staid and polite. He made her a bow and said gravely, "You will need a little time."

Bess was mildly surprised that he did not want to undress her. Or perhaps he was so polite he would not do such an intimate thing without being invited. Bess gave him a radiant smile and went into the bedchamber. She disrobed slowly and freshened herself with the scented rose water, hoping he would come in and find her undressed. When he did not, she donned a cream silk night rail embroidered with damask roses and climbed into bed. When he still did not come, she decided to call him. To her dismay she found she could not call him *William*. Instead, she called out, "You may come in, Will; I'm ready."

He came to the foot of the bed and gazed at her with adoring eyes. "You are so very beautiful." He reached out his hand as if he wanted to touch her hair but dropped it as if he did not dare touch her. Then he blew out the candles and undressed in the dark.

Bess smiled into the darkness, thinking him excessively shy. Perhaps she would have to make the first advance. She felt the bed dip as he slipped between the covers, and she cautioned herself to be ladylike with him.

The moment Syntlo was in the bed with her, his staidness disappeared. His hands roamed her body, and she had never known a man to become this excited this quickly. She reached out and learned that he was naked. The moment she touched him, he groaned, and gasped, and cried out incoherently, bucking against her soft thigh. To aid his haste Bess tried to remove her nightgown.

"Elizabeth, I can't wait," he gasped, pulling up the silk garment and mounting her. He thrust wildly, and Bess was stunned by his need. She opened her thighs and yielded to him generously, trying to adjust her body's timing to his. She hadn't experienced the sex act for two years and would have preferred he go a little slower this first time.

"Elizabeth...ohmigod... Elizabeth!" He arched and spent just as Bess felt her first flutter of arousal.

His arms went around her, and he buried his face in her breasts. "I'm sorry, I'm so sorry, my dearest. Forgive me, Elizabeth?"

At first Bess thought he was apologizing for coming too fast and leaving her unsatisfied. She stroked his hair gently.

"I didn't mean to hurt you—forgive me for being such an animal!" he begged.

Bess realized he was apologizing for forcing sex on her. "Will, you didn't hurt me, and you're certainly not an animal." She sat up and lit the bedside candles.

"I love you so much; how could I have done that to you?" The look of shame and agony on his face was hard for her to fathom.

"It's all right; you didn't hurt me."

"Really? Oh, God, you have no notion how

much I enjoyed it. You excite me beyond anything I've ever experienced. Bess, you're so understanding about a man's pleasure."

"Will, making love can give a woman pleasure too."

He laughed and shook his head. "You don't know the excitement or the pleasure I felt. It's different for a man. A lady could never experience anything so...carnal."

Bess wanted to laugh. No, she wanted to cry. What she really wanted was to be brought to climax. She deliberately licked her lips and lay back down. When he blew out the candles and moved against her, Bess knew she'd be ready this time. He kissed her tenderly, and she arched against him invitingly. Her thigh brushed against his groin, and she felt him flaccid and soft. He kissed her again, and she thrust the tip of her tongue to tease him.

"Good night, Elizabeth...thank you."

Bess lay staring up at the bed canopy long after she heard his breathing slow into sleep. *All men are not created equal!* She realized that she had deliberately chosen St. Loe because he was the antithesis of Cavendish. Bess simply did not want to love another. She told herself that she did not want all that passion and pain ever again. St. Loe was a good man; it would be a good marriage. She did *not* regret it!

As Bess lay beside her new husband, the hollow, empty feeling inside her belly was like ravenous hunger, only worse. "William," she whispered two hours later as she slipped into blessed sleep. But it was not William who filled her dreams that night, nor was it the new husband she had wed.

A voice like black velvet whispered in her ear. "You've never been loved by a man of your own age—a man in his prime." Bess turned and gave herself up to his arms. "Sable bedgown...black stallion...impale you...naked for a week...peak of your arousal...sheathe myself to the hilt...second coupling...writhe for an hour." The third time he made real love to her, cherishing and worshiping her with his body until she dissolved in liquid tremors and yielded everything he ever wanted from her.

The following day, when Bess and Syntlo arrived at Brentford, they enjoyed a private celebration with her family. The newlyweds had been excused from Court, and Bess decided to use this time to move her family back to Chatsworth. She couldn't wait to show Sir William the magnificent house she was building and, in turn, show off her new husband to her noble friends in Derbyshire.

Jane and Marcella totally approved of Bess's marriage to St. Loe and treated him with almost reverential respect. Her daughter Francie seemed a little reserved in her welcome to her new stepfather, but Bess's sons, now nine, eight, and seven, vied with each other for Syntlo's attention. Little Elizabeth and Mary, who were four and three respectively, showed no fear of the gentle man with the close-clipped gray beard, and both climbed onto his knee as they had on his previous visits.

While Bess busied herself packing up the entire household, St. Loe purchased spices, artichokes, olives, wine, and anything else he could think of that was plentiful in London but might be in short supply in Derbyshire.

Before she left, Bess gathered a good supply of dragonwort to be certain she avoided conception. She may have taken another husband, but Cavendish was the only man who would ever father children on her. It was quite a cavalcade that set off on the Great North Road, for both of them took their personal servants, and Bess took most of her household staff, including her children's tutors and nursemaids.

On the journey the newlyweds were never alone until their bedchamber door closed each night. The bridegroom was so profoundly affected by sharing his bed with his bride that his excitement seemed to increase rather than diminish. When he fell asleep each night, he was the most sexually sated, replete man in the realm, who had no notion that his beloved *Elizabeth* lay awake beside him, aching and unsatisfied.

When Chatsworth came into view, Bess felt almost dizzy with happiness. She had come within a hairbreadth of losing it, and she vowed never to put it in jeopardy again. She had courageously taken the reckless chance that if she postponed selling it to pay the crippling debt to the Crown, fate would intervene on her behalf. Standing before her dream home, Bess knew she had done the right thing. She had gambled and she had won!

Sir William was suitably impressed with Chatsworth, whose pleasure gardens alone covered five miles.

"Chatsworth is my great passion," she told him, with tears of happiness in her eyes.

"As you are mine, my dearest. I want you to start building again. I want you to finish it."

"Thank you, Will, that is the best wedding present you could ever give me."

Bess lost no time. She immediately hired men to dig limestone to make plaster, and others to mine coal from her estate's shallow pits to fire up the lime kilns. With the aid of her stewards, Francis Whitfield and Timothy Pusey, Bess hired masons, joiners, slaters, and glaziers. She sat down and penned a letter to her dear friend Sir John Thynne at Longleat, asking him to let her have the services of his artistic plasterer. She signed the letter *Elizabeth Cavendish,* saw her mistake immediately, and, crossing out *Cavendish,* substituted her new name, *St. Loe.*

Sir William was in his glory. Domesticity was new to him, and he delighted in playing father to his ready-made family. He was exceptionally generous, unfailingly kind, endlessly patient, and tirelessly supportive of anything Bess wished to do. His father had left him a large inheritance, which he was happy to spend on his new wife and children.

Syntlo had been at Chatsworth only a fortnight when he received a dispatch from the queen, requesting his immediate return. Elizabeth wished to move her Court to Windsor for the rest of the summer and could not manage without her captain of the guard and chief butler of England. Bess hid her disappointment and told him she would pack immediately.

"My dearest, there is no need for you to return. I want you to stay here and enjoy your summer with the children. The queen may order me about, but she may not order my wife. As soon as I get back to Court, I shall pay off your debt. That will put Her Majesty in a sweet temper. I shall miss you terribly, but you love it here, and your happiness is all I desire."

"Oh, Will, I shall miss you too. You are so kind and generous." And after he had gone, Bess found that, indeed, she did miss him. He had indulged her every whim, and she could do no wrong in his adoring eyes. She soon busied herself in building the third story of Chatsworth and also took on a new project so that her every waking hour was filled. Since the law stated that she could claim any land that she improved, Bess enclosed an additional twenty-five acres at Ashford with hedge and ditch and called it Lark Meadow.

Sir William faithfully sent a wagonload of supplies up to Chatsworth every week, including books and candies for the children, and along with cloves, ginger, dates, and figs, he sent Spanish embroidery silks for Bess. His letters were touchingly affectionate and always began, *My own, more dear than I am to myself.*

Toward the end of summer, Frances Grey arrived from Bradgate for a visit, and Bess was appalled to see how much weight her friend had gained. Frances had to be helped in and out of a chair, and once she sat down she preferred to remain there all day gossiping.

"Well, Lady St. Loe, I'm very proud of you. The ladder of success is climbed one marriage at a time. How the devil did you catch him?"

Bess knew better than to take offense at anything Frances said. "Marcella insists it was my breasts."

"Perhaps, darling, but I'd be more inclined to think it was the red hair and your resemblance to the queen. He's probably been in love with Elizabeth for years."

Bess smiled. "I have all his affection now."

"And all his money and lands, I should hope. Have you ever met his dissolute brother, Edward, the black sheep of the family?"

"No. It is difficult to imagine a dissolute St. Loe."

"Edward is a vicious swine. That's why Sir William is a model of respectability, to silence the scandals of his brother. Edward married a rich widow after poisoning her old husband. Within a month she, too, was dead, and poison was again rumored. Then he turned his attention to the bride their father had selected for Sir William and married her himself. The family disowned him; that's

427

why Sir William got all the Somerset and Gloucestershire lands when his father died."

Bess felt disloyal gossiping about the St. Loes. She would ask Will about it. He would tell her the truth; he had too much honor to lie. Bess changed the subject. "How is Catherine liking it at Elizabeth's Court? I never get to see her, since she is always on duty during the day, and I am on duty at night."

"Poor Catherine. Whatever will happen to her without a husband when I stick my spoon in the wall? I wrote to Queen Mary before she died, asking her to set aside her edict that Catherine not marry. Now I suppose I shall have to write Elizabeth. Bess, if aught should happen to me, will you ask the queen to find a suitable husband for Catherine?"

Bess felt alarm. "Frances, are you ill?"

Frances shrugged her shoulders. "It's the dropsy, I'm afraid. I never seem to pee much these days, no matter how much I drink."

"Oh, my dear, I am so sorry. I'll get Marcella to brew you some agrimony; I'm sure it will help. Would you like to go to bed?"

Frances winked. "I've spent enough time in bed since I wed my young equerry. Never mind, Bess, at least I shall die with a smile on my face!"

Before Bess knew it, autumn was approaching and Sir William arrived to escort her back to Court at Windsor. He had paid the tuition for young Harry and William Cavendish to go to

Eton College, which could be seen from the towers of Windsor Castle. The rest of the children would remain at Chatsworth with Bess's mother, Jane, and Marcella.

The reunion was like living her wedding night all over again, and Bess decided that, when they were back at Court, she would try to gently instruct Sir William to display less sexual excitement and learn more staying power.

The accommodations at Windsor Castle were extremely hospitable, not only for the queen and her attendants, but for Lord and Lady St. Loe. Their apartment was more spacious and luxurious than at Westminster Palace and even had two bedchambers. They often entertained their friends at Court, and once a week her sons visited from Eton College, which was directly across the river.

As the months went by, every hour that Elizabeth was not closeted with Cecil, she spent with Robin Dudley. Bess was mildly surprised that here at Windsor he had gradually gained complete and open access to Elizabeth's chambers. The secrecy had fallen away. The couple rode together every morning in Windsor Great Park; they hunted, hawked, shot at the archery butts, and strolled hand in hand along the grassy banks of the river.

When Bess questioned Mary Sidney about the progress of the queen's foreign marriage negotiations, Mary let her in on a secret. "My brother's wife, Amy, suffers from a malady of the breast. The doctors say she has less than a year to live. All these marriage negotiations with France, Spain, and Scotland are a sham to buy them time. Robin says Elizabeth will wed him when he is free."

The following week, when neither Bess nor her husband were on duty and they could spend the night together in their own chambers, Bess brought up the subject of Elizabeth and Robin being lovers.

"Bess, you are quite wrong. The queen is a virgin."

She looked at him in astonishment. He had been Elizabeth's captain of the guard when Tom Seymour was her lover. How could he delude himself?

"Men find her enchanting and gather about her like bees around a honeypot with their sexual fantasies. But she would never allow an intimacy of any kind."

Bess studied him for a moment. It came to her in a flash that *he* was one of those men who had sexual fantasies about Elizabeth. And then a second thought occurred to her. When Sir William married her, he had been a virgin, or next thing to it! His trouble did not stem from shyness; he was completely inexperienced. In a boy it would have been delightful; in a middle-aged man it was not. Bess smiled her secret smile. She would have to take him in hand, as Frances Grey had once indelicately put it.

"Will, darling, would you help me with my gown?"

He was beside her in a moment, his eyes alight

with eagerness. "Are you sure you don't want me to call your maid?"

She slid her arms about his neck. "I want *you* to undress me, darling. I love the feel of your hands upon my body."

Bess had never been disrobed as quickly in her life. He pulled the silk nightgown over her nakedness. "Slip into bed, Elizabeth," he said urgently, moving to blow out the candles.

"No, Will, I don't want to get into bed, and please leave the candles burning so I can watch you undress."

He licked his lips in a fever of excitement and tore off his doublet and linen shirt. He hesitated, then his hands moved on.

When he hesitated, Bess moved toward him and pushed him down on the bed. She removed his boots and her hand moved to his codpiece.

"Bess, don't," he said desperately. "I'll spend."

"Yes, my darling, you'll spend. And then you'll spend again." She unfastened the laces on his codpiece, and his sex sprang free of its confinement. She encircled him with her fingers and began to caress him.

Will groaned and gasped and began thrusting in a frenzy of excitement. Bess knew he could last no more than a minute. She leaned over him, palmed his testes and rolled them together, then her fingers tightened on his erection and she felt him explode. The pearly drops of his semen arced like a fountain onto the nightgown that covered her breasts and belly, and he collapsed onto the bed in ecstasy.

His eyes devoured her as she moved over him and took his hand. Then she deliberately rubbed his ejaculation over her belly and up across her lush breasts. She encircled her nipples with his fingertips until they stood erect. The material turned transparent. "It feels hot and wet through the silk."

"My God, Bess, I want you!" He was hoarse with desire.

"There is no hurry; we have all night. Why don't we finish undressing?" She helped him remove his remaining garments, then slipped the wet night rail from her body. She slid naked against the length of him and touched her lips to his.

With a low moan he thrust his tongue into the hot cave of her mouth, and Bess felt his sex start to rise against her soft thigh. She whispered against his lips, "You are a very selfish lover, my lord. I will build and climax just like you, if you arouse me." He gazed at her, not quite believing, but with hope in his eyes. She guided his fingers to her high mons, separated the red-gold curls, and found her woman's center with his fingertip.

"I have a tiny bud; can you feel it? If you play with it, my passion will be aroused. Then, when you enter me and slide your hardness across it, the bud unfurls, and as my desire builds you will give me delicious pleasure."

When he stroked her bud with the pad of his finger, Bess moaned softly to show him she enjoyed what he did. When he slipped a finger into her sheath, she writhed to encourage him. "Bess, I can't wait," he gasped intensely.

She smiled into the candle glow. He was calling her Bess. Elizabeth had vanished. "Neither can I. Hurry, darling." When he mounted her and plunged deep, Bess made a splendid show of her enjoyment. She cried out his name and screamed as she felt a mild climax. She knew that bringing her to fulfillment would give him more pleasure than he had ever known before. And if they were lucky, next time would be even better. She would never experience a grand passion, but a little of the emptiness would be gone.

Sir William's duties demanded he arise with the dawn. When Bess opened her eyes, she found her husband, already bathed and dressed, gazing down at her with adoration. He sat down on the edge of the bed. "Bess, I've decided to leave all my lands in Somerset and Gloucestershire to you, to be passed on to your children."

"But surely your brother is entitled to a portion of the estates if we have no children together?"

"My brother is debased. He taints everything he touches. The lands are mine to do with as I please. I know you have debts, my dearest, and my estates will give you security."

Bess knew just how vulnerable Sir William was to her. He wanted to give her the moon and the stars, but she did not wish to be accused of manipulating him to make herself wealthy at his family's expense. "Will, I don't want to be the cause of trouble between you and your brother. As your wife I am legally entitled to one third of your estates, and I am more than satisfied with that."

After her husband left, Bess began to shiver for no apparent reason. She slipped on a warm bedgown and moved toward the fire. As she stood looking down into the blue flames, she had a premonition that something evil hovered close by. She turned and peered into the shadowed corners of the bedchamber, unable to dispel the nameless disquiet she felt.

TWENTY-EIGHT

When news of the death of the Earl of Shrewsbury was brought to Court that winter, Bess was deeply saddened. She was convinced that this was what her premonition had been about. Death sometimes had a foreshadowing that could not be denied. These days she never allowed her thoughts to dwell on Lord Talbot, but after the news of his father's death, she could not get him out of her mind.

Queen Elizabeth declared a day of mourning for her premier earl, and Bess put on her black dress whose sleeves were embroidered with gold leaves and acorns. She sat down to pen a letter of condolence to Talbot but had no idea what she would say to him. She ran her fingers over the soft material of the gown and saw herself reclining on the window seat in the magnificent black and gold bedchamber at Shrewsbury's house.

Then, though it hadn't happened, she pictured the dress lying abandoned on the carpet while she lay in Talbot's arms, oblivious to the world and everyone in it. They had all but become lovers that afternoon. He had been on the brink of domination, and she had been on the verge of submission. Whenever they saw each other, they engaged in the compelling steps of some strange mating dance. What was the irresistible lure that drew them together?

It was purely a physical thing, Bess told herself, that was the reason it was so seductive. If they had coupled, would they have touched each other's hearts or souls? She would never know. With an effort Bess abandoned her daydreaming and focused on the letter she must write.

When she reread the condolence letter, it was formal and stilted, and to her dismay she had addressed it to Lord and Lady Talbot. But he was Lord Talbot no longer. He was now Sixth Earl of Shrewsbury, lord lieutenant of Derbyshire, Nottingham, and Yorkshire, and the chief justice north of the Trent. As well as wielding immense power, he was the wealthiest man in the realm. A smile touched the corners of her lips. He had been dominant and autocratic before; what in the name of God would he be like now? Bess quickly rewrote the letter to the Earl and Countess of Shrewsbury and signed it *Sir William and Lady Elizabeth St. Loe.*

When Frances Grey, Duchess of Suffolk, died suddenly in the spring, Bess was devastated. She cried for days, and the only thing that brought her out of her grief was the thought of her friend's daughter, young Lady Catherine Grey, who was now all alone in the world. When Catherine was growing up, Bess had often mothered her and called her *poppet,* and the young woman now turned to Bess for comfort.

Catherine was a lady of the queen's Privy Chamber, rather than a lady-of-the-bedchamber, and Elizabeth made a special show of taking her late cousin Frances's daughter under her protective royal wing. Queen Elizabeth discussed Catherine's plight with Bess.

"The thought occurred to me that I might adopt Catherine; what do you think, Bess?"

"Adopt, Your Majesty? Lady Catherine has just turned twenty-one; surely she is too old to be adopted."

"Mayhap you are right, but it would certainly send a strong message to that presumptuous Mary Stuart that there are other heirs to my Crown of England besides herself!"

Bess hid her feeling of cynicism. She should have realized that Elizabeth seldom did anything unless it enhanced her political position. Elizabeth was a master of deceit and loved the role. Bess gathered her courage. She had promised her friend Frances that she would ask the queen to allow Catherine to marry. Here was her opportunity. She took a deep breath and plunged in.

"Your Majesty, I believe Frances would want you to find a suitable husband for Catherine. Queen Mary declared that Lady Catherine Grey must never wed, and Frances wrote to her, begging her to alter that cruel edict."

"Cruel? I see nothing cruel about it. Rather, it was politically astute of my sister. Lady Catherine Grey is the heiress presumptive to *my* throne. It would be suicidal of me to permit her to marry and produce heirs of her body. It would be an open invitation for some madman to pull me from my throne and replace me with another. I will hear no more from you on this subject! Do I make myself clear, Lady St. Loe?"

"Crystal clear, Your Majesty." Bess realized that Elizabeth was a queen first and foremost, a woman second, and a woman of compassion almost never.

Bess was in low spirits. She was superstitious and believed that death always came in threes. Shrewsbury had died, and then her dearest friend, Frances, who had been so generous to her in the early days. Bess found herself wondering fearfully who would be next. Who would be the third to die?

Bess wasn't alone in her superstition; the Court was steeped in it. Mary Sidney told her of an astrologer her sister Kitty had consulted, so Bess asked Mary to arrange for him to come to Court. It would be an evening of entertainment, held in the St. Loe apartment, with just a few intimate friends.

Lettice Knollys and Catherine Grey came, as well as Mary Sidney and her sister, Kitty, along with their brothers Robin and Ambrose Dudley. The astrologer, Hugh Draper, who was also rumored to be a sorcerer, arrived with his two assistants. They gave everyone present a sphere and then proceeded to cast each guest a horoscope for their future.

All those present were relieved that no deaths were foreseen, but an amazing number of marriages were predicted. Robin Dudley, Lettice Knollys, Catherine Grey, and even Bess had future marriages show up on their spheres. The evening was declared a success, and everyone left in a happy state of mind. This all changed, however, the following night when Bess and Sir William supped together.

St. Loe had something to tell Bess, and he waited until Otewell Greves cleared the table and poured them wine.

"Bess, a few days ago my brother came up to London, and I informed him that I intend to change my will and leave all my lands to you."

"Oh, Will, I know he will make trouble for us, I feel it in my bones." Bess set down her wine goblet and clutched her stomach. "Dear God, I feel it in my belly!" she said shakily.

Sir William gulped down the contents of his goblet and rushed around the table to Bess. "Dearest, what is it?"

Bess moaned and gripped the edge of the table. "Will...the pain is cutting me in half...it feels as if I've been poisoned!" She tried to stand but was taken by a spasm of agonizing cramps and rolled to the floor, pulling the tablecloth and its contents down with her.

Otewell Greves came running. "Fetch Cecily, her maid," Syntlo shouted in panic. "Fetch the queen's doctor!" Suddenly, Sir William himself doubled over with gripes. "The food or the wine has been poisoned!" he gasped.

Bess bit her lips to keep from screaming at the searing, burning pain that knifed through her. "Cecily, quick, bring olive oil!" Bess held her nose and gulped down a few mouthfuls of oil, then immediately began to vomit. By now her husband was rolling about the carpet with his knees drawn up to his chin. "Will, drink the olive oil!" Bess cried between bouts of spewing.

They were put to bed in separate bedchambers, and the Court physicians eventually came to tend them. The doctors concluded that indeed Lord and Lady St. Loe had been poisoned, and if it had not been for a remedy of sorts being at hand, the lady might have died. Sir William's condition was far graver than his wife's, however, and the doctors did not know if he would recover.

Within two days Bess was on her feet and helping to tend Sir William, who lay listless, with a green-tinted pallor. She dosed him with syrup of balm to soothe the irritated lining of his stomach and prayed fervently that her husband would not be the third person to succumb in the trinity of death.

Syntlo's recovery was excruciatingly slow, and Bess tended him with loving hands and gentle patience. His liver had been affected by the poison and he became yellow and jaundiced, but gradually Bess nursed him back to health. She noticed immediately that the ordeal had aged him, and her heart was filled with pity when he did not regain his former wiry strength.

The queen ordered an immediate inquiry into the disturbing near-tragedy that had taken place at her Court. Elizabeth, who had a morbid fear of poison and ate and drank as little as possible, always used a food taster for anything that passed her lips. Suspicion immediately fell upon the astrologer, Hugh Draper, who was the only stranger who'd had access to the St. Loe rooms.

When he was arrested and sent to the Tower, along with his assistants, it was learned that Sir William's brother, Edward, had been seen frequenting the astrologer-sorcerer's establishment in Red Cross Street, and the Court was abuzz with the shocking news that Edward St. Loe had tried to murder William and Bess.

"Darling, they won't arrest Edward unless you press charges against him." Bess would have felt much safer with Edward St. Loe in the Tower with his evil associates.

"My dearest, I have no proof that Edward

was involved, but even if I had, the scandal would be horrific. For your sake I don't want notoriety connected to the St. Loe name. There is a better way to be sure no further attempts will be made upon us. Today I made an indenture to hold my lands jointly in both our names. When I die you will get all the lands, so the incentive for Edward to get rid of me has been removed."

"Oh, Will, you are so generous. How can I ever thank you for all you have done for the children and me?"

"Consenting to be my wife is all the thanks I will ever need. You fill up my heart, Bess."

She could not help feeling guilty, for though she loved Sir William St. Loe, she was not *in love* with him, and Bess wished with all her heart that it could be otherwise.

"You need a change of air, dearest. A summer at Chatsworth will do you a world of good. I'll go over to Eton College and make the arrangements for the boys to take their holidays."

"You are coming too, Will. You look positively haggard these days. Elizabeth works you far too hard." Bess knew he would never criticize the queen, so she did it for him.

The week after they arrived at Chatsworth, Bess's stepfather, Ralph Leche, passed away. After the funeral Bess crossed herself, realizing this was the third death. The following week Sir William received a dispatch from the queen, requesting his immediate return. Elizabeth had decided to move her Court to Greenwich Palace for the summer and could not manage without her captain of the guard and chief butler of England.

"Damn Elizabeth; she treats you like a lapdog. The minute you leave her side, she calls you to heel." Bess vented her anger, because Syntlo looked as if he needed a rest. "I shall come back with you. It is my duty as your wife to see that she doesn't work you day and night!"

"My love, I am used to the queen's whims and know how to take care of myself at my age, I should hope. I think you should stay here to comfort your mother in her loss. The summer is so short, my dearest. Spend it with the children and your family. Perhaps you will get the third story of Chatsworth finished this year."

Bess felt humbled. He was such a devoted man, who always put her needs before his own. She felt torn, but in the end Chatsworth won. Bess was afraid that it always would.

When he returned for her at the end of August, however, Bess regretted her decision. Her husband looked as if he had aged ten years in one short summer. He was stooped and his pallor was yellowish, making Bess fear that the poison he ingested had permanently damaged his liver.

Marcella dosed him with the herb allheal, which had a hot, biting taste and was extremely good for the liver and spleen. The jaundice disappeared, but unfortunately the stoop was permanent.

When the door closed on their luxurious bedchamber at Chatsworth, Bess was happy that Syntlo became excited at the thought of sleeping with her, but an hour later, when he had not been able to achieve an erection, she became concerned.

Sir William flung himself from the great carved bed in frustration. "I'm sorry, Bess, I'm useless!"

"It's all right, Will, it doesn't matter."

"It matters to me! My God, I've dreamed of you every night. You wouldn't believe how erotic those dreams were, and now this!"

"Come back to bed, Will. Perhaps it was something I did, or didn't do. Come, we'll try again."

After much persuasion he got back into bed and lay staring at the canopy. Realizing he was afraid of failure, Bess moved close and lifted his arm about her. Then she began to kiss him. Her kisses were not aggressive or demanding in any way, but soft and gentle. Slowly, she stroked her hand down his chest, across his hip, then cupped him with the palm of her hand. When he grew half-erect, she closed her fingers about him and squeezed. Then, with featherlike strokes, she drew her fingers up his shaft to the head and pulsed her fingertips until he engorged with blood.

He gasped and moved over her immediately to mount her, but his erection shriveled instantly. Bess was willing to keep trying, but Sir William was not. "It's too humiliating. I'll never be able to satisfy you."

"Hush, Will," Bess soothed, "it's probably the herbs Marcella dosed you with. It will be fine tomorrow. Let's get some rest." She enfolded him in her arms and cushioned his cheek against her breast. It was another hour before she heard his breathing alter and she knew he slept.

As she lay quietly beside him, her heart overflowed with compassion. She didn't believe that their sex life was completely over, but she was wise enough to realize that this episode of failure and frustration would not be the last.

Bess was most happy the Court had moved from Greenwich back to Windsor before she returned, not only because their apartment at the castle was so spacious, but because her sons were close by at Eton. Queen Elizabeth's birthday was September 7, and Windsor was a hive of activity, preparing for the celebration.

A great masque was being planned. The Presence Chamber would be decorated to look like an underwater kingdom, and those invited would be costumed as Neptune, Poseidon, water sprites, and mermaids. The days leading up to Her Majesty's birthday were filled with frenzied activities.

There was a great hunt, then a medieval tournament with jousting. There was a large hawking party and daily contests with rich prizes at the archery butts. The courtiers were almost worn out before the big day arrived, yet at her birthday masque, Elizabeth danced until dawn.

Bess helped Elizabeth out of her crystal-encrusted gown and long green wig. The dressing room adjoining the queen's bed-chamber was in chaos, with garments lying everywhere, but Elizabeth told Bess to leave it and attend to it later, after the queen had three or four hours of sleep. Bess withdrew to the anteroom, sank down in a soft chair, and put up her aching feet.

She didn't awaken until after nine o'clock and wondered why one of the other ladies-of-the-bedchamber hadn't come to relieve her. Mary and Lettice both must have slept late. Bess stood up and stretched. It would feel good to get out of her gown and climb into her own bed. She went through to the queen's bed-chamber and drew back the heavy curtains on both windows.

"Good morning, Your Majesty; it has gone nine o'clock."

"Good morning, Bess; that was the most glo-rious birthday celebration I've ever had!"

Bess held Elizabeth's bedgown, and the queen slipped her arms into the sleeves and wrapped it about her slender body. When Bess went into the dressing room, she was appalled at the disarray that met her eyes. She began to tidy up immediately and opened the huge wardrobe to put away some of the gowns. Bess was very efficient and methodical and had the dressing room tidy in short order.

Bess heard Robin Dudley's voice and paused in what she was doing, thinking she should withdraw so they could be private.

"Amy is dead!" Robin's deep voice seemed unnaturally loud.

"At last!" Elizabeth's voice sounded exultant.

"She was found with a broken neck at the bottom of the stairs."

"What? You brainless, clumsy, stupid fool, Robin! By Christ's precious blood, you've ruined everything! Was this your idea of the perfect birthday gift for me? Amy was supposed to die in bed with the doctors hovering about her! How could you have committed this insanely stupid act?"

"Elizabeth, I didn't kill her!" Dudley's voice quivered with emotion.

Bess sank down upon a stool, her knees turned to water. She remained as still and silent as she could.

"You bloody fool, Robin. I don't cavil at murder, if it can be dressed up as something else, but this is beyond all disguise! The entire world will accuse you, but worse, it will point its accusing finger at *me* and condemn *me!*"

"Elizabeth, stop it. On my honor I had nothing to do with my wife's death. If it was not an accident, then it was suicide!"

"It was murder, you fool! If not by you, then by your worst enemy, to prevent you from marrying the queen."

"Cecil! He's the only one with enough power, enough cunning and determination!"

"Cecil has been away for weeks negotiating a peace with Scotland. Take your bloody hands off me! It isn't what has happened that matters, it's what it appears to the whole world—and believe me when I tell you it appears that we have murdered your wife so that we can wed. If this crime can be proved against you, you will lose your head, you clumsy fool!"

"I wouldn't be the first lover you've abandoned to the block."

Elizabeth gasped. "Lord Dudley, you will be taken to Kew under house arrest until there is an inquest into your wife's death."

"I understand, madam," he said coldly.

Bess heard him withdraw, and Elizabeth let out such a cry of anguish, Bess came to the door of the dressing room. Elizabeth stared at her in horror, as if she had forgotten her presence in the adjoining chamber.

"What in the name of hellfire are you staring at? You sly bitch, listening at keyholes! Don't you dare to look at me like that. You are nothing but a bloody hypocrite, Bess Hardwick. You and Cavendish poisoned his wife so he could wed you!"

Bess stiffened with outrage. "That is a lie, Your Majesty. I would not take my happiness at the cost of another woman's pain and suffering."

"I would!" Elizabeth said defiantly. "I have! I had some damned good teachers." The

447

queen's amber eyes glittered dangerously. "If you open your mouth outside this chamber, I'll see that it's closed permanently."

"Yes, Your Majesty." Bess swept her a curtsy. "May I withdraw?"

"Yes, get out!"

When Bess reached the antechamber, the door opened and Cat Ashley entered. Elizabeth's cries and curses could be heard all over the apartments. "What has happened, Bess?"

"Something terrible, Cat. She experiences everything with the same deep passion I do. You had better let her scream and rage until she gets it all out."

TWENTY-NINE

While Robin Dudley was banished from Court, the queen did not dance all night. She retired to her bedchamber at a decent hour, but in the antechamber Bess was still kept awake for hours as she listened to Elizabeth's sobbing. Though Bess had been offended and hurt at the angry words Elizabeth had hurled at her, she decided not to leave her Court appointment as lady-of-the-bedchamber. She fully understood this was a terrible time for the queen, and Bess refused to desert her.

In the New Year the inquest into the death of Amy Dudley returned an open verdict, which neither cleared nor condemned Robin

Dudley. It was good enough for Elizabeth, however, who immediately welcomed him back to Court. Though she no longer sobbed the night away, Bess could see that Elizabeth was taut as a harp string, living on her nerves, pretending indifference that she was being laughed at all over the world for her scandalous behavior with her horse master.

Each day Bess saw her grow thinner and paler, until finally she gathered her courage and spoke to Elizabeth. "Your Majesty, I presume upon our long acquaintance. Your gaiety is forced, as worry over something eats away your soul."

The Queen fixed Bess with a haughty glare. "Your presumption is pure arrogance, Lady St. Loe." Then Elizabeth heaved a deep sigh. "I am at a crossroads. One path leads to my fulfillment as a woman—the other to my fulfillment as a queen. By Christ's precious blood, you have had three husbands; can I not have just one—is it too much to ask?"

"Your Majesty, I am fulfilling my destiny, as you must fulfill yours. You do not want or need my advice. Our choices in life are difficult, but as you know they are unavoidable."

In the months that followed, Elizabeth honored Robin Dudley constantly, first with a pension, then a license to export pelts and furs. Following this she bestowed upon him the levies on all imported wines and silks, and it was rumored that an earldom was being considered.

Most courtiers surmised that the queen

was about to throw caution to the wind, but Bess knew differently. Robin was receiving these favors from the queen as compensation for a marriage that would never take place. Elizabeth had chosen the path that would lead to her fulfillment as a great queen.

Bess's eldest daughter, Frances, turned thirteen, and Bess knew the time was ripe to arrange a good marriage for her. One of the most prominent men in Nottingham was Sir George Pierrepont, whose ancestors had lived at Holme Pierrepont for generations. Naturally, such a prominent family had enjoyed the hospitality of Chatsworth, and Bess had not missed the fact that Sir George's heir, Henry, was only two or three years older than her daughter Francie. Not only was Sir George impressively wealthy, a shrewd Bess could see that his health was deteriorating from either gout or rheumatics, and it would not be long before young Harry inherited everything.

Bess discussed the matter with Syntlo, who promptly offered to furnish their beloved Francie with a sizable dowry. Not to be outdone by her generous husband, Bess decided she would give Francie one of her manors upon her daughter's marriage. Bess penned a letter to Sir George and Lady Pierrepont, opening negotiations, and decided that if the reply was favorable, she would visit them at Nottingham on her way to Chatsworth.

Bess had no sooner dispatched the letter than Lady Catherine Grey knocked on Lady St. Loe's door, asking to speak with her in private. When Bess saw the worried frown on Catherine's face, she bade her sit and dismissed the servants. "Catherine, poppet, whatever is amiss?"

"Oh, Bess, I am cursed with impulsiveness. I have done something that seemed so exciting and romantic at the time, but now I am afraid that I acted foolishly."

"Oh, darling, your mother was often impulsive; we cannot help the traits we inherit."

"You know that Teddy Seymour and I have known each other since we were children. I'm afraid I've been indiscreet with him."

Bess laughed. "Well, I'm amazed you've kept your virginity this long. When you were no bigger than pissants, you couldn't keep your hands off each other!"

Catherine blushed profusely. "Bess, we were secretly married when the queen moved the Court to Greenwich."

"By God's precious blood, Catherine, it's tantamount to treason to have wed without Elizabeth's permission! Oh, you foolish child, I could shake you till your teeth rattle!"

"But we are in love, Bess," Catherine declared, as if this made it acceptable.

"Elizabeth is jealous of anyone who loves. Who was your witness at this secret marriage?"

"Edward's sister; it was before she died so suddenly." Tears flooded Catherine's eyes.

"Tragic though that was, it is extremely

fortunate for you that your witness cannot carry tales."

"Dear heaven, don't you think the queen will forgive me?"

"Poppet, don't be so naive; she never forgives anyone anything, not where her crown is concerned."

"Bess, whatever shall I do?"

"Destroy the legal document immediately. Get Edward to France and deny everything, as I shall certainly do if I am ever questioned about this reckless affair!"

Bess told no one of her conversation with Lady Catherine Grey, not even her husband. Though the time for her to leave for Chatsworth for the summer months was fast approaching, Bess was loath to leave St. Loe. He looked far from robust, and he had never regained his sexual ability. As a result they now slept in separate bedchambers.

Syntlo could not bear the humiliation, even though Bess would have preferred to share a bed for companionship and warm affection. She did thoroughly understand how sensitive Will was about his impotence, but in actual fact Bess had not felt sexually satisfied since Cavendish had died.

Bess now found herself torn between her children and Chatsworth and her duty to her aging husband. Whenever she criticized Elizabeth for working him too hard, however, Syntlo sprang to the queen's defense, and Bess realized Elizabeth Tudor could do no wrong in her husband's eyes.

Bess put off leaving until the end of July, when suddenly she learned something she did not want to know. Lady Catherine Grey came to her in secret late one night and burst into pitiful sobs. "Oh, Bess, whatever shall I do? I am with child!"

Bess stared in horror at Catherine's belly. The girl was corseted so tightly, it was a wonder she hadn't killed herself and the child she carried. "You knew you were pregnant when you confessed the marriage to me!" Bess accused.

"I refused to believe it. Edward is in France, and I have no one to turn to, Bess."

Bess relented and put her arms about Catherine, wishing with all her heart that her dear friend Frances were still alive. "There, there, poppet, don't cry. Babies won't be ignored. Once you are impregnated, childbirth is inevitable, I'm afraid. You must throw yourself on the queen's mercy, confess all, and beg her forgiveness. It is your only hope, Catherine."

"I cannot, I cannot," she sobbed. "You must tell her for me."

Bess vividly recalled Elizabeth's words about Catherine Grey marrying: *I will hear no more from you on this subject! Do I make myself clear, Lady St. Loe?*

"Dry your tears, darling. I'll do the next best thing. I'll ask Robin Dudley to beg Elizabeth to treat you with mercy, Catherine. The queen refuses him very little these days. I'm sure he will do me this favor." Bess fervently hoped she was not giving her false hope. Once again Bess put off leaving for Chatsworth, feeling that she could not desert Catherine in her plight.

In a couple of days, Bess found an opportunity to speak in private with Dudley. "Robin, young Catherine Grey has done something that will anger the queen, and I will take it as a personal favor to me if you will approach Elizabeth and pour soothing oil on the turbulent waters it will stir up."

"Bess, my dear, you know I would do anything for you."

"Lady Catherine is almost seven months pregnant."

Dudley laughed. "How ironic that Elizabeth appointed Catherine Grey because of her virtue."

"Her virtue is not ruined—she is *wed* to the father."

"She's secretly wed?" Robin was surprised; there were few secrets at Court to which he was not privy.

"She's married to young Edward Seymour," Bess said quietly.

"What? She must be mad; the pair of them must be mad! You want me to tell Elizabeth that the heir presumptive to her throne is about to give birth to her own heir? And, even worse, that the father is royally connected to the late King Edward the Sixth's mother, Jane Seymour?"

"Dear God, to me they are just two youngsters in love. Now, I clearly see this strengthens her right to the succession and could be inter-

preted as deliberate treason, but, Robin, her entire family is dead—Catherine has no one to plead her case."

"Aye, and her father and sister were executed for *treason*. Elizabeth won't be merely angry, she'll be incensed!"

Bess anxiously waited for news regarding the queen's reaction to Catherine's delicate situation, but she heard nothing until August 16, when she learned that Lady Catherine Grey was in the Tower of London. Bess immediately sought audience with the queen but was refused. Next she looked for Robin Dudley, but he seemed to be avoiding her.

Bess voiced her indignation to her husband, who, as captain of the queen's guard, had been responsible for arresting Catherine and escorting her to the Tower. "Elizabeth is being unfair. 'Tis too sharp a punishment for a girl who is seven months gone with child!"

"The young Earl of Hertford is being brought back from France. He'll likely bear the brunt of the queen's anger," St. Loe soothed.

"Will, in my experience Elizabeth treats men far more leniently than she does females; there are very few women she likes."

"She likes you, my dear."

Bess hoped and prayed that St. Loe was right.

Four days later, on August 20—Bess's fateful day on which she had been evicted from Hardwick and married Cavendish—Sir

William St. Loe's second-in-command knocked on the door of their Windsor apartment and handed his commanding officer a warrant. The queen was placing Lady Elizabeth St. Loe under arrest and ordering her to the Tower. St. Loe, visibly upset, began to wring his hands. He could hardly speak for the lump in his throat.

Bess herself was staggered. She resorted to anger, which had always served her well in times of trouble. "How dare she do this to me? She has had all my loyalty since she was twelve! We pledged our undying friendship to each other. The redheaded daughter of Satan cannot do this!"

"She is the queen, Bess; she can do anything."

"She can bloody well rot!"

"Bess, please stop. You must obey this warrant; you have no choice, my dearest. I swear to you it will be for a few days only, while you are questioned about what you know of Lady Catherine Grey's unlawful marriage. Pack some things, dearest. I shall send food and wine and whatever else you need every single day."

"I need my freedom, Will. I don't think I can bear to be incarcerated."

"You are a strong woman, Bess; you can bear anything you have to and bear it with grace and dignity."

Lord God, how little you know me, Syntlo. I can bear anything, but not with bloody grace and dignity!

Bess decided to take her maid Cecily with her, and the guard waited patiently while she and Bess packed an overnight bag. She refused to allow her husband to accompany her, knowing how it would upset him, so Syntlo gave his second-in-command money to give to Edward Warner, the lieutenant of the Tower, in order to secure the best possible accommodation for Lady St. Loe.

Bess swept into the Tower of London wearing her best gown, refusing to be cowed by this ridiculous false arrest. But underneath her bravado she was secretly relieved that she had not been taken into the Tower through Traitor's Gate.

She was housed in the Bell Tower, the same one where Elizabeth had been imprisoned, though not in the same chamber. Through the small window she could see the Beauchamp Tower and what had become known as "Elizabeth's Walk," where the young princess had been allowed on the tiles between the two towers. Bess suppressed her anger for three days, and when at the end of that time she had neither been questioned nor received any word from the Queen's Court, her anger erupted into fury. "Go back to Windsor, Cecily. I don't need you here, doing everything for me. If I don't at least tend to my own needs, make my own bed, and stoke my own fires, I shall run mad. You will visit me each day and fetch what I need. Today I want pen and paper, lots of it. None shall be spared my scathing letters!" It was extremely galling to Bess, adding insult to injury, that she was imprisoned in one tower while Hugh Draper, the man who had poisoned Syntlo and herself, was housed across the courtyard in the Salt Tower.

Bess wrote to Elizabeth, to Cecil, to Robin Dudley, and to Syntlo. Her husband was the only one who replied.

> *My own sweet Bess:*
> *I have spent hours upon my knees to the queen on your behalf and feel hopeful about a speedy release. For your own sweet sake, I deny myself the pleasure of coming to you, so that Elizabeth's wrath will not be visited upon you further. I am sending coal for your fire and the scented candles you love. Tell Cecily of your needs, and I shall fill them immediately. Be brave, my darling. Somehow I shall appease the queen.*
> Your faithful and loving
husband, Syntlo

Bess threw the letter on the fire. "You cannot appease a tyrant!" She lit one of the scented candles Cecily had brought, hung up her fresh clothes, and handed her serving woman the linen that needed to be laundered. "Would you bring me a mirror tomorrow, Cecily?"

Bess's nature did not adapt well to being confined; she had far too much energy. She loved to embroider, but after three solid hours of peering at a tapestry she was working on, she was ready to throw it on the fire. She had no option but to play a waiting game with the queen and at times felt more sorry for Syntlo than she did for herself. No doubt Elizabeth had forbidden him to visit his wife, and he did not have the guts to disobey his queen. The dear man was now impotent in every way.

At the end of September Catherine Grey gave birth to a son. Though she was confined to the Tower along with her young husband, the lieutenant of that fortress, Warner, was kind enough to allow the new father to visit his son, and all gave thanks that the mother and child were healthy.

As October slowly evolved into November, a hope kindled in Bess's heart that Elizabeth would release her for Christmas. It would be unthinkable to spend the Holy Days imprisoned in the Tower. She wrote letters to her mother, her sister Jane, and her aunt Marcella. She advised Sir William about the New Year's gifts for her children and occupied herself with Chatsworth's accounts, which were brought to her every month by James Cromp, who was in charge in her absence.

Bess also wrote to Sir George and Lady Pierrepont to negotiate the espousal of their son and her beloved daughter Frances, but she received no reply.

Sir William's daily letters described his duties to the queen regarding her festive plans for Christmas and New Year's and for an upcoming progress Elizabeth planned early in the year. He told her that he beseeched the queen daily for her release and encouraged Bess to write to Her Majesty and beg her forgiveness. Bess was livid; she'd be damned if she'd *beg* for forgiveness when she had done nothing wrong!

Bess's hope of being released before Christmas was dashed as December came and went without any word of a reprieve. Bess became depressed when she realized she had been in the Tower for four long months and there seemed to be no light at the end of the tunnel. More and more Bess had the feeling that she was very much *alone* and felt as if she had been abandoned. Wrapped in solitude, she had far too much time for reflection and introspection.

She had no patience for Will's letters with the pathetic dried teardrops on the paper. *If only he were stronger; if only he would command the queen, instead of beseeching her. I don't need a man who will go on his knees; I need a man who will go and pull Elizabeth through a bloody knothole!* Bess knew Cavendish would have done it, but William St. Loe was not William Cavendish. Bess sighed. She could not ask pears of an elm tree. Finally, Bess admitted to herself that in times like this, she did regret marrying Syntlo, as the Earl of Shrewsbury had predicted.

By the end of January, Bess began to experience disturbing dreams, then she had her old recurring nightmare, where she lost everything. Was it possible that she could really lose everything? Even her life? Her anger was gradually being replaced by apprehension, which slowly but surely grew into full-blown fear.

It began to dawn upon Bess that perhaps she was not here because of anything Catherine Grey had done. Perhaps she was here because she knew too much about Elizabeth! Not many people knew that Thomas Seymour had been her lover; even fewer knew that she had possibly been carrying his child. How many had known that when Seymour married Catherine Parr, Elizabeth had lived with them at Chelsea in a ménage à trois? All who knew for certain—besides herself—were now dead!

Bess realized she also knew more about the queen's intimacy with Robin Dudley than any other living, breathing person. She had even witnessed their conversation when Elizabeth had taken it for granted that Robin had poisoned Amy so he could wed her. This imprisonment was a warning for Bess to keep her mouth shut. She fervently hoped it was only a warning, because there was a more permanent way of ensuring her silence! She could not confide her fears to her husband. She would never make him privy to the secrets she knew, and St. Loe would never believe Elizabeth capable of wickedness.

Her fear grew stronger throughout February. Her incarceration became intolerable when she thought about spring. The Tower ravens were starting to mate, and their caws were raucous. The snowdrop would give way to the crocus, then daffodils would blanket the gardens. Bess was ready to sell her soul to be astride a horse, to feel the wind whipping her red hair about her shoulders. She ached to tuck her children into bed; her heart longed for Chatsworth. She had been held in close confinement for six endless months and feared that if she did not soon escape her cage, she would go mad.

Perhaps because spring was in the air, Bess suddenly found herself with no sexual release. Since Cavendish had died she had managed, one way or another, to suppress her sexual needs. Never fully satisfied by Syntlo, Bess had channeled her sexual energy into restarting the building at Chatsworth and overseeing and expanding her vast landholdings, while performing her Court duties and still fulfilling her roles of wife and mother.

However, now that she had nothing to do but think and worry, her body turned traitor on her and began to ache for comfort and fulfillment. Her dreams became erotic, which only filled her waking hours with an intense longing, making her feel as if she were about to come out of her skin. All this compounded the fear that she was losing her mind. Bess was fast approaching the moment when she considered death preferable to imprisonment.

PART FOUR

THE COUNTESS
LONDON 1562

❖

Alas, my love! Ye do me wrong
To cast me off discourteously:
When I have loved you for so long,
Delighting in your company.
Greensleeves is all my joy,
Greensleeves is my delight,
Greensleeves is my heart of gold,
and who but My Lady Greensleeves.

ANONYMOUS

THIRTY

When Bess opened the door to the loud knock, the warder announced, "Ye have a gentleman visitor, Lady St. Loe."

"It's about time," she answered peevishly as the warder departed to bring him. Bess was angry with her husband, and she was beyond pretense. Though she knew he had kept away for her own good, she needed her husband's strength to lean on, his shoulder to cry on. Suddenly, fear gripped her by the throat. *He has come to deliver bad news.... He has come in person to soften the blow!*

As the dark shadow fell across the threshold, her black eyes went wide in stark terror, then she stared in disbelief at the tall figure who stepped into the chamber and secured the door. "Shrewsbury," Bess whispered.

"Bess, why in the name of God did you not get word to me that you were incarcerated?" he demanded angrily.

"You came," she murmured in wonder.

"Of course I came, and would have come a hell of a lot sooner if you had sent for me."

"Shrewsbury," she repeated whimsically.

He towered above her for one endless moment, then swept her into his arms. He was knight errant and savior rolled into one. He was the strongest, most powerful man she had ever known, and he had come to rescue her. Bess melted against his iron-hard chest and offered up her mouth for his ravishing.

She reveled in the sheer strength of his arms as he wrapped them tightly about her and held her secure in an all-powerful embrace. His mouth descended upon hers in total possession and instantly ignited a flame that blazed up out of control in seconds. Bess had never felt so weak and vulnerable and feminine in her life. Overwhelming relief mingled with the hot passion she felt and rendered her ready to surrender to him body and soul.

Shrewsbury had never felt more a man in his life. His response to Bess and her plight made power surge through his veins, giving him the heady feeling of omnipotence. He felt exultant that he had the means to give her everything she needed. In one fell swoop he would free her, yet bind her to him forever!

Bess responded blatantly to his virility. She did not want to think, only to feel, and he made it so easy. She gazed up into his brilliant blue eyes as if she were seeing his compelling face for the first time. He was so virile and magnetic, she could hardly bear waiting for him to take her. Her eyes closed, her mouth curved sensually, and she offered herself up to him, her supple, luscious body promising to do all his bidding.

Talbot's sure fingers undid the buttons of her gown, then he slid the heavy, brocade sleeves from her shoulders so she could slip her arms free. Now bared, her arms wound about his neck as she went on tiptoe to fit herself against him. The top of the dark green gown fell about her waist, revealing a frothy seafoam-green shift. "How utterly feminine to wear enticing undergarments even when there is no one to see them."

The straps of her petticoat proved no obstacle to Talbot; she was bared to the waist in seconds. "Your skin is as pale as priceless alabaster from being in this damned place." He swallowed hard. "Your breasts are exquisite, more beautiful than I ever imagined, and I swear I've imagined them every day of my life."

Bess licked her lips with the tip of her tongue. "Mistress Tits, you called me. Do you remember?"

"I recall every word we've ever exchanged, as well as every lusty thought I've ever had about you, Vixen."

Her hands went of their own volition to the fastenings on his doublet. "Hurry!" she urged.

His face was too taut with desire to smile, as his arousal mounted savagely. He threw off his jacket and tore the buttons from his linen shirt in his great haste to feel her naked flesh against his own.

When Bess saw his heavily muscled chest covered with its pelt of blue-black hair, it drew her lips instantly, then her tongue, and finally her teeth, as desire took control of her. As her passion mounted by leaps and bounds, her fear diminished, then vanished altogether as the powerful emotion of lust obliterated all else.

When his hands swept her gown to her ankles, the froth of petticoat followed. Bess stepped from the circle of clothing and kicked it aside impatiently. Clad only in lacy stockings, the red-gold curls on her mons looked like flaming tongues of fire.

"Vixen." He wanted to touch it, taste it, and thrust into it, all at once. His fingers threaded possessively through the tendrils, and his hot palm pressed over her pubic bone, yet she was so much hotter than his hand, he felt scalded.

Bess's fingers tugged insistently at his remaining garments. He helped her to bare his flesh, and once more she kicked aside the heap of cloth that lay at their feet.

He lifted her onto his jutting shaft and gasped at the deep pleasure he felt. She clung to him as if her life depended on him, as in actuality it did!

Both of them were in such need of immediate gratification, the thought of the bed never entered their minds. Shrewsbury took two steps, pushed her against the stone wall, and impaled her with his iron-hard weapon until it was seated to the hilt.

Bess cried out with sheer pleasure-pain as she frenziedly wrapped her white thighs about him, needing every inch he could give her. Their burning lips fused, then, open-mouthed, they moaned incoherent, dark words against each other's sensitized flesh.

He thrust savagely, like a stallion with a mare, and was ready to spill before her, but not much before. He hung on for a tormented minute and was rewarded by an exultant feeling when he heard her scream as she spent with him.

"Shrew...Shrew...yes, oh, *yes!*" She collapsed upon him and would have fallen to the floor if the strength of his body had not supported her.

He swept her up and carried her to the bed, knowing full well her legs were too weak for her to stand. He sat her on the bed, combed his fingers into her flaming, disheveled hair, and lifted her face to his. "My beautiful Vixen. We are so alike. We give all and take all at the same time."

Her eyes were heavy-lidded with need. "It's a match made in either heaven or hell, and at the moment neither of us cares which." He was like too-potent wine she had quaffed greedily, and she was now intoxicated with his power and thirsted for more. She felt mesmerized at the sight of his supple body, entranced by his male scent, and insatiable for the taste of him. Shrewsbury was all male—hard, demanding, dark, dominant, and dangerous—and he appealed to every one of her womanly senses.

Then the kissing began. Neither of them could stop. If Bess thought she had been in danger of going mad before, it was nothing compared to the insanity that gripped her now as she willfully urged him to steal her senses. Now, as before when he had taken her to his black and gold bedchamber, Bess wanted his hands and his mouth on her body; she wanted his long, thick, marble-hard manroot filling her emptiness. She arched her hips beneath him, squirming and rutting until his cock swelled against her woman's burning center. She drew up her knees, sliding them up his hips, then allowed her thighs to fall open in blatant invitation.

He breached the portal in a heartbeat, wanting to go slow, to draw it out forever, but he could not. His body had a will of its own. His thoughts mocked him—he knew he'd have to have her a hundred times before he could pleasure her slowly and sensually. This time he did not have to wait even a moment for her. Bess arched up off the bed with a cry that echoed his own. Both matings had been primal, all thrusting tongues and feverish, driving lust, as his hard flesh beat and pounded against her softness. Yet still his sexual energy was not all spent.

He withdrew his phallus from her sheath and moved down her body until his face was level with her belly. He kissed her and caressed her, rubbing his cheeks against her silken skin, tasting her, inhaling her woman's scent, learning her essence.

Slowly, Bess opened her eyes and the room stopped spinning. When she looked down she saw her breasts still rising and falling from her wanton exertions, then she looked beyond them to where his dark head lay against her belly, his mouth still lavishing her with adoration.

It began to dawn on her what they had done. They had both committed adultery!

Never had she allowed her heart to rule her head, and in truth she hadn't this time. But she had certainly allowed her *body* to rule her head. Guilt washed over her. Strangely, the guilt she felt had nothing to do with her present husband. Rather, it was for betraying Cavendish with a lover. Bess reached out her hand until her fingers touched his blue-black hair. "Enough," she whispered.

"Let me make love to you again, Bess." His face was still hard with desire.

"What we did had nothing to do with love—it was lust, pure and simple." Honesty made her admit, "It was magnificent and exactly what I needed, but it was lust."

Shrewsbury knew that lust was not all he felt for this glorious woman, but he kept a wise silence.

Bess sat up and tossed back her disheveled mane. "Shrew, I have betrayed my husband, and you have betrayed your wife. We cannot undo it, but we can make sure it never happens again."

Never again? You must be mad to ask the impossible. His sensual mouth curved. Bess could no more deny herself such passionate pleasure than he could. Reluctantly, he reached for his clothes, finally remembering why he had come. "Tomorrow I shall come again and take you to the interrogation room. It shouldn't be long after that when you will be freed." As Bess went to retrieve her petticoat, he spoke urgently. "Don't dress! Let me see you nude until I leave."

She hesitated only a moment. He had brought her so much pleasure, how could she deny him such a fleeting favor?

After Shrewsbury departed, Bess realized he had brought her more than pleasure—he had banished her dark fears, restored her hope, and given her back her confidence. Her resilience was renewed, as she pondered how much longer she would have to remain in the Tower of London. Bess smiled a secret smile. She had been here seven months; she could do the rest of her time standing on her head, she decided with bravado.

As promised, Shrewsbury returned the following day. Bess kept a cool distance between them, knowing that his closeness would make mincemeat of her resolve. As a tangible reminder of their wantonness, she held one of his shirt buttons that she had picked up from the floor. When she tightened her fingers, the sharp mother-of-pearl cut into her palm.

In the interrogation room Shrewsbury questioned her about her knowledge of Lady Catherine Grey's marriage, how long she had known of it, and if she had aided and abetted the girl to deceive the queen. Bess told him the truth, as was her wont, and she saw Talbot's mouth quirk with amusement. Impatiently, she confessed her privy thoughts. "My incarceration has little to do with Catherine—it is a warning to keep my mouth shut about all the secrets I guard!"

Talbot put a quick finger to his lips. "When I take you before the council, admit nothing, deny all."

"Is it because you are a senior member of the privy council that you were chosen to interrogate me?"

"That and because I am chief justice of the north, where your home and property are located. However, I wasn't chosen, Bess; I insisted it was my right." He moved toward her and took her hand.

Bess felt an immediate physical response to his powerful masculinity. She hovered on the brink of going into his arms but caught herself in time. She opened her fingers, revealing the shirt button and her bloodied palm. She lifted her black eyes to his and saw raw desire blaze up in them. Her lashes came down to conceal her own desire as he took her hand to his lips and tasted her blood. She took back her hand and replaced it with a tiny barb. "My blood is not nearly blue enough for you, milord."

He cocked an amused brow. " 'Tis not blue at all, Vixen."

"You arrogant raptor," she whispered, adding the insult to the toll she would make him pay before she was done with him.

When Bess was questioned by the privy council, they took their findings and their recommendations to Principal Secretary Cecil, who was aghast to learn that Lady St. Loe was

473

still in the Tower. Cecil advised the queen to release her friend immediately, and on March 25, a fortnight after Shrewsbury's initial visit, the door of her cell was unlocked.

Bess stepped across the threshold, vowing never to become a victim again. In the past, whenever a supplicant had come to her, she had put herself in their shoes, enabling her to empathize with them. Bess decided never to do that again. From now on she would steadfastly maintain her own point of view, self-serving though that might be.

Her reunion with her husband was touchingly affectionate. His genuine tears of relief made her overlook his shortcomings. She told herself that if she had wanted a hard-as-nails man who threw his weight about and dominated all in his path, she should not have wed William St. Loe, who was a gentle man to the bone.

He presented her with a velvet-covered casket, which took her breath away when she opened it. He had bought her a pendant and earrings of deep blue Persian sapphires to welcome her home and help erase the deep guilt he felt over not visiting her in the Tower. "Will, these are finer than any of the jewels you have given Elizabeth. I thank you from the bottom of my heart."

"Elizabeth needs jewels to make her look radiant—you do not, Bess."

She kissed him. "That's the loveliest thing you've ever said to me, my dear."

Not until May did the council declare that no marriage had ever taken place between Lady Catherine Grey and young Hertford. Any children of their union were therefore bastards, and the pair was confined indefinitely to the Tower for "unlawful carnal copulation."

Now that Lady St. Loe was free, all her fair-weather friends at Court flocked back to her. She was invited to every social function, and Bess attended, delighting in showing off her fashionable wardrobe and growing collection of jewels. Because of her forced absence she was more gay and witty than ever, fending off Shrewsbury's secret overtures and enjoying Queen Elizabeth's favors as if nothing had ever happened.

But as spring gamboled toward summer, Bess knew she must have a serious talk with her husband about her future. "Will, I want to leave early for Chatsworth this year."

"I think that is a splendid idea, Bess. It will give you more time to spend with the children."

Bess took a deep breath. "Will, I shan't be returning to Court in the autumn. I plan to take up permanent residence at Chatsworth."

"But what about Elizabeth, my dear?"

"What about her? She proved that she can manage very well without my services."

"You haven't forgiven her!" he said with amazement.

"Of course I've forgiven her; forgiving comes easily to me. Forgetting, however, is something I shall never do."

"Bess, I love you so much. I shall miss you dreadfully."

"Will, I want you to think seriously about retiring from Court and coming with me. Cavendish died from the stress of overwork; don't delude yourself that it cannot happen to you."

"Bess, the queen needs me." St. Loe's words were so sincere, they almost brought tears to her eyes. *Within the hour of your death, a dozen others will rise up to replace you. Elizabeth will give you a state funeral if she's feeling generous that day, and that will be that.* Bess could not bring herself to destroy his ideals. "The decision is yours, Will, but promise me you'll think about it?"

Bess, along with her two sons who were on summer holiday from Eton College, departed for Chatsworth. When they arrived at Nottingham, she put them up at the best inn, along with their body servants, and proceeded to Holme Pierrepont with her maid Cecily. Her fears about Sir George and Lady Pierrepont shunning her because of her arrest were groundless. Up here in Nottingham they did not concern themselves with the Court affairs of London and knew very little of the sad business of Lady Catherine Grey.

Lady St. Loe and Sir George dealt very well together. After she regaled him with horror stories of what the Court of Wards could do to his heir unless young Henry was wed, she told him the generous amount of her daughter Frances's dowry and that the young couple would receive the deed to one of Bess's manor houses once the marriage was solemnized. The betrothal documents were signed, and Lady Pierrepont invited Frances Cavendish to stay with them for the summer so the espoused couple could get to know each other better. By the time she left, Bess congratulated herself on a clever piece of business.

When Bess arrived at Chatsworth, she was greeted with open arms, not only by her children, but by her mother, Elizabeth, and her aunt Marcy. Bess kissed Francie, then scooped up young Elizabeth and Mary and swung them about, trying to listen to them all at once.

"How dare that wicked bitch imprison you for thirty weeks?" Marcella demanded, her jowls quivering in outrage.

"Thirty-one weeks," Bess corrected her, then laughed. "Queens have to be wicked or they would soon lose their thrones. At any rate I am out of my cage now and intend to exercise my freedom like never before!"

Bess's mother kissed her. "It's good to have you home, darling."

"I hope you mean that, Mother, for I'm here to stay. Have you selected a new husband yet?" Bess teased.

"Speaking of freedom, I've decided not to

saddle myself with anyone as burdensome as a husband. Not that Ralph and I weren't devoted, but there is definitely something to recommend widowhood."

Bess stared at her mother in disbelief. Her own widowhood had been the nadir of her life, and she still did not know how she had survived it.

"Oh, darling, I could bite my tongue!"

Bess embraced her mother. "I'm never going to live in the past again—carpe diem."

Marcella made a moue with her lips. "All these fancy French phrases—you cannot deny Court gave you a sophisticated polish."

Bess wrinkled her nose. "I think that one is Latin, but I'm not sure. I might have a bit of polish, but I'll never be an intellectual, thank God!" She surveyed her daughters with pride. Elizabeth, now seven, was definitely the beauty of the family. She loved pretty dresses and had a sweet, obedient nature. Little Mary, on the other hand, looked exactly what she was: a red-haired imp of Satan with a stubborn mind of her own.

"Your brothers are no doubt at the stables reacquainting themselves with their horses and dogs. I want you to join them for a little while, because I have something very important to discuss with your sister Frances."

Hand in hand, mother and daughter strolled out into the vast garden and sat down beside a lily pond. As Bess gazed fondly at her daughter Frances, she couldn't get over how like her father she was. Dark, with laughing eyes, Frances was a Cavendish down to her fingertips.

"Francie, I've finalized the espousal between you and Henry Pierrepont. You haven't changed your mind about Harry, have you?" Bess watched her daughter's face carefully to see her true reaction and saw a smile of pure delight suffuse it.

"I think he's in love with me," Frances confided.

"But what about you, Francie? I've been in *love,* and I've been in *like,* and believe me, love is better."

"Well, I think I might be in love, but I have more good sense than to let Harry know," Frances said with a wink.

"Lady Pierrepont has invited you to stay with them for the summer so that you can get to know them and they you. But you must promise me that if you have doubts about spending the rest of your life with Harry, you will come to me immediately. Years ago I made a promise to your father that I would see you made a good marriage. Henry is heir to the Pierrepont estate, and you will never want for anything, but as well as material wealth I want your happiness above everything else."

"I promise. Thank you for being the best mother in the entire world. May I have some new clothes?"

"We will dazzle them with your wardrobe, Francie. A woman cannot have too many gowns, or riding habits."

"Hunting clothes!" Frances giggled, as her mother laughed at the pun she made.

Bess could hardly believe her daughter was fourteen. A lump came into her throat as she remembered how afraid she had been when she first found out Cavendish had made a baby in her. *Thank God and all his Apostles that I did nothing foolish to rid myself of this precious child, whom I love and adore!*

THIRTY-ONE

With renewed vigor Bess rode over her lands daily. Sometimes her children rode with her, but her sons, now twelve, eleven, and ten, were more interested in their own pursuits, and Bess was often free to roam far afield with the summer wind whipping her red tresses into a tangle. She loved to ride in Sherwood Forest, which was alive with birds and other game.

She ordered a thousand billets of wood to be cut and stacked ready at all times to fill Chatsworth's great fireplaces whenever the day was cool and damp. Chatsworth's mill was repaired, and Bess made improvements at Ashford Manor, Lark Meadow, and Doveridge. The Chatsworth acreage alone covered over ten miles, Ashford had eight thousand acres, and Doveridge another five hundred, so Lady St. Loe was the greatest landowner in Derbyshire, after Shrewsbury.

The livestock on her landholdings was considerable. She had forty oxen for drawing heavy carts, and five hundred ewes, most of which had just lambed. She had an equal number of rams and ordered that most of them be castrated so they could be fattened for market and sold as wethers, since she needed fewer than a score of rams for breeding purposes. Her tenant farmers also bred milky herds of Charolais cattle and, of course, some huge Yorkshire pigs and boars. All were fed by crops grown on her own acres, and there were still enough fields left to grow wheat for Chatsworth's bread and barley for its ale.

The late mornings and afternoons were given over to finishing the building of Chatsworth. Bess wanted a porch across the entire front face of Chatsworth and battlements built on the roof in the same matching stone. Whenever she heard of a religious order falling on hard times or the estate sale of a nobleman, Bess was there to buy up their treasures for Chatsworth. She acquired more tapestries than her magnificent house could display but squirreled them away for future use, for once Bess acquired an objet d'art, she vowed never to part with it.

Bess arose at dawn, and when she saw that the sunrise turned the sky red, she knew there would be a summer thunderstorm before the day was over. Deciding to take her ride early today, she headed into Sherwood Forest, where deer could be spotted at dawn or sunset.

She was delighted to see a hare dash across her path, and shortly after she watched a gray fox pursue it. She paused beside a stream and watched a couple of otters swimming together. She realized by their antics that they were a mated pair.

In the distance Bess heard a hunting horn and was surprised as the high notes traveled closer, now accompanied by the baying of hounds. She rode through the green canopy of trees toward the racket and suddenly found herself face to face with a dozen huntsmen. All wore the white-hound badge of the Talbots, and then she saw Shrewsbury himself with a dead stag thrown across the broad rump of his great black hunter.

He flung himself from the saddle the moment he saw her and issued an order for his men to fall back. They obeyed immediately, taking the dogs with them.

Bess's pulse quickened the moment she saw him. *Why does he have the power to make me feel alive?* The corners of her mouth lifted only slightly as she looked down at him from her saddle. "You are poaching on my territory—but, then, it wouldn't be the first time, would it?"

"If you are speaking of the Tower, I was openly invited, Vixen."

Bess hid her amusement. "I didn't write to thank you for my release, because I paid you in advance."

"You have a cruel tongue."

"Not always. It can be teasing, playful even."

"I am well aware and can think of other uses."

"All wickedly intimate, no doubt."

As they dueled with words, the sexual tension between them coiled ever tighter. Shrewsbury shortened the distance that separated them and placed a possessive hand on her velvet-covered knee.

"You are a bold devil, when I have the whip hand," she teased, rolling the handle of her quirt between her palms suggestively.

"If you don't cease making that provocative gesture with your whip, I'll show you just how wickedly intimate I can be."

"I believe you already did that—twice. Surely at your age you have learned control?"

"Bess, you haven't the faintest idea just how much control I'm exercising at this moment. I want to pull you down in my arms and tear that black riding habit to ribbons. What outrageous color are your undergarments today, Vixen?"

"Crimson. You shouldn't be touching me at all with the blood of the stag on your hands."

"If you're really wearing crimson, it won't show."

"You'll never know, will you?" She tossed back her hair in a challenging gesture.

His eyes flashed a warning she should have recognized. His bold hand went up inside her riding skirt and she heard material tear as he ripped a handful of petticoat and flourished the brilliant silk victoriously, then shoved it inside his leather jack.

"You black devil," she hissed, raising her riding crop.

"Lash me with it, and see what happens," he goaded.

Bess licked her lips and laughed at him. "You'd like that, wouldn't you, Lucifer, but I shall be the picture of decorum."

Talbot searched her face, then his banter dropped away and he became earnest. "Bess, will you ride with me sometime?"

She looked directly into his piercing blue eyes. "Of course, since you covet this part of Sherwood Forest that I own. I will ride with you, hunt with you, converse with you, even dine with you, but I won't fuck with you, Shrew, so don't ask."

You shall, my beauty, you shall!

"Since you are amenable to dining with me, I invite you to Sheffield to celebrate the wedding of my son and heir next month."

Bess caught her breath. Shrewsbury's heir would be the greatest catch in England, and she wondered what blue-blooded heiress Talbot would accept as his daughter-in-law. "And who is the lucky bride?" she asked lightly.

"Anne Herbert, the Earl of Pembroke's daughter."

Bess almost choked with chagrin that William Herbert and his gossipy countess had struck such a profitable alliance for their daughter. Until this moment Bess thought she had done exceedingly well for her daughter Frances, but young Harry Pierrepont's fortune paled into insignificance beside young Francis Talbot's. With an effort Bess restrained her tongue. "How lovely. I shall look forward to receiving the invitation."

His eyes never left her face. "You haven't said you'll accept."

Bess smiled. "I accept your invitation; it's your proposition I decline."

"We'll see," he replied with generations of inbred arrogance.

Bess wheeled her mount and galloped off, but the ache in the pit of her belly was a direct result of the close proximity of the dark devil she left behind, as was the hardening of her nipples against her crimson silk undergarment.

"Peste take it! That wretched Anne Herbert has pulled off the match of the decade for her daughter. She has espoused the girl to Shrewsbury's heir!"

Marcella raised bristly brows. "I warrant it was Talbot and William Herbert who did the deal. The Countess of Pembroke likely had naught to do with it."

"The mere fact that she's a countess had everything to do with it. Nothing less than an earl's daughter would do for blood-proud George Talbot!"

Bess's secretary, Robert Bestnay, brought her the post, mentioning that there was an unusual amount today.

"Well, speak of the devil," Bess said, as

she sorted through the envelopes and found one decorated with the crest of the Earl and Countess of Pembroke. She tore it open and scanned the contents. A small shriek escaped her lips. "God damn and blast it! Not only is their porridge-faced daughter marrying Francis Talbot, their snot-nosed son, Henry Herbert, is to marry Catherine Talbot, Shrewsbury's eldest daughter, on the same day."

"Well, well, there's nothing like keeping their fortunes in the family," Marcella observed shrewdly.

"Shrew never mentioned a bloody word to me!"

"Shrew?" Marcella's eyebrows twitched upward.

Bess tossed her head as her cheeks flushed. " 'Tis the name I call Shrewsbury, among others. Gertrude Talbot must be a cold-hearted bitch. Her daughter Catherine cannot be much more than ten. I think it's shameful!"

"When the fortunes involved are as large as Shrewsbury's, they must be protected by early espousals. You have a hard head for business, Bess; I'm surprised at your attitude."

Bess wrinkled her nose as her innate honesty came to the fore. "I'm just pea-green with envy that it's not my children who are marrying into the Talbot family." As Bess finished reading the letter, another small shriek erupted. "Anne Herbert says she's looking forward to staying at Chatsworth for a few days. Ohmigod, everyone who is anyone will be coming!"

She flung down the letter, and slowly a look of radiance transformed her face. "They'll all die with envy when they see my house. Robert, get James Cromp for me—Francis Whitfield and Timothy Pusey as well. The battlements must be finished before next month and all the excess stone carted away from the grounds."

There were letters from Nan Dudley and William Parr, Marquess of Northampton, informing her they were attending the wedding and hinting for an invitation to Chatsworth. Bess saved Syntlo's letter until last, yet it brought the most startling news of all. Her Majesty Queen Elizabeth would be traveling north to attend the double wedding and would be staying at Haddon Hall, which was only a couple of miles away. "I can't believe it— I'm about to entertain the queen and the entire Court at Chatsworth!"

Bess spoke with the gardeners and the entire inside staff—now considerable—and told them what to expect. She consulted with the gamekeeper to make sure there was a good supply of both red and gray partridge. She inspected the blue livery of her footmen, as well as the bed linen, silver, plate, and china. She took stock of the wine cellar, then sat down at her desk to make a long list of supplies and spices for Syntlo to purchase in London and ship up to Derbyshire. She told her musicians and harpist to learn some new dances and songs, since the queen's courtiers loved music only second to gambling.

All three stories of Chatsworth were now completed, and Bess knew nothing in the north could compare with it. Sheffield Castle, of course, was larger, with far more servants and costlier furnishings handed down through generations of Talbots, but Chatsworth from top to bottom reflected Bess's impeccable taste.

Once she was satisfied that her magnificent house was in order, her thoughts turned to her own wardrobe. She wanted to look spectacular for the wedding and outshine them all. She called her head seamstress to her solar and invited her mother and sister Jane, since they also would need new gowns.

Bess examined a bolt of cloth of gold and another of silver tissue, but both were becoming so commonplace at Court, Bess shook her head. "No, I intend to wear my Persian sapphires and want something that will show them off to perfection."

"Your breasts will do that, darling," her mother supplied.

"I think I'd like a gown of sapphire blue, cut very low in front."

"Velvet or brocade, madam?" asked the seamstress.

"Both are too heavy for summer. I think taffeta; it rustles and whispers so deliciously."

"La, anyone would think you were out to catch a man, darling."

"I think Bess dresses for other women, mother. She always manages to make them look dowdy by comparison."

"Thank you for noticing, Jane," Bess said, laughing.

"Will I line the sleeves with silver tissue, Lady St. Loe? That is always so effective against a deep jewel-toned gown."

"No, I don't want hanging sleeves. I want puffed sleeves, slashed with cream silk." Bess took up a sketch pad and a piece of charcoal. "I want the very latest fashion—let me show you." Bess drew a framed collar that stood up in a flared semicircle behind the head. "I want this in cream color to show off my bright hair. Perhaps it could be edged in blue brilliants to match my sapphires." Bess sighed. "If only I could sew real sapphires on my gowns, but only Elizabeth can afford such indulgences."

"Would you like sapphire or cream undergarments, madam?"

Bess thought for a moment, then smiled her secret smile. "How about something totally unexpected, like jade green?"

The seamstress blinked, but did not dare to suggest something less flamboyant. Instead, she changed the subject. "I have the chamois riding breeches ready, madam."

"Oh, wonderful, I'll try them on. Tell Cecily to fetch my tallest black riding boots and that tight little doublet with the brass buttons."

Bess donned the male attire and admired the ultrafeminine effect in the polished silver mirror.

"Bess, you don't intend to actually wear those things in public, do you?" her mother asked with disapproval.

489

"They will be absolutely perfect for riding astride, don't you see?" Bess asked, spreading her legs wide apart and running her hands over the soft buff suede that covered her hips.

Her mother blanched. "Riding astride is something a lady would never do either."

"Who the devil said I was a lady? And where is it written that a woman cannot wear breeches and sit astride her own horse on her own land?"

A knock on the solar door interrupted her. Bess opened it to find Robert Bestnay.

"I'm sorry to disturb you, ma'am, but Cromp is below and says he must speak with you immediately."

Bess ran lightly down the broad staircase that led to her office, unmindful of her unconventional attire. "James, is there some sort of trouble?"

"There is, ma'am. A couple of days ago, Tim Pusey had trouble collecting some of your tenants' rents. I sent him back out with instructions to accept no excuses, but it has precipitated some sort of riot."

"Riot? Which tenants are giving trouble?"

"It's the Chesterfield tenants, I'm afraid."

"Let's go," Bess said decisively, taking up her riding gloves and crop from the hall table.

At the stables a groom hurried to saddle her favorite mare, but she stopped him. "No, I'll ride Raven; he's faster. Don't put a sidesaddle on him." She threw her leg across the black stallion, and before they were out of the stable yard, she urged Raven to a full gallop.

A huge crowd had gathered in the village of Chesterfield, and bloody fighting had obviously erupted, but the arrival of the Earl of Shrewsbury had put a temporary stop to the rioting.

"These are my tenants; what the devil business is it of yours?" she demanded.

His eyes devoured the woman before him astride the stallion. He watched her hungrily as she dismounted, dug her fists into her hips, and planted her legs firmly apart in a stance of confrontation. "I'm making it my business. It's too close to my property of Bolsover for my liking; riots have a way of spreading if they're not nipped in the bud."

Bess addressed Tim Pusey, who was nursing a black and swollen eye. "What is this trouble about?"

It was Shrewsbury who answered her. "The farmers who work Hardwick haven't had any wages for weeks, so they refuse to pay their rent."

"How do you know this before I do?" she demanded angrily.

"Bess, there is little that happens north of the Trent that I don't know about."

She bristled that it should be so. "If they refuse to pay their rents, I'll clear the bloody land and put sheep on it!"

"Bess, they have no money—they hardly have food."

She stared at him. *Well, well, who would have guessed the great Earl of Shrewsbury has a compassionate nature?* "I'll speak to my brother about this," she informed him loftily.

"That will do damned little to solve the problem. James Hardwick has allowed his property and landholdings to go to rack and ruin."

"Are you saying my brother is to blame for this trouble?" she demanded angrily, furious because what Shrewsbury said about James was all too true.

"He's useless." Shrewsbury's piercing blue eyes narrowed, challenging her to refute him.

Bess bit her lip and acknowledged the truth of his words. "James doesn't have a good head for business. I make a better man than he does."

Shrewsbury's eyes traveled up her shapely legs and came to rest on her breasts thrusting beneath the male doublet. "You, Vixen, are all woman, and never more so than dressed in those provocative riding breeches." He wanted her astride him, not her stallion.

"Black brute," she murmured, secretly pleased that he thought her provoking.

Angry voices rose up around them. "Will you let me handle this? I could easily put down a riot by force—I have an armed guard of forty soldiers in my pay—but force isn't the answer here." He didn't wait for her reply but raised his voice to the men milling about them. "There is a job for any man who wants one in my lead and coal mines."

Bess remounted her horse and added her voice to the earl's. "I, too, have coal to be mined, and sheep to be tended." Suddenly, Bess remembered what it was like to have absolutely nothing, and her heart constricted.

"I'll allow a week's hunting on any of my lands to fill your larders. If there's aught else you need, speak to my stewards."

The crowds gathered about Bess and the earl to offer their thanks. The mounted pair slowly walked their horses through the throng, uncomfortable with the display of gratitude.

"Ride with me," Shrewsbury said quietly.

Bess urged Raven forward with her heels, and the two black stallions galloped abreast until the village was left behind and they entered a copse of beech trees. Their horses slowed, then stopped as the riders looked at each other. Shrewsbury urged his mount closer to hers until their stirrups touched. "Christ, I swear you're dressed this way to provoke my lust."

"I'd rather provoke your temper."

"Look at the effect you have on me, Vixen." His hand indicated his swollen groin. "Can we not be secret lovers?"

She lifted her chin. "It would take more than six stiff inches to tempt me to sin."

"Seven," he corrected.

They stared for a moment, then both burst into laughter at the absurd things their sexual desire made them say to each other. Bess sobered. "I shall speak to my brother about Hardwick. Thank you for aiding me today."

"Bess, it is always my pleasure to *serve* you." The double entendre gave him the last word.

You are a witty devil when the spirit moves you. We could have such fun together, damn you to hellfire!

493

THIRTY-TWO

Since she was practically on the doorstep, Bess rode straight to Hardwick Manor, deciding not to go home and change her clothes first. The male attire would lend her authority for what she had to say to her brother.

As she rode up to her old home, Bess realized how much she loved it, in spite of the fact that the small manor house had fallen into a dilapidated state. She reined in and sat staring at it, remembering how devastated she had been that day when they had been evicted. Her heart ached for its sad state of disrepair, and she felt a wave of guilt wash over her, because she had transferred her affection to Chatsworth.

She remembered the promise she had made to this house: *I will be back to claim you!* And she had kept that promise. But she had gotten it back for James because Hardwick was his birthright, and look what he'd done to it. Anger replaced her sadness and guilt. Why couldn't James be a man? Why couldn't he make the five hundred acres of Hardwick pay?

She swung down from the saddle, tethered Raven to a tree, and strode up to the front door. She rapped with her riding crop, then walked in. Bess dismissed the servant who approached and spoke directly to her sister-in-law. "Where is he, Lizzie?"

The young woman stared in disbelief at Bess's attire, then indicated the parlor.

Bess swept into the room with weapons primed. "James Hardwick, while you sit here bending your elbow, your workers are rioting because they cannot pay their rents!"

"Lady St. Loe," he mocked, "welcome to my humble abode."

"Don't use that tone with me, you idle son of a bitch."

"You always did swear like a man; now you've taken to dressing like one. Are you growing a cock under those fine breeches, sister?"

"If I were a man, I'd take a horsewhip to you. Now, explain what's happening at Hardwick."

The sneer dropped from James's face and was replaced by a sullen, morose look. "I can't make a go of it, Bess. I've tried and tried. Either the crops fail or the sheep die of foot rot. This spring I couldn't even sell my wool. They said it was inferior quality, and it was so tick-infested, I had to burn it."

"Dear God, James, you have to be a better manager. You know sheep must be dipped to keep them tick-free. You should know that successful farming takes hard work and good management. We as landowners have a responsibility to our tenants."

"I haven't collected rents from Hardwick's tenant farmers for months—I know they cannot pay," he said defensively.

"That's all very well, but what about those who work for you and rent from me? No wonder fighting broke out in Chesterfield, if my tenants have to pay rent when yours don't! Why haven't you done something about this mess?"

"You're the one who's filthy rich. Why haven't you?" he asked bluntly.

"In case you've forgotten, I spent the last eight months in the Tower."

"You likely deserved it; you always were a meddling bitch."

Bess took a menacing step toward him and raised her riding crop. Behind her she heard Lizzie scream. "Don't hurt him—James spent a month in Fleet prison for debt."

Bess swung around and stared at her young sister-in-law. Her shrewd glance swept back to James and her black eyes narrowed. "How did you get out?"

"I borrowed the money to pay the debts."

"You mortgaged Hardwick?" Bess accused.

When James nodded she stepped forward and brought her crop down across his shoulders.

He snatched it from her hand. "How the hell else could I get money? Marry it, like you did?"

"You bastard!" Bess snatched up the iron poker and advanced on him. He backed up in a hurry, knowing what her temper was like when riled. "Why didn't you come to me?" she demanded.

"Pride, I suppose."

"You have no bloody pride. Look at this place!"

"I've just borrowed some money to make repairs," he said defensively.

"Cancel the loan instantly. I'll pay for the repairs and fix the roof. I'll also loan you money to get more livestock and put in some crops."

"You've always wanted Hardwick, and this is your way of getting your grasping hands on it."

"James, you have horseshit for brains. Don't you realize I could buy the place cheap from your creditors?"

He knew she spoke the truth and agreed to let her fix up the house and loan him money for livestock. But Bess had no idea that the moment she made the improvements, James intended to sell the accursed place and move to London.

On the day of the double wedding, Bess decided they needed two carriages to take them to Sheffield, since she did not want her sapphire taffeta crushed and creased. Her mother, wearing blush pink, and her two young daughters, in identical white dresses with pink sashes, went in the first coach with her, and her three sons went in the second coach with Marcella and Jane.

Syntlo was not with them. He was escorting Queen Elizabeth from Haddon Hall and had ridden over to Chatsworth last night to spend a few hours with his family. Bess had been appalled at his frail appearance. Not only was he stooped and gray, he was thin as a rail. All the women had fussed over him, feeding him and mixing him possets to increase his appetite, but he had assured them he was feeling quite well. Bess, however, decided to speak with him about taking a break from his duties, once this wedding was over.

Bess's coach and the queen's arrived at precisely the same moment. Robin Dudley accompanied the queen on horseback. Bess took this opportunity to introduce her two younger daughters to the queen.

Elizabeth looked down at the elder. "I am your godmother, and you are my namesake."

Young Elizabeth, almost eight, sank into a graceful curtsy and murmured, "Your Majesty, I am honored."

The queen looked at Bess. "This one is a Cavendish, all right." The queen's eyes slid to the smaller of the pair with the bright red curls, who stuck out her tongue. "This one's a Hardwick, may God help her."

Bess rolled her eyes at Robin, who couldn't hide his amusement. Bess envied Queen Elizabeth her gown. It was white satin, embroidered all over in a diamond-shape pattern with jet beads. On the bodice, interspersed with the jet beads, were real diamonds. "You look magnificent, Your Majesty."

"But you are wearing the latest style, I see. That framed collar does glorious things for your hair. I shall adopt the fashion immediately."

Bess waited for the queen to precede her, but Elizabeth spoke up. "We shall go forward together to greet our hostess and see what the mother of the bride is wearing."

"I wager she'll be wearing Tudor green to honor you, Your Majesty," Robin guessed.

As Gertrude Talbot rushed down the castle steps to greet her queen, Elizabeth murmured, "Good God, that's not Tudor green! Whatever shade is it?"

"Goose turd, I'd say," Bess murmured behind her fan.

The queen gave a great bark of laughter. "I miss your wit, Lady St. Loe, when you are absent from Court."

Gertrude Talbot shot Bess a look of loathing. She was a short, plump woman who would not have been attractive no matter what she wore. Making matters worse, her features were set in a condescending look that was permanent. "You honor us, Your gracious Majesty."

"I do indeed," Elizabeth said rather caustically. "Why isn't the Old Man here to greet me?"

Shrewsbury seemed to materialize from nowhere, his tall, dark figure casting its powerful shadow over them all in the brilliant morning sunlight. He sketched an elegant bow. "The two loveliest ladies in the realm; welcome to Sheffield."

"I refuse to share that honor with Mistress Tits," Elizabeth said crudely, and the four of them were transported back to the day they met at Hampton Court.

Dudley laughed so hard, he choked, and the queen wiped tears of mirth from her eyes. Bess and Talbot joined in the laughter, but their amusement was a private thing, apart from the others. They had an intimacy that was secret and could never be shared.

The Earl and Countess of Pembroke joined them, and all made their way to Sts. Peter and Paul's Church, which was on the grounds belonging to Sheffield.

Syntlo joined Bess in the church, which bulged at its consecrated seams with noble guests. The child brides brought a lump to Bess's throat, and she offered up a quick prayer that the young girls were making happy marriages.

The religious ceremony seemed to be over in the blinking of an eye, and the guests thronged from the church to partake of Sheffield Castle's hospitality. Large families were the fashion, and the nobility had brought all their children. Bess's sons and daughters immediately went off with Talbot's brood, together with the offspring of the Herberts, the Howards, and the Stuarts.

The reception was on a lavish scale, comparable with anything the queen's Court ever put on. The banqueting chamber held a formal dining table that accommodated all sixty adult guests, while the young people sat at smaller tables. A liveried footman stood ready to serve behind every second chair.

Bess had never seen so much silver plate all at one time. The price of the heavy sterling cutlery alone would have fed an entire town for a year. The paintings and the tapestries on the walls were of course priceless and had been handed down through generations of Talbots since medieval times. Bess tried not to stare, but to own such riches was almost beyond comprehension.

After dinner, when they moved to one of the ballrooms and Bess was immediately approached by William Parr for a dance, she cast an inquiring glance at her husband.

"Go and enjoy yourself, my dearest. I'm not up to dancing these days, but I know how much you love it."

With a pang Bess watched him join a group of older men who did not dance and knew he would be happier talking with William Herbert than partnering her on the ballroom floor. As the hours flew by, Bess danced every dance, partnered by all the earls and lords who had ever made her acquaintance and some who hadn't until tonight. Finally, she found herself being swept into Shrewsbury's arms in a lively galliard.

Beneath her tiny cream ruff, the huge sapphire sparkled in the cleft between her breasts, and she saw his eyes on it.

"Magnificent," he murmured.

"Thank you; 'twas a gift from Syntlo."

"I wasn't referring to the sapphire."

When she ignored the innuendo, he bent close. "You could be wearing diamonds and emeralds, my beauty, if you'd let me buy them for you."

She glanced up at him with a challenge in her black eyes. "How about the infamous Talbot pearls?"

Shrewsbury threw back his dark head and

laughed. "You are the most audacious woman I've ever known, and it attracts me like a lodestone."

"Men always want what they cannot have," she said lightly.

"Apparently women are the same, or why would you covet the pearls?"

Bess was well aware that the only way a woman could get the pearls was by becoming the Countess of Shrewsbury, yet when he alluded to the fact that she could never have them, it rankled her. "Shrew, you keep your pearls and I'll keep my virtue."

She felt the muscles in his arms bulge, hard as iron, as he lifted her high in the galliard, and she felt weak with longing. She watched his pupils turn black with desire as her jade silk undergarments were revealed, and in that moment she knew she wanted him desperately. To talk and touch in the crowded room was sheer torture.

He whispered intensely, "You're starving for it. Why do you deny me, deny yourself?"

She looked up into his eyes. "Do you want the truth? It's because we are both married; that's the only reason I deny you."

"Syntlo cannot possibly satisfy you. He was an old man when you married him, but now he's a frail shadow of his former self."

"All the more reason why I cannot betray him."

"So you'll live like a nun just to honor an empty marriage vow you should never have made in the first place."

"You once thought me rather fetching in a nun's habit."

They were level with the ballroom doors, and he pulled her through them before she knew what he intended. "No, Shrew!" She tried to release her hand from his, but his powerful grip tightened and he almost dragged her along the gallery that led out to the gardens. "Christ, I won't ravish you!" he growled.

Damn, if only you would, how simple it would make everything.

They ran through the night-scented gardens, across manicured lawns, passing a fountain of dancing waters, to the seclusion of a giant yew walk that had sheltered lovers and their secrets for over a century. Bess made no outcry, knowing the scandal would be horrendous with the nobility for witness.

He took hold of her other hand and looked down at her face outlined by moonlight. "You've invited everyone to Chatsworth save me," he accused.

"I'm entertaining Her Majesty, for God's sake. I can't be distracted by you."

"Then you admit I distract you?" His arms closed about her and he pulled her close against his long, hard body.

"You are well-aware of what you do to me, you black devil. You are like Lucifer, tempting me to sin."

"Loving is no sin, Bess."

"Damn you, it isn't love, it's lust!"

"We are two passionate soulmates who have found each other."

"We are two oversexed people who can't keep their hands off each other!"

"You don't seem to have any trouble resisting me."

"Shrew, if I dared to let down my defenses, I'd devour you!"

He groaned, and his mouth came down on hers with a hunger he had never known before. With his lips still against hers, he demanded, "Do you know what it did to me, watching you dance with all those other men, knowing their hot hands were on you, their eyes devouring your luscious breasts, hoping for a glimpse of nipple?"

"Shrew, for God's sake, don't kiss me again. You know we can't stop." For answer his mouth took hers and ravaged it.

Bess pulled away from him angrily. "This is insanity. We cannot carry on like this. It's your son and your daughter's wedding! 'Fore God, if you don't control yourself, we'll be coupling under the hedge like a pair of gypsies!"

Suddenly, they both heard someone shouting. They stopped talking and listened. There seemed to be a general outcry from the castle. "Obviously something's wrong; go quickly," she urged.

Bess waited a few minutes, then, keeping to the shadows, made her way across the gardens and back to the castle. She was in time to watch George Talbot, Earl of Shrewsbury, gently pick up his countess, Gertrude, from where she lay on the floor and carry her up the great ornate staircase to her private apartments. Gertrude's three ladies-in-waiting followed, wringing their hands.

Bess joined Syntlo, who was standing with the queen and Dudley. "What happened?"

"Some sort of seizure. Fortunately, Shrewsbury has his own physicians at Sheffield. Too much excitement, I warrant," Elizabeth declared.

Anne Herbert spoke from behind her fan, although it did little to muffle her words. "Gertrude was arguing with her son Francis, my new son-in-law. He and his bride wanted to retire from the reception, and Gertrude wouldn't hear of their being alone. Apparently, she's a termagant with the children, likes to exercise complete control over them. Her girls are frightened to death of her."

Elizabeth raised her plucked eyebrows. "I knew we could rely on you to give us a full accounting, Lady Herbert."

Anne Herbert's skin was so thick, the pointed barb did not penetrate. "Now that Francis is a married man, he decided to challenge Gertrude's authority, and suddenly she turned red as a turkey wattle and fell to the floor."

"She probably just fainted and needs to rest," Bess murmured.

"Mmm," Anne Herbert pressed her lips together before she pronounced her diagnosis. "Gertrude's left side was completely paralyzed—couldn't speak, couldn't get up. Looks serious to me!"

"I hope not," Bess murmured fervently, suffused with guilt.

Her Majesty looked at the Countess of Pembroke. "How fortunate that you are here to take over as our hostess, Anne."

"Oh, I suppose as the other mother of the bride and groom, that is true." Anne Herbert lifted her fan and raised her voice. "Everyone, do carry on; the Countess of Shrewsbury simply fainted from the heat. All she needs is a little rest. William, do have the musicians play the grand march so the newlyweds can circle the ballroom before taking their leave."

"We are in competent hands now," Elizabeth said with a straight face, while those about the queen were biting their lips to keep from shouting with laughter.

"Syntlo, I think perhaps you'd better order up the carriages. We'll return to Haddon Hall rather than stay overnight at Sheffield. Robin, give our excuses to Shrewsbury and tell him to let us know how poor Gertrude fares tomorrow."

Sir William St. Loe took leave of his wife and murmured, "Her Majesty has a horror of sickness. Good night, my dearest. I shall ride over to Chatsworth tomorrow, duty permitting."

Shrewsbury returned with Dudley to bid Elizabeth and her entourage farewell, then he assured the remaining guests that Gertrude was resting comfortably.

When Bess decided to round up her family, she found her three sons enjoying a wrestling match with Gilbert Talbot, an affable youth who had inherited his father's dark looks.

Her eyes turned speculative immediately and a seed of ambition was sown. *It is high time I started thinking about the future of my children.* She turned and saw Shrewsbury watching her from the doorway.

"Bid Lord Talbot good night and thank him for his hospitality," she bade her sons as they reluctantly stopped their horseplay. She watched them make their bows and leave the room with Gilbert following them. Bess approached Shrewsbury and laid her hand on his sleeve. "Anne Herbert says she cannot talk or walk."

He nodded. "Her doctor assures me she'll recover, but I don't have much faith in the damned quack."

"I'm so sorry." She searched his face. "See how guilty you feel now!"

He covered her hand with his. "You are wrong, Bess. I am incapable of feeling guilt over anything I've said to you or done with you. However, you look racked with guilt, my beauty, so I shall desist in my unseemly behavior toward you while Gertrude suffers this indignity. I promise."

He sounded absolutely sincere. Could she believe him? Bess lowered her lashes. "Good night, my lord. Please send me word on how she fares."

THIRTY-THREE

The next sennight was the busiest time Bess had ever known in her life. She entertained Her Majesty Queen Elizabeth and the courtiers who had accompanied her north. Chatsworth was a raging success and the envy of every single one of her guests. She took this opportunity to ask the queen to excuse her from her Court duties for at least a year and heaved a sigh of relief when Elizabeth gave her permission.

Before Syntlo returned to London with the queen, Bess spoke to him about her two eldest sons. "Will, this is Henry's last term at Eton, and of course his future is set. He will inherit all my Cavendish holdings, so I needn't worry about him, other than finding a suitable heiress for him to wed. It's William's future I'm concerned with. I'd like him to go into the law; it's the most lucrative profession in England. I should know—a great deal of my income has gone into their coffers over the years."

"I think that's an excellent idea. William will have to attend Cambridge, of course. The tuition will be no problem, but I believe it's devilish hard to get in there."

"Will you make inquiries, my dear?"

"Of course I shall, and let me know the moment you set a date for Francie's wedding."

"And what if Her Gracious Majesty has conflicting plans?" Bess asked archly.

"I shall be at Holme Pierrepont for Francie's wedding, come hell or high water, I promise you."

Bess knew he was the most devoted stepfather in the world and thanked God for it. She bade him a tender farewell and begged him not to make himself ill with overwork.

"Don't worry about me, my dearest. Marcella has packed me a year's supply of everything from calf's jelly to syrup of figs."

Bess rolled her eyes. Marcella believed if the bowels were kept open, the rest of the body would be right as a trivet.

With all her company gone, Bess retired early. She did her best thinking in bed these days, where—unfortunately—there were no distractions. She thought about the notes she had received from Shrewsbury telling her that Gertrude's speech had returned somewhat, and with bed rest her doctors hoped she would soon be walking. There was nothing improper about the letters, except for the greeting. Both had begun *My Dear Nun*.

The corners of Bess's mouth lifted with irony. She was, indeed, living a nun's life, and Shrewsbury's reminder told her clearly that this need not be so. Bess put carnal longings aside and thought about her children. An idea had been bubbling in the back of her mind and she decided this was the perfect time to examine it closely. If the Herberts had married two of their offspring to Talbots, why couldn't she do the same? Bess had five children who were unespoused and Shrewsbury had four.

Of course, blood-proud Talbot, descended from Plantagenets, would likely die of apoplexy if she suggested such a thing. Her children were all Cavendishes and none of them titled. But her daughters *could* become titled through marriage, if she reached high enough and played her cards right. Bess pictured young Gilbert Talbot. He could very well become Earl of Shrewsbury someday, making whomever he married a countess. Then there was Charles Stuart, the Countess of Lennox's son, whom her daughter Elizabeth had sat with at the wedding banquet. He was cousin to the queen and in line of succession to the throne! Bess tucked these ambitious thoughts away for the present and sighed. *If wishes were horses, beggars would ride!* The first order of business was setting a wedding date for her daughter Frances and getting the newlyweds settled close by at Meadowpleck on the River Dove.

The wedding of Frances Cavendish and Henry Pierrepont took place at Holme Pierrepont the first day of September. It was not a large wedding, because the groom's father, Sir George, was in ill health. When Sir William St. Loe, the bride's stepfather, arrived from London, it was obvious to all that he, too, was a sick man.

With a heavy heart Bess took her husband

home to Chatsworth. Both of them knew he would never return to Court. All that autumn she nursed him and mothered him, knowing full well that his days were numbered.

Whenever Syntlo was strong enough, he sat in Chatsworth's magnificent library, wrapped in a lap robe, occupying himself with correspondence. Bess sat with him doing her accounts at her carved oak desk.

He looked up from a letter he had just reread, which he had received a week ago from Cambridge University. "I'm sorry, my dearest, it looks hopeless for getting young William into Cambridge. This is the second time I've applied and the second time they've turned him down. It seems all the places are filled."

Bess threw down her quill and took a turn about the room. "It's not your fault, Will. 'Tis the bloody class system. If he were a young lord or heir to an earldom, they'd be standing on their bloody heads to find a place for him, but plain Master William Cavendish doesn't stand a chance!"

"I wrote to Shrewsbury a couple of days ago, asking if he could help."

Bess's hand flew to her throat. "Ohmigod, Will, you shouldn't have done that!"

"Why not, my dear? He's the best fellow in the world, and his influence is so far-reaching that if anyone can help it's Lord Talbot."

"I don't want to be obligated to him," Bess tried to explain.

"Don't be upset, my dearest. He is lord

lieutenant of Derbyshire, as well as chamberlain of the royal exchequer. He's also a close personal friend of yours. I don't think he will mind in the least using his influence on our son's behalf."

Bess's cheeks flushed, and she moved over to one of the tall windows to keep him from seeing the agitation on her face. Suddenly her pulse began to race as she watched the tall, unmistakable figure of Shrewsbury ride in. She turned from the window. "He's here now! Are you sure you're up to this, Will?" Bess wasn't at all sure she was.

Shrewsbury removed his heavy riding cape and gloves and handed them to the butler. "I'm here to see Sir William."

"Yes, Lord Talbot, they are expecting you. Would you follow me to the library, my lord?"

Shrewsbury felt his heart skip a beat at the thought of seeing Bess. So far it had been the longest, dreariest winter he could ever remember, and he hadn't seen her once. A hundred times he had looked for her when riding over the acres of their adjoining property, and scores of times he had almost ridden to Chatsworth to visit her. So when he received the note from Syntlo, he rejoiced because he finally had a legitimate reason to go.

The moment he crossed the threshold of the library, his senses were filled with her. As she came across the room to greet him, he saw that her pale gray velvet gown was embroidered with pearls. Her sleeves were slashed with jonquil silk, making her look like spring sunshine. He imagined her brilliant yellow undergarments, and his body reacted immediately. His eyes fastened on her beautiful face and he knew why his life was dreary. He had been starving for the sight of her.

She held out her hand. "Lord Talbot, it is more than kind of you to come."

He took her long, slim fingers to his lips, then, before he released them, rubbed the ink stain on her index finger with his thumb. She wore a fragrance of verbena, and he thought he had never smelled anything so intoxicating.

"Forgive me for not rising, Lord Talbot."

For the first time Shrewsbury realized Bess's husband was in the room. He felt himself staring in shock at the shriveled man beneath the lap robe and gave himself a mental shake. "Sir William, I came as soon as I had your note." He could not bring himself to ask after Syntlo's health. He could see with his own eyes the man was dying.

"Bess is upset with me because I asked for your help."

"I could never be upset with you, Will; it just seems such an imposition to expect Lord Talbot to solve our family problems."

"It is no imposition at all, Lady St. Loe. I've already written to the dean of Cambridge, recommending William Cavendish be admitted to Clare Hall next Michaelmas when the term starts."

"There, Bess, you see? I told you he was the best fellow in the world."

"How will I ever thank you, Lord Talbot?" Bess asked stiffly.

Damn it, Bess, don't look at me that way! I am no whoremaster ordering you to pay with your body. He cursed himself. He knew he couldn't even look at her without revealing how much he wanted her.

Bess lowered her lashes. "Would you care for some brandy, my lord, or some hot cider perhaps?"

"No, nothing at all."

"Oh, please, stay a little while and tell Will how things are at Court." Her dark eyes implored him, and he suddenly realized Syntlo would have few visitors. His face softened. "All right, I suppose hot cider will keep out the cold on my ride back to Sheffield."

With a pang he saw the grateful look she threw him before she left the room. He cleared his throat and sat down beside Syntlo. "I was at Court only a month before I was called home. My wife's condition has steadily deteriorated." Shrewsbury was an intensely private man who could never reveal the shouting matches that went on between Gertrude and the children. She blamed them for her affliction, and a day did not go by that did not end in her loud recriminations. He knew she was her own worst enemy, and her carping had brought on several small seizures. The young Talbots now avoided their mother whenever they could, and though he would like to do the

514

same, he spent time with Gertrude to take the brunt of her behavior upon himself. He put it down to a mental affliction and tried to treat her with kindness.

Syntlo murmured his sympathy and pursued the subject closest to his heart. "What is Her Majesty up to these days?"

Shrewsbury tried for a light note. "She's not married yet, if that's what you're asking." When Syntlo didn't laugh, he continued, "The council has proposed Archduke Charles of Austria. An Anglo-Spanish alliance would be a balance against the French."

Syntlo closed his eyes as a spasm of pain cut into him. When it eased he smiled. "Elizabeth plays the marriage card with such adroit skill."

"It all boils down to religion, playing the Catholics against the Protestants. It's an act she and Cecil perform with ease."

Bess returned with a footman who carried a heavy silver tray holding steaming goblets of cider. She carried a cup to Will that contained a mixture of chamomile, balm, and opium. He was no longer able to eat, but the posset eased the agony in his belly.

She handed Shrewsbury a goblet of cider and took her own to the fireplace. He watched her push the poker into the glowing coals and wait for it to get red-hot. He took his goblet over to her and held it out. When she plunged in the hot poker, the cider hissed and the aroma of spiced apples rose up about them.

She looked up into his eyes, and in the firelight he saw the mauve shadows of fatigue beneath hers and thought them beautiful. He murmured low, "The winter *will* pass...spring *will* come." She nodded her understanding, and he knew a lump had come into her throat to prevent her from speaking.

He sipped his cider, wanting to take her in his arms and ease her anguish. He knew he must put space between them for decency's sake. He gulped down the contents of the goblet and set it on the mantelpiece. He glanced over at Syntlo and saw he was beginning to doze. He put his finger to his lips and quietly made his way to the library door.

Bess followed him, and together they descended Chatsworth's elegant staircase. She waited in silence as the butler handed him his cape and gloves then tactfully moved away.

"Thank you," she whispered.

"Cambridge is—" His words halted as she shook her head.

"Thank you for keeping your promise to me."

Sir William St. Loe died in early January, long before the first spring flower could struggle through the cold earth to lift its face to the pale sun. Queen Elizabeth ordered a day of mourning for her faithful captain of the guard and chief butler of England but did not honor him with a state funeral.

Bess accompanied her husband's body to London. She knew the long trip would be too arduous in the winter weather for her mother and Aunt Marcy, so she asked her sister Jane to go with her. Bess's three sons, all at Eton College, joined their mother for the funeral. Sir William St. Loe was buried in the church of Great St. Helen in Bishopsgate, beside his father, Sir John St. Loe.

After the interment Bess took her sons to visit their father's grave at St. Botolph's in Aldgate, which was only a stone's throw away from Bishopsgate. Inside her chest, Bess's heart felt heavy as lead. She realized she had never stopped mourning Cavendish, and here she was burying another husband. It all felt so unreal. How on earth had she outlived three husbands? What had she done to deserve life? What had they done to deserve death? Strangely, she remained dry-eyed, but once again she recognized the numb feeling that engulfed her, turning her emotions to stone.

By the time she got home to Chatsworth, Bess was exhausted. She retreated to her own private suite of rooms, which she loved so much, yet found she could neither sleep nor eat. The frightening part was that she could not even feel.

She reread Syntlo's will. Bess knew he had left her all his lands and manors in Somerset and Gloucestershire, but the great ruined monastery and lands at Glastonbury were a complete surprise. They had been married for four and a half years, and because of his dedicated duty to the queen, they had spent much of that time apart. Bess looked down at the will again. Syntlo had been devoted to her. Though she had had a genuine affection for him, he had loved her far more deeply than she had loved him. Why didn't she feel guilt? Sorrow? Anger? Dear God in heaven, why didn't she feel something?

Downstairs, the Earl of Shrewsbury offered his condolences to Bess's mother and Aunt Marcy. Jane rushed upstairs to inform Bess of his arrival.

"Give Lord Talbot my apologies, Jane. I don't wish to see anyone."

"But, Bess, it's the Earl of Shrewsbury. I cannot refuse him."

"I can, and have many times," Bess said without emotion. "Please leave me alone, Jane."

Reluctantly, Jane approached the small group in the beautifully appointed receiving room. "My sister sends her profuse apologies, Lord Talbot, but she cannot see anyone this evening."

Talbot stared at her as if she were mad. "Did you tell her it was me?"

Jane flushed with embarrassment. "It's not personal, my lord. Bess has isolated herself."

"I assure you it *is* personal. Would you be good enough to inform her that if she doesn't come down, I shall go up?"

Jane stood rooted to the floor, while Bess's mother uttered a shocked, "Lord Talbot!"

Marcella stepped forward with great

authority. She knew there had been something secret and intimate between Bess and "Shrew," as she called him, for some time. "You'd best go up, my lord earl. It will take someone with a will stronger than hers to snap her out of her trance."

Shrewsbury needed no urging. He took the stairs two at a time and located Bess's rooms with unerring instinct. He knocked but did not wait for a reply. Without hesitation he opened her chamber door and walked in.

"Who gave you permission to come up here?" Her voice was remote.

"I don't ask permission for my actions."

She was standing by a tall window, holding something in her hands. The black gown she wore gave her the look of a wraith. As he drew close he was shocked at how pale and bloodless her face looked. He reached out firmly and took the object from her hands. She offered no resistance. He found himself looking down at a gold-filigreed book studded with precious rubies. When he opened the cover, two portraits were inside, one of Bess, the other of William Cavendish.

"Splendor of God, you are still mourning Cavendish!" He ignored the sharp jealousy that rose up in him, set the book down on an occasional table, and lifted her into his arms. He carried her to a cushioned settle by the fireplace and sat down with her in his lap. With infinite tenderness he cradled her against his heart. "Bess, let go, let go."

He stroked her hair, marveling that the

firelight turned it to flame beneath his hands, and felt her body shudder. His arms tightened about her, holding her secure, holding her safe, and waited with infinite patience for the ice that froze her heart and her emotions to start to thaw. "You've been strong long enough. Let go...let me be your strength."

Her body began to shiver, in spite of the warmth of the fire, and he stroked her back, over and over. Gradually, he felt some of the rigidity leave her. In a little while he heard a low sob, then a long shuddering breath, and finally the floodgates opened, letting out all the dammed-up emotion that had been impossible for her to release until this moment.

She clung to him for an hour, crying and sobbing, then abruptly she stopped and was racked with a fit of hysterical laughter. Next she shot up from his knee and swept about the room in a terrible temper tantrum that encompassed the gamut of cursing, screaming, and breaking things. The storm was electrifying to the man who witnessed it. It was a magnificent, passionate rampage that made Gertrude's petulant tirades pale into insignificance.

Then Bess began to talk, confessing all her shortcomings, all the things that covered her with guilt, ending with an about-face, self-righteously defending herself. Finally, she crawled back into his lap and began to cry again.

Shrewsbury shook his head in tolerant wonder. Bess was the most passionate creature he had ever known, and he loved her beyond reason. He allowed her to cry for two more minutes, then said firmly, "That's enough, my beauty." He sat her up and began to unfasten the back of her gown.

"What are you doing?" she demanded.

"Undressing you."

Her tear-drenched eyes widened in shock. "You cannot do that!"

"Don't be utterly ridiculous, of course I can. I'm going to undress you and put you to bed." He went about the business matter-of-factly, as if he had undressed her every night of her life. Beneath her mourning gown and black petticoats she was wearing the plainest shift he'd ever seen. "Christ, is this some sort of a penance? You'll be wearing sack-cloth and ashes next."

She didn't laugh but looked at him woefully. He slipped off her stockings and garters with an iron control that amazed him and went to her wardrobe for a bedgown. He selected a soft lamb's wool that would keep her warm in her big, empty bed. He held it out to the fire for a minute before he thrust her arms into it and pulled it snugly about her middle. Then he swung her up into his arms and carried her through to her adjoining bedchamber. He pulled back the covers, tucked her into bed, then bent to light a fire in the marble fireplace. He set the chimney draught carefully, then went to all four windows and closed the heavy drapes. Outside, it had begun to snow, and he knew it would be a cold ride home. He lit a candle and carried it to the bed. Her eyes were closed in sleep; her lashes, still wet with tears, made dark shadows on her cheeks.

As he descended the great carved staircase, he saw three apprehensive faces gazing up at him. He knew it must be close to midnight, knew they had heard the screams and the crashes, and knew they expected some sort of explanation. Instead, he quieted their fears. "She's sleeping like a baby. Tomorrow I think she'll be back to her old self."

He climbed into the saddle and urged his horse from Chatsworth's warm stables. Suddenly, he didn't mind the snow at all. His blood ran hotly in his veins. The mere thought of Bess would keep the bitter cold at bay.

THIRTY-FOUR

Bess received many letters of genuine condolence, but the ones from her friends and acquaintances in London urged her to return to Court. Most of them offended her sensibilities, and she read them aloud to the women of her family.

"Just listen to what Anne Herbert writes: *There are no better hunting grounds for a husband than here at Court.* And listen to this from Lettice Knollys: *Do ask Her Majesty to make you a lady-of-the-privy-chamber. At the moment there is only Blanche Parry, Mary Stafford, and myself, and the men at Court are positively randy!*"

"The woman has no decency; hasn't she ever heard of a widow's mourning period?" her mother asked.

"They are out of fashion at Court. Rich widows are snapped up like trout flies," Bess explained.

Marcella remarked, "You will certainly make a very rich prize for some ambitious man, my dear."

"I shall *never* marry again. My money, my manors, and my lands will go to my children. My wealth will not go into a husband's coffers; I worked too damned hard for it." *Besides, there is only one man in the world who makes me feel alive, and he's been married since he was twelve.*

The month of April forced winter to loosen its icy grip, and spring came with a rush. Bess took full advantage of the milder weather and rode out each day inspecting her acres, her tenant farms, and their newly sown crops. Lambs were beginning to dot the rolling hills, and her heart filled with anticipation that wildflowers would soon blanket the meadows.

Bess was grateful that Shrewsbury had kept a discreet distance, but she knew it would not last. Each time she rode out, she was prepared to encounter him and knew in her heart that sooner or later he would come. The antagonistic relationship they had had for years had undergone a drastic change. He was still the most arrogant man alive, but she had seen the way he looked after his people, had seen the kindness he'd extended to her own tenants, and she knew firsthand his generosity. She finally acknowledged that Lord Talbot was a good man, a fair man, and a kind man. He was moral in every way, except where Bess was concerned. He always contended it was love they felt for each other, while she was adamant that it was lust. But now she began to suspect that her feelings ran too deeply. She must guard her heart against him at all costs—if it was not too late. He had allowed her three months' mourning, and she knew he would come soon.

Bess was surprised by the contents of a letter she received from her old friend Sir John Thynne. He told her that he was coming to Derbyshire to look at several properties. He wanted to see the finished Chatsworth and hinted that he would like to become her neighbor and renew their longstanding friendship. He told her that he had been considering a property called Abbot Stoke, in Lincolnshire east of Sheffield, but that the Earl of Shrewsbury had outbid him.

Bess tucked the letter away in her desk until she could think of a polite way to discourage him. She suspected that Sir John had more than friendship in mind. A beam of sunlight fell across her desk, and she realized she was far too restless to stay indoors. She decided to ride over to Meadowpleck and visit Francie and her new husband. Her daughter had been deeply saddened by the loss of her stepfather, and Bess hoped that the lovely spring weather would lift her spirits.

Heartily sick of wearing black, Bess donned a fuchsia petticoat before covering it with her black riding habit. On her way to the stables, she bent to pick a crocus and Shrewsbury's words came back to her: *The winter will pass...spring will come.*

Bess cantered toward the River Dove, breathing in the clear Derbyshire air as if it were the elixir of life. She spotted a baby rabbit and wondered if Francie would make her a grandmother this year. She didn't feel old enough to be a grandmother, but she was thirty-three, older if she admitted the truth.

She saw a horseman in the distance, and her heart did a somersault. Just for a moment she experienced panic. Should she turn tail and make a run for it? Bess laughed at her own foolishness. He'd give chase immediately *and* capture the quarry! She must never take the defensive with the compelling devil, or she'd be as powerless as yon baby rabbit.

She did not lessen her pace until he reined in and stood directly in her path. White teeth flashed in his dark face. "Such an eager welcome—how did you know I was coming, my beauty?"

Bess lifted her chin. "I'm not your beauty."

"You are, you know," he contradicted.

"And I had no idea you were coming!"

"You're a liar, Bess. You knew I'd come; mayhap not today, but soon."

Bess knew she must not lose her temper. She was a respectable widow; she would act sedately. Her lashes swept her cheeks. "Lord Talbot, I am in mourning."

He laughed out loud. "Your petticoat is showing."

"You black devil!" she spat, yanking her riding habit down to cover her boots.

"No need to pretend with me, Vixen—I know you inside and out."

Bess gasped, "You lewd, crude beast!"

He grinned wickedly. "That's what makes me a perfect match for you, my beauty."

Suddenly, Bess began to laugh. "Why do you taunt me apurpose when you know I get angry as fire?"

"I like to rouse your passion. Anger is part of your passion—the only part I can rouse without making love to you."

"Shrew, please stop."

"Bess, the open door to freedom lies before you. Surely you have the courage to cross the threshold and come to me?"

"God in heaven, you're like a pit bull when you want something."

"You would no longer be committing adultery, my beauty, so don't give me that excuse."

"But *you* would!" she cried.

He laughed. "Let me worry about my own sins, Bess." He dismounted and held up his arms to her. "Come, walk with me by the river. I want us to talk."

More than anything in the world she wanted to walk with him, talk with him, but she knew that if he put his arms about her and kissed her, passion would overwhelm them. "I will walk with you if you promise not to touch me and if you give me your word we will have a normal conversation that isn't unseemly."

His piercing blue eyes searched her face intently for a full minute to see if she was serious. Then he dropped his arms, allowing her to dismount on her own, and began a normal conversation. "I bought a piece of land in Lincolnshire—thought I might try my hand at building a house like Chatsworth."

"Abbot Stoke! Sir John Thynne told me in his letter you outbid him. He's interested in buying property in these parts."

"God damn Thynne, the only thing he's interested in is you!" His hands closed over her shoulders and he shook her. "Promise me you won't marry again! Christ, they'll all be sniffing about you like dogs after a bitch in heat."

Bess clenched her teeth. "This is unseemly!"

"Fuck unseemly! You'll have so many proposals, you'll be married again before the year's out!"

"Shrew, don't insult my intelligence. I shall never leg-shackle myself again! The moment I marry, all my wealth and lands become the property of my husband in the eyes of the law, and I know the law very well. What is mine I intend to keep for my lifetime, then it passes to my children. Every manor, every acre, every penny!"

"Thank God you have decided to use your brains. Marriage is like prison, a life sentence. It eats your soul; it's hell on earth."

"I'm sorry yours has been like that, Shrew. It can be hell, or it can be heaven."

His hand cupped her cheek. "Bess, I want my piece of heaven—I know I'll have it only with you."

She covered his hand with hers and held it while she touched her lips to his palm in an intimate gesture. How stubbornly blind she had been. As surely as she was his weakness, he was hers. Yet he was her strength too. He was everything she needed, everything she wanted. She could no longer go on denying it to herself. He had known for years it was inevitable; what had taken her so long?

Bess suddenly realized with clarity that after Cavendish she had been afraid to love again, for when love was taken away, it was too painful to bear. That's why she had married Syntlo, to keep her heart from being torn asunder again.

"What are we going to do?" she whispered.

His arm slipped about her and drew her close to his side possessively. "We are going to make plans to be together, of course. Whenever we can, wherever we can. I'm going to Court tomorrow. I'll take care of all the exchequer business and council business in short order, then we'll have the whole summer before us. I'll take you to Wingfield Manor, Rufford Abbey, Buxton Hall, Worksop, Welbeck...all of them. You have a passion for houses, Bess—I want you to get to know mine. Some you'll love, some you'll loathe, like Tutbury Castle. It's so damp, moss grows on the walls."

"Shrew, you go too fast."

"You will come?" he demanded intensely.

"Yes," she said softly, "I'll come, but aren't these places crawling with servants?"

"Each has a staff of caretakers, but nothing like the horde at Sheffield Castle. I'll make sure the servants are discreet. Neither of us wants a scandal that will reach the ears of our children."

"Nor our queen," Bess cautioned.

"Spend the afternoon with me. We'll ride up into the Peaks, away from civilization. We won't encounter a soul." He made the pledge to her as though he could control the universe, and in that moment they both believed he could.

As they galloped together, they laughed as if they were children without a care in the world. Then they climbed their mounts for almost two hours, going ever higher, until they crested the tallest peak. They reined in and sat in their saddles, holding hands, looking down at the rivers and valleys far below.

"Do you realize, my beauty, that between the two of us, we own as far as the eye can see?"

He sounded like a god standing on Olympus. The corners of her mouth lifted with the wonder of it all. "Does it intoxicate you?"

"Not nearly as much as you do, Vixen."

Two weeks later Bess received another letter from Sir John Thynne in the morning post. He told her he had heard a rumor that her old home, Hardwick Manor, was for sale, and if it were true he was most interested in the property.

Bess flung down the letter and summoned Robert Bestnay. "Find James. I need him immediately."

James Cromp was not only Chatsworth's steward, he had been a friend to Bess for more than sixteen years, because they kept no secrets from each other. When her secretary returned with Cromp, she questioned them both. "Has either of you heard a rumor about Hardwick being on the market?"

"Hardwick Manor and lands?" James asked in disbelief. "I would have come to you immediately."

"I've just paid the bills for all the repairs," Bestnay said. "It can't be true."

James looked hard at Bess. "I put in the last of the new stock last week.... I wouldn't put it past him."

"That rotten swine!" Bess cursed. "Robert, I want you to ride into Derby to the chambers of Messrs. Funk and Entwistle and bring one of them to Hardwick." She glanced at the library clock. "James and I will meet you there around two."

At precisely one o'clock, Bess, accompanied by Chatsworth's steward, arrived at Hardwick. She held on to her temper as she inspected the repairs on the beloved old manor, then asked her brother, James, to show her the new flocks of sheep and herds of cattle she had purchased. She asked him what crops he planned to sow and gave him every opportunity to confess what he had done. When he was not forthcoming, Bess asked casually, "What income did Hardwick bring in last year?"

James looked affronted at the question. "Nothing. You know I had to put a mortgage on it to get out of debt," he said defensively.

"With the new livestock, what income do you expect this year?" she asked innocently.

"The first year I'll do well to even make the mortgage payment. This place has never paid for itself, Bess."

"Then you don't think it's worth much?" she asked lightly.

James changed his tune immediately. "I wouldn't say that. The manor comes with five hundred acres and two tenant farms. It's strange you should ask; I was thinking only yesterday about putting it up for sale."

"Only yesterday? And what price were you thinking of asking?"

"Five hundred pounds."

Bess showed surprise. "So much?"

"I have to pay off the mortgage and have enough left to get a house in London."

"London, is it? That can be very expensive."

"It's none of your damned business!"

"None of my business?" Bess's voice was deceptively low. "When I've just paid for repairs on the manor and bought you all new livestock?"

"I didn't ask—you offered. Besides, you can afford it, Lady Moneybags."

"James, I could strike you. Not for the petty names you call me; I have a thick skin. It's your deceit that angers and sickens me! Behind my back you have put Hardwick up for sale with an agent in another county."

"Hardwick is my birthright—I can sell it if I wish!" he shouted.

"Then you can sell it to me. Ah, we have visitors, I see." They made their way from the stables back to the manor. "James, I believe you have met Master Entwistle, Attorney at Law? I asked him to meet me here to handle my purchase of Hardwick."

James was thrown off balance by the unexpected turn of events. He was also wary of his sister's attitude. She had such a temper, he was amazed that she wasn't cursing and shouting. But the presence of her attorney told him that she was serious about buying Hardwick. He knew she had money, so perhaps this was his golden opportunity to unload the place that for years had been a millstone about his neck. "Come in, gentlemen. I think we can do business, if the price is right."

"You say five hundred pounds is the asking price, James?"

He was prepared for a session of hard bargaining. Five hundred was a steep price for a property like Hardwick, and Bess was an extremely shrewd businesswoman. "Five hundred—worth every penny."

"What do you think, Cromp?" Bess asked her steward.

"In my opinion the price is too high," Cromp said flatly.

"Master Entwistle?" Bess asked politely.

The attorney frowned. "One pound an acre in these parts is unheard of. Ten or twelve shillings is the going rate for Derbyshire property. You have to take into account what the income will be, Lady St. Loe."

"Oh, I believe I can make the property pay, Master Entwistle. My stewards know what they are about. In this case I am prepared to be generous; I have no objection to five hundred pounds."

"Then it's a deal? Five hundred pounds?" James asked eagerly.

Bess nodded. "It's a deal. Draw up the papers, Master Entwistle; get the deed, James." Bess turned to her secretary. "Bestnay, you have those bills for the repair work on the manor. What is the final tally?"

"New roof and gutters, replacing the beams throughout, rebuilding a chimney, and repairing two walls and wainscoting comes to a round figure of a hundred pounds. Another fifty pounds was spent on outbuildings for a new cattle barn and sheep pens, making a tally of a hundred fifty pounds, my lady."

"Cromp, what did you pay for the new livestock?"

"A hundred pounds, my lady."

James turned purple in the face. "God damn you, Bess, that leaves me with only two hundred fifty pounds!"

"Oh James, didn't I tell you? I purchased your

mortgage. Master Entwistle, what is the amount of the mortgage on Hardwick?"

Entwistle cleared his throat. "Two hundred fifty pounds, Lady St. Loe."

"You bitch! You greedy, grasping jade! You've buried three husbands and taken their land; now you are trying to get *mine!*"

"Yours? I have the papers to prove that Hardwick is now mine."

"You clever bitch! You are just laughing at me on the inside!"

"No, James, on the inside I am crying." A great lump welled up in her throat, preventing her from speaking for a moment. She arose from the table and looked through the window at the ancient oak tree. It took only a minute or two to compose herself, then she walked back to the table. "Master Entwistle, be good enough to burn the mortgage on Hardwick and draw up an agreement of sale for five hundred pounds. As my brother said, Hardwick is worth every penny—at least to me."

The papers were drawn up, signed, and duly witnessed on the spot, and Bess left with the deed to Hardwick in her hand. "Would you register this for me immediately, Master Entwistle?"

"Yes indeed, Lady St. Loe." He tucked the deed into his leather portfolio. "Such dreadful news about the Countess of Shrewsbury."

"What news?"

James Cromp broke it to her. "The countess passed away last night. It was the talk of Derby this morning."

"And Shrewsbury away at Court, poor man. So sudden; it will be such a shock to him."

"Yes...a shock indeed," she managed, rendered almost speechless by the unexpected news. Bess rode back to Chatsworth in complete silence. For once she allowed her steward and secretary to take the lead, while she followed at a slower pace, lost in deep thought. The moment she arrived at Chatsworth, she sought out her mother and aunt and blurted, "Gertrude Talbot is dead!"

"When?" Bess's mother asked with disbelief.

"Apparently, it happened last night. Shrewsbury's at Court. It'll take him two or three days to get home. I don't know what to do. Should I go or stay away?"

Her mother looked at her oddly. "Of course you must go."

Marcella fixed Bess with a knowing look. "As a good neighbor and dear friend, the natural thing for you to do is go immediately. You must take our condolences and see if there is anything you can do to help until Shrewsbury can get home."

"Yes, of course. I'll ask Francie to ride with me; she's known young Anne Herbert all her life."

THIRTY-FIVE

Lady St. Loe, accompanied by her daughter, was met by Gertrude Talbot's bereaved ladies-in-waiting. They were red-eyed and in a state of complete agitation. Bess realized they were fearful for their appointments once Shrewsbury returned when one of them blurted in distress, "He hates the very sight of us."

One of the ladies said, "Would you care to see the countess, my lady? She is lying in the chapel."

"No, no," Bess demurred quickly. "We've come to see the children."

"The wicked young devils are in dire disgrace. They are the cause of this."

Bess was appalled at what they were saying. She looked about at the army of servants, who were busy draping the windows with black. "I'd like to see them, please."

"The young ladies have their own governesses, and the gentlemen their tutors. We have nothing to do with the young Talbots."

Bess put the woman in her place immediately. "That is a blessing for them. Inform whoever is in charge that I am here. Shrewsbury won't take it kindly that I've been kept in the entrance hall." Bess dealt with a whole battery of Talbot servants before she was taken to an upstairs sitting room and allowed a private conversation with the three young Talbot girls, Catherine, Mary, and Grace.

Twelve-year-old Catherine burst into tears, and Bess gathered her in her arms. "There, there, darling, get it all out."

"I want Father to come, but I'm afraid what he'll do to us."

"Catherine, my dear, he won't do anything. He loves you."

Grace, who was only nine, said, "We killed her; we're all going to burn in hell."

Bess's heart went out to the child, and she picked her up and sat her on her knee. "Grace, someone has been filling your head with nonsense. You didn't kill your mother. She has been ill for a long time, and God has taken her to heaven to live with the angels."

Grace looked up at Bess with solemn dark eyes as she digested the words. The door opened and Francis Talbot and his young bride, Anne Herbert, came in. "Oh, I'm so glad you came, Lady St. Loe," Anne said.

"You may call me Bess now that you're a married woman."

As Anne and Francie embraced, Grace made an announcement. "Bess says we didn't kill her—God did."

Young Gilbert Talbot joined them, and when they were all together, they found the courage to tell Bess of the terrible argument Francis had had with his mother and how the rest of them had joined in the shouting match to support their eldest brother. When his mother laid about him with her walking stick, she fell to the floor in a seizure and died.

Bess talked to them for hours, doing her best

to take away their guilt and assure them they would not be blamed. She knew they all felt considerably better for talking about it openly. Finally, Grace asked, "Will Father punish us?"

"No, my darling, he will not," Bess promised. "I shall write him a letter and leave it with your big brother Francis. Your father will likely be home tomorrow. He loves you all very much. Your welfare will be his only concern."

In the letter Bess told Shrewsbury that his children were blaming themselves for their mother's death. *I know you will take away their guilt, as you took away mine. You have an infinite supply of strength and compassion and an amazing ability to comfort. My heart goes out to the children, and to you also, Shrew.*

That night, as Bess lay abed, her thoughts were filled with him. Before he left for Court, they had pledged to become discreet lovers with a long, beautiful summer lying before them. Instead, Shrewsbury was returning to a dead wife, a big funeral, and a long, circumspect period of mourning with the eyes of the kingdom upon him. Gertrude's death had changed everything.

In spite of the fact that she felt cold and shivery, Bess finally fell asleep. Gradually, she felt a warmth against her back that slowly seeped into her limbs. She stretched as the delicious heat crept over her entire body. Suddenly, she realized he was there in the bed with her, and she turned eagerly into his arms. "You came," she whispered in wonder.

He took her whispered words into his mouth,

then murmured against her lips, "Of course I came."

She melted against the molten heat of his body and opened her mouth for his ravishing. Bess moaned with longing. He was easily the most attractive and sexually arousing man she had ever encountered. Her breasts and belly ached with need. She wanted his hands and his mouth on her body, she wanted his long, thick, marble-hard manroot filling her emptiness, but above all, above everything else in the world, she wanted to be Elizabeth, Countess of Shrewsbury.

"Are you mad?" He pulled away from her and quit the bed. "You're only a servant."

Bess sprang from the bed to confront him, uncaring that she was naked with her disheveled hair tumbling about her shoulders. "I am Bess of Hardwick—just as good, if not better, than any in the land!"

"Well, at least your name is apt," Lord Talbot drawled. "You certainly make my wick hard."

She flew at him and raked his dark, arrogant face. "Bastard! Whoreson! Ravisher!"

He began to laugh. "You openly invited me, Vixen."

"I've changed my mind; I won't fuck with you, Shrew. I won't be your mistress. No bedding without a wedding!"

"You set too high a price on yourself! You will never become Countess of Shrewsbury."

"I shall, I shall!" she vowed.

Bess awoke with a start and sat up in bed.

She was covered with a fine sheen of perspiration and didn't know where she was for a moment. She lit a bedside candle and saw with relief that she was at Chatsworth in her own beautiful bedchamber. The dream came flooding back to her. She realized it was made up of memories from the past. Shrewsbury had always desired her, but only as his mistress; it went without saying that she could never be anything more. She had deliberately suppressed her deep feelings for him for years, but now that he was a free man, she could deny them no longer. Her heart told her that she loved him. Then, as clearly as if he was in the room with her, Bess heard the man she loved say: *You will never become Countess of Shrewsbury.*

Bess drew up her knees and wrapped her arms about them. She sat hugging herself for an hour, deep in thought, then slowly the corners of her mouth lifted and she whispered into the flickering candlelight, "I shall, I shall!"

Two weeks had passed since Gertrude Talbot's large funeral, which all the northern nobility, except for Bess, had attended. Her married daughter, Frances, and husband, Henry Pierrepont, had represented her. Bess and Shrewsbury had not seen each other since the afternoon they had ridden alone in Derbyshire's magnificent peaks.

It was the last day of May, and twilight descended in the gardens of Chatsworth.

When Bess heard the dinner bell clang, she sent her daughters inside for their evening meal. She lingered in the rose garden, breathing in the heady fragrance produced by a warm afternoon followed by a cool evening. When she glanced up from admiring a full-blown bloom, Shrewsbury was coming toward her.

"How I've missed you," he said simply.

"How are the children?"

That they were her first concern told him exactly why they spoke of her on a daily basis. The older ones had such deep admiration for her, while little Grace was besotted with her, demanding to know why Bess couldn't be her mother. "They will be all right, I think. We've become closer. Thank you for talking to them. Your understanding words comforted them."

"I didn't attend the funeral; I couldn't bring myself to play the hypocrite."

"I understand that, but why are you avoiding me, Bess?"

"Everything has changed."

"Nothing has changed," he contradicted flatly.

"Will you take dinner with me?"

"Can we be private?"

"Of course."

Bess had been waiting for him to come. She had planned exactly what she would say, what she would do. Since she was a young girl she had been taught how to catch a husband, and the lessons she had learned would stand her in good stead now.

Bess's mother and Marcella offered the earl their condolences and politely withdrew. Bess ordered dinner be served in her private sitting room, then she took him directly upstairs. The moment the door closed, he reached for her.

"No, Shrew."

"Why the devil not?"

"We have to get something clear. Please sit down. This is difficult for me to say, Shrew; please try not to interrupt me."

He folded his long length in a leather chair and waited.

"I've been avoiding you because your status has changed. You are now a widower, and I want to make it clear from the outset that I won't marry you." She saw him slant an eyebrow at her but was relieved when he did not interrupt.

"I know that you covet the land I own in Sherwood Forest, and I know you would love to own Chatsworth. I'm fully aware of the benefits you'd reap from a business merger between us. Our land runs together and would not need to be managed separately, but for the first time in my life, I have a considerable income and no debts to speak of. I am a wealthy widow who has already received two proposals of marriage, so I don't want another one from you."

"Who the devil—" His words were cut short by the appearance of a footman who brought their dinner.

Bess hid her amusement at the perfect

timing of the interruption. "We'll serve ourselves. That will be all," she instructed the
footman, who bowed and withdrew.

"Don't ask me who the proposals came
from. I don't want you to get angry—you are
far too possessive of me as it is." She indicated
the food. "Come and eat before it gets cold."

He came up out of the chair and took two
long strides, swallowing the distance that
separated them. "To hell with the food. Was
it John Thynne?" he demanded.

"No, it wasn't Sir John, though his correspondence hints at it." She smiled up at him
and laid her hand upon his cheek. "It doesn't
matter who it was, for you have all my heart."

He groaned and enfolded her in his arms.
"Bess, Bess, don't do this to me—you know
I've loved you forever. I don't want your
lands, I just want you."

Men want what they cannot have, Bess
reminded herself sternly, and will move heaven
and earth to get it—I devoutly hope, she
added, crossing her fingers. "Darling," she whispered her first real endearment to him, "if you
start kissing me, we'll never get to the food.
We won't often be able to dine so intimately;
let's enjoy it while we have the chance." Bess
knew that while they talked and ate, she had
a small measure of control, but once he started
to make love to her, all her control would be
swept away by his passion.

Beneath the silver covers were a brace of
plump partridge crisped in wine, followed
by a venison pasty, redolent with leeks and

herbs. She served him a hearty helping of each and poured them wine. She was acutely aware of his gaze, which never left her face. "For all the notice you are taking of your food, I could have served sheep brains."

"I'm starving for you; all I can taste is breast." He threw down his napkin and moved around the table. Then he lifted her up and slid beneath her.

"I'm not finished," she protested breathlessly as the heat from his thighs seeped up through the material of her gown.

"I'm not started." He lifted her hair from the nape of her neck and set his lips to it. He was already full and hard, but when he felt his cock throb with every heartbeat, he began to lick and suck her neck, unable to resist a passionate love bite.

Bess gasped as his hands came up beneath her breasts and cupped them possessively, loving the exquisite sensations he aroused as she felt her nipples harden with desire. "Darling, there's no need for haste. I want you to stay all night." She knew her words inflamed him, for his hands slid from her breasts to lift her skirts and stroke her naked thighs above her gartered stockings.

"I've waited an eternity to hear those words from your lips." The food was forgotten as his fingers stroked her. His hungry mouth took possession of hers, and as his insistent tongue slid inside, he thrust a long finger inside her sheath and thrust deeply, rhythmically. The way her sugared walls closed over his finger told him her body responded instantly, hungrily, to his foreplay, and he thanked God for this woman whose passion matched his own.

She clung to him as he brought her to shuddering climax with his fingers and knew this was just a foretaste of the dark velvet pleasuring he would give her this night. She felt his impatient hands on the fastenings of her gown and knew that any moment he would rip it from her in his haste.

She slipped from his knee and smiled as he protested. "I want to undress for you. Curb your impatience and watch me. It gives me unbelievable pleasure to see the desire blaze up in your eyes when you look at my body."

The intense, hard look on his face thrilled her as she moved about the chamber, drawing the heavy brocade drapes across every window. Next she lit a long taper and set ablaze the dozens of candles in ornate silver candelabra. Then, very slowly, with sensuous deliberation, she unfastened the sedate gray silk gown and let it slither in a pool about her feet.

The impact of her tangerine undergarments made him draw in a swift breath of appreciation. Her clothes matched her personality perfectly tonight. Beneath her serene exterior lay a riot of flagrantly shocking color that revealed her passionate sexuality. Then, beneath that, he suspected there were dark erotic layers whose depths had never yet been plumbed.

She slowly stepped out of her petticoat, and as she flung it away, it flashed an arc of brilliant color across the candlelit chamber. She stood before him now, her sinuous body clad only in a short shift and black lace stockings. As she inched the shift up her thighs, she uncovered startling tangerine garters that held up her black stockings, but even more arresting was the riot of red-gold curls that covered her high mons.

Bess slowly licked her lips in a deliberately provocative gesture as she paused for a full minute before lifting off her shift to reveal her breasts. She knew the arousing effect they had on him and knew the wait would heighten his anticipation.

He looked his fill, in a growing agony of need but thoroughly enjoying the splendid show Bess put on for him. Her body was so lush, it spoke a language of its own, crying out to be mated often, and mated well. And it promised untold rewards for the man bold enough to accept the challenge of arousing and satisfying the towering passion she had held in check for so long.

"You make the most beautiful mistress any man could wish for in his wildest dreams."

"Shrew, I don't want to be your mistress. That's a demeaning position where a man pays a woman for sexual favors and only a small step up from being a whore. I want us to be lovers, equal in every way and completely free in every way. Promise?"

He was ready to promise her anything and give her the earth as well. He stripped off his clothes in a fever of need and tossed them away impatiently as he stalked his prey. He gathered her up and lifted her onto his engorged phallus. He did not need to tell her to wrap her legs about his back. He could feel the texture of the black lace stockings against his skin, as well as the heated flesh of her naked thighs where the stockings left off. The contrast was so erotically arousing, he plunged up into her with a savage thrust and felt her nails claw his back. Her velvet sheath lured him deeper, and, unable to remain standing a moment longer, he took her to the floor so that he could bury himself all the way inside her. She felt like scalding honey, and his balls tightened so pleasurably, he growled deep in his throat like a wolf with its mate.

It was such a swift, dominant possession, Bess writhed beneath his big powerful body, relishing the fierce hunger he unleashed as he pounded into her, holding nothing back, like a rampant male animal. The mating became ferocious, with both of them making fierce demands upon each other. Bess loved the things he did to her, loved his hard hands on her body and the way they made her feel. He knew how to arouse her passion to madness. Her sheath gripped him convulsively as he buried his maleness inside her, harder and deeper with every savage plunge.

When her moans turned to gasps and a scream began to build in her throat, her lover took possession of her mouth, taking her love cries into himself, muffling her vocal response to keep them private from any who might be awakened by their passionate coupling. He felt her first flutters, knowing she was building to orgasm, and timed his climax accordingly. They spent together in an explosion that robbed them of breath and coherent thought. Then they collapsed together, his great weight pinning her to the floor as she sprawled beneath him in wanton abandon.

Shrew withdrew his weight and sat back on his heels. "That was spectacular, my love, and well worth the wait." He stroked her breasts, softening now with surfeit. "Your body is so lush, I want to watch you walking about without your clothes."

When Bess hesitated, he said, "Surely, you're not shy with me?"

"No, love. Your anointing was so thorough, I'm full of you."

He laughed. "I'm sorry—it's been so long." He picked up her goblet of wine and a clean napkin. "Open for me, beauty." He dipped in the linen and watched with avid eyes as she let her knees fall apart, then arched her mons for him. She shuddered as he laved her in wine, then dabbed her dry. "Let me carry you to bed."

"I thought you wanted to watch me walk."

"Later—the wine has given me other ideas." He lifted her high against his heart and carried her through to the adjoining chamber. He laid her on the bed and, lifting one of her legs, removed the black lace stocking with its bright garter. Then he lifted her other leg and did the same. He kissed her bare toes, then drew the tip of his tongue along the high arch of her sole. "First, I want to watch you writhe again."

Bess drew in a swift breath, knowing where his tongue would lead. She was not disappointed, though he teased her unmercifully with the length of time it took to reach his goal. But once he did, she couldn't believe how quickly he was able to arouse her again. As she watched his dark head moving between her legs and felt the thrusts of his powerful tongue, the intimacy of the act drove her wild. When her climax came, it was so hard and fast she arched high off the bed, thrusting her mons against his hungry mouth. When he withdrew his tongue and covered the inside of her thighs with kisses, she thought her very bones would melt. When she could speak again, she said, "That felt so lovely, I want to do it to you. Get the wine; I want to drive you wild."

Shrewsbury came up out of a deep sleep and his pulses began to race the moment he knew whose bed he occupied, whose woman's scent enveloped him, and whose lips brushed against his. To be awakened by a kiss from Bess was a fantasy he'd indulged in for years. His cock began to fill, and he reached for her with joy. "Sweetheart, I'll never have enough of you."

Bess laughed softly. "Darling, that's very flattering, but I woke you because it's four o'clock. You must go now."

He groaned as her words rubbed harshly against the grain of what he wished to do. "I can't leave you," he protested stubbornly.

"You must. Though I am mistress of Chatsworth, I don't believe I can allow you to tuck your long legs beneath the breakfast table across from my mother and Marcella."

He groaned again, realizing the truth of her words. Their liaison must be kept secret to guard her good name and to protect the children. Reluctantly, he swung his legs from the bed as Bess lit the bedside candles. His eyes began to search out his clothes, scattered in haste across the chamber, but his gaze was drawn back to the woman on the bed. She reached for her bedgown, and he watched her cover her beautiful breasts and shoulders. "If I had my way, I'd never let you get dressed again. I'd keep you naked in a locked chamber whose only furnishing was a bed."

Bess smiled. "A lavish compliment indeed. Now I'll give you one." She came around to his side of the bed and sank to the carpet between his naked thighs. "For the first time in years, perhaps for the first time in my life, I feel replete. I enjoy matching you in sensuality. Your body has the ability to satisfy mine, as you always promised me it would, and I thank God for it."

He cupped her face between his hands. There were so many things he wanted to say, but there was no time. "You are a part of me. When can I come again?"

"Darling, you cannot. June arrives with the dawn. My sons are finished college; they will be home any day. They are far too old and wise for us to pull the wool over their eyes."

"Hell and damnation!" he swore, searching his brain for a solution to his dilemma. He could feel her lush breasts brush against his testes and he wanted to hold her forever. "I'll make Rufford or Worksop a safe haven for us. I'll send you a note."

As Shrewsbury rode home in utter frustration, his thoughts were obsessed by the woman he had just left. She might be replete, but he was not, and strangely it had little to do with sex. Making love with Bess most of the night had certainly left him sated, but at this moment he was more dissatisfied than he'd ever been in his life. He wanted to be with her morning, noon, and night. He wanted to talk with her, make her laugh, ride over their acres together, eat with her, bathe with her. He wanted her to share his houses, share his children, share his life. He wanted to carry her to bed every night and wake up every morning with her beside him.

He longed to cover her with jewels, swathe her in fur, and shout to the world that she was his and his alone. He wanted to possess her, body and soul, and he knew he would not know a moment's peace until she fully committed to him and vowed her eternal love. A foul oath fell from Shrewsbury's lips. All Bess wanted was her bloody freedom! She had made him promise they would be lovers and nothing more.

His knees gripped his stallion's belly and his resolve hardened. She thought she could wrap him about her little finger. She had extracted the promise so she would be free to leave him any time she chose, and in a vulnerable moment he had given his word. Well, some promises were made to be broken, and this was one of them. Freedom was the last thing he'd let her have. He would mount a relentless campaign and force her to yield to his wishes. He would be satisfied with nothing less than complete and unconditional surrender.

THIRTY-SIX

Bess was well aware that George Talbot, Earl of Shrewsbury, was more than a match for her. If anyone in the world had a stronger will than she, it was Shrewsbury. He was so dominant, he even imposed his wishes on Elizabeth Tudor when the mood took him.

At the moment Bess knew that Shrewsbury was in thrall with her, but she also realized that he wouldn't let her have her own way for long. If she wanted that wedding ring on her finger, she would have to plan her strategy with cunning. He had been trapped in a loveless marriage most of his life, and now that he was at last free, it would take extremely clever maneuvering to get him to put his neck in the noose again.

Bess acknowledged that if Shrewsbury had not suddenly become a widower, she would have been more than content to be secret lovers for the rest of their lives. Wild horses could not have dragged her into a fourth marriage; she was far too ambitious for her children to pour the wealth she had accumulated into a husband's coffers. But Shrewsbury was different. He was the wealthiest and most powerful peer in the land, with eight principal houses and castles, in addition to the ones in London and at Chelsea on the riverside. He owned vast tracts of land in five counties and was lord lieutenant of three of them. He was also her heart's desire.

Bess asked herself, what was the irresistible lure that attracted her? Was it the man himself, his wealth, his houses, his power, or his noble title? She was honest enough to admit that she was in love with all of these things. He represented the greatest challenge of her life. Not only did she want him with all her heart, she needed him to love her enough to make her Elizabeth, Countess of Shrewsbury.

He sent her a gift of rubies. It was an exquisite brooch in the shape of a crescent moon. Bess smiled her secret smile and pinned it to her gown so that it curved provocatively about one of her nipples. Two days later Bess received his note inviting her to meet him at Worksop Manor. She blithely ignored it. A second note arrived, furiously demanding why she had not kept their rendezvous. She sent a very sweet reply explaining that his invitation had come too late for her to change her plans.

He wrote again, giving her the time and place for their next tryst, and Bess read his towering impatience between the lines. Though she longed to go to him, Bess was determined to listen to her head and not her heart. She wrote back and explained that her sons had just arrived home and that it would be impossible for her to get away.

His next letter was not an invitation, it was an ultimatum. He threatened that if she did not come to him at Worksop, he would come to her, no matter the consequences. The next day Bess arrived at Sheffield on horseback with all three of her daughters in tow. Shrewsbury greeted her with formality, his blue eyes blazing his anger at the games she was playing.

Bess hid her amusement. "It was such a beautiful day for a ride. June is such a lovely month, don't you think?"

"Too lovely to waste," he said pointedly. "It's almost over!"

Her heart hammered at the sight of him, and she was thrilled to the core that he could not hide his frustration. "My daughters wanted to visit yours, and of course Francie and Anne Herbert have been friends all their lives. Since they are both newlyweds, they will have much to talk about."

"My son and Anne may be married, but

they have separate households here at Sheffield until they become old enough to cohabit," he said repressively.

"Shrew, they are mad in love. 'Tis cruel to keep them apart. Still, they do say abstinence builds character." She watched the muscle in his jaw clench like a lump of iron.

Bess saw Grace peeping over the banister of the ornate staircase and called to her gaily, "Don't be shy, darling. We've come especially to see you."

Grace ran down the stairs and Bess caught her and swung her around in the air. "Don't you ever slide down the banister? That's what I love to do."

Grace looked at her father's forbidding face and said, "We're not allowed to."

"But your father loves to play games!" Bess said mischievously.

"Not *this* particular game," he warned Bess.

She chose to ignore his warning, thoroughly enjoying the undercurrents of sexual tension that coiled between them. Bess saw his other daughters and Anne hovering up on the landing. "Why don't we all go for a ride? You can show me about Sheffield's great park; it's too lovely to spend the day indoors."

The young ladies were so eager to join Bess and her daughters that Shrewsbury had little choice in the matter. At the stables his two older sons, Francis and Gilbert, decided to join the party. "I should have brought my sons along. You boys would have such great fun together. Why don't you come and visit them at

Chatsworth?" she suggested, ignoring Shrewsbury's grimface.

"May we come too, Bess?" Grace begged.

"It's very rude to invite yourself, and you must
not call the lady *Bess,*" her father said sharply.

"I gave the girls permission to call me Bess,
Lord Talbot, though you may call me Lady St.
Loe if you prefer." She watched him grind his
teeth and knew she was teasing him unmercifully. "My lord, you are welcome at
Chatsworth anytime, providing you bring
your lovely daughters of course."

They all set off at a gallop across the park,
but Shrewsbury took a firm hold of Bess's reins,
forcing her to remain at his side. "I don't
like this game, Vixen."

"That is obvious. Your face is as dark and
forbidding as a thundercloud. Are you not
pleased to see me, after I rode all the way to
Sheffield?"

"You did not need to come all this way.
Worksop Manor is only half the distance."

"Oh, darling, don't you think I'd like to be
at Worksop this moment? Just the two of us?
Don't you know how I long to be in your
arms, to have you carry me to bed and make
love to me all night?" Bess cupped her breasts
and brushed her thumb across the ruby brooch
that encircled her erect nipple. "I ache for you.
Every night I lie abed, tossing, turning,
burning for you, and when I finally fall asleep,
my dreams are so shamefully carnal, the blush
never leaves my cheek." She knew her words
were convincing, because she spoke the truth.

"Bess, you must come to me! You were never meant to be a nun, and I'm living like a bloody monk!"

"It's difficult when we must be so careful. For me to stay away all night would prompt questions."

"Then come to me through the day," he demanded in desperation.

"At nightfall will you let me go?"

"If I say no, you won't come."

She gazed at his mouth. "Then lie to me," she begged.

Grace turned her small palfrey and cantered back to them. She looked at Bess with great dark eyes and said earnestly, "Father says you can't be my mother unless you marry him."

"Grace, not one more word!" her father ordered.

"It's all right, Shrew. Children need to have their questions answered. Grace, your father has to observe a mourning period to show his respect for the mother of his children."

"How long is a mourning period?"

"Traditionally, it is a year."

"A year! I can't wait a year!" Grace cried.

"That's enough, Grace. Go back to your sisters. Lady St. Loe and I wish to speak privately."

The child obeyed her father, albeit reluctantly.

A heavy silence hung between them. When Bess summoned the courage to glance at him, he was looking at her with speculative eyes. "Bess—"

"Don't you dare to ask me!" she warned.

"Don't you see it would be the answer to everything?"

Bess felt as if a great red rose bloomed in her heart, and her knees turned to water. Her plan was working, he was on the verge of asking her, but of course it would be on his terms. How tempting he was! If only she could put her children second to her own desires. As the woman and the mother warred within her, her resolve hardened; Shrewsbury's terms would not be nearly good enough for Bess. With a great effort she schooled her features and looked him directly in the eyes. "You have stolen my heart, and I freely give you my body. Isn't that enough, Shrew? Must all I have achieved go to enriching the vast Talbot empire?"

"Splendor of God, Bess, how many times must I tell you I don't want your wealth? Don't you realize how much you would gain?"

"I wouldn't gain anything unless you died, and I cannot bear to think about that." Suddenly, the reality of her words were brought home to her. A cold hand squeezed her heart and withered the rose that bloomed there. "Let's go on as we are. I vow I'll come to you this week at Worksop. Get rid of the servants."

"Tomorrow?" he demanded.

"No, no. At the end of the week...I'll come Friday."

"Swear it!"

Before Bess and her daughters took their leave, Francis Talbot and his bride, Anne Herbert, cornered her.

"Bess, will you use your influence with Lord Talbot? We want to be allowed to set up our own household," Anne pleaded.

"I shall be sixteen soon. I'm a man, yet Father treats me as a child. We are chaperoned day and night. We never have a moment alone together without the prying eyes of a hundred servants!"

Bess's heart went out to them. Privacy for a Talbot was a rare commodity. "Francis, use your ingenuity. You are heir to a half dozen places in the vicinity that are far more private than Sheffield. Take your bride for a ride in the country to one of the Talbot estates that is more secluded. Some of the manors are quite romantic, I believe, with only skeleton staffs."

On Friday morning Bess chose a favorite deep purple riding habit and selected outrageously frilly lavender undergarments to go beneath it. She gathered a few toilet articles, her hairbrush and kid slippers, and carried them down to the stables. She chose a sidesaddle, as befitted a lady, and rode out from Chatsworth before her family awakened.

Though the hour was extremely early when

she arrived at Worksop, Shrewsbury was there before her. A sigh escaped her lips as his powerful hand reached up to grasp her mount's bridle and lead her into the stables.

"You look ravishing, Vixen."

A sultry laugh escaped her lips. "And a damned good thing I do, since that's clearly your intent."

"Ready when you are, milady." He held up his arms.

Bess glanced about the stables.

"No grooms; we are absolutely alone."

Her breath caught in her throat at the mere thought of being alone with him in a stable. He wore tight leather riding breeches and a white shirt, unbuttoned to the navel. Her mouth went dry at the sight of such rampant virility, and she went down into his waiting arms in a flurry of lavender petticoats.

His mouth, already hard with anticipation, took possession of hers and she opened her lips, inviting his tongue to master her. She could feel the hard shank of his thigh thrust between her legs, and she gripped it with her own thighs and pressed her breasts into the solid wall of his chest. The kiss robbed her of all strength, and when he withdrew his arms to look down at her, she staggered a little. With a husky laugh she raised her skirts to her knees. "You'll have to help me with my riding boots."

He stared at them, then swallowed hard. "Christ, no. I want everything else off, but we'll keep the riding boots on for now." He picked her up and carried her to a stall piled high with fragrant hay, then he laid her back and carefully undressed her, kissing every delicious part of her body as he exposed it, until she lay completely naked except for the black riding boots.

She watched through half-closed eyes as he stripped off his own clothes, revealing the magnificent, hirsute body that had invaded her dreams since she was a young girl. He kissed the inside of her thighs above the boots, then moved up to her belly, teasing and licking her navel with the tip of his tongue. When he tasted her breasts, she knew it gave him untold pleasure. He toyed with them endlessly, weighing them on his palms, stroking them until they quivered, tonguing the bright tips until they turned into hard little berries, then sucking them whole into his mouth as if they were succulent fruit. Slowly he raised himself up and mounted her, and her boot-clad legs wrapped about his lithe torso.

"I swear I'm so hard, I could break off inside you."

"Mmm, then I could take it home and pleasure myself day and night. I've always wanted a cock."

"Vixen, you say the most outrageous things, and they make me insatiable for you."

"*Insatiable* is a lovely word, and a stable is surely one of the most erotic places there is to make love." She reached down to stroke the intimate place where their bodies joined, then she encircled him with her fingers and squeezed rhythmically. "The smell of the stable, the prickle of the hay under my bottom, the sight of your brute stallion trying to nip my mare's neck with his savage teeth—they do wild and wicked things to my blood."

"Tell me what you want, beauty."

"When you've ridden me, I want to ride you, you black devil!"

It was a unique experience for Shrewsbury to be alone at one of his manors, and the pair of lovers took complete advantage, enjoying the gardens, the trout stream, and even the kitchen. He watched, entranced, as Bess, clad only in her frilly petticoat, cooked them an omelet garnished with herbs from the garden for their lunch. They had also picked strawberries for their dessert, and as Bess began to wash them at the sink, his arms slipped about her to distract her with caresses. Laughing, she fed him strawberries between kisses and lamented that they had no cream.

"I'll give you cream," he promised wickedly, sliding his bold hand up her bare leg beneath the lavender silk.

With a squeal she deftly eluded him, and he chased her from the kitchen, along a passageway covered with portraits of his Talbot ancestors, and up a great winding staircase. When she reached the top, he was almost upon her, and knowing there were only bedchambers to run to, she climbed onto the polished banister and slid all the way back down to the ground floor.

He was after her in a flash, his long legs descending the steps two at a time. He vaulted the last six in time to catch her as she went sailing off the carved newel post. They fell in a heap of petticoat, tangled legs, and laughter, sprawled together like children who had suddenly found themselves without supervision. As they lay catching their breath he said, "I think we need an afternoon nap."

"I think we need a bath."

"We can do both, if you'll come upstairs with me."

"Persuade me," she purred.

"If you come up to the master bedchamber, I have something for you I know you'll love," he tempted.

"Is it big?"

"Would I give you anything small?"

"Is it hard?"

"Would I give you anything soft?" he teased.

"I'm baffled; give me another hint."

"Mmm, let's see—it's round, it has a thick shank, and it will bring you endless pleasure." He stroked the backs of his fingers across the swell of her breasts. "The sight of it alone will make you gasp."

"It's oversize, like everything else about you?"

"I promise it will be a snug fit."

"How can I resist?" She rolled to her knees, set her slippered feet to the priceless oriental stair carpet, and took off up the steps, knowing he would catch her before she reached the top. The corners of her mouth went up as she felt one hand slip about her waist, while the other slid up her petticoat to fondle her bottom.

"Did you know you have a heart-shape bum?"

"I didn't know an earl was allowed to use such common language."

"There's lots of things you don't know about me yet."

She turned and wound her arms about his neck, fitting her lush body to his. "Will you teach me?"

He picked her up, carried her into the master bedchamber, and sat her on the edge of the bed. "It will take me a lifetime. Now, close your eyes and hold out your hand."

Bess did as he bid her and wriggled her fingers suggestively, thinking she knew exactly what he would put in her hand. But Bess was wrong. As her fingers closed over the ring, her eyes flew open in surprise to see a huge rose-cut diamond, surrounded by emeralds. "Oh, it's exquisite!" She slipped it onto her finger and found it a perfect fit. Though suddenly her heart was singing, her head told her she must make a token protest. Her eyes sought his. "Shrew, I can't accept a ring. It's a symbol that irrevocably binds me to you." She held her breath, hoping he would say that was exactly what he intended, that he loved her madly and couldn't live without her.

"Damn it, Bess. It's a love token, nothing more! I want you to have the very best. Don't deny me the pleasure of giving you things. You have beautiful hands—I want to see your fingers sparkling with jewels."

She ran the tip of her tongue about her lips. "I would never deny you the things that give you pleasure." In one sensuous movement she lifted off her petticoat and let it slide to the floor beside the bed.

During the next hour Bess made good her promise, yielding everything to the man who aroused such heady, violent passion in her. Finally, though they were both sated, he could not bear to withdraw from her warm, languorous body, and they lay together with her legs still cradling him and his face buried in her glorious hair. In this intimate position they drifted to the edge of slumber, isolated from the universe in a cocoon of love.

They did not hear the ardent voice of the young man who opened the door of Worksop and lifted his young bride over the threshold. They did not hear the soft laugh of the young woman as she shyly allowed her husband to take bold liberties with her.

"Francis, what about the servants?" she whispered nervously.

"Anne, sweetheart, we'll use the master bedchamber. If there are any servants about, they'll think it's my father in there, and they won't dare open the door."

She allowed him to coax her up the winding staircase, longing to be alone with him in a room with an actual bed, yet afraid of the demands his powerful young body would make on her. His possessive hands were already on her breasts, and she could see the bulge between his legs. Outside the door she tried to pull back.

"Don't be afraid, Anne. I won't hurt you; I love you." With determination Francis Talbot swung his bride into his arms and turned the doorknob.

As the heavy oak door swung open, it creaked on its hinges. Bess's lashes fluttered on her cheeks. Her lover stirred and brushed his lips against her temple.

"Father!" Francis Talbot blurted out in horror, setting his bride's feet to the floor.

Shrewsbury rolled off Bess and yanked the cover over her nakedness. "Splendor of Christ, what are you doing here?" Shrewsbury thundered. "Don't bother to tell me; it's obvious, you young lecher!"

Anne gasped and ran like a frightened rabbit.

"Oh, no," Bess breathed as she realized what she had done. What were the odds of them coming to the same place on the same day? The moment Shrewsbury absented himself from Sheffield, Francis had obviously seized the moment.

Francis stood his ground. "I wouldn't have come if I'd known you were here with your whore!"

Shrewsbury shot from the bed and grabbed his son by the scruff of his neck. "Apologize!" he demanded.

Red in the face, Francis looked truly sorry.

"Forgive me, Lady St. Loe, I had no idea you were Father's mistress."

His father cuffed him across the ear. Francis staggered slightly and fled downstairs.

"Shrew, go after him. None of this is his fault." Bess padded from the bed and picked up his clothes. "Go, darling. I'll speak with Anne." She flung on her petticoat and searched the upstairs chambers until she found the young woman she had known since Anne was a baby.

"I'm so sorry, Bess."

"Anne, what can I say? We are in love, just like you and Francis. Come help me dress and we'll talk."

Wearing her purple riding habit, with every hair brushed and coiled in place, Bess entered the downstairs drawing room, holding the bride's hand. When Anne saw the intimidating figure of her dark, dominant father-in-law, she began to tremble, but Bess squeezed her hand to imbue her with courage. "Don't be angry with them, Shrew. It's all *my* fault. I suggested they come here."

His blue eyes narrowed, and his voice took on an icy tone. "I've just explained to Francis that we are going to be married. Show them your betrothal ring, darling." His eyes blazed their accusation, but somehow he managed to keep his tongue clamped between his teeth.

The moment Francis and Anne left Worksop, Bess and the earl had a towering row. She was covered with guilt for inadvertently causing their sexual relationship to be revealed but was furious that he thought her so devious and calculating, she had done it apurpose so she would be compromised. She slapped his dark, cynical face and departed without another word.

THIRTY-SEVEN

The next morning Shrewsbury arrived at Chatsworth, determined to settle matters once and for all. With blazing eyes Bess took him into the library and carefully closed all the doors. He propped himself on the edge of her carved oak desk, while she paced up and down the room like a tigress. She knew she must convince him that she had not set a trap for him, so she snatched the offensive position before he did.

"Why did you have to lie to them? If you did it out of some ridiculous chivalrous notion that it would save my reputation, you have insulted me. If it was to save your own face, you've just made matters worse."

"I didn't lie to them; we are going to be married," he said implacably.

She knew by his tone that he would have it all his own way. He would concede her nothing. He was a law unto himself, and she protested with the only argument she could think of. "You are the Earl of Shrewsbury. You cannot marry the minute your wife dies; the scandal would be horrendous! My reputation would be blackened beyond redemption. They would say I trapped you into marriage because I am an avaricious bitch! My own brother accuses me of marrying one man after another to acquire property." She stopped before him and threw out her hands. "If I married you my name would be dragged through the mud from one end of England to the other."

He reached out and took firm hold of her hands, forcing her to stop pacing. He spoke quietly. "Women will always gossip about you, Bess, because they are jealous of your beauty and envious of your sexual attraction." He slanted a dark brow. "Do you really care what people think or say about you?"

"I don't care what they say, so long as it's true! I am no plaster saint! I freely admit to being ambitious. But what nobody seems to realize, including you, is that I am more ambitious for my children than I am for myself! Don't you think I would love to be Countess of Shrewsbury and lord it over everyone?"

"Then marry me, for Christ's sake!"

"No, Shrew, I'm returning to Court," she said quietly.

"I forbid it!" He jumped up, grabbed her by the shoulders, and shook her like a rag doll. "I forbid it, do you hear me?" He was in a towering rage and determined to show her who was master. "At Court you attract men like bees to a honeypot! I let you escape me once; I'm not such a bloody fool as to let it happen again!"

"Are these arrogant commands your way of saying that you love me, you black devil?"

"Oh, Vixen, you know I love you—I adore you!" His arms enfolded her and held her tight against his heart. "If you'll marry me you can have your damned lawyers draw up any kind of a marriage settlement you want. If you're happy, I'm happy."

"I'm going to be the next Countess of Shrewsbury!" Bess made the announcement to her mother, Jane, and Marcella as if she didn't quite believe it.

Her mother and Jane were absolutely speechless. Marcella looked at her with startled admiration. "What a clever girl you are, Bess. I told your mother when you were still a child that you would be our salvation, and my prophesy has always proven true."

"But Shrewsbury is the most powerful earl in the land," her mother protested. "Are you certain his intentions are honorable?"

Bess threw back her head and laughed. "I know the difference between a proposition and a proposal—I should, I've had more than my share of both!"

"Bess!" her mother reproved. "You'll have to watch your tongue and your temper, or you'll lose him, mark my words."

"We are well-suited. 'Tis a match made in heaven!" Bess laughed as if she had just said the funniest thing in the world and hurried back up to the library to write her letter to her lawyers.

The women looked at each other and shook

their heads in disbelief. "Do you think it's true?" asked her mother doubtfully.

Jane said, "It's quite possible. Bess isn't like other people; she's unique."

"But they are both so dominant and willful. Their strong personalities are so totally unsuited, they will clash every day of their married life." Her mother shuddered. "What could possibly have attracted him?"

Marcella pursed her lips. "It's the breasts— it's got to be the breasts. There is no other answer!"

It was now impossible for Bess and Shrewsbury to see each other alone. There could be no flagrant behavior between the earl and the lady he intended to make the Countess of Shrewsbury. Though the upcoming marriage was not yet common knowledge, once their families, their lawyers, and their servants knew, there was no hope of keeping it secret.

Bess gathered her sons and daughters together and gave them the momentous news that Lord Talbot, Earl of Shrewsbury, was going to be their stepfather. Her sons were aware of the great power and prestige of Shrewsbury, who had made it possible for William to be accepted at Cambridge. Her young daughters were more interested in the prospect of having three new sisters to play with.

When Shrewsbury told his children he was going to marry Lady St. Loe, they were overjoyed. The older ones would have a confidante and a buffer against their autocratic father, and the younger ones would have a mother who not only laughed and played games but actually gathered them in her arms and sat them on her knee.

At Bess's insistence Shrewsbury brought his family to visit at Chatsworth for a few days, and little Grace Talbot fell in love with the place. It was such a beautiful new house, in stark contrast to the massive and gloomy Sheffield Castle and the fortified Wingfield, where she had spent most of her life.

Bess and Francis Talbot became allies when she promised to see that he and his bride would get their own wing at Sheffield once she was officially his stepmother. And when she saw that her eldest son, Henry Cavendish, and Gilbert Talbot were becoming fast friends, she promised to persuade Shrewsbury to allow them a grand tour of Europe, as the earl had had in his youth.

Bess seemed undaunted at the prospect of doubling the size of her family and becoming mother of twelve, and to help Shrewsbury get used to the idea, she suggested they make a progress together that would include all her properties and all his. When Bess saw romantic Rufford Abbey, she was so enchanted that Shrewsbury knew he had found the place to take her for their honeymoon and began to make secret plans.

In the meantime the Earl of Shrewsbury's attorneys met with Lady St. Loe's and began to thrash out a marriage settlement. His lawyers were appalled that he was willing to concede so much and argued against it. Hers were astonished that she was driving such a hard bargain, when any other woman in the realm would have taken him on any terms whatsoever. The negotiations between the lawyers went back and forth, dragging on for three weeks to a stalemate.

The earl's impatience grew daily, until finally he declared he had had enough. He and Bess sat down together with their lawyers and dictated how the papers were to be drawn up for their signatures. Bess would be entitled to a wife's share of the vast Talbot wealth, which encompassed money, land, estates, lead and coal mines, ironworks, and a thriving wool market with overseas exports. And in a separate document she also was allowed to retain her Hardwick, Cavendish, and St. Loe land-holdings and the income they brought in for her lifetime, to be passed in succession to any children she and the earl might produce together. The only exclusion was Chatsworth, and a legal paper was drawn up deeding her magnificent house to her eldest son and heir, Henry Cavendish. On top of everything else, Shrewsbury very generously agreed to give her other two sons, William and Charles, considerable lump sums of money when they became twenty-one.

When all the legal documents were signed, sealed, and witnessed, Shrewsbury heaved a great sigh of relief and proceeded with the secret plans he was making for their wedding. He took

Bess's family into his confidence, telling them his intent to carry her off and swearing them to secrecy so they wouldn't spoil the surprise.

On a gloriously warm day in August, Shrewsbury arrived at Chatsworth with only a groom in attendance. "I want you to ride out with me today."

"Shrew, you know we cannot run off alone. Besides, I'm trying to pack all the things I'll need to take to Sheffield."

"I'd like your opinion on a piece of property." He knew that nothing in the world was closer to her heart than land. "It will be perfectly proper; I have a groom with me, and you can bring Cecily along if you're worried about your damned reputation."

"All right," she agreed with a radiant smile. There was a serious matter that Bess wished to discuss with him, and this might be the perfect opportunity. She had long harbored the ambition of betrothing a couple of her Cavendish children to Talbots but had never dared broach the subject, especially in light of all the concessions he had made in her marriage settlement.

Her head told her to wait until they were securely married before she revealed her ambitions, in case he became incensed at her audacity. But her conscience nagged at her to be open and honest in her dealings with him, and she decided to speak of it today if she got the chance.

When they rode into Nottinghamshire, Bess

realized they were going in the direction of Rufford Abbey, on the edge of Sherwood Forest. "Is this property close to Rufford?"

He heard the excitement in her voice. "Extremely close," he admitted.

"You black devil, if I'd known of such a property, I would have bought it for myself!"

"Vixen, you are going to have to stop thinking in terms of *yours* and *mine*. From now on it is *ours*."

"Do you truly mean that?"

"I do," he vowed solemnly. "What's mine is yours"—he slanted an amused brow at her—"though obviously what's yours you are determined to keep, you avaricious little jade."

Her laugh was sultry. She knew he was mad in love with her and ready to give her the moon and the stars. "Let's visit Rufford. I vow 'tis the most romantic place I've ever seen."

He pretended reluctance but gave in to her wishes and sent his groom and Cecily ahead to warn the servants of their impending arrival. When they came to the first stream, they let their horses drink, and Shrewsbury lifted her from her saddle and sat her before him between his thighs.

She reveled in his great strength and lifted her mouth to his for the first kiss they had shared in weeks. She wondered if she dared make love on the forest floor and arrive at Rufford flushed and disheveled, with every Talbot servant guessing correctly what they had been up to.

His arms encircled her, his hands captured her breasts, then he bent his head to whisper in her ear. "I have abducted you, beauty. We will share a bed tonight. I give you no choice in the matter."

Bess thrilled at his possessive tone and knew a protest would be useless. Once Shrewsbury made up his mind about something, it was impossible to dissuade him. And why would she do such a ridiculous thing anyway? It seemed they had waited a lifetime.

He dismounted and lifted her down to him, and the two horses contentedly nibbled the lush green grass that sprang up against the cloistered walls of the ancient abbey. He took Bess's hand and led her beneath a stone arch into a small open courtyard, surrounded by a secluded covered walk. "I want us to exchange vows today, here in the abbey's chapel. I want it to be simple and private. Will you marry me, Bess?"

She was taken by surprise. "You brought me here to get married today?" *It is August 20, my fateful day, and the day I married Cavendish all those years ago.* Her eyes sought Shrewsbury's, and suddenly, realization dawned on her. *He knows. ... He knows exactly what day it is. He is determined to lay the ghost of Rogue Cavendish to rest.* The corners of her mouth went up. "Yes, I will marry you, yes," she said quickly.

At dawn this morning, when she'd first opened her eyes and realized it was her wedding anniversary with William, she had said her final farewell to the father of her children. She knew he would approve of this marriage that would elevate her to the highest ranks of the nobility, and not only because of the advantages it would provide for their Cavendish children. He would heartily approve of her finding a great love once again.

When they entered the chapel hand in hand, a priest awaited them at the altar. Cecily and the groom, sitting in a side pew, were their only witnesses. Bess suddenly felt shy, as if she were becoming a bride for the first time. She looked up at the darkly handsome man at her side and felt tears flood her eyes. Lovingly, he raised her hand to his lips, then drew her down to kneel beside him while they pledged their vows.

The priest solemnly charged Shrewsbury: "Wilt thou have this woman to thy wedded wife, to live together after God's ordinance in the holy estate of Matrimony? Wilt thou love her, comfort her, honor and keep her, in sickness and in health, and forsaking all other, keep thee only unto her, as long as you both shall live?"

Shrewsbury squeezed her hand. "I will."

He has just vowed to be faithful to me for the rest of his life—and he means it! Her heart overflowed with love.

Now the priest was charging her, adding two more questions: "Wilt though obey him and serve him?"

"I will," Bess promised. *At least I'll try!* She added the qualification silently.

Shrewsbury let go of her right hand and took hold of her left. He removed the huge diamond and emerald ring from her finger and slipped on a wide gold band, set with matching stones. "With this ring I thee wed, with my body I thee honor, and with all my worldly goods I thee endow." He then slipped the priceless betrothal ring back onto her third finger.

He has just made me the wealthiest woman in England, after the queen! Bess suddenly felt dizzy. She heard the priest pronounce them one flesh and knew that they were now man and wife. She felt her husband's arm slip about her and draw her into the vestry to sign the register, which lay open on a refectory table. As their witnesses joined them, the groom smiled down at her and handed her the quill. Bess hesitated, her mind going blank for a moment, then a radiant smile transformed her face and she signed with a flourish, *Elizabeth, Countess of Shrewsbury.*

The bridegroom added his signature to the chapel register, then he enfolded her in his arms. "May I kiss the bride?"

Bess laughed up into his face. "I've never heard you ask before." She lifted her lips and was amazed that he did not ravish her mouth. The kiss was perfect.

When he lifted his mouth from hers, he murmured, "Bess, this is easily the happiest day of my life—I want it to be happy for you too. We are going to steal a whole week alone together."

"Oh, Shrew, I *am* happy—you've fulfilled all my dreams!"

"Once, years ago, you asked me to give

you a wedding ring; you asked me to give you my name, do you remember?"

"I was being very wicked. You were married—I knew it was impossible."

"But you'll never know how much I longed to give you those things. Bess, you are my true sweetheart. I've never been in love before. You're the first...and the last."

She stood on her tiptoes to brush her lips against his. "I shall love you forever."

With arms entwined they made their way along the cloisters to the adjoining manor house, all built from the same beautiful old weathered stone. Bess sighed. "This place is so romantic."

He brushed his lips across her temple. "That's why I chose it for our honeymoon. I wish we had longer than a week."

She looked up at him, starry-eyed. "I am only just beginning to realize that you are a romantic at heart."

He swept her up into his arms and carried her into Rufford. It wasn't until he set her feet down on the ancient stones that she realized a score of servants had gathered in the hall to await their arrival. One by one the steward, housekeeper, cook, laundress, footmen, maids, gamekeepers, gardeners, grooms, and body servants either bowed or curtsied and said respectfully, "Welcome to Rufford, Countess."

Bess caught her breath. "How lovely of you to welcome me. I can see you were all in on the secret. It is the best surprise I've ever had." Bess won their hearts immediately.

Cecily came forward and curtsied. "Lady Talbot, all your things are upstairs, even your portable bathing tub."

"How on earth did you manage to spirit everything away without my knowledge?" Bess asked, utterly confounded.

"It was simple enough," Shrewsbury teased. "You were closeted with lawyers and couldn't see what was going on under your nose." He dipped his head to whisper in her ear, "If you hurry, there will be lots of time for us to bathe before dinner."

Bess decided two could play a teasing game. She blushed and reached up to whisper back, "No, no, Shrew, if we bathe together, they'll all know!"

He kept a straight face. "Nonsense. Talbot servants are trained to notice nothing of a salacious nature."

"That's a relief."

"That they are well-trained?"

Her laugh was sultry. "No, that you intend to be salacious!"

"I love you, Vixen."

"You'd better, you black devil!"

Upstairs, he had chosen adjoining rooms for them so they would have extra space. Cecily had brought Bess so many clothes they took up an entire double wardrobe; then of course there was the huge bathing tub. Shrewsbury decided one of the chambers would be their bathing and dressing room, the other their bedchamber.

One of his gifts lay across the bed. Bess

saw it immediately and lifted it to her cheek to caress the delicate material. It was a white silk bedgown, edged in white fox. On the breast was embroidered a gold coronet with her new initials above it: *E.S.*

"Shrew, it's exquisite, but woefully impractical."

"What do you mean?" He knew she adored beautiful lingerie.

"My lover is impatient—he'll tear it to tatters."

"Then leave it on the bed and we'll just look at it."

"Not a chance! Perhaps my husband has more patience than my lover?"

"I doubt that, my beauty."

But miraculously, as he began to undress her, Bess found his hands amazingly gentle. He handled her as if she were precious and fragile as porcelain. When they were both naked he lifted her tenderly and carried her into the adjoining chamber, where the bathing tub of steaming water awaited them. He stepped in first to make sure it was not too hot, then gently scooped her up and eased them down into the water, with her in his lap.

She rested her head against his shoulder and gazed up at him in wonder. He was so big and dark and dangerous-looking that gentleness was the last thing she expected from him.

"Did I not just vow to cherish you?" he murmured, lifting her fiery hair from the nape of her neck and nuzzling it sweetly. He wrapped his arms about her, kissed the tip of her ear, then whispered all the things about her beauty that enchanted him. "The curve of your back is so sinuous, it makes me want to stroke you like a feline—stroke you until you purr. Your waist is so small, I can span it with my hands. One of my favorite things to do is splay my fingers out across your rib cage, like this, then slowly move them up beneath your breasts, like so. You have so many soft, silken places I like to touch, and the most exciting part is your eager, passionate response to everything I do to you, my beauty. You allow me to indulge all my fantasies. What man hasn't dreamed of bathing with his beloved? Holding you captive in my lap allows me to touch and caress all your most intimate, vulnerable places."

He dropped a kiss on the top of her head, and his possessive hands stroked down her body until they captured her hips. He lifted her slightly so that his thick shaft lay in the cleft between her legs, then his fingers threaded through the red tendrils that covered her mons. He toyed with her lightly, arousing her, but taking great care not to bring her to climax.

Before the water cooled, he took the soap between his hands and rubbed until he created a rich, thick lather, then he stroked the cream over every inch of her body, turning her skin to the texture of velvet. Bess shuddered at the exquisite sensations his knowing fingers aroused, yet his ministrations were strangely soothing, making her feel languid and very much loved.

"Let me lather you, darling."

"No, sweetheart, if you touched me it would be all over. I want to enjoy my state of arousal a little while longer. I have a perfect night planned for us."

He stepped from the tub and knelt down to her. Then he lifted the sponge and trickled water over her shoulders to remove the creamy lather. He wrapped her in a thirsty towel and carried her to the bed, gently patting her dry. Then he gazed down at her, worshiping her with his eyes and then his lips. He touched her with such reverence, Bess felt as if she were floating on a cloud. He feathered kisses into her hair, touched his lips to her temples, her eyelids, her slanting cheekbones, and finally he kissed her lips with such heart-stopping tenderness, Bess almost cried with happiness.

He gazed into her eyes and whispered lovingly, "I want the consummation of our marriage to be perfect for you." Then, without lust, he made real love to her, cherishing and worshiping and honoring her with his body until she dissolved in liquid tremors and yielded her heart and soul to him.

THIRTY-EIGHT

A velvet box sat beside Bess's plate at the breakfast table, and her husband schooled his impatience for her to open it. She dallied over her bread and honey, and sipped her chocolate slowly to tease him, until she herself could stand the anticipation no longer. Finally, she cast him a saucy glance from beneath her dark lashes and lifted the lid.

He watched intently as her face became suffused with surprise, then disbelief, then possessiveness, and finally joy. She lifted one of the eight-foot loops of pearls with reverence, marveling at their size and lustrous opalescence. She knew they had been brought from the Orient by the first Earl of Shrewsbury and that they were now priceless. "Oh, Shrew," she breathed raptly as she lifted them over her head.

He came around the table and kissed her deeply. "I warrant you are the first Countess of Shrewsbury whose luminous beauty eclipses that of the pearls."

They spent the summer day outdoors, enjoying the setting that seemed to have been created especially for lovers. Rufford had three streams that meandered through its secluded grounds, and the gardens were walled with the same lovely weathered stone as the cloisters. The wide flower beds held a profusion of delphiniums, larkspur, carnations, nicotine, and stocks. The wooded walks were edged with heavenly-scented lavender and rosemary. Lupines and harebells danced on the warm summer breeze, and flowering vines and English roses climbed up every wall and stone archway.

They held hands and talked and kissed and made endless plans for their future together, as lovers have done since the dawn of time. They knew their time alone would be fleeting, and they reveled in their isolation.

Shrewsbury had brought his favorite cook to Rufford, and as the newlyweds sat across from each other in the formal dining room—behaving with decorum before the servants but devouring each other with their eyes—everything they ate tasted like ambrosia.

Each successive day mirrored the first. After a night of passionate lovemaking, he presented her with another rope of the fabulous Shrewsbury pearls at the breakfast table. It was like an epilogue to his loving, thanking her for the deep pleasure she brought him, telling her that she lingered in his consciousness, and hinting at the coming night's possibilities. He seemed completely under her spell, bewitched by her special magic.

They went for long rides with Bess sitting between his thighs, they went hawking, and fishing, and lay on cushions in a wooden punt as it drifted across the abbey's small lake. Whenever she touched him the blood flowed thick and hot in his veins and flooded his loins with a sweet, heavy ache. Bess was aware of how her loveliness affected him by the way his avid eyes devoured her. He was always close enough to hear the rustle of her petticoat and inhale her intoxicating woman's scent. She could bring him fully to life by just a look or a touch. She filled his senses and fired his imagination. Sometimes both of them were overcome by the most violent, most savage passion,

585

and at other times they rolled in the long grasses, helpless with laughter.

When dusk descended they always went for a romantic walk in the gardens, lingering in the night-scented darkness until the moon came out and turned everything to silver. Then he carried her to bed, oblivious of the servants who did their best to give the lovers privacy. Their week stretched to eight days, then nine, but finally, reluctantly, they made plans to ride to Sheffield after one more precious day alone together.

Bess raised the lid of the antique jewel casket, lifting the strands of priceless pearls, then letting them slide through her fingers so that the reflecting candlelight made them shine with a deep luster. "Now that I have all eight strands, I think I shall have my portrait painted wearing the pearls."

"Wearing *only* the pearls," he suggested huskily.

Bess knew immediately what he wanted. She waited until he went into the dressing room to shave, which he did every night before he made love to her, then she quickly undressed and adorned herself with the ropes of pearls. She stood before the mirror admiring her reflection, allowing the strands to fall about her naked body in different provocative ways.

As they slid across the smooth flesh of her breasts and belly, it thrilled her to think she was wearing a fortune in precious jewels. How many women had been so indulged?

Cleopatra perhaps? Helen of Troy? *Even Elizabeth Tudor has nothing so fine as these!*

Bess gathered up all eight strands and wrapped them close about her throat so that the pearls fell down her back in an opalescent waterfall. They were long enough to loop beneath her bottom cheeks, making her look like a nautch dancer from a prince's harem.

In the mirror she saw the tall, dark figure loom behind her. His face was taut with desire, his eyes black with passion. She felt his fingers trace down her spine, setting her all ashiver, then his hands began to caress her bottom, stroking in circles that went ever smaller until his fingers slid into the deep cleft of her cheeks, seeking pleasure points she didn't know she possessed.

She felt the engorged head of his phallus rub against her, urgent and throbbing. Her buttocks tightened as a spasm quivered up her back and slithered between her legs to her woman's center. Bess was reeling from the dark, erotic sensations he was arousing in her. She felt the hot, wet glide of his tongue trace down her neck and across her shoulder, and fire snaked through her breasts and down into the pit of her belly.

When she moaned his name, he gathered her up and took her to the bed. He placed her in a prone position on her hands and knees with her beautiful bottom arched in the air and curved his long body over hers. When he thrust into her sheath, the sensation was new and strange to Bess, but almost immediately she realized this position allowed him to stroke across her bud directly, stimulating her to climb and build from the moment he entered her.

His hard body fell into a powerful rhythm, and hers began to move with his. Her hands clutched the bedcovers as they plunged together, riding one surging wave after another in uninhibited splendor. Both could feel the loops of pearls rolling sleekly between their bodies, creating a delicious friction across the curve of her bottom that made them feel decadent.

When his hands took possession of her full, lush breasts, glorying in their weight, Bess began to cry out her intense pleasure. They exploded together and he pulled her back against him, shuddering as he unleashed a final surge of raw passion.

Much later, after the storm had abated, she sat up in bed, cradled between his legs so they could talk. Bess asked, "Shrew, do you want more children?"

"Splendor of God, don't you think we have enough?"

She laughed with relief. "I do indeed; I don't want to start all over again with babies."

"We will have enough to do arranging suitable alliances for the nine children who are not yet espoused," he pointed out.

"Shrew, I meant to speak of this before we were married, but you were so impetuous, you didn't give me a chance."

"Sweetheart, if it's about our children,

can't it wait? We will be at Sheffield the day after tomorrow. All too soon they'll be dominating our lives again."

"Darling, I've already waited too long to broach this subject. I have great plans for their futures, and I need your approval."

He finished his wine as he listened to her talk and knew he had never felt so replete and happy in his life.

"I intend to dower all of my children generously. Upon their marriage each will get one of my manor houses and five hundred acres of property."

"That is more than generous, my love," he murmured, closing his eyes contentedly.

"I want our children to found a great dynasty, and it must all be set out exactly, stating who is to marry whom and assigning lands and assets. It must be signed by both of us and given to the lawyers so they can draw up the legal documents."

"Mmm, darling, set all your ideas down on paper and I'll look it over." He moved down in the bed and gathered her against him. "I love sleeping with you; my bed will never be cold again."

The following day a light summer rain was falling, and Bess spent the entire morning sitting at the desk in the cozy paneled study that was tucked off the main hall. She had thought about these marriages between their Cavendish and Talbot children for so long, she knew just exactly who would be paired with whom.

Bess wanted Gilbert Talbot for her youngest daughter, Mary. He stood a very good chance of becoming Earl of Shrewsbury someday and making her daughter a countess. Of all Shrewsbury's sons, Gilbert was most like his father, dark with an attractive air of arrogance, and she knew Mary, with her fiery curls and stubborn temper, was most like herself. *It will be a match made in heaven; they will be just like Shrew and I.*

Since her eldest son, Henry Cavendish, would get Chatsworth, Bess wanted Grace Talbot for her daughter-in-law. She had a special place in her heart for Grace, and since the child had already fallen in love with Chatsworth, what could be more fitting? Harry was a few years older than Grace and would have to wait to consummate the marriage, but it would give him time to sow some wild oats and enjoy his tour of the continent before he settled down.

In her enthusiasm Bess made a few blots and spelling mistakes, so she took great pains to write out a fresh copy before her husband saw it. Her heart filled with pride as she signed it, *Elizabeth, Countess of Shrewsbury.*

"Bess, where the devil are you hiding? The rain has stopped, and I warrant the woods are filled with deer. Let's ride into Sherwood and see if we can bag one. It's our last day here."

She knew he loved to hunt and agreed to ride out with him. "I have to change, but I promise I won't be long, darling. While you're waiting for me, you can look over the matches I have proposed for our sons and daughters."

He watched her walk away from him, then turn to look over her shoulder with an inviting glance. Her lure was potent; surely she didn't expect him to put his mind on the serious business of espousals when all he wanted to do was help her change her clothes. His eyes scanned the paper on the desk, curious to know what she had been plotting. When he saw that she had paired two of her children with two of his, he threw back his head and laughed, totally amused at how outrageous she could be.

That afternoon Bess did not bring up the subject that was foremost in her mind. He had read her proposals, and that was a good start. She would give him a little time to reflect and come around to her way of thinking.

While her husband and his gamekeeper dressed and hung the stag he had shot with a single arrow, Bess helped Cecily with the final packing, and the servants carried their baggage down to the hall in readiness for an early departure to Sheffield. Though she was loath to leave Rufford, Bess was looking forward to her new position as Countess of Shrewsbury and mistress of Sheffield Castle. She couldn't wait to start redecorating their private wing and putting her personal stamp on everything in the Talbot empire.

Shrewsbury bathed and changed his bloodied clothes, then joined his wife for a glass of wine before dinner. "We've been so happy here,

Bess. Let's pledge to come back often, just the two of us."

She raised her glass, then glanced down at the paper still lying on the desk. "We mustn't forget to take this." She gave him a brilliant smile. "What do you think about my clever idea?"

"Surely you jest! Sweetheart, you can't be serious?"

The smile left her face. "I've never been more serious in my life. This is very important to me, Shrew."

"Who my children marry is of tantamount importance to me too, believe it or not." His voice dripped with sarcasm and arrogance. "Wherever did you get this preposterous idea?"

"I got it when you married two of your children to two of William Herbert's!" Bess could feel her anger rising quickly.

"William Herbert happens to be the Earl of Pembroke. Our children are equal in name and wealth."

Bess felt as if her cheeks were on fire. "So you actually think my Cavendish children are not good enough to wed with Talbots, you arrogant swine!"

"I think no such thing."

"Then what do you think?" Bess cried furiously. "Let's be plain with each other!"

"All right. Since you ask, I will be plain. These things are for me to decide, not you. I will not allow you to be the boss and make the decisions. It's highly amusing that you just assume I will let you have all your own way. You obviously think because I love you deeply, I will allow you to rule me. But I will not, nor will I allow you to run roughshod over me or manipulate me. Bess, I will be master in my own house."

"You brute, how dare you speak to me like this!" She hissed like a feline ready to unsheathe her claws.

"You are a woman, a very beautiful woman, and up to now that has allowed you to have your own way about everything. You have had men dancing to your tune all your life. You may have been able to wrap your other husbands about your fingers, Bess, but not me, my darling. I am not other men, as you will soon learn."

"Don't you dare to threaten me, you black beast!" He had immediately taken the offensive position, which left her with no option but to defend herself. "I would not be doing my job as a mother if I did not look after my children's best interests!"

"Your ambition is insatiable. It consumes you and everything in your path like wildfire. I won't allow it to destroy us!"

Bess picked up the inkstand from the desk and hurled it at him. It missed, but the ink splattered, then pooled on the priceless Persian carpet.

His icy blue eyes narrowed. "You forget yourself, madam. You are behaving like a common fishwife."

"And you're behaving like a bloody Talbot hound!"

"I think the servants have heard enough. When you are ready to beg my pardon, I will be upstairs," he said coldly.

"I wish I'd never married you!" she screamed.

"But you did," he said quietly, "and you also vowed to obey me. Bess, make no mistake, I will bring you to heel if I have to."

She gasped, speechless, as he turned his back on her and left the room. She stood there, stunned that she did not hold him in the palm of her hand. "To hellfire with you, Shrewsbury!" She put her hands to her temples and felt her blood pounding. *Son of a bitch, son of a bloody bitch! Bring me to heel, begod! I'll show him; I'll leave him! I'll go home to Chatsworth! Tonight!* Bess summoned her maid. "Cecily, we are leaving. No, don't bother with the damned baggage." Bess raised her voice in total defiance. "And you know what you can do with your bloody pearls too!"

The following morning Bess's mother and Marcella were amazed to find her sitting at the breakfast table.

"What are you doing here?"

"I live here," she snapped.

"Where's Shrewsbury?" her mother ventured.

"Never utter that name in this house again!" Bess summoned her secretary. "Robert, bring the accounts up to the library."

Marcella rolled her eyes. "We are in for a monumental battle of wills between the earl and his new countess, I'm afraid."

Bess's mother whispered, "It's a miracle it lasted this long."

Bess threw herself into her work. After the accounts were done, she visited her tenant farms, ordered the necessary repairs, and she waited for Shrewsbury to come. When he did not she inspected her mines and rode over to Hardwick, where a great seam of coal had just been discovered. She vowed to herself that when Shrewsbury came she would be ready for him. But Shrewsbury did not come.

During the next week Bess raved and cursed and swore and threw things. Then she flung herself on her bed and sobbed. When she was finally drained of her temper and her self-pity, she began to think more clearly. She still felt that the betrothals were right, but she admitted that she had been wrong not to broach the subject before they were married. When he came she would admit it.

Bess managed to fill her days, but her nights were endless. She missed Shrewsbury so much, she thought she would surely die. *Damn the man, why is he taking so long to come?* She answered herself. *Because he's arrogant, and stubborn, and willful, and expects everyone to do his bidding without question!* She pressed her lips together, knowing she had just described herself. What if he never came? The thought was unendurable. What if he was finished with her? She'd never live down the scandal—she'd be a laughingstock! Yet deep down it was another matter that was breaking her heart. She loved him madly, more than she'd ever admitted, more than she'd ever realized, and obviously a thousand times more than he loved her! What in God's name was she going to do?

Bess cringed at thoughts of going to Sheffield, begging for forgiveness. She had too much pride; it would choke her! She concocted a dozen plots that might bring him to Chatsworth but abandoned them, knowing he would see through her deceit. She hadn't slept in a week and in desperation took a full bottle of malmsey to bed with her.

Bess awoke, terrified. The room was empty, stripped bare. She ran downstairs and found the bailiffs carrying off everything she possessed in the world. Bess begged and pleaded and cried, all to no avail. Outside, all her lovely possessions were being piled on a cart. She had been put out of her beautiful house and had nowhere to go. Fear washed over her in great waves. Panic choked her. When she turned around, the cart was gone, her family was gone, and even Chatsworth had vanished. Bess had lost everything she had in the world. The suffocating terror mounted until it engulfed her, the waves of fear almost drowning her. The hollow, empty feeling inside her belly was like ravenous hunger, only worse: Shrewsbury was gone! She was overwhelmed with helplessness, hopelessness.

Bess awoke and heard herself crying his name, "Shrew...Shrew." As she lay trembling, recovering from the nightmare, she knew that she never wanted to be alone again. She had done this to herself. She had been too pushy and had tried to dominate him. Shrewsbury was a man who would not be controlled by a woman, and therein lay his great attraction. And the only thing that was keeping them apart was her pride. She had always accused Shrewsbury of being too blood proud, but she suddenly realized her own towering pride was every bit as great as his. We are a good match—nay, we are a perfect match! she told herself.

By the time dawn arrived, Bess knew what she must do. "Cecily, what happened to that outfit I designed especially for my first entrance to Sheffield Castle as Countess of Shrewsbury?"

Cecily hid a smile. Bess spoke of her "entrance" as if she were the queen. "I'll speak to your sewing women, my lady; it must be finished by now."

As she stepped in front of her mirror to inspect her appearance, Bess knew she looked spectacular. The tight-fitting cream velvet jacket showed off her high breasts to perfection, and the brilliant peacock velvet she had chosen for the full skirt contrasted dramatically. Beneath it, her three petticoats were in varying shades of the same color, while her gloves and riding boots were made of soft kid leather, dyed peacock color to match her skirt exactly. The outfit was sewn all over with seed pearls, as if they had been scattered by a careless hand.

The pièce de résistance, however, was the saucy hat with its sweeping ostrich feather that curved down one side of her flaming tresses and tucked beneath her chin. Bess adored the hat; it made both the outfit and her look absolutely ravishing. She carried her hat and gloves downstairs and was just about to send orders to the stable to have Raven saddled, when a footman announced that the Earl of Shrewsbury had arrived.

Bess drew in a swift breath, and her pulses began to race madly. She watched the tall, dark figure stride into the room and felt his presence dominate it. "You came," she murmured in wonder.

His eyes swept her from head to foot. "I came to bring you to heel, Vixen."

Her eyes flashed and her chin went up as a defiant phrase sprang to her lips. Bite your tongue, Bess, he's baiting you, her inner voice whispered. "Say what you have come to say, my lord, I will listen," she said evenly.

"I've come to take you back to Sheffield with me, where you belong. From now on you will be an obedient wife." He paused to give his ultimatum emphasis. "If you refuse, the marriage is over, here and now. I won't ask you again, Bess."

You are not *asking* me now, you black devil, she thought wryly but bit down on her wayward tongue. "Since you give me no leeway, it seems I must obey you, my lord husband." She quickly pushed away thoughts of all she intended to take with her. *Just go; don't keep him waiting.* Bess pinned on her hat and picked up her gloves. "I'm ready, my lord." Though her words were soft, there was nothing meek about her demeanor as she sailed through Chatsworth's front door, like a ship proudly flying her colors.

When she saw the carriage, she bit her lip. *Damn, he wants me to arrive like a lady. I was looking forward to a wild gallop.* "How thoughtful of you to bring the carriage for me," she said softly. She did not see the look of amusement Shrewsbury quickly masked as he climbed into the saddle. *It's just as well we are not riding together. I couldn't keep this charade up for ten miles!*

Bess made a triumphant entrance into Sheffield Castle just as she had planned, with her husband, the earl, at her side. He was extremely proud of this beautiful, vibrant woman as she stood in the Great Hall before hundreds of Talbot attendants and servants. "Ladies and gentlemen, I have the great honor of presenting my wife, Elizabeth, Countess of Shrewsbury."

Bess thanked every single person who welcomed her, and it was two hours before Shrewsbury could maneuver her up to the library and shut the doors so they could be private. She unpinned her hat, and he took it from her and set it aside. Then he opened the desk drawer, took out a document, and placed it in her hands. She read it quickly, breathlessly, hardly daring to believe it espoused her daughter Mary to Gilbert Talbot, and his daughter Grace to her son Henry Cavendish.

Her fingers traced his signature and his seal.

As her eyes sought his, her heart was singing. "Shrew, why did you do this?"

"It is a reward for your obedience," he said solemnly.

"You arrogant swine!" She flew at him, ready to rake his face.

With a whoop of laughter, he pinned her arms behind her and gathered her close. His demanding mouth descended on hers, mastering her, then his lips softened in a kiss that was perfect. He lifted her and sat her on the edge of the desk to explain his reasoning. "That night at Rufford, when my anger cooled, I began to see the advantages of what you proposed. I saw that it would keep our wealth in our own family and benefit not just our children but our grandchildren and their children for generations.

"When I awoke and found you gone, I couldn't believe it. I was ready to murder you. I was incensed that you would put anything before our love, even the welfare and interests of your own children. And then it began to dawn on me that you were fighting for a principle, and you were ready to sacrifice everything for what you believed in your heart was the right thing for them. You were not only willing to risk the wealth and title, you were ready to sacrifice your own happiness. I thought that was rather a noble gesture, Bess, and I was proud of you."

Bess was speechless. *He thinks I'm noble! Thank God he doesn't know I was on my way here to beg him to take me back!*

He cupped her face and lifted it for a kiss. Then his glance was drawn lower. "You look ravishing, Vixen." The backs of his fingers stroked down her cheek and over the curve of her throat and over the swell of her breasts. *Thank God she came with me. I almost had heart failure when I saw her all dressed up for London.* His fingers unfastened the tiny pearl buttons, and her lush breasts spilled into his possessive hands. Their desire flared up instantly, threatening to consume them.

Bess glanced down at the wide polished surface of the desk, assessing its possibilities. How many titled ladies had lain naked across this massive desk in the Sheffield library? None, she'd be willing to bet. "Shrew, as Countess of Shrewsbury, I'd like to set a precedent!"

EPILOGUE

Summer 1567

The Earl of Shrewsbury had taken his mining engineer to Hardwick to find out if the land held any more valuable coal deposits. Bess lingered in front of her beloved old home, which was now empty. As her husband rode up the dusty path, his eyes were drawn to her. She was almost forty, but in her pale green muslin, she still looked like a young girl. He knew he loved her more every day.

"Who are you talking to, my beauty?"

"I'm talking to Hardwick Manor."

"Do you suppose it can hear you?" he asked quizzically.

"Of course. I'm telling it all the fine plans I have for it."

Laughing, Shrewsbury bent down and lifted her before him in the saddle. "Suppose you tell me," he suggested indulgently, slipping possessive arms about her.

"I'm going to make Hardwick the most beautiful house in all England. It will be the envy of all who see it!"

"What about Chatsworth?"

Bess laughed. "Oh, I just built that for practice. Hardwick Hall will eclipse it in every way."

"Hardwick *Hall*, is it?" he teased. "What about poor old Hardwick Manor?"

"Oh, I shan't pull it down. It will be the heart of the new house. I want Hardwick to be a glorious celebration of light and happiness. I intend to build a fairy-tale palace of glass, with its towers touching the clouds!"

"Towers?" Shrewsbury was bemused.

"Yes...six of them! I was six when my family was evicted from Hardwick."

Shrewsbury suddenly realized the motive that was driving her to transmute the shabby manor into an elegant palace that would be beyond compare. It was the same passionate ambition that had transformed a farmer's daughter into a countess. His arms tightened about her. She was vibrant, self-confident, invincible almost, and yet the seeds of insecurity still lay buried within. Suddenly, more than anything in the world, he wanted to make her laugh. "Of course, you intend to emblazon your noble monogram across this great mansion?"

"Oh, Shrew, what a marvelous idea! On top of each tower I shall have my initials in six-foot-high solid stone."

Shrewsbury laughed. "My darling, I was jesting!"

"Don't you dare laugh at me. The queen puts her bloody Elizabeth Regina on everything in sight. I'm a Talbot now, and everyone knows the Talbots are far more noble than the Tudors—we are descended from Plantagenets, don't you know?"

Her husband shook with laughter, but Bess blithely ignored him. "I see nothing amusing about letting future generations know that Hardwick Hall was built by Elizabeth, Countess of Shrewsbury."

He nuzzled her neck, and his thumbs moved up to stroke beneath the swell of her breasts. "I am reputed to be the wealthiest man in England, but I can see you are determined to beggar me before you are done."

Her sultry laugh rang out happily. "I shall certainly try my very best, you black devil!"

AUTHOR'S NOTE

Bess Hardwick lived to be over eighty years old. The two magnificent houses that she built, Chatsworth, "The Palace of the Peaks," and Hardwick Hall, "More Glass than Wall," are among the finest examples of Britain's stately homes, which can still be visited today.

Through her Cavendish children, Bess founded a dynasty that included her granddaughter, Arbella Stuart, the earls and dukes of Devonshire, the dukes of Portland, the duke of Newcastle, the earls of Burlington, and the marquess of Hartington, who married Kathleen Kennedy, sister of President John F. Kennedy.